"A Man's Mistress Often Fares Far Better Than His Wife!"

The color siphoned from Jarina's face. Of all payments he could have expected in return for the favor she asked of him, *that* possibility had never even come to mind. He slipped an arm about her waist and pulled her against him. His mouth came down on hers, gently at first, then with more persistence, molding her lips to his, then parting them with his tongue.

Engulfed in the heady brandy scent of him, Jarina was helpless to even think, and her confused mind whirled drunkenly in the path of his assault. His tongue plunged boldly into her mouth, then retreated and plunged again and again, teasing and tormenting her until wild sensations unlike anything she had ever felt jolted through her entire body.

When he finally dragged his mouth from hers, she was breathless and shaken and on the verge of tears. Before she could protest his uninvited familiarity, he broke the embrace and pressed a gown into her hands. "I'm going up on deck for a while," he said. "If you want privacy while you dress, you'd best enjoy it now. It will be in short supply during the voyage home . . ."

PASSION'S PRICE

LINDA ANDERSEN

CHARTER/DIAMOND BOOKS, NEW YORK

PASSION'S PRICE

A Charter/Diamond Book/published by arrangement with
the author

PRINTING HISTORY
Charter/Diamond edition/October 1990

ISBN: 1-55773-398-8

Charter/Diamond Books are published by The Berkley Publishing
Group, 200 Madison Avenue, New York, New York 10016. The
name "CHARTER/DIAMOND" and its logo are trademarks be-
longing to Charter Communications, Inc.

PRINTED IN THE UNITED STATES OF AMERICA

10 9 8 7 6 5 4 3 2 1

PASSION'S PRICE

Chapter One

January 24, 1807
Wyeburn Plantation, Virginia

The late afternoon sun streamed through the narrow stone-mullioned windows, striking the leaded panes and casting a diamond pattern across the dark oak paneling. At the far end of the room, opposite the cavernous fireplace, a ripple of feminine laughter wafted up from the huge four-poster bed. Her raven hair tumbling wantonly down around her shoulders, Evelyn Landon sat amid the rumpled sheets, rummaging through an ornately carved jewel box. She lifted a ring from the box and slid it over the third finger of her right hand. A look of smug satisfaction spread slowly across her features as she extended her arm to allow the large ruby to catch the sunlight. "Do you think Jared will give me your mother's jewels once we are married?" she inquired of the dark-haired man lying beside her, his hands folded behind his head.

Damon Cunningham's gold-spoked eyes narrowed as they roamed freely over Evelyn's naked form, and the corners of his hard mouth lifted into a wry smile. "You are terribly certain my brother is going to marry you," he taunted, withdrawing one hand from behind his head to fondle a breast.

"Jared is only your half brother," Evelyn reminded him. Her coral lips turned out in a childish pout as she glanced at him from beneath her lashes. "And yes, he will marry me. I will make him marry me. God knows he has kept me dangling these eight years past."

Damon snickered. "I can't quite conceive of anyone *making* Jared do anything. And you know full well he has no intention of marrying you. You may have succeeded in luring him into your bed, my dear, but the man is not going to start paying for what he has always been able to get for free."

Evelyn flashed him a venomous look. "You would do well to assist me in getting Jared to the altar rather than amuse yourself with making light of my maiden state. Everyone in the commonwealth knows you have no legitimate claim to Wyeburn. Until my position in this household is secure, neither will yours be."

A ribald comment regarding Evelyn's imagined maidenhood sprang to the tip of Damon's tongue, but he judiciously kept the retort to himself. Hoisting himself up on one elbow, he snapped the lid of the jewel box shut and removed it to a bedside table. "I don't want to talk about Wyeburn and I certainly don't want to talk about Jared," he said brusquely. Sliding an arm beneath Evelyn's knees, he gave her a hearty jerk that put her flat on her back before shifting his weight so that she was lying beneath him.

Irritation creased her brow. "Haven't you had enough?"

Damon's lips moved down the perfumed column of her throat. "Of you, my dear, never," he said huskily. His breath was hot against her skin. "Besides, I get a fiendish delight out of taking you on my brother's bed."

Evelyn extricated her hand and held it up to the light, her gaze held captive by the glittering ruby. "Half brother," she murmured absently.

January 24, 1807
Southampton, England

Jarina squeezed her eyes shut and choked back a shriek of terror as something soft and furry scuttered across her foot in the darkness. *A rat!* Anguish burst inside her chest and the tears that had been threatening all day reared up again, but she choked those back too. The persistent rocking of the ship and the stink of the bilge made her sick to her stomach, but this was no time to be wallowing in self-pity, she reminded herself as she huddled miserably behind the chests of Birmingham hardware that had been loaded on board earlier that day. In a few hours, the merchant ship *Pegasus* would sail with the tide. Until it did, she had to be quiet lest she give herself away. When her absence was discovered, there was certain to be a commotion, and a substantial reward posted for her safe return. She had to stay hidden until the *Pegasus* was too far out to sea to warrant turning back.

Her breath caught in her throat as a shaft of light pierced the blackness, and male voices followed heavy footsteps through the maze of cargo that filled the hold.

"Take care ye don' drop that, now, Jacky, or the cap'n will take it outa yer pay, and it don't come cheap. That's some smooth drinkin' ye're holdin' there, lad. It don't bite back like some. If we're lucky, there'll be a dram or two left in the bottle they're nursin' up there now. And then, I'll treat us both to a taste the likes of which ye'll ne'er get in an alehouse."

"I never seen Captain Cunningham put away as much as he has tonight," came a younger, more clipped voice. A Yankee voice. "Him and the young gentleman been going through this brandy like it was water."

"If ye had the troubles the cap'n has by half, Jacky, ye'd want to drown yerself in a bottle too. What with the fines and taxes them Tories stuck him with, he'll be hard pressed to turn a profit this voyage."

Suddenly, the men stopped talking. In the smothering silence that followed, Jarina's heart pounded so loudly she was certain they could hear it. She gritted her teeth to keep them from chattering and pressed herself even farther into the corner, making herself as small as possible.

After a moment's silence, the younger man started talking again. "It's rumored, Angus, that Captain Cunningham 'tends to sell out when we return to Virginia. If he does, I'm thinking I might buy me a tract of land out toward the Blue Ridge and take up farming. 'Tis a warming thought, having a few fine acres to pass on to my sons when I'm gone. What of you, Angus? What will you do with yourself if the captain sells the *Pegasus*?"

Jarina never heard the older man's mumbled reply. A panicked scream tore from her throat as a sinewy hand snapped around her wrist in a biting grip and yanked her to her feet.

"Hold the lantern up, Jacky, so we can see what we gots here!" Angus exclaimed. His hand tightened on Jarina's wrist as she tried to squirm free.

Jarina recoiled from the light that flared in her eyes and turned her head aside so the men could not see her face, but Angus caught hold of her chin and twisted her face back to the front, his grip so tight she felt as though the bones in her jaw would be crushed.

" 'Tis a laddie! A wee bairn," Angus announced, his sharp eyes raking down over slender hips encased in boy's breeches. "Thinkin' to steal the cap'n blind, are ye, boy?" he demanded, giving her a stern shake when she did not answer. "Speak up, lad! What harbor rat sent you to do his dirty work? What were ye out to steal?"

Terror flared in Jarina's eyes. If the men turned her over to the authorities, her identity would be quickly ascertained and she would be returned to Hamilton Hall before morning. "I-I wasn't stealing," she stammered. "Honestly, I wasn't!"

"Then what are ye about, lad? Are ye a deserter? The cap'n don' take kindly to deserters. Ye cause more trouble'n ye're worth, what with them Tories always seizin' our ship to search for ye."

Jarina shook her head as vehemently as she could under the old man's restraining grip. "No, sir. I'm not a d-deserter."

"A runaway then?"

She swallowed hard, but said nothing.

Angus chuckled and released her chin. For an instant, Jarina thought he was softening toward her, but that hope was soon dashed. Still gripping her wrist, he dragged her out of the corner. "C'mon, lad. We're goin' up to see the cap'n."

With a strength she did not know she possessed, Jarina wrenched her hand free. Whirling about, she darted into the shadows.

"The lantern, Jacky! Hold up the lantern!"

"Where'd he go, Angus?"

"Ye can't hide from me long, lad," the older man called out. "I'll catch ye, sure, and when I do, ye'll be answerin' to Cap'n Cunningham as to why ye're down here skulkin' about his cargo!"

Molly McGuire wriggled her bottom provocatively against Jared Cunningham's lap, and a giggle burst from her throat as he lowered the front of her bodice and nestled his brandy snifter into the warm valley between her breasts. "You're a comely wench, Molly," he drawled, a slight pause in his words betraying that he had long since surpassed his limit of the amber liquid. "But I'm wondering, are you worth what I paid for you?"

"Hah!" Rising to the bait, Molly glared at him in feigned indignation. "Worth 'at and more! Me and

Kate both, we're cleaner 'n virgins and can show you a better time 'n you'll get anywhere in Sou'ampton!"

Beneath strongly arched black brows, a wicked gleam danced in Jared's gray eyes. "Oh, can you now?" he teased, casting a bemused glance across the table at his business partner who was likewise occupied with Molly's friend. Turning his attention back to the girl seated on his lap, he lifted the snifter from its warming shelter and passed it beneath his nose, all the while studying her. *Much more of her squirming on my lap*, he thought, *and I am liable to take her right here and now.* "Tell me, Molly, just what can you show me that I've not yet seen?"

Molly pursed her rouged lips and traced a forefinger along the line of Jared's firm, clean-shaven jaw as she gave that question some consideration. Then a delicious twinkle sprang into her eyes. She leaned forward and whispered into his ear.

Jared threw back his head and his loud guffaws filled the ship's cabin. "Accomplish that feat, you naughty girl, and I'll double your price!" He lifted his glass in Stephen Landon's direction. "To a night worth remembering, Stephen, my man! And to a job well done. Between your friends and my money, we make a formidable team."

The younger man tore himself away from the well-fleshed bosom that had been commanding his attention. "I should like to see the look on Roswell's face when he learns customs is holding his profits for debts against the crown," he said with a lopsided grin. His face colored as an exploring hand worked its way between his legs. "Do you suppose they'll tell him before or after the wedding?"

Molly snorted contemptuously. "Slimy mutton-monger," she spat. "I can't but feel sorry for the little missy what's marryin' him on the morrow. Her da sold her to him for a hundred quid, he did, and the duke not bein' normal and all."

Kate bobbed her head in agreement. "I wouldn't want for nothin' to be in that 'Amilton girl's shoes come night when the duke claims 'is 'usbandly due. Lady Marbury let one o' the girls go to 'im last summer, and by the time the duke was finished with our poor Lilly, she 'ad to be stitched up. Lady Marbury was fit to be tied, she was, 'cause Lilly died anyways, even after Lady Marbury paid for the doctor."

The chance to earn an extra sovereign never far from her thoughts, Molly slipped a hand inside Jared's white silk shirt and splayed her fingers across his broad, powerfully muscled chest. "The Duke of Roswell might be nobility," she cooed in a low sultry voice, picking up where her friend had left off, "but he ain't half the man you are, Captain Cunningham. I wouldn't warm his grace's bed for all the gold in England!"

Jared placed his glass on the table and shifted Molly to his other knee. He leaned back in his chair and his brows drew together and down above his long, slightly hooked nose in a pensive expression as he contemplated the girl before him. A lock of wavy black hair fell haphazardly over his broad, high forehead, lending a careless elegance to his hawkish features, but there was nothing either careless or haphazard about the driving masculine energy that exuded from his tall, muscular form. "Not even if he made you a duchess?" he inquired with a cunning smoothness that warmed Molly's blood.

Grinning, she wrapped her arms about Jared's neck and pressed her bosom against his granite chest. "Not even if he made me queen."

Stephen Landon laughed. "You should be so lucky, Jared," he said. "Since she was old enough to walk, Evelyn's had her sights dead set on being the next Duchess of Wyeburn!"

Jared's expression became closed and unreadable.

" 'Twould serve her right to have you return to Wyeburn with a wife in tow," Stephen continued, oblivious to the subtle change in Jared's mood. "Though I would have only the greatest of sympathy for the poor girl unlucky enough to land you for a husband. Not only would she have to contend with your nasty temper, Evelyn would claw her eyes out!"

Molly bolted upright and both she and Kate chimed in unison, "I'll marry you!"

Stephen looked appalled. "Absolutely not!" he blurted out, then quickly amended his outburst. "You two beauties would not do at all. Besides, I could tell you a thing or two about our dear Jared here that would make your skin crawl. No decent lass will have him!"

Molly began to pout. "But, I'm not decent. I never have been!"

Jared assuaged Molly's wounded pride by sliding one hand beneath her skirt to caress her thigh. "I assume you already have a candidate in mind for this distasteful deed," he said dryly.

Stephen shook his head. "Only a list of qualifications. First, she must be in utterly dire straits. That way, she will be willing to wed you on a second's notice, knowing nothing about you, and she would be so grateful for being rescued from the depths of hell that she would even swear to make no claims against either your person or your wealth. Secondly, she must be so hideously ugly that you will have no qualms about depositing her at Wyeburn and returning to your more . . . ah . . . interesting pursuits in Alexandria."

One dark brow angled upward.

"But then," Stephen said, reconsidering, "were she a beauty, dear Evelyn would turn fairly green with envy. And the girl must, at all costs, be free of the pox." He made a show of consulting his watch. "I believe we have just enough time before the *Pegasus* sails to scour the waterfront in search of such a—"

Stephen's words were cut short by a brief but violent commotion just outside the door.

Jared thrust Molly aside and sprang to his feet as the door crashed open. Angus and Jacky barged into Jared's cabin, both men trying in vain to subdue one desperately reluctant prisoner.

"Caught 'im in the hold, sir," Angus said, grunting as an elbow gouged him in the ribs. "A runaway—*Eee-oow!*"

At a motion of Jared's hand, the two men released their squirming catch who then sprawled inelegantly at Jared's feet.

"The lad could use a taste of the strap," Angus complained, surveying with displeasure the teeth marks on his hand.

A head of crudely cut, dark auburn curls reared up and Jared was transfixed with a half-terrified, half-furious glare of the deepest, purest blue he had ever seen. For a moment, he just stared, his surprised gaze held captive by those beautiful long-lashed eyes, then dropped to linger on the swell of a decidedly feminine bosom beneath the threadbare flannel of a boy's shirt.

Jared grinned, his even white teeth flashing in brilliant contrast to his deep tan. "Either you're getting old, Angus, or your eyesight's failing you. This is no lad." He gripped a slender, softly muscled upper arm and hauled his prize to her feet.

Shame burned in the girl's cheeks as six pairs of eyes riveted to the vicinity of her bosom, and she attempted to shield herself from their prying gazes with her free arm.

"By Jove, it *is* a lass!" Angus exclaimed. "And a right bonny one too!"

Molly yanked her bodice back up over her own generous bosom and eyed the unwelcome newcomer with haughty disdain. "Looks a might skinny, if you ask me."

The girl whipped her head around to stare, first at Molly and then at Kate, and Jared knew by the way she blushed all the way to the roots of her hair that she had correctly assessed the situation. He jerked his head toward the door. "Out!"

Molly let out a wail of protest as Stephen forcibly guided both her and Kate toward the door, but she quieted the instant he pressed a gold guinea into her palm. Before the door closed, both women's voices could be heard on the companionway as they plied Angus and Jacky with a detailed accounting of their charms.

Jared's grip tightened on the girl's arm and he pulled her nearer the lamp. Grasping her chin, he tilted her face up.

She flinched, but did not look away, and what she saw terrified her. There were no lingering traces of youth to soften the hard edges of stern, almost severe, features that hinted of a maturity gained through hard work and bitter lessons learned rather than the mere passage of time. His white ruffled shirt was open at the neck and the black hair that swirled across his broad chest made him even more frightening to behold. He could not be termed "pretty" by any measure; the foreboding black brows, prominent cheekbones, and the obdurate set of his lean, thrusting jaw disallowed that assessment entirely. He was a tall, powerfully built man who could easily destroy her entire future at whim. Suddenly one of those menacing black brows quirked upward. "Is Angus right? Are you a runaway?"

She swallowed audibly. "Y-yes, sir."

"From what, girl? The law? A cruel master?" Then another thought occurred to him, and he added, "Or perhaps a repulsive husband?"

She blanched.

Annoyed when she did not answer him, Jared abruptly released her. "What is your name?"

She swallowed again. "Jarina, sir," she whispered, then hastily added her mother's maiden name, "Jarina Davies."

"Jarina Davies," Jared repeated in a low, thoughtful voice. He folded his powerful arms across his chest and proceeded to walk slowly around her, his gray eyes assessing every inch of her, and it was all Jarina could do not to quake in terror beneath his probing scrutiny. Perhaps he knew who she really was. Perhaps an alarm had already been raised and this man was mentally counting his reward money. Perhaps—

A muted chuckle drew Jarina's attention toward another, younger man with light brown hair and warm brown eyes and an elegant silk cravat knotted at his throat. "I had her ordered especially for you, Jared," he said. Laughter sparkled in his eyes as they swept over Jarina in open appreciation, and she found it impossible to believe that anyone would dare joke with the fire-breathing giant hovering over her.

Jared glowered at the other man. He again grasped Jarina's chin and forced her to look at him. "Why my ship? Why did you stow away on the *Pegasus?*"

"B-because it was the only American ship in p-port, sir."

"Do you have any kin?"

She hesitated. "No, sir."

Jared dropped his hand.

Fighting the urge to rub her abused jaw, Jarina nervously moistened her lips. "Please don't put me ashore, sir. I-I'll work for my passage. If that's not enough, you can sell me into indentureship when we reach the colonies. I don't eat much and I'll not cause you any trouble. I'll do anything you want."

"Do you have any diseases?" Stephen asked suddenly.

Jared crossed to the door and yanked it open. "Stephen, you are testing my patience. Get out before I decide to do you bodily harm."

"But, Jared, look at her! She's perfect! And just think of Evelyn's reaction when she sees her!" Without warning, Stephen swept into a dramatic bow before Jarina and said with exaggerated reverence, "Stephen Landon, Esquire, at your service, your grace."

Jarina cast Jared a questioning glance.

"Out!"

Stephen turned to Jared and bowed again. "Your grace."

"Out!"

On his way out the door, Stephen gave Jarina a broad grin and a wink. All too soon he was gone, and Jarina could not help wishing he had been the one to stay behind, for this other one frightened her terribly. But, the thought of being returned home frightened her more.

He came to her and Jarina choked back a cry of fright as he slid his long, tanned fingers in her chopped curls. "Who did this to your hair?" he demanded.

"I-I did, sir."

Jared drew his hand through her shiny chestnut curls and let them spring away from his fingers. "A pity. You have such beautiful hair, m'lady."

Jarina chewed on her bottom lip, but said nothing. She could hear him rummaging about the cabin behind her, yet she dared not turn to see what he was doing. Then he returned to her and she caught the glimpse of a blade from the corner of her eye. Seized with panic, she darted out of his reach. "What are you going to do to me?"

Irritation darkened Jared's face as she backed into the wall and shot a terrified glance at the knife in his hand. Then that brilliant blue gaze lifted to his face and he inexplicably felt his heart slam against his ribs. A man could lose himself in those eyes, he thought. He had never seen eyes so lovely, so blue, so scared. He felt a twinge of remorse for having frightened her. He sighed wearily. "I'm merely going to trim your hair," he said. "You did yourself a grave injustice when you lopped off those lovely locks. My only wish is to make you more presentable by softening the ragged edges you left behind in your haste to disguise yourself as a boy. Now, come here."

On legs that felt as though they were made of water,

Jarina moved to stand before him. Something in his severely chiseled face and his silky voice utterly terrified her, and when he took her by the shoulders and turned her away from him, it was all she could do not to bolt to freedom.

As Jared combed his fingers through her thick, full curls and proceeded to slice off an inch here, a smidgen there with the finely honed blade, he took the opportunity to study her closer. She was of a pleasing height, with the top of her head fitting just under his chin; and her auburn curls were soft and shiny and sweetly scented as only hair that is freshly washed can be. Her skin was the color of fine alabaster, and was so delicately textured that he could see the tiny violet veins that shadowed her eyelids whenever she blinked. She had a straight little nose and a generous mouth that was the same deep rose as the azaleas that bloomed at Wyeburn in the spring. He circled around her to trim the curls that framed her slender oval face and her gaze lifted to his; and he was once again struck by the depth and purity of the blue in her eyes.

Then her stomach let out a growl of protest, and Jared saw her cheeks pinken in embarrassment.

Grinning down at her, he playfully rumpled her hair as he would a child's, then stood back to admire his handiwork. "That will have to do for now," he said.

Before Jarina could thank him, the bits of hair he had shaken loose tickled her nose and she sneezed.

Jared put the knife away, then went to the door and summoned his servant. After speaking in low tones with the man for several moments, he closed the door and turned back to Jarina to find her staring at him, fear and uncertainty marring her lovely eyes. He had never seen such long lashes. "Angus will bring you something to eat," he said.

At the mention of food, Jarina's stomach rumbled again, and she folded her arms defensively across her middle. "I'm not hungry."

Jared chuckled. "I don't think your stomach would agree with you on that point, m'lady." He motioned toward a chair. "Sit down."

Jarina did not move. Her time was quickly running out. If he had no intention of taking her to America, then she needed to find someone who would. She took a quivering breath. "Sir, I-I must know . . . what you intend to do—"

"I've not yet decided what I am going to do with you. You have placed me in an awkward position, love. In all my years of sailing, I've only had to deal with one other stowaway. Usually my reputation precedes me, and most men are inclined to keep their distance."

Although he had spoken lightly, the implication in his words brought all manner of unpleasant suggestions to mind. "Your reputation, sir?" she asked warily.

Jared had not missed the sudden evacuation of color from her face. His expression softened. "Jarina, whatever else you may think of me, you may rest assured that I am not a monster who devours young girls for breakfast," he chided gently. "I am, however, a hard taskmaster. Anyone who works for me earns every pence of his wages. I've no patience for laziness, and those inclined to sloth soon learn to look elsewhere for their dole."

Jarina fidgeted. She did not doubt that the captain's reputation as an exacting employer was well deserved. Indeed, to her he looked like someone who would be difficult, if not impossible, to please. Still, she had to try. Her future depended upon it. "I am not afraid of hard work, sir," she said.

While he did not dispute her claim, he found the mental picture of Jarina down on her hands and knees, wrecking her loveliness with menial labor, offensive. Then another pastime came to mind, one he did not find offensive in the least. If anything, he found the very idea almost too pleasurable. In spite of the fact that she was clothed like a cabin boy, Jarina was the perfect combination of youthful innocence and beguiling temptress, and he knew he would not tire of her soon. That she appeared to bathe regularly did not hurt her standing in his eyes either.

Just then, Angus returned to the cabin with a tray. The smells of chicken and hot coffee caused Jarina's stomach to clamor loudly and her mouth to water. She had not eaten all day, and, in spite of her denial, she was famished. She cast a glance at Jared from beneath her lashes and caught him watching her. "We can discuss your future after you have eaten," he said firmly. "Right now, I think you had best devote some attention to your stomach."

This time when he indicated where she should sit, Jarina did not balk.

Seated across the table from her, Jared leaned back in his chair and observed her from beneath partially lowered lids while she ate.

Damn, she was beautiful!

Were she not, he would have no trouble deciding what to do with her. What he should do is give her a stern lecture on the dangers that awaited young girls who defied their elders and take her back home where she would no doubt have her ears boxed and be sent to bed without any supper.

Instead, he found himself entertaining the idea of taking her to his own bed and keeping her there until they reached Alexandria. If she proved worth keeping, he might even set her up in her own house where he could come and go at will, whenever the fancy struck him. But, first, he would get her out of those horrible clothes.

God's teeth! What was wrong with him? He knew full well that to warm his own bunk during the long cold voyage home while denying his men similar comfort was to invite mutiny. So, why did he want her?

As she ate, Jarina saw her benefactor fill his brandy snifter twice, and her alarm steadily grew. The man on whom she was depending to help her leave the country was unquestionably drunk. Yet, what was she to do? The only other ships in port flew His Majesty's colors. She dared not seek asylum on one of them. Her only hope for escape lay in convincing this man to allow her to stay on board.

With a deceiving calm, Jarina dabbed at her mouth with her napkin, then placed it on the table beside her empty bowl. She lifted her gaze to Jared's face. "I guess I was hungrier than I thought. Thank you."

A small smile touched Jared's mouth. "You're welcome." He drained his glass and placed it on the table.

Jarina's gaze flew to the nearly empty bottle on the table, but he made no move to reach for it. Instead he stood up and went to his locker. "You may wear this for now," he said, returning with a pale pink gown. "I have an abiding distaste for women in breeches. When we reach Alexandria, I will buy you some new gowns. You will find, my dear, that when it comes to the matter of gifts, a man's mistress often fares far better than his wife."

The color siphoned from Jarina's face. Of all the payments he could have extracted in return for the favor she asked of him, *that* possibility had never even come to mind.

Jared chuckled and the abrupt sound made her flinch. "You need not look as though you have been sentenced to the gallows," he teased, coming around the table toward her. "My mistresses have been known to fare quite well, actually."

Jarina's heart pounded with the slow, steady beat of a death knell. Was it possible that in her haste to flee Hamilton Hall she had simply traded one madman for another? "But, you don't even know me," she said in a choked whisper. "And I know absolutely nothing about you, sir. Not even your name!"

A slow, portentous smile spread across Jared's features as he came around the table toward her. Placing a hand beneath her elbow, he guided her to her feet. "An oversight on my part, I confess, but one easily remedied. I am Jared Cunningham, sea captain, merchant, and full owner of one hundred fifty thousand acres of the finest land in the State of Virginia."

Before Jarina had a chance to digest even that small bit of information, he slipped an arm about her waist and pulled her against him. His mouth came down on hers, gently at first, then with more persistence, molding her lips to his, then parting them with his tongue.

Engulfed in the heady brandy scent of him, Jarina was helpless to even think, and her confused mind whirled drunkenly in the path of his assault. His tongue plunged boldly into her mouth, then retreated and plunged again and again, teasing and tormenting her until wild sensations unlike anything she had ever felt jolted through her entire body. His hands forged a trail of glowing warmth down her back to cup her buttocks and pull her hard against him, and his mouth left hers to travel down her neck and press smoldering kisses into the rapidly fluttering pulse in the hollow of her throat before returning to capture her lips once again.

When he finally dragged his mouth from hers, she was breathless and shaken and on the verge of tears. Before she could protest his uninvited familiarity, he broke the embrace and pressed the gown into her hands. "I'm going up on deck for a while," he said. "If you want privacy while you dress, you'd best enjoy it now. It will be in short supply during the voyage home." Taking her by the shoulders, he spun her around and planted a hearty smack on her derrière. "Hop to it, my dear, unless you want to be caught with your bottom bared."

Chapter Two

With a gasp of indignation, Jarina whirled around to confront him, but he was gone. The door slammed loudly after him, and she heard his voice raise in a drunken ditty as his footsteps faded.

She groaned. What had she done? The man intended to make her his mistress, and she had just stood there like a witless fool, giving him her tacit consent by her failure to voice even a single objection. And now she was trapped. She could either go along with the distasteful arrangement or go to him and tell him she had misunderstood his purpose. Even as drunk as he was, she did not think he would force her to his bed if she informed him she had changed her mind. What he would do, drunk or not, is put her ashore. Of that she was certain.

Every fiber of Jarina's being told her to flee this ship and the inebriated lunatic who captained it while she still had the chance. His ardor had left her mouth bruised, and her skin still burned where his hands had roamed. Had she anywhere else to take refuge, she would already be gone, for his bold touch had awakened something in her that was at once pleasurable and unsettling. She was sure she would die if she were forced to endure any more of his brazen caresses.

Then William Osterbrook's pimply visage rose to the forefront of her memory, along with the fetid odor of garlic and decay that clung to his fleshy form. The thought of the duke's meaty hands pawing at her body in such a shameful manner on their wedding night and every night thereafter for the rest of her life sent a shudder of revulsion rippling through her.

The choice she had was really no choice at all. She could either become the mistress of a man who terrified her, or the wife of one whose mere presence made her want to gag.

With that repugnant thought still fresh in her mind, she hastily stripped off her flannels and breeches. Even becoming a kept woman was preferable to returning to Hamilton Hall and the obscene debacle that awaited her tomorrow morning at St. Michael's Church.

She donned the pink gown, all the while casting fearful glances at the closed door. She had an inclination that Captain Cunningham was the type of man who would burst into a room without first knocking; and should she be caught undressed, as he had so crudely suggested, she doubted he was gentleman enough to turn his back.

There. It was done. The gown was big on her and dragged on the floor, but for that she was grateful. She had neither the stockings nor slippers to do the gown justice, and the ill-fitting brogans she had been wearing had rubbed such blisters on her feet that she was unable to put them back on. The gown's high-cut waist was gathered just below her breasts with a matching velvet ribbon. It was a summer gown, with short, puffed sleeves that left her arms bare to the chill night air; and no amount of tugging at the low bodice was sufficient to cover her bosom decently. What alarmed her most, however, was that the material of it was so fine and so sheer one could almost see through it, revealing wickedly that she possessed no chemise to wear under it.

She wished he had not insisted she wear it. Goose-flesh erupted on her skin, and she rubbed her arms in a futile attempt to warm them. Perhaps when he saw how impractical the gown was, he would change his mind.

As if it mattered, she thought miserably. Before the night was out, there would not even be the pretense of a gown between them. Hysteria welled up inside her and burst from her throat in a choked laugh as the absurdity of her situation struck her. Before the night was out, she, Margaret Jarina Hamilton, a well-brought-up young lady of impeccable lineage and unquestionable virtue, would become the mistress of a raw colonial she had known less than an hour.

Then she heard the clank of the anchor winch and felt the ship lurch.

Footsteps pounded the deck overhead. The ship heeled, nearly sending Jarina sprawling. Regaining her balance, she hurried to the large bowed window that stretched across the aft of the cabin and knelt upon the seat to peer out into the darkness beyond. The harbor lights that bobbed in the distance seemed to be moving away. To Jarina, it felt as if a giant hand had suddenly taken hold of the ship and was pulling it through the water.

There was a soft knock at the door and Jarina sprang off the window seat and whirled around just as Angus entered the cabin. Stunned by the difference made in her appearance by the simple change of attire, the old man stared at her in open-mouthed amazement. "Blessed saints," he whispered aloud. Suddenly a scarlet stain crept up his neck and he hastily lowered his gaze. "I've come to clear away yer dishes, lass," he mumbled. "The cap'n, he said to tell ye he'll be down shortly."

Jarina's stomach knotted. She could not go through with this. She would be sick if she went through with this. "Sir, please—"

Angus looked up from the table where he was placing the dishes on the tray. "Aye, lass?"

Even in her panic, Jarina knew it was too late to go back now. She tried to smile. "I-it was nothing."

Bewilderment creased the Scot's brow as he stared at her. "Is there anything else ye'll be wantin', lass?" he asked.

I want to go home! A terrible ache swelled in Jarina's chest as she realized that she might never see her home or her father again. She shook her head and turned away before the old man saw the rush of tears that flooded her eyes.

All too soon, she was left alone again with her fears and the creaking of the ship's timbers for company.

Pressing her palms against her cheeks, she paced anxiously. Surely being a man's mistress could not be all that difficult, she thought, fighting to contain her burgeoning terror. All she had to do was lie there and let him take his pleasure. It was the same thing required of a wife, except a wife was not supposed to enjoy it and a mistress was supposed to pretend she did.

With a sigh of exasperation, Jarina plopped down on the window seat and glared at the closed door. A lot you know, she silently admonished herself. A sneaked kiss behind the hedgerow with the vicar's twelve-year-old son when she was but ten was hardly sufficient apprenticeship for becoming a paramour.

At least a man's mistress, unlike his wife, was not bound to him by law.

Jarina's breath caught in her throat. Why did she not think of that before? She was not married to Captain Cunningham, therefore, he had no legal hold on her. Even if she were forced to share his bunk during the voyage, as soon as they reached the colonies, she could flee. She would find work, and when she had enough money saved, she would send for her father.

Suddenly, the future did not seem so bleak.

But what if he got her with child?

Jarina's brows drew together and she chewed her bottom lip as she pondered that one. If a woman of questionable virtue had little chance of acceptance by polite society, a woman who bore a child out of wedlock had absolutely none.

Unless, of course, she passed herself off as a widow.

So caught up was Jarina in fabricating solutions to the various obstacles she might face that she failed to hear the approaching footsteps.

The door swung open. Startled out of her reverie, Jarina sprang to her feet and her face colored hotly as her nemesis strode into the cabin on a blast of arctic air. He was whistling merrily and had a bottle of brandy in each hand, and there was an appreciative gleam in his gray eyes as they swept over her that made her feel naked and vulnerable beneath his devouring gaze.

Jared placed the bottles of brandy inside his locker, then turned and extended a welcoming arm in her direction. "Come near the stove where it's warmer. You will take a chill if you insist upon standing by the window."

Catching her bottom lip between her teeth, she crossed the cabin to stand before him, and her heartbeat escalated to a furious gait when his strong arms slid possessively about her and he drew her close.

She stood stiffly, trying not to shrink away from the overpowering bouquet of spirits that clung to him like an aura. But when Jared's lips brushed down the curve of her cheek and across her temple to tease her ear, an involuntary shudder rocked her body, and she jerked her face away.

Jared drew his head back to look at her. Golden lights danced in his gray eyes as he studied her with thinly veiled amusement. "Are you afraid of me?" he asked.

Yes! Jarina wanted to cry out, but she choked back the response, unwilling to add humiliation to insult by admitting her fear, especially when he almost seemed to be laughing at her. "No, sir," she whispered. "I-I merely do not know how to please you."

"You may begin by dropping the 'sir'," Jared said. He lowered his head to hers. "My name is Jared. Use it."

She swallowed hard. "Yes, si—Jared."

A pleased look flickered in his eyes. "Again."

"J-Jared."

His lips traveled downward, planting moist kisses on her throat and on the soft swells of flesh above the bodice of her gown. His hand moved up to caress her breast through the thin fabric of her gown, his long sun-browned fingers teasing the sensitive peak that responded to his touch with unnerving swiftness. "Put your arms around me," he commanded huskily.

Unable to think clearly over the conflicting emotions he was arousing in her, Jarina obeyed.

The innocent, yet seductive, feel of her slender arms circling his waist was Jared's undoing. His arms closed around her like bands of steel and he crushed her to him, smothering her cry of surprise with his mouth. The intensity of his kisses scorched her lips and stole the breath from her lungs. Her head began to reel in confusion as a small flame of pleasure ignited deep down inside her and began to spread its dizzying warmth throughout her body. Without realizing that she did so, she entwined her arms about his neck and clung helplessly to him as he worked his magic on her.

Her reluctant yielding to his caresses snapped the remaining threads of Jared's restraint. Knotting his hands in the fabric of her gown, he separated the fragile armor with a rending tear.

In panic, Jarina tore her mouth from his and shoved him as hard as she could.

The ruined gown slid off her shoulders, baring her to the hips, and Jared's eyes burned with unbridled passion as they beheld her naked beauty.

Uttering a horrified gasp, Jarina caught the gown and snatched it back up over her breasts, but when she would have fled, Jared moved his foot, deliberately trapping the gown's hem beneath his boot. A low, pleased chuckle sounded deep in his throat. "You're a fresh sight for even my jaded tastes, my dear," he said, smiling at her as he began to unbutton his shirt. "I fear come morning I shall awake to find you were but a dream, if a lovely one."

Jarina's frantic gaze sought the door, then riveted on the man before her who was calmly, methodically, removing his clothes. A sick feeling of hopelessness jelled in her stomach. She had struck a bargain with the devil, and now she would pay the price he demanded of her.

Jared's hands moved to the buttons at his waist, and Jarina squeezed her eyes shut and choked back a groan of despair.

Jared took Jarina's hands and eased her fingers open, freeing the gown of her tortured grip, and it slithered to her feet. "Look at me, sweet."

Struggling for self-control, Jarina opened her eyes. She kept her panic-stricken gaze fixed on Jared's face, not daring to let it drop lower than his chin, lest she unwittingly witness his nakedness. Jared showed no such restraint. He reached out to stroke her cheek as his gleaming gaze caressed the rest of her. "For someone who professes not to be afraid," he said gently, "you are trembling like a terrified child."

To be called a child nearly destroyed Jarina's resolve. She was trying very hard to be sophisticated and nonchalant about all this, yet she was failing miserably. "I-I'm cold," she stammered.

Jared slid his fingers into her hair and drew her toward him. "Then come here and let me warm you."

This time there was not even the gossamer fabric of the pink gown to shield her from the heat of his hard-muscled body as he bound her to him, crushing her naked breasts against the broad wall of his chest as his lips descended to claim hers. His hands moved downward to knead her buttocks, and some small part of her resistance shattered beneath the molten warmth that exploded deep inside her. An involuntary moan of pleasure burst in her throat and she slumped against him, unable to fight the strange new sensations he was arousing in her with his masterful touch. His closeness and the warmth of his hands on her bare skin sent an intoxicating heat spreading down her legs, turning them to jelly; and her body began to quiver with an intense, pulsing need. She did not protest when Jared lifted her in his arms and carried her to the bunk.

Still kissing her, he gently lowered her to the mattress. With a lightness of touch that set every nerve in her body to tingling, he trailed his fingertips down the length of her arms and back up along their soft warm insides, then repeated the motion along her thighs. He kissed and petted and stroked every inch of her sensitive flesh until she thought she would die of pleasure, and when his hand moved downward to caress her most private place, she ceased to think at all. Jared lowered his weight to hers and parted her thighs with his knee.

Then a terrible blistering ache spread between her thighs, jolting her out of her passion-induced stupor. She clenched her teeth to keep from crying out, but the sensation was so intense her back arched and she ground the back of her head into the pillows. Tears of pain stung her eyes. She tried to push him away, but he caught both her hands in one of his and drew them up over her head, pinning them to the wall. Seized by panic, she struggled furiously, but her movements only served to further flame his desire for her, and in her attempts to wiggle out from under him she inadvertently succeeded in driving her hips against his. Again and again he thrust deep within her, until she no longer had the strength to do anything but lie there with tears of helpless anger streaming down her face while he had his way with her.

The tumultuous storm over, Jared relaxed against her and drew her into his arms. His touch was gentle as he stroked her naked hip and tenderly kissed her. "Thank you, m'lady. I needed that," he whispered huskily into her ear, savoring the soft warmth of her body against his. He reached up to brush her tousled curls back from her face, then drew back in bewilderment when his hand touched wetness. Jarina squeezed her eyes shut and turned her face away. She refused to look at him, and Jared's stomach knotted at the dawning awareness that her tears were not the result of passion's release. He shifted his weight off her.

His gaze dropped, first to the crimson smears on her thighs, then to his own bloodied member, and the dawning awareness of what he had just done both sobered and sickened him. He would never in a million years have believed she was a virgin. Even now, with the night's evidence staining the quilt on his bunk, he found the truth hard to swallow. Had she not come to him of her own free will? Had she not teased and lured him with her enchanting beauty, alternately resisting, then yielding to him with the skill of a practiced courtesan? Had she not met his impassioned thrusts with a hungry eagerness that matched his own? Had she not entered into this liaison fully cognizant of what was expected of a mistress?

Jared drew a ragged breath. "Why did you not tell me you were a virgin?"

A tear streamed down her temple and into her hair, and Jarina reached up to wipe it away with the back of her hand. "I-I didn't think . . . it m-mattered."

"You didn't think it mattered? My God! What a fool you are! Do you honestly think I would have been stupid enough to bed you had I known you were untouched?"

Jarina bit down on her bottom lip, but the sob es-

caped anyway. In spite of the high value men placed
on virtue, he did not seem at all pleased by hers. Instead, he was behaving as though she had just contami-
nated him with some dreadful disease. She wished she
had not given herself to him. She wished she had never
come here.

Suddenly feeling spent and exhausted, Jared rolled
onto his back and stared glumly at the rafters overhead.
A fine pickle he'd gotten himself into this time, he
thought. He'd managed to make it to the age of thirty-
six without falling prey to the machinations of scheming virgins and their matchmaking mothers, and here
he was, snared by his own carelessness in a trap he'd
spent most of his adult life trying to avoid. "So, what
happens now, love?" he asked quietly. "Do you scream
rape and send me to the gallows? Or is there another
game you play? Tell me, Jarina. What price do you demand of me? Do I pay for my folly with my purse or
with marriage?"

Thoroughly humiliated by the unfair accusations,
Jarina flung herself away from him with a strangled cry
and burst into tears.

Jared squeezed his eyes shut and mouthed a silent
curse. Never in his life had he felt like such a cad. If
he were any kind of a gentleman at all, he would swallow his pride and do what was right. He would marry
the girl.

Except that he didn't want to marry her.

He hadn't wanted to marry anyone since that
wretched day eight years ago when he had nearly proposed to Evelyn.

He had been a young man of twenty-eight when he
fell in love with Evelyn Landon. He'd caught but a
glimpse of her as her carriage had overtaken him on
West Road, and he had spent the next hour cursing his
mount's lame leg; had his horse been fit, he would not
have hesitated to give chase, for Evelyn's exotic splen-

dor had been permanently etched in his mind. There
was something oddly familiar about her, something he
could not quite place. For days to follow, he scoured
the streets of Alexandria for anyone who might give
him a clue to her identity, and at night, he dreamed
of burying his hands in luxuriant tresses the color of
a raven's wing and of ruby lips begging for his kisses.

A week later, he received an invitation to a Fourth
of July picnic at Fair Oaks.

He nearly turned down the invitation. He had not
been to Fair Oaks since he was a child, even though
the plantation bordered his own, and his memory conjured up less of the elegant Fairfax County estate than
of the bitter quarrel that had erupted between his par-
ents during their last visit there.

Still, the tantalizing, seductive, oriental perfume that
permeated the invitation drew him like a hound to the
hunt, and he accepted.

And his search ended.

The jet-eyed beauty who had been haunting his
dreams was mistress of Fair Oaks; the infant he barely
remembered from his last visit to the plantation was
now a woman.

All day long, he could not take his eyes off her.

"Shouldn't you return to your guests now?" he asked
her when they finally reined in their horses after a brisk
run across the countryside.

Evelyn slid to the ground and yanked the yellow
scarf from around her head, freeing her dark locks from
their modest restraint and letting them tumble wantonly down over shoulders. "You are my guest," she
said. Then she flung the scarf across his stallion's eyes,
causing the Arabian to start. "Bet you can't catch me!"

By the time Jared got his horse under control, Evelyn
was halfway across Goose Run, her skirts hiked up
around her waist, baring her shapely calves as she
jumped from rock to rock in the middle of the rapidly
flowing creek.

Jared urged his horse into the water.

Evelyn cast a frantic glance over her shoulder as the distance between them closed, then squealed as Jared dipped low and caught her around the waist, lifting her clear of the water. They were both were still laughing when he lowered her to the opposite bank. He dismounted and sank to the ground beside her. Evelyn's eyes grew dreamy as she threaded her fingers through Jared's thick black hair and drew his head down to hers. "My very special guest," she murmured against his lips.

Jared lost his soul in that kiss.

They made love on the creek bank beneath a willow canopy. Jared was neither surprised nor dismayed to learn that Evelyn was not a virgin. Nor did he care. All that mattered was the feel of her heart beating next to his.

"I searched all over for you," he whispered into her hair as she lay in his arms, her fair skin flushed in the aftermath of their lovemaking. "I didn't know where to find you. No one seemed to know who you were."

"I knew who *you* were," Evelyn said offhandedly. She disentangled herself from Jared's arms and sat up. "In fact, I know a great deal about you."

Jared chuckled and reached up to twirl a dark curl about his finger. "Such as?"

Evelyn turned her head and pressed her cheek against Jared's hand. "Such as, you are the catch of the season. You are the richest man in Fairfax County. You own more land than anyone in Virginia, more than the Randolfs and the Carters combined. And you are a duke."

Merriment danced in Jared's eyes. "I'm afraid you've been misinformed on that last one, my dear. The duchy of Wyeburn was dissolved when my grandfather fled Dorsetshire."

"But, you *would* be a duke," Evelyn persisted, "if your family had remained in England."

"Perhaps."

"And if you married me, I would be a duchess."

One corner of Jared's mouth twitched uncontrollably. "Are you proposing?"

Evelyn feigned horror. "To a mere duke! Never!"

"Good. Because when the time comes, *I* want to do the asking."

Reconsidering, Evelyn frowned. "Now, if you were a prince . . ."

Grinning, Jared pulled her down to him. "You would be a princess," he finished for her.

Evelyn giggled. "A very wealthy one."

For the next three months, Jared could be found at Fair Oaks more often than not. He could not get enough of Evelyn Landon. He loved her recklessness, her bold passions. There was nothing pretentious about Evelyn. She was selfish. She was greedy. And, in bed, she was insatiable.

By the middle of October, the *Pegasus,* newly outfitted and loaded with molasses and tobacco, was ready to sail, but Jared was not. Although he had already bid farewell to Evelyn, he could not resist returning to Fair Oaks one last time before putting out to sea.

He intended to ask her to be his wife.

His spirits were high as he rode into the yard and dismounted. He could not wait to see the look on Evelyn's face when she saw her betrothal gift. No mere ring for his princess. In his waistcoat pocket, carefully wrapped in white velvet, was an emerald and diamond tiara.

He did not bother knocking. Evelyn had given him a key, and he used it now to let himself into the house. From upstairs, he heard her laughter. Anxious to see her lovely face again, he started up the stairs.

"Yes. Oh, yes!" Evelyn cried out, her voice growing louder as he reached the landing. He took the remaining stairs two at a time.

As Jared neared Evelyn's bedchamber, he heard her

moan, a low, primal, animal sound punctuated with the unmistakable creak of bedslats.

He froze.

In the middle of the bed, in all her naked glory, was Evelyn on her hands and knees, with her head thrown back in wild abandon and her eyes squeezed shut, her breasts slapping together rhythmically as Charles Cabell rammed into her from behind.

Jared slipped from the house unseen. Sick with revulsion and loathing, he goaded his horse to a killing speed. When he reached Alexandria, he took the tiara from his pocket and hurled it into the Potomac River.

Never again, he swore, would he allow his reasoning to be clouded by a woman's charms.

Jared rolled off the bunk and went to the table. His hand shook as he refilled his glass.

What was he going to do now? he wondered. Only a few hours ago, he had been celebrating his final contact with England. He'd had his fill of priggish British civil servants and watery-eyed tax collectors. He had planned to return to Virginia, sell the company, and spend the remainder of his life at Wyeburn where he belonged. And he had planned to do so with a clear conscience, knowing that in his entire adult life he had never cheated a man, forced himself upon a woman, or fathered any bastard children.

Now all that had changed. In one drunken evening, he had managed to commit the second of those crimes, and possibly even the third.

Jarina's gut-wrenching sobs tore at Jared's liquor-strained senses, and he turned to her, no longer able to put her out of his mind. Going to the bunk, he worked the covers from beneath her hips, then lay down beside her and drew the quilt up over them both. "Go away!" she shrieked, but he slid an arm beneath her shoulders and rolled her toward him. She tried to pull away, but he held her tightly, cradling her head against his chest with his hand and wishing impotently that he could do something to ease her grief. He had seen women weep before—Evelyn had mastered the art—but not like this. Unlike the tears Evelyn shed, tears which welled up in her eyes without reddening them only to roll prettily down her cheeks one at a time, Jarina's were scalding and copious, drenching his chest, and her sobs jerked her entire body with spasms of wracking misery.

He did not know why her tears should affect him so; she was a woman, scheming and deceitful as were all women, and unworthy of his respect. Had he not had that lesson well drummed into him by his mother and Evelyn Landon and countless others like them? He doubted Jarina was all that different.

After a while, Jarina gave up fighting him and sagged weakly in his arms. Weariness and the day's trials overcame her, and she slipped into an exhausted sleep, her slumber punctuated by an occasional muffled hiccup against his chest.

Jared pulled back so that he might gaze down on her, and what he saw did not sit well within his mind. With her swollen, tear-ravaged face, she no longer looked the beguiling seductress, but more like a battered, broken child. A child whose innocence he had destroyed. But she was no child. God, how well he knew that! Yet, who was she? Why, and from what, was she running? She was too fine-boned to be of common stock and her body did not appear to have been ill-used. Her skin was smooth and delicately hued, and her slender white hands soft and uncallused. He recalled her voice, cultured and softly accented, and he knew she was no waif from the streets.

Everything about Jarina told him she had to have come from a family of some importance. If that were so, he knew it would not be long before the law was breathing down his neck, demanding her return. In his mind, he could already see himself swinging from a gibbet in payment for her abduction, and the sight was not a welcome one.

Jared lifted a tangled curl back from Jarina's face and pressed his lips to the erratic pulse at her temple. "What am I going to do with you, my little stowaway?" he whispered. But no answer was forthcoming, and he was unable to shake the cold dread that gripped him as he felt the hangman's noose tighten around his neck.

Chapter Three

Dawn had already filled the cabin with its faint gray light when Jarina jerked awake. Her eyes flared wide and her body stiffened as she realized she was cradled in a man's arms with her cheek pressed against a powerful, naked chest. For a bewildered moment, she could not remember where she was. Then her face flooded with color as the memories came rushing back to her, filling her with shame and revulsion. A cry of anger welled in her throat, and she placed her palms flat against that broad chest and shoved as hard as she could, but Jared lay unmoving in a deep, dreamless sleep, with one arm wrapped securely about her middle. Jarina tried unsuccessfully to lift the arm off her. Like the rest of him, it was hewn of iron and weighed as much, and there was not an ounce of fat beneath the sun-bronzed skin to soften the well-defined contours. She gritted her teeth and began scooting down the length of the bunk, gradually working her way from beneath the imprisoning arm.

At last she freed her head and sat up. "Rutting beast!" she hissed. Her eyes blazed as they swept over Jared's naked body. " 'Twas your notion to make me pay for my passage with my virtue, and when I attempt to comply with your wishes, you accuse me of seeking to blackmail you! If I had a knife, I would cut off your mighty cock and throw it to the fishes! See then what a big brave man you are with no weapon to perform your vile deeds!"

Clambering over him, she climbed out of the bunk. Then she yanked off the covers and hurled them to the floor. "I hope you freeze to death!"

Jared did not even stir.

For a moment, Jarina just stood there with her teeth chattering, clenching and unclenching her fists as she glared down at him in impotent frustration. She longed to knot her fingers in his thick black hair to shake him awake and make him listen to her as she assaulted him with every damning curse she could think of, but her courage was rapidly waning. Even in sleep he had no cause to fear her as she did him. Sudden tears stung her eyes and she turned away, furious at both her own cowardice and the impossible situation in which she had entangled herself. No man would have her now. She was ruined, and she had only herself to blame.

Alternating between cursing him and cursing herself, Jarina snatched up the boy's breeches and flannel shirt she had worn on board the ship and hastily dressed, her hands shaking as she fumbled with the buttons. She refused to spend another moment in this cabin. She did not know where she might hide; she only knew she had to get away from that unscrupulous drunkard who dared call himself a captain. She would find the old man who had found her hiding place in the hold and who had brought her dinner last night, she decided. He would help her. Picking up her shoes, she tiptoed across the cabin to the door and quietly, carefully, turned the knob.

"I wouldn't go out there if I were you," Jared said in an ominously quiet voice.

Jarina whipped around to find him sitting on the edge of the bunk, holding his head in his hands as though it were too heavy to be supported by his neck.

He glared up at her through pain-glazed eyes. "The men bathe up on deck this time of morning," he said tersely. "If you leave this cabin now, you are likely to see more than you bargained for." He let go of his head and straightened his back. "Come here. I want to talk to you, and I don't want to have to shout to be heard."

Both fury and fear building rapidly inside her, Jarina raked him with a damning gaze. "We have nothing to discuss," she said icily. "You made your opinion of me and my motives quite clear last night."

Anger flared in Jared's bloodshot eyes. "Don't test me, Jarina. I am in no mood this morning for your little games."

"So you do remember my name," she spat, knotting her fists and eyeing him with contempt. She was determined not to let him see her fear. "After last night, I am surprised you would remember your own. Your mind is well-pickled, Captain!"

The muscle in Jared's cheek twitched. "I am not a patient man, Jarina," he said with a deliberate calm that made her resolve crumble and her knees threaten to buckle beneath her. "Nor am I above using force when provoked. It does not please me to know I shall likely be paying the rest of my life for a single moment of stupidity. Believe me, letting you remain on board this ship was not the act of a man in full possession of his senses. However, whether you like it or not, your well-being lies entirely in my hands. You have a choice. You can either learn to obey me, or accept the consequences of your actions. Now, come here."

A blinding hatred unlike anything Jarina had ever known welled up inside her. He had her backed into a corner and he knew it. Angry tears brightened her eyes, and a thousand obscenities sprang to her lips, begging to be heaped upon his arrogant head. But her fury was outweighed by her fear of being returned home, and she knew she had no choice but to surrender to his demands. Despising herself for not having the courage to defy him, she put down her shoes and reluctantly crossed the cabin to stand before him, painfully aware with each step she took of his cold gray gaze boring into her, reminding her in no uncertain terms of the power he wielded over her. She was completely at his mercy, and that galled her to no end.

A small smile of amusement twisted Jared's mouth. "It's good to see you possess some common sense after all," he said dryly. "For a moment, I feared you might be stupid enough to try to disobey me."

Something inside her snapped. In a high rage, she brought up her hand with the intent of slapping that silly smirk right off his handsome face, but something in the look he gave her caused her hand to freeze in midair. Jared stared for a moment at her upraised hand, then turned his cold, steely gaze upon her face, and Jarina knew that if she struck him, the penalty he would extract from her would far outweigh any satisfaction she might gain from expressing her anger. Barely able to see him through the bitter tears that pooled in her eyes, she closed her hand into a fist and let it drop to her side. She had been completely cowed by a single look. "I hate you," she choked.

"I'm sure you do," Jared said wearily. He patted the mattress. "Now be a good girl and sit down."

Pricked by his patronizing tone, she sat, not where he indicated, but at the foot of the bunk, as far away from him as she could get.

Jared frowned and started to say something, then seemed to think better of it. Resting his forearms along his thighs, he dangled his hands between his knees and stared at the deck. Several long, uncomfortable seconds passed before he spoke. "Jarina, I apologize for hurting you last night. When I suggested you share my bed, I had no idea you were a virgin."

Jarina's bottom lip trembled. "What did you think I was?" she asked, unable to keep the hurt from her voice. "A tavern whore?"

"Actually, it would have been better if you were. It would certainly simplify matters."

A tear streamed down Jarina's cheek and she reached up to wipe it away with the back of her hand. "I have no intention of trapping you into marriage, if that's what you think."

"It's not what I think. Even if you tried, you would not succeed. I could easily discredit your word, and your character would suffer greatly in the process. No, Jarina, I have a far better solution in mind than dragging your name through the mire.

"When we reach Alexandria," Jared continued, "I will have my attorney establish a trust in your name. You will receive a handsome allowance—"

"I don't want anything from you."

"You will receive a handsome allowance," Jared repeated, disregarding her objection. "Enough to allow you to live in comfort the rest of your days, or until you marry, whichever you choose."

Jarina speared him with a look of resentment. "And if I don't want your money?" she asked. "What will you do? Force it upon me?"

Jared did not deign to answer that. Tired of her needling, he eased his large frame up off the bunk, slowly, as though each small movement pained him, and carefully made his way to the door. "There's fresh water by the basin. I suggest you remain in this cabin until I return unless it is your wish to be treated to a saltwater dousing up on deck along with the rest of the men." He started to open the door, then stopped and turned back to look at her. "Jarina, this is going to be a long voyage. Try not to make it any longer for either of us."

At the sound of the door closing behind him, Jarina vented her frustration on the quilts lying on the floor at her feet, giving them a savage kick. How dare he talk down to her as though she were a mere child! And what was wrong with her? Had she no tongue in her head? Or was she such a quivering coward that she could only voice her anger when he was not awake to hear her heated words?

Well, no more! she vowed. He was just going to have to learn that she was a force to be reckoned with, and not some mindless trollop he could use to satisfy his vulgar needs, then discard. When he displeased her, she would tell him so. When he ordered her to his bed, she would refuse him. Never again would she quake in fear before his demands or grant him the satisfaction of seeing her reduced to tears.

For several long seconds, Jared stood outside his cabin door, toweling his wet hair. Annoyance creased his forehead as last night and the memory of Jarina's tortured weeping returned to torment his already unsettled conscience. She had come to him in desperate straits, and he had used her, too drunk to even notice that she was a virgin. The best thing for all concerned would be for him to bring the *Pegasus* about and take Jarina back to Southampton, but the thought of the authorities waiting to seize his ship and clap him in irons the moment they docked rendered that alternative out of the question. Jarina had best learn to accept her lot.

She was sitting on the window seat with her feet tucked beneath her when he entered the cabin. Her back was toward him as she sat staring out the window, and he saw her shoulders stiffen, the slight movement her only acknowledgment of his presence.

Tossing the damp towel on the back of a chair, he donned his breeches. He poured himself a healthy dose of brandy and downed it in a single swallow. Then he went to his desk and sat down, stretching out his long legs and closing his eyes, to wait for the hammering in his head to abate.

In the silence that yawned between them, Jarina felt her courage rapidly slipping away. Why did he not say something? Had she not only been dismissed, but forgotten as well? Or was he merely waiting for her to speak first? She took a deep breath to try to calm her mounting apprehension. Why was he torturing her like this? Even his bellowing placed less of a strain on her frayed nerves than did this terrible, pulsing silence.

Finally, unable to bear the torturous wait any longer, she lowered her bare feet to the floor and swung around on the seat to face him. Suddenly she felt very foolish as it became evident that tormenting her was probably the farthest thing from his mind. His eyes were closed and there was a wrinkle of pain between his brows like one she had often witnessed on her father's forehead the morning after a night of overindulgence. Something inside her softened toward the man sitting before her now. He was but human after all.

There was no denying that he was a fine-looking man, Jarina grudgingly admitted, her gaze sweeping over his tall, broad-shouldered frame as he lounged in the chair, unaware of her perusal. Had circumstances been different, she might have even been attracted to him. Physically, he was magnificent. He was the lover of her imagination, the carefully embroidered fantasy, the unattainable standard against which all other potential suitors paled in comparison. But that was where the similarity ended. Whereas the Adonis of her dreams was kind and gentle and solicitous, reality had burdened her with a man who was forceful and domineering and who took what he wanted as though it were his God-given right.

Any compassion she might have felt for him faded as her resentment flared. She hoped he suffered dearly for his indiscretion. She hoped he felt utterly wretched. He deserved to be in pain. Her wandering gaze fell on the bottle of brandy on the table, and she gloated, reveling in the knowledge that her handsome lord was not infallible. Like any mortal man, he had been tested by a liquid mistress.

It was unfortunate that Jared chose that instant to open his eyes, for Jarina's resolve nearly fled under his cold, unsparing glower. "Do you find my discomfort amusing?" he asked caustically.

Stunned that he had so deftly discerned her thoughts, she hastily shook her head. She was no longer feeling so smug, and her toes curled into the floor in an unconscious retreat.

That slight movement did not go unnoticed. His attention drawn to the angry red blisters on her feet, Jared felt a very small part of his ill humor begin to subside. She must have walked miles in those miserable shoes, he thought, and he made a mental note to find some unguent for her. He brought his gaze back up to her face, and was mildly surprised by the defiance he saw in her eyes as she boldly returned his stare. It was a welcome respite from the cowering deference he usually elicited in people. "How old are you?" he asked.

"Eighteen."

A small smile tugged at the corners of his mouth as he remembered himself at that age. Obstinate. Headstrong. Invincible. "So young," he mused aloud.

Immediately, Jarina's expression became defiant. "I am not stupid."

"I never said you were."

"It was implied. So young. So pretty. So like a woman. Why don't you simply say *so stupid?* It's what men usually mean when they make a comment like that."

"Such harsh words, Jarina. I cringe to think you include all men in your bitter assessment." He hefted his tall frame out of the chair and came to her. Bending down, he placed a gentle kiss upon her lips. "Not all men deserve your condemnation," he said softly, a quiet understanding in his gray eyes. Then he straightened up and rumpled her tangled curls. "Only some of us."

He turned away from her and only then did Jarina let her rancor show. Conceited oaf! She ached to show

him just how much condemnation she could summon
for the likes of him!

Sufficiently recovered from the aftereffects of the previous night's revelry, Jared went to the washbasin
where he picked up the leather strop and began sharp-
ening his razor, cognizant of Jarina's wide-eyed gaze
following his every move. When he finished with the
strop and tossed it aside, he heard her expel her breath.
Little fraud, he thought, stifling a chuckle. For all her
bravado, Jarina was scared to death of him.

Yet he was quite pleased with her, he realized with
some surprise. Her guilelessness excited his passions far
more than any planned seduction. It was a pity they
had gotten off on such poor footing last night. Jarina
would make a delightful mistress, and he could think
of nothing that would give him greater pleasure than
to take her in his arms and make sweet, passionate love
to her.

After a few minutes, when he finished shaving, he
turned to find that she had placed her feet up on the
window seat and was sitting with her arms wrapped
around her drawn-up legs and her head resting on her
knees. Her eyes were closed and her long lashes threw
shadows on her fair cheeks. In the bright sunlight that
streamed in through the window, she looked no more
than fourteen, hardly old enough to be sharing his
table, much less his bed. He picked up a dry towel and
wiped his face. "Are you hungry?" he asked.

She straightened and opened her eyes to look at him,
and this time Jared did not fail to see the lingering fear
in their blue depths before her expression once more
became guarded. She shook her head.

Jared chuckled softly. "I am not an ogre, Jarina.
Someday you may even grow to like me."

His ridiculous assumption rankled and an apprecia-
ble number of cutting rebukes sprang to the tip of her
tongue, but she kept silent.

Annoyance flickered in Jared's eyes when he realized

no retort was forthcoming. Shaking his head, he went to the locker. "You have me curious, love," he said as he began dressing. "You do not look to have been abused. From all outward appearances, I would guess you come from a fine family and enjoyed the trappings of a comfortable, if not extravagant, existence. Why did you run away?"

Jarina stiffened slightly and suddenly she felt as though steel bands were tightening around her chest, cutting off her air. She took a deep breath, thankful Jared's state of undress gave her an excuse to keep her gaze modestly averted. "My guardian promised my hand in marriage to a man I abhor," she said in a low, hollow voice. "Because my betrothed is man of some importance, I was given no say in the matter. As our wedding day neared, I found I could not go through with it."

Jared looked thoughtful. "Wealthy?"

"My guardian?"

"The man you were to have married."

She nodded.

"Titled?"

She hesitated, then nodded again.

Jared looked vaguely amused. He had yet to meet a woman who would turn down both money and position. "I assume you have a good reason for not wanting to marry him."

A small tremor rocked her body as she remembered the day her father had broken the devastating news to her. He had been clearly upset over something, although he would not tell her what, and he seemed in that moment to have aged ten years. She said slowly, "I don't love him."

Jared pulled on a seaman's sweater knit of coarse dark wool. "Did it ever occur to you that perhaps your guardian knew what was best for you?"

There was a condescending note in his voice that set Jarina's teeth on edge. Why did men always think women incapable of deciding their own futures? "If you knew my betrothed, sir, you might better understand my reluctance," she said, struggling to keep the irritation from her voice. She still avoided his gaze. "His belly hangs to his knees and his wig crawls with vermin and he reeks of sausage. It doesn't matter to me that he is either wealthy or titled. I would rather die than marry him."

She had so exactly described Roswell that Jared was momentarily taken aback, but he swept the duke's visage from his mind without further thought. "Then you are a fool, Jarina," he said flatly. "You should have married the man for what he could offer you and sought your pleasures elsewhere."

She jerked her head up to look at him and her eyes were wide with dawning horror. "Do you mean, take a lover?" she asked incredulously. Her voice, little more than a shocked whisper, suddenly became louder as her surprise gave way to anger. "My God! You do me a grave injustice to even suggest such a thing! Do you honestly think I am the type of woman to swear fidelity to my lord only to deceive him the moment his back is turned?"

Jared sat down beside her on the window seat and began pulling on his boots. "You need not look so self-righteous, my dear. Women do it all the time."

"In your circle of friends perhaps. Not in mine!"

Oddly touched by her naiveté, Jared reached out to trace the line of her jaw with his forefinger. "Then I envy you your friends," he said softly.

Jarina jerked away from his touch and sprang to her feet, white-hot fury blazing in her eyes. "Were I a man, I would call you out for your impertinence! First you insult me, and now you mock me! Is it not enough that I relinquished to you the only thing of value I possessed? Must you also belittle me and ridicule the truths I hold dear?"

Jared sighed wearily. "No one is mocking you,

Jarina. Nor was it my intent to question your integrity.
I was merely trying to point out that marriage and love
are seldom compatible bedmates, and it's often wise to
separate them entirely. Your convictions are com-
mendable. They are simply not very realistic." He
stood up. "I must go up on deck for a few hours. I trust
you will find something to occupy your time during my
absence."

Again she had been dismissed, and the thought that
he could so casually shunt her aside while she still
seethed with pent-up rage was a slight she would not
soon forgive. He had goaded her into a fine temper, and
now, when she wanted nothing more than to give him
a piece of her mind, he had turned his back on her and
was walking away as though she were nothing more
to him than a bit of sport with which he grew easily
bored. He reached for the door and her anger soared.
"Jared!"

He stopped with his hand on the brass knob and
turned to look at her.

In spite of the fact that she was trembling and that
it took nearly all her strength to stand her ground and
not back down, Jarina drew herself up to her full height
and faced Jared squarely. She lifted her chin and met
his emotionless gaze straight on. "What of your wife?"
she asked. "What would you do were she to go behind
your back to seek solace in another man's arms?"

For a moment, he did not move, but the abrupt contraction of his pupils told Jarina that she had struck
a nerve.

The slow, lazy smile that then spread across Jared's
features did nothing to disguise the proprietary glint
in his gray eyes, and there was something frightening
in the way he was looking at her. "Quite simply, my
dear," he said, fixing her with that terrible smile as he
opened the cabin door. "I would kill them both."

Chapter Four

Jared barked at the helmsman. "You're luffing your sails. Point her into the wind!"

It annoyed Jared that the crack in the mast was not spotted before leaving port. He turned to the first mate and said curtly, "Tighten the fore topgallant stays and send someone aloft to inspect the rigging. If she keeps straining, we'll have no choice but to bring her down."

"Aye, aye, sir." Silas Crawford sucked in his breath as he spoke. "We'll get her squared away."

Crawford hurried off.

Jared's eyes narrowed as he observed the seaman's hasty departure and he wondered if the man had taken to drinking while on watch. He had no wish to lose his ship in a squall simply because his first mate had grown careless. He turned his attention to Stephen who was cautiously making his way up to the quarterdeck with one eye closed and his face set into a grim mask.

Stephen peered up at Jared through the eye he had managed to pry open. "G'morning," he mumbled.

"Good afternoon," Jared corrected wryly.

Stephen grimaced and rubbed his throbbing temple. "Is it my imagination, or did we have a stowaway on board last night?"

"You should know. You suggested I marry her."

The younger man groaned. "No wonder I dreamed I had paid a magistrate a hundred pounds to leave his warm fire to come out to the *Pegasus* in the middle of the night and perform the ceremony. Tell me, Jared, was she as beautiful as I remember, or was that, too, a dream?"

Beautiful. And dangerous, Jared thought, his irritation piqued. There had been a definite challenge in Jarina's eyes earlier when she asked him what he would do were his own wife to seek solace in another man's arms. Both the question and his response continued to gnaw at him, for they exposed him as a hypocrite. It did not matter to him that other married women of his acquaintance took lovers with a regularity that bordered upon the obscene. His reply to Jarina had been no idle threat; should the woman he marry ever play him false, he would kill her. Yet what troubled him most was that it was Jarina of whom he had been thinking at the time. He did not know why he should feel so possessive toward her; he intended to wash his hands of her as soon as they docked in Alexandria. His disposition thoroughly soured, he started toward the companionway. "Join us for dinner and see for yourself," he said irritably.

Stephen's brows dipped in bewilderment as Jared disappeared through a door beneath the quarterdeck. Surely the girl was not still on board? Then he gripped the taffrail with both hands as his stomach convulsed. "Holy Mother *machree* . . ."

Jared came upon his servant just outside the cabin door. The Scot's wiry legs bowed beneath the weight of the bolts of cloth he held in his arms. "I knocked, sir, but the lass dinna answer," Angus said. A look of concern creased his weathered face. "Ye think she's a'right in there?"

Jared made no attempt to disguise his foul mood. "I'm sure she is, Angus," he bit out as he took the bolts of cloth.

Not knowing what he had done to incur his master's displeasure, Angus held up a small bundle tied within a scarf. "I found this 'mongst the cargo, cap'n," he said warily. "I think the lass must've dropped it last night."

A muscle in Jared's cheek jerked as he regarded his servant, and it was all Angus could do not to shrink away from the contempt in that glacial glare. It didn't happen often that his master was like this, but when it did, Angus swore he would willingly give his right arm for the luxury of waiting out the storm as far away from Jared as possible.

Jared claimed Jarina's bundle. "Mr. Landon will be dining with us this evening, Angus. You will handle the arrangements, of course."

The grayed head bobbed up and down. "Aye, cap'n. Will ye be wantin' anythin' special? I mean, does the lass—"

"Jarina will adapt her tastes to that which is available," Jared snapped. "If there is nothing else, you are dismissed."

The Scot mumbled a hasty reply and hurried to do his master's bidding, leaving Jared to glare at his departing back in contempt. Something special, indeed!

It had been a mistake to let Jarina get under his skin, he thought. How much easier she would be to forget were she some simple-minded twit he could use to satisfy his lust then toss aside without further regard. Instead, she had to stick that damned defiant chin of hers up in the air and peer down her nose at him as though he were a lowly commoner to grovel at her feet.

Jared shifted the bolts of cloth to one arm and opened the door. It was time Her Highness learned just who gave the orders around here.

But even that, he realized when he entered the cabin, was going to have to wait. Jarina, the little minx, was gone.

*   *   *

Jarina wrinkled her nose in disgust as her gaze wandered about the cramped infirmary. Dimly illuminated by a tiny salt- and grime-encrusted portal high on one wall, the cabin was dusty and ill-kept. A peculiar odor—like rotting gammon—pervaded the air. In the glass-fronted lockers built into one wall, surgical instruments were carelessly heaped rather than being arranged in any useful order, and many of them appeared as though they had not even been wiped clean before being put away. Bitter bile rose in her throat, and she had to swallow hard to keep from being sick. Her father would be appalled to see a surgery so poorly maintained. His own offices were never less than immaculate, and he religiously boiled his instruments after every use.

Placing her shoes on the floor just outside the door, she stepped into the sick bay, and her disgust gave way to anger as she swiped at a cobweb that stretched across the doorway. The custodian of this infirmary should be drawn and quartered! And Captain Cunningham! What manner of man was the captain that he would permit such filth on his ship? Had he such little regard for the welfare of his men that he would risk their lives by allowing them to be operated on with befouled instruments and treated with medicines that had long since gone rancid? She grimaced at the odor that emanated from a pot of salve and hastily replaced the lid. Something had to be done about this place. Immediately.

Rolling up her sleeves, she marched to the lockers and yanked open a door. She did not care whether the ship's surgeon happened to return or not. Indeed, she hoped he did, for she was inclined to give him a piece of her mind.

One by one, she removed from the locker the various lancets and scissors and trocars. She discarded those that were damaged beyond repair and placed the others in a pile to be taken later to the galley and boiled clean, her ire fueled by the needless waste brought about by neglect. So intent was she on the task that she did not hear the approaching footsteps behind her.

"You bloody cur! Get yer thievin' hands off my tools!"

Jarina's heart leaped into her throat and a handful of delicate whalebone forceps clattered to the floor. She whirled around and found herself face to face with a balding, bug-eyed man brandishing a large butcher knife. Her eyes widened in stricken terror as he came toward her.

"What do you think ye're doing, boy, messing 'round down here and going through them tools like they belong's to you?" the man demanded. He wiped one hand on his soiled apron. "You know bloody well this bay's off limits without my say-so. Just you wait 'til I get you up to the cap'n! He'll strip the skin off yer scrawny back. You'll think long and hard 'fore you go stealin' again."

Jarina's mouth had gone slack as she listened to the man's tirade, and now she stared at him in wide-eyed disbelief. "Are you the . . . surgeon?" she asked, edging away from him until her back was against the wall.

"The surgeon!" the man shrieked, and his eyes seemed ready to pop out of his head. Suddenly he laughed. "Hee, hee! Now, if that ain't a funny one! The surgeon!"

Jarina's fear gave way to anger. "You said one needs your approval to come in here."

The man scratched his belly with the knife handle. "So I did."

"If you are not the ship's surgeon, then who is?" Was the man so addlepated he could not comprehend a simple question?

He took another step toward her and Jarina gasped as he raised the knife to her throat. There was a wild, almost crazed look in his bulbous eyes. "Now, you just watch yer mouth, boy, and don't you go usin' that high-and-mighty tone with me!"

Jarina flattened herself against the wall, but there was no escaping the point of the blade that pressed into the soft flesh under her chin.

"Ye're all alike, you Tories," the man spat. "You like to sign on with Yankee vessels 'cause the pay's better'n what you can get anywheres in England, but you think ye're too good to rub elbows with American—" He broke off in midsentence, and if it were possible for his eyes to protrude any more, they did. "Well, I'll be hanged! If you ain't the cap'n's whore! Ye're the stow-away Angus caught in the hold. I was wonderin' if the cap'n was gonna keep you on to warm his cock on the cold voyage home." He lowered the knife and a lewd grin spread across his face. "You got nice tits, girl," he said, tapping the flat of the blade against the under-side of a breast. "Real nice tits. You gonna open that shirt of yers and let me get a good look at what ye're hidin' in there? You know, if ye're nice to old Fitch here, I just might put in a good word with the cap'n, and when he tires of you—"

"Fitch!" Jared's deep voice reverberated throughout the bowels of the ship like a cannon blast, nearly send-ing Jarina to her knees in relief. The dirty man jumped away from her and spun around to face his employer.

"She was stealin' my tools!" Fitch waved the knife in Jarina's direction. "Caught her redhanded, I did! She was in here goin' through my—"

"Silence!"

"But, cap'n—"

"Another word, Fitch, and I'll take that knife and cut out your cursed tongue!"

Jarina sidled around the man and started toward Jared, but was brought up short when he turned his gaze on her. His gray eyes blazed with a cold fury that seemed to burn right through her. "What are you doing in here?" he demanded.

For a moment, she just stared at him, hurt by the accusation in his eyes, and when she finally did summon the courage to speak, her voice shook so badly she wanted to die of embarrassment. "M-my shoes . . ." she managed to get out, hating herself for stammering. "They rubbed b-blisters on my—"

"Get to the point," Jared snapped.

"I-I was looking for some salve."

"You was stealin' my tools!"

"I was not!"

"She was, Cap'n Cunningham! I swear it! I seen her with my own two eyes. When I come through that door, I caught the thievin' guttersnipe goin' through the lockers and dumpin' my tools on the deck."

"I was cleaning up your filthy mess!" Jarina shot back. "This place is a disgrace. It's a pigsty! Sewers are cleaner. And you dare call yourself a surgeon!"

Fitch bristled. "Now, you listen here. I can saw off a leg as good as any of them fancy doctors—"

"That will be enough!" Jared bellowed. His face was dark with a barely contained rage that threatened to explode at the slightest provocation. He glared at the other man long enough to drive home an unspoken warning, and Fitch visibly recoiled. Then he looked at Jarina and said with a quiet, deadly calm that was far more portentous than any barked command, "You will return to our cabin, young lady, and you will stay there until I give you permission to leave it."

Jarina opened her mouth to object, then stopped short as she realized the precariousness of her situation. To talk back to Jared now, before one of his men, would be to force his hand, and she doubted that he would allow his authority as captain of this ship to be undermined by letting her disobedience go unpunished. Swallowing both her pride and her seething anger, she gave him a slight, barely perceptible nod in acknowledgment of his command and started toward the door.

Fitch snickered.

Jarina froze. She might have to bow to Jared Cunningham's lofty edicts, but she owed that whining, knife-wielding, foulmouthed excuse for a surgeon not one whit. He had insulted her. He had threatened her. He had touched her in a manner she found revolting and unforgivable. She would be damned if she would stand there and allow him to snigger at her behind her back.

Knotting her hands so tightly her nails gouged her palms, she slowly turned until she was facing Jared. With a measure of self-control she knew she would be hard put to ever duplicate again, she lifted her head and met his warning glower with a look of unnerving calm. "One more thing, Captain Cunningham," she said, her tone deceptively serene, "Please inform Mr. Fitch that this 'thieving guttersnipe' is *not* a whore."

That said, she turned away, her head held high, and calmly exited the infirmary.

She kept her pace unhurried until the sick bay was well behind her, then broke into a panicked run. Dear God, what had ever possessed her to succumb to such a fool temptation? There was no telling what Jared would do to her now.

For the first time since running away from Hamilton Hall, Jarina wondered if she had made a mistake by not marrying the Duke of Roswell.

She had nearly reached the aft cabin when she remembered that she had left her shoes lying outside the sick bay door. Stopping to catch her breath, she worried about returning for them. After a moment's hesitation, she decided against it. She did not want to provoke Jared any more than she already had. She started toward his cabin, then changed her mind. Ill-fitting as they were, they were the only shoes she had and she did not want to take a chance on losing them. She turned back to retrace her steps, but the sound of forceful, angry, rapidly approaching footfalls brought her to an abrupt halt and sent her flying in the opposite direction. In her haste, she nearly collided with Angus on the companionway stairs. The sympathetic look Angus gave her before scurrying out of her way did nothing to alleviate her fears. If even Jared's man pities me, Jarina thought frantically, just what savagery is he capable of?

Just then, Jared's deep voice seemed to literally swallow her as he shouted a command ordering all hands on deck. Gripped in a paroxysm of terror, Jarina took the remaining stairs two at a time and did not stop running until she was safely inside the cabin.

This must stop! she screamed inwardly, trying to get a grip on herself as she collapsed against the closed door. To let Jared see her like this would only confirm how easily he could intimidate her, and once that happened, she would be forever at his mercy. If she were to survive this voyage she was going to have to make it perfectly clear to him that she was not some spineless female given to quaking in fear every time he arched a brow or bellowed like a wounded bull. *Nor do I have any intention of being his mistress*, she fumed. The undisciplined, swaggering libertine was going to have to seek his pleasures elsewhere.

But, thirty minutes later, when he entered the cabin, one glance at his rigid face forced Jarina to the conclusion that Jared was neither undisciplined nor swaggering. Never in her life had she seen such controlled, exacting fury. Were there ever a fine line between passion and violence, Jared trod that line now, and Jarina shuddered to think what would happen should he ever cross it.

He did not speak to her immediately, but stalked to the window where he folded his arms across his chest and stood, feet apart, and stared grimly out at the gray sea. Everything about him—his angry stance, the tautness of his muscles, the unyielding set of his shoulders—attested to the unvented rage that seethed within. That he was able to keep a grip on his temper at all was no small feat, Jarina realized, and she felt her hard-won composure slip a notch. She nervously clenched and unclenched her hands. She opened her mouth to speak, then thought better of it. It would be best, she decided, to simply stay out of his way until his mood improved.

Moving silently in an effort not to draw attention to herself, she cautiously made her way toward the door.

Behind her, Jared stirred. "I did not give you permission to leave this cabin," he said sharply.

Her hand froze on the doorknob and she whirled around to meet his hard, cold-eyed stare. Frantically, her mind scrambled for an explanation.

Jared snapped his fingers and pointed to a chair. "Sit down."

Her heart pounding in her ears, Jarina reluctantly obeyed. The small distance between the door and the chair might as well have been an uncrossable chasm, because by the time she reached the chair and slid onto it, her knees were all but knocking together. Despising herself for being such a coward, she folded her hands in her lap and lifted her chin to fix Jared with what she hoped was a convincing look of bored indifference.

Jared regarded her silently for some moments before speaking. "My men have all been informed that you are under my protection. They are also aware that any undue attention toward you will be severely punished. You need not fear a repeat of this afternoon's performance in the sick bay."

Some of the haughtiness left Jarina's expression. She swallowed and tried to force a smile of gratitude, but her mouth refused to cooperate. "Thank you," she finally managed to get out.

Jared glowered at her. "Do not thank me. It is a captain's duty to protect his passengers from the unwanted advances of his crew. I was fulfilling my obligations. Nothing more."

His biting words stung more than Jarina would have

ever imagined possible. She felt a warm flush of humiliation creep over her face. To her horror, her bottom lip began to quiver. She hastily bit down on it and averted her gaze.

Jared paced the floor like a restless cat. "I regret that you were forced to endure Fitch's assault," he continued. His harsh tone made his apology sound more like a reprimand. "He has assured me it will not happen again."

"He should be relieved of his duties," Jarina mumbled ungraciously, unable to keep the tremor of hurt out of her voice. "The way he maintains the surgery is a disgrace."

Jared's pacing stilled. "What did you say?"

Jarina lifted her gaze to Jared's face. "I said, Mr. Fitch should be relieved of his duties."

"If he is, young lady, you will be damned hungry by the time we reach Virginia. Fitch is the ship's cook."

"But, I thought—"

"He is the cook. There has not been a surgeon on one of my ships for the past five years. I do not require one. In my experience, they are a self-serving lot, loath to pull their own weight when their medical services are not required, and generally to be found drunk when they are. When necessary, Fitch can perform an acceptable amputation. For anything less serious, each man is responsible for himself. I have discovered that men are less likely to go running to the sick bay for every trivial ailment that befalls them when there is no one there to lend a sympathetic ear to their complaints."

By the time he finished speaking, Jarina was gripping the edge of her chair seat with both hands. Her face had taken on an ashen hue. "That's . . . disgusting," she choked. "I would rather die than let that filthy man touch me!"

"Unless you have plans to go climbing about the rigging, my dear, your chances of requiring Fitch's skills are nonexistent. Should you need anything in the way of medical attention, you will come to me. Below decks is off limits to you. I don't want you wandering there again. The men's quarters are located there, and I am too busy a man to be burdened with worrying about your safety. When I am not with you, you will venture no farther from this cabin than the quarterdeck."

Jarina felt uncomfortably like a naughty child who had just had her ears boxed. Gritting her teeth to keep her chin from quivering, she rose from the chair, and it took every shred of self-control she could muster not to crumble beneath the icy blast of his gaze. Her chin inched upward. She had to grip the back of her chair to steady herself, and she swallowed spasmodically several times before she could speak. "It was not my intent to cause you worry," she said in a low, hollow voice. "Nor to be a burden."

Jared studied her long and hard, and something akin to hatred passed over his features. "From the moment I decided to let you remain on board this ship, you have been both a worry and a burden. Every time I look at you, I am reminded that I traded a single night of pleasure with a willing whore for a naive schoolgirl who wouldn't know how to please a man if her life depended on it."

Raw hurt mingled with shock in Jarina's eyes. She suddenly felt sick to her stomach. "I am sorry my inexperience offends you," she spat, lashing out. "But I told you last night I did not know how to please you. If my abilities fell short of your expectations, then you have only yourself to blame for being such an inept teacher!"

The instant the words left Jarina's lips, she knew she had gone too far. The anger in Jared's eyes turned hard and purposeful as he closed the distance between them. His hands shot out and Jarina froze in anticipation of the expected blow, but instead of striking her, he caught her around the waist and swung her up into his arms. A strangled cry of surprise wrenched from her throat. She tried to fling herself away from him, but he merely tightened his hold on her. His strong fingers bit into the tender flesh of her waist and thigh. He carried her across the cabin and dumped her unceremoniously onto the bunk.

Jarina rolled toward the wall and scrambled to her knees, but before she could get away, he seized her ankle and jerked, sending her sprawling face down across the quilt. The mattress shifted beneath his weight, and he caught her hands and dragged them behind her. She tried to pull free, but he transferred both her wrists to a single hand and easily held them captive. He rolled her onto her back, trapping her hands beneath her, and broke the effectiveness of her kicks by thrusting his knee between her thighs. With one leg imprisoned between his, all she could do with her free leg was kick aimlessly without striking her target. She lunged upward in a desperate attempt to break his hold on her, inadvertently driving her loins against his hard-muscled thigh, and the intimate contact sent waves of shock spiraling through her. Jared's eyes met hers and her panic rapidly evaporated into thick, nauseating fear.

With his free hand, he began to slowly, deliberately unbutton her shirt, and with every inch of flesh that was exposed to his view, her alarm grew. The last button undone, he tugged the hem free of her breeches and folded each half of the shirtfront back as far as it would go, baring her to the waist. He brought his passion-inflamed gaze back up to her face. "Lesson number one," he said in a low, husky voice, touching the responsive peak of a breast with his fingertip as his eyes burned into hers. "Never taunt a man unless you expect him to rise to the challenge." He cupped her breast in his hand and his caress deepened, bringing an involuntary groan to her lips.

"Don't touch me!" she cried out, and shrank away from him, but he merely increased the pressure on her wrists until she gasped and arched her back, and her breast strained against his palm.

His gray eyes smoldered. "Lesson number two. Don't fight me. No matter how hard you try, I will always win." He stroked her warm, smooth flesh. "Such delicate skin, Jarina," he murmured. "So flawless. So sensitive to the slightest touch."

She twisted and writhed beneath him, but there was no escaping either the hold he had on her hands or the gentle assault of his long, tanned fingers as they skimmed across her breasts. "Let go of me!" she wailed. "Dear God, no—!"

He lowered his head to her breast and his lips burned her skin as he pressed a kiss to the taut nipple. His mouth opened around it and he alternately teased it with his tongue and gently sucked until sharp stabs of pleasure-pain shot through her body, igniting an intense heat that made her feel as though she were on fire. Just when she thought she could bear it no longer, he directed his attention to her other breast and the torture began anew. She whimpered and, without realizing that she did so, arched her back more, her body craving what her pride rejected. Her hips rose up off the bunk. Jared slid his hand beneath her buttocks and lifted her even higher, pulling her hard against his thigh.

A convulsive shudder rocked her body. Squeezing her eyes shut, she flung her head from side to side. "Stop! Oh, please, stop—"

Without easing up on the pressure he was exerting between her thighs with his knee, Jared moved his lips up her throat, leaving behind a trail of burning kisses. "Lesson number three," he whispered into her ear. "No man is deceived by false modesty. Your body betrays you, my dear. It tells me what you want, even as you try to resist me."

Her body jerked with repressed sobs as she struggled to deny the truth of his words and get her rampaging emotions back under control. She vehemently shook her head. "No, that's not true!"

"Oh, but it is true," he said, his voice hoarse with his own restrained passion. "I have complete control over you, Jarina. I can make you moan with pleasure and your body ache with desire."

"No!"

He pressed his lips to the rapidly jumping pulse in the side of her neck. "I can make you so addicted to my touch, you will beg me for it."

She gritted her teeth and twisted, but everywhere she moved, his lips followed.

"Shall I make you beg, Jarina? Shall I make you come crawling to me and beg me to take you in my arms and satisfy your needs?"

Scalding tears streamed down her face and collected in her ears. "You bastard!" she choked. "I would sooner marry that human swine who calls himself my betrothed than to ever go willingly into your arms!"

A sharp knock sounded on the cabin door.

A scowl marred Jared's brow. "You will come to me," he said thickly, ignoring the interruption.

"I'll see you burn in hell first!"

"You will come to me and you will beg me to pleasure you."

A sob broke in her throat. "No!"

The knock came again, louder this time, and more insistent.

Swearing savagely, Jared abruptly released his hold on her and surged up off the bunk. "Damn you, come in!"

Shaking so badly she could hardly make her limbs do what she asked of them, Jarina somehow managed to sit up and pull her shirt closed just as the door opened and Angus came into the cabin. Shame burned in her cheeks as she caught the Scot's look of concern, and she hastily averted her gaze, thoroughly humiliated that anyone should see her in such a disgraceful state. Her hands trembled as she buttoned her shirt.

Angus shifted uncomfortably, and his shoulders hunched before Jared's hostile regard. "Beggin' yer pardon, sir, but we've a sail off the port quarter. Mr. Crawford thinks it might be a man-of-war. He wants to know, Cap'n, should he change tack and outrun her?"

Jared turned to Jarina and stared at her long and hard.

Feeling his eyes on her, she lifted her head and met his gaze, and her heart skipped a beat. His cold scrutiny made her uneasy, and she did not understand why he was looking at her like that. She sniffled and wiped her tear-streaked face with her fingertips.

Jared turned back to his man. "Tell Crawford to run out the stern chaser, but keep her on the present course. We've nothing to hide. If it is a warship, we'll let her intercept. Keep me informed, Angus."

The old man's head bobbed as he backed out the door. "Aye, Cap'n, that I will."

As soon as the door closed after his servant, Jared turned on his heel and went to his desk. Unlocking a drawer, he removed a leather case that had seen many years of use and began sorting through the papers contained within. When his attention did not return to her, Jarina realized that she had been dismissed. Again. And, for once, she was glad.

No longer trembling uncontrollably, yet still afraid to move for fear Jared would remember her and want to resume the unpleasant business that had been interrupted by his servant's arrival, she scooted off the bunk and smoothed the covers, erasing the evidence of the struggle which had just taken place there. Then she straightened her rumpled clothing, all the while casting anxious glances at Jared's back. But he did not turn around. He did not even seem to notice that she was in the room.

Perplexed by his sudden remoteness when only moments ago he had been all too attentive, she went to the wash basin and bathed her reddened eyes, quietly at first, then louder, deliberately making distracting sloshing sounds with the water as she splashed it over her face.

Still, Jared ignored her.

Not certain whether she was more disturbed or relieved by his silence, she kept her gaze fixed on him while she dried her face. She was prepared to bolt for the door should he turn and come toward her.

His quicksilver mood changes terrified her. He could be utterly charming one moment and deadly the next. Before his servant's timely interruption, his passions had run high. Now he was cold as stone and his movements terse and businesslike as he inventoried the documents in the leather case.

And she was completely forgotten.

Again, a knock sounded at the door.

Jared strode across the cabin and opened the door. He stood there for several minutes, conferring with Angus in low tones. Finally, he closed the door and turned to her. The muscle in his cheek twitched. "We are being overtaken by a British man-of-war. There is a strong chance the officer in command will want to board and search the *Pegasus* for deserters. To refuse to cooperate would be to endanger both my ship and my men, and I will not do that." He paused to give his words time to sink in, then added in a low, meaningful voice, "Not even for you."

The color drained from Jarina's face and her eyes grew wide and round. He was going to put her on the British vessel and send her back to England! She slowly shook her head in disbelief and opened her mouth to plead with him, but all that came out was a strangled, "*No . . .*"

At the look of guileless horror in Jarina's eyes, some of the tension left Jared's face. Gone was the furious

virago who had sworn she would see him burn in hell
rather than yield to his caresses, and in her place was
a vulnerable, terrified child. If she were that afraid of
being returned home, then she was not likely to point
a finger at him for abducting and raping her. "I am not
sending you back to England," he said quietly. "Just
do as you are told, and everything will proceed without
incident."

Relief surged through her like a tidal wave, and she
nodded jerkily, placing her trust—and her life—in his
hands. If he couldn't save her from being returned to
the Duke of Roswell, no one could.

Jared took a deep breath to calm his nagging doubts.
If the *Pegasus* were boarded by the Royal Navy, he
would not be able to keep Jarina's presence secret. To
even try would be suicidal. Yet, he could not risk allowing any of the officers to get a close enough look at her
to be able to recognize her. As much as he wished to
have the question of her identity answered, this was neither the time nor the place. Not when his own freedom
was at stake.

Noting her inappropriately clad form, he silently
cursed himself for destroying the pink gown he had
given her to wear last night. It might not draw less attention than her breeches, for Jarina was a striking
beauty, but it would certainly prompt fewer questions.

There was only one solution.

"You are going to have to get out of those clothes."

Bewilderment clouded her eyes. "But, they're all I
have."

"Take them off. If you are seen dressed like that, you
will only arouse suspicion."

"I can hide!"

"There is no place on this ship where a man determined to sniff out a deserter will not be able to find
you." He paused as Jarina's eyes riveted on the torn
pink gown she had folded earlier and placed on the foot
of his bunk. She lifted a questioning gaze to his face

and he shook his head. "I'm afraid I have no more gowns for you to wear. I am not in the habit of transporting women's garments in my locker. That one, as fate would have it, was left behind by a delightful woman who fled my bed only moments before the arrival of her irate husband."

He shrugged indifferently and Jarina felt her face grow warm as she remembered the strumpet he had been entertaining when she was hauled into his cabin and dropped at his feet. She was not so naive as to think a man as commandingly virile as Jared had not had numerous such women, but for the first time she wondered just *how many.* And a small flame of jealousy flickered to life in her breast.

As Jared watched the myriad changing emotions play across Jarina's face, it was not hard to guess what she was thinking, and he regretted losing his temper with her earlier. She was a child, and, until he had forced himself upon her, a virgin. Yet he continually expected her to play the part of the worldly paramour, well-learned in the ways of men. Why? Was it because he truly believed she was inherently as faithless and conniving as his mother had been? As Evelyn Landon was? As were the other females who looked to him with one eye on Wyeburn and the other on his wealth? Or because, deep inside, he feared she might be different, and that he would be forced to reckon with her as an individual and not lump her into the same mold as the other women of his acquaintance? He frowned. It would seem he had a great deal to feel guilty for these days, and that did not sit well with him at all.

Doing an abrupt aboutface, he yanked open the door and called for Angus. Then he turned back to Jarina with a stone-faced surliness that masked his own churning uncertainty. "Do as you are told, Jarina," he said curtly. "Take off your clothes."

Chapter Five

The seventy-four gun H.M.S. *Meeker* closed in swiftly on the *Pegasus* while two frigates hovered on the horizon, ready to give chase. Up on the quarterdeck, Stephen shook his head and whistled. "She's loaded for bear," he commented. "If they open up with those thirty-two pounders, they'll blow us right out of the water!"

Jared lowered the glass and passed it to his first mate. His expression was solemn. The warship's gundecks had been cleared for action, and red-coated marines were already positioned in the rigging, their muskets trained on the American merchantman. Protecting Jarina was going to be the least of his worries.

"Holy shit!" Silas Crawford muttered as he focused the glass on the carronades mounted fore and aft. "Did you get a look at those smashers? A shot from one of them will rip a hole in our hull the size of Delaware!"

"Like t' see 'em try," retorted Pete Riddle. "You just point out yer man, Cap'n, and tell me which side you want his hair parted on. Old Betsy and me, we'll take care of it." He lovingly patted the brass barrel of the long twelve mounted on the merchantman's quarterdeck.

Jared smiled. Peter Riddle had been with him from

the company's beginnings. He was a crusty veteran of both the Northern and the New York-New Jersey campaigns, and a more skilled, more loyal seaman would be hard to find. Jared turned and glanced back at the rest of his crew. Armed with everything from cutlasses to blunderbusses fitted with spring bayonets, the men waited in expectant silence for his orders. "Keep your pants on, Pete," Jared cautioned. "The last thing I want to do is get into an artillery duel with a ship of the line."

Meanwhile, in the cabin, Jarina clutched Jared's dressing robe tighter around her and nervously chewed her bottom lip as she observed the man-of-war's approach from her perch on the window seat. It was a floating fortress, more than double the size of the efficient merchantman, and was well armed. Jarina lost count of the number of gunports on the starboard side as the warship overtook the *Pegasus* and slipped from her view.

A soft knock at the door brought her to her feet with a start. Gathering the length of Jared's robe to keep from tripping over it, she crossed to the door and opened it. Angus entered the cabin carrying two buckets filled with hot water. "It's almost time," he said as he emptied the buckets into the copper hip bath that had been placed near the stove. "Ye gots all ye need?"

Jarina glanced about the cabin. The bolts of fabric had been stowed away and her small bundle unpacked, the few belongings she had brought with her placed in Jared's locker. Oils and soaps and fresh towels had been arranged on the floor beside the tub. The pink gown had been turned to hide the torn side and draped across a chair as though she planned to don it after her bath. She nodded and said uncertainly, "I think so."

She's scared to death, Angus thought, noting her pallor. The sharp glint in his old eyes softened. "Ye'll be a'right, lass," he said gently. "The cap'n knows what he's about."

"I hope so," she murmured. Jared's plan might be a good one, but she could not help hating him for it. Never in her life had she been subjected to so many humiliating, lustful stares as she had since coming on board this ship, and the thought of having to endure yet another was almost more than she could bear. Not until Jared pointed out that she might be recognized should anyone get more than a brief glance at her did she reluctantly concede to his demands.

Concern creased the Scot's brow and he opened his mouth to speak, then thought better of it. There was nothing he could say to ease her fears. Nor did he wish to bring Jared's foul temper down on his own head for interfering where he had no business. "I'll be right outside the door, lass, if ye needs anything," he said instead and picked up the empty buckets.

Jarina nodded, but said nothing. Her spirits heavy with foreboding, she turned away and began untying the belt that held Jared's robe closed at her waist.

Just then, an explosion ripped through the air, shattering the calm. Overhead, hurried footsteps pounded the quarterdeck. The *Pegasus* lost speed and foundered, and was thrust into a back and forth rocking motion that drove Jarina's stomach into her throat. She whirled around. Her eyes were wide and terror was frozen on her face. "They're firing at us!"

Angus stopped with his hand on the door. "'Twas only a warning shot, lass, fired across the bow to tell us they'll be wanting to board."

It felt as though they were sinking. Jarina gripped the back of a chair, certain she was going to be sick.

Angus gave her a sympathetic smile and hurried from the cabin.

The door closed after him and Jarina was left alone with her fears. As she listened to the bustle and the shouted commands up on deck, her mind leaped from one frantic conclusion to another. Finally, she had to shut out the confusion of disturbing sounds and thoughts altogether lest she make herself ill with worry. Jared had told her explicitly what he expected of her and Angus had assured her that Jared knew what he was doing. She had no choice but to obey and hope for the best. With trembling hands, she untied the knot at her waist and let the dressing robe slide to the floor. Then she stepped into the tub and sank down in the hot water to await the next stage of Jared's plan.

Up on the main deck, Jared greeted the ten-man boarding party with an air of cool indifference that immediately put the officer in command, a short, pale-eyed lieutenant, on the defensive. After a hasty round of introductions, Lieutenant Stendhal drew himself up to his full height, which fell a good head short of Jared's six feet, three inches, and said brusquely, "Captain Cunningham, I am under orders to search your ship for deserters from the Royal Navy, and to inspect your cargo. I must caution you that refusal to cooperate will—"

"I am well aware of the consequences, Lieutenant," Jared interrupted. "I have no intention of hindering you in your duties. I am, however, growing weary of these countless searches. I time my voyages to insure the greatest profits, and with each unnecessary delay, my cargo diminishes in value. If you will have your men begin their search straightaway, you and I can proceed to the quarterdeck where you may peruse the ship's log and my papers at your leisure."

Lieutenant Stendhal noticed that both Midshipman Haywood and the marines in his charge were looking to Captain Cunningham for their orders. His resentment flared. *I give the orders around here!* he wanted to shout, but he dared not. His last boarding had resulted in a melee that left fourteen men wounded and one dead. Another such mistake, and he was guaranteed to find himself facing a court-martial board.

Jared focused immediately on the officer's hesitation and pressed to his advantage. He removed a sheaf of papers from his leather case and handed them to the tall, skinny, pimple-faced midshipman. "Here is the bill of lading. You will notice that the content of every chest is inventoried in detail. You may open any of the chests you want. All I ask is that you have a care for the items contained within, and that your marines keep their bayonets out of the woodwork. This voyage to England was my last and I already have a buyer for the *Pegasus.*"

Midshipman Haywood bobbed his head a shade too eagerly, betraying both his lack of sophistication and his utter terror of the tall, dark-haired American issuing the directive. "Yes, sir! We won't damage a thing, sir. I swear it!" No sooner were the words out of his mouth than the youth caught Lieutenant Stendhal's glower of impatience. Realizing his error, he blushed a bright crimson.

Giving the midshipman a glare that promised he would deal with him later, Lieutenant Stendhal barked a curt order. As the marines jumped to do his bidding, he turned to Jared and said shortly, "I want all your men on deck and I want to see your muster roll."

Jared's smile did not extend to his eyes. "Everything you require is here, Lieutenant," he said icily as he handed him the leather case. "Muster roll, citizenship papers, articles of indenture. Your fellow officers have yet to find a deserter on one of my ships and I don't anticipate that you will now."

Lieutenant Stendhal gritted his teeth. Insolent colonial! Determined to prove Jared wrong, he ordered, "Your men, Cunningham. On deck. Immediately!"

Jared folded his arms across his chest and studied the officer through hooded eyes. "My men *are* on deck," he said evenly.

From one corner of his eye, the lieutenant saw the glint of sunlight on metal and turned his head to find the business end of a Turkish scimitar hovering only inches from his neck. He lifted his gaze to the grinning countenance of a one-eyed sea dog sporting a gold ring in his right ear. Something indefinable in the man's expression made his blood run cold. He glanced around him at the other seamen, all well-armed, and a strong sense of déjà vu gripped him. All had their eyes fixed on him. They were waiting, he knew, for him to make a mistake. Any mistake. A vague uneasiness jelled in the pit of his stomach. Without another word, he located the ship's roster and scanned the list of names and duties, and a quick head count ascertained that the correct number of men were on board. Or, at least, on deck. Eager to be away from this bloodthirsty bunch of ruffians, he returned the muster roll to the leather case, then turned to Jared and said, "I will review the rest of these documents in your cabin."

"I'm afraid not, Lieutenant. My wife is in our cabin, and at the moment she is disinclined to receive visitors. Perhaps the quarterdeck will be more to your liking."

A knowing look reflected in the officer's colorless eyes. So the American scum was hiding something after all. A smug half-smile dimpled the corners of his mouth. He would play along with the pretense for now, but if Captain Cunningham thought to be rid of him without a thorough search of his cabin, he was in for a surprise. "I am quite comfortable here," he said in a syrupy voice that revealed more than it masked.

Jared was not misled for one second by the Englishman's sudden agreeableness. He knew exactly what was on the officer's mind; Lieutenant Stendhal was playing right into his hands.

An ominous quiet hung over the ship as Lieutenant Stendhal studied the ship's papers, and Jared could not help wondering how Jarina was faring in his cabin.

"It would seem your papers are in order," Lieutenant Stendhal said at last. He handed the leather case back to Jared. "You have gone to great lengths to document the identity of every member of your crew. Were other merchant captains so conscientious, my job would be a great deal easier."

Jared's expression was carefully guarded. "My papers are always in order," he said flatly. "You and your men are going to have to look for your *deserters* elsewhere."

Lieutenant Stendhal bristled at Jared's meaningful emphasis on the word "deserters," but was saved from commenting by Midshipman Haywood's appearance topside. "The cargo checks out, sir," the boy said as he handed the bill of lading to his commanding officer. Lieutenant Stendhal passed it to Jared. "I had the men open a score of chests at random, and each one contains exactly what the records state, without exception," Midshipman Haywood said. He cast Jared an apologetic glance and his thin face reddened in embarrassment.

The exchange did not go unnoticed. "Did you search the entire ship?" Lieutenant Stendhal snapped.

The youth nodded. "All but the captain's cabin, sir."

"Fine. We shall make a quick search of Captain Cunningham's cabin, and then we will let him be on his way." Lieutenant Stendhal started aft, but was abruptly stopped as Jared's hand closed around his arm.

"I told you, Lieutenant, my wife is in there."

The officer shook off Jared's hand and his pale eyes burned with determination. He was going to see this blasted colonial hang. "My men and I will leave this ship *after* I have had the opportunity to look inside your cabin," he said tersely. Without waiting for Jared's approval, he marched to the doorway beneath the quarterdeck and descended the companionway stairs.

Jared made no real attempt to stop him. The invasion of his cabin was a contingency he had anticipated. It was also a part of the plan he had outlined to Jarina.

He prayed she would not disappoint him now, for her sake as well as his own.

Without even the courtesy of a knock, Lieutenant Stendhal opened the door to Jared's cabin and barged inside, only to be brought up short by the sight of a very shapely young woman rising from her bath, a towel wrapped about her head and water streaming down over her lush curves. She gasped when she saw him and her hands flew to cover herself. Then, with a half-choked shriek, she sat back down, sending soapy water surging over the sides of the tub. Lieutenant Stendhal hastily exited the cabin and yanked the door shut. He whirled around and came up hard against a broad, unyielding wall of muscle and fury.

His face turned a deep scarlet and his entire life flashed before his eyes as he realized his blunder. "I am terribly sorry, Captain Cunningham," he blurted out. "When you said your wife was disinclined to receive visitors, I had no idea you meant—"

"You have insulted me and you have embarrassed my wife," Jared ground out through clenched teeth. His gray eyes blazed. "You can be certain I will report your conduct to the British Naval Attaché in Washington."

Lieutenant Stendhal blanched. "My good man, it was not my intention to—"

"Get off my ship," Jared ordered. "Get off my ship or I will have you thrown off!"

Behind the closed door, Jarina huddled in the now chilled water, her heart thumping mercilessly as she listened to the heated exchange. Jared's plan had worked! The officer had satisfied his curiosity without getting more than the briefest glance at her. Her only regret was that she had chosen that precise moment to stand up to work a cramp out of her foot. But then, perhaps that was just as well, she concluded, coloring, for her error had lent an air of authenticity to the ruse.

The angry voices moved away from the door and

Jarina lost no time getting out of the tub and drying off. She yanked the towel from around her wet hair and tossed it aside, then hastily donned her shirt and breeches. In Jared's locker, she found a pair of wool stockings which he had unpacked from her bundle and was just reaching down to put them on when another thought stopped her cold. She straightened. Just why had Jared gone out of his way to protect her when he could very easily have turned her over to her own countrymen and washed his hands of her? He had made it quite clear that he loathed the very sight of her. He had called her a naive schoolgirl who wouldn't know how to please a man if her life depended on it.

He is right, she thought miserably. She did not know what pleased a man. She could cook and clean and manage a household with reasonable skill. She knew how to get the best bargains at the village market. She could coax a lush garden out of thin soil. She could turn a bobbin of string into fine lace and a bolt of plain muslin into an elegant gown. And, from the hours spent assisting her father in the surgery, she could prepare a plaster or lance a boil or bring down a fever as well as any practiced physician. But, of men she knew fearfully little. And of Jared, she knew nothing at all.

Yet, what did it matter that she displeased Jared Cunningham? She did not like him. He had insulted her. He had forced himself upon her. He continually treated her as if she were a child. And he had a vicious temper.

It mattered because she could not bear the thought of spending the entire voyage in the company of a man who despised her.

It mattered because, whether she wished it or not, he was all she now had in the world; and some perverse, illogical, unreasoning, totally emotional part of her begged to be loved by him rather than hated.

It mattered because she wanted it to matter.

The *Pegasus* lurched in the water as her sails were

hoisted. Jarina breathed a sigh of relief at the knowledge that they were once again on their way. Angus came to the cabin to remove the tub and wet towels, and again awhile later to light the lamps as the shadows lengthened. Jarina's empty stomach rumbled noisily and the Scot cast a startled glance toward the window seat where she sat.

She smiled sheepishly. "Will it be much longer until supper, Angus?"

"No more'n an hour, lass," he said as he returned the flint and steel to the tinder box. He paused on his way out the door. "Will ye be wantin' a biscuit to tide ye over 'til then?"

"No, thank you. I can wait. Angus?"

"Aye, lass?" Once more he stopped and turned to her.

It was on the tip of her tongue to ask him where Jared was, but she could not make her mouth form the words. She shook her head. "It was nothing."

Angus watched her sadly. Never in his life would he forget the look of torment that had haunted her tear-filled eyes when he had come to the cabin earlier to warn Jared of the approaching warship. Damn the cap'n! Didn't he know the lass was just a wee bairn who couldn't possibly understand what she had done to upset the safe predictability of his life? She'd turned his world upside down, she had, and now she was paying for it.

Not long after Angus left, Jared returned.

Jarina bolted up off the window seat, relief surging through her at the sight of him. "Your plan worked!"

He looked at her, but said nothing, and her spirits plummeted. She did not know what she had done this time to annoy him. She had followed his instructions to the letter. By all rights, he should have been pleased.

He had brought back her shoes. He placed them on the floor beside the door. When he straightened, her gaze flew to his face, searching for some clue to the cause of his distant mood, but there was none. Just like old man Gilliam who visited her father at the surgery several times a week to complain about the stiffness in his joints or the ringing in his ears or the sad state of the monarchy in general, she thought. Her father said Mr. Gilliam was cross because he was lonely, but she found it hard to be so gracious. As far as she was concerned, the old man was contrary and bad-tempered because other people let him get away with it. Just like they let Jared get away with it. Her gaze followed him as he strode past her to the desk and returned his leather case and his ship's papers to their proper places. Yes, she decided, he is just like old man Gilliam.

Jared motioned toward the bunk. "Get over there and sit down."

Jarina's heart seemed to stick in her throat. Her eyes riveted on the bunk and she stood there numbly, just staring at it, her courage flagging as all too recent memories flooded her thoughts. She looked up and caught him watching her, and her revulsion for the bunk paled beside her fear of what he might do should she disobey him. Old man Gilliam had merely annoyed her. Jared terrified her. A sick feeling churned in her stomach. She reluctantly did as she was told, cutting a wide arc around him as she crossed the cabin.

Armed with a pot of salve and several small rolls of soft linen bandage, he went to the bunk and sat down beside her. "Remove your stockings."

She hastily complied.

But when he reached for her foot, the thought of him touching her bare skin sent a wave of hot color flooding over her face and she pulled away. "I can do that," she blurted out. She reached for the pot of salve.

Ignoring her protest, Jared grasped an ankle and firmly placed her foot across his thigh.

Taken aback by the unexpected move, Jarina jerked her head up and startled blue eyes met gray, but before she could say anything, her stomach let out a long agonized growl. Humiliated to the core, she lowered her eyes.

Jared could not help noticing the way her long sooty lashes threw shadows across her delicately boned cheeks. His gaze dropped to her lips, soft and inviting in the golden glow of the lamp, and he silently cursed himself for wanting to savor again their moist sweetness. She was too young to be anyone's mistress. She should be at home in her own bed rather than here in his, tempting him. He should have handed her over to Lieutenant Stendhal and been done with her. Yet he had chosen to keep her here, a constant reminder of a single drunken night that had forever altered the course of his life. Why? Out of kindness? Surely not. It had never been his habit to be kind to anyone unless he had something to gain, and he saw no cause to start now. No, he kept her here because he wanted her. He wanted her more than he had ever wanted a woman and that galled him because he could find no logic in his reasoning. She was probably the only woman he had ever met who found his advances disagreeable. Yet, rather than discourage him, her rejection only made him all the more determined to have her.

Her stomach growled again.

Jarina caught her bottom lip between her teeth and stubbornly refused to look up, even though she could feel Jared's gaze on her. Her face grew warm beneath his lengthy scrutiny.

Jared frowned. If she expects me to coddle her, he mused, opening the pot of salve, she is going to be disappointed. He had neither the time nor the inclination to cater to the whims of an eighteen-year-old girl whose foolish notions about love had led her to flee marriage to a well-heeled aristocrat who could have given her anything her heart desired.

Jarina flinched when Jared touched the cold salve to the raw flesh on her heel, then gradually relaxed as a soothing numbness set in. There was something disconcerting, almost erotic, in the tanned darkness of his fingers against her white skin as he applied the salve to her foot and wrapped it in bandages. Darkness and light. Worldliness and innocence. Visions of those strong hands touching her in other, forbidden, places flashed through Jarina's mind, causing her pulse to quicken and kindling an odd warmth deep down inside her. She hastily brushed the unseemly imaginings aside, uncomfortable with the effect they had on her. She found his gentleness unnerving.

Jared tied the ends of the bandage and reached for her other foot. The crease between his brows deepened as his gaze focused on a particularly bad lesion. Taking care not to hurt her, he applied the salve to her foot and began wrapping it with the strips of linen. "When we reach Alexandria, I will buy you shoes that fit," he said, annoyed with himself for not noticing last night how bloodied her feet were.

Jarina bridled. "I did not ask for new shoes," she said stiffly.

"Don't test me, Jarina."

She failed to heed the note of caution in his voice. "I was not testing you," she retorted without thinking. "I was merely reminding you that I want nothing from you."

Jared's hands stilled on her foot, and when Jarina glanced up, she found his cold, impenetrable gaze fixed on her. "I am only going to say this once, Jarina, so you had better listen very carefully," he said slowly. "Until you marry, I will put a roof over your head. I will provide for you. I will give you whatever protection and comforts my money can buy. But I will not tolerate your niggling over the circumstances surrounding your presence here. Start showing a little grace and learn to accept your lot and you will find that I can be a fairly reasonable man to deal with. Fail, and you will suffer the consequences. I can make your life hell, my dear, and don't you ever forget it."

How could she forget when he never missed an opportunity to remind her? Tears of impotent anger stung her eyes and her chest constricted. Afraid she was going to shame herself by bursting into tears, she averted her gaze and clenched her jaw in a desperate attempt to keep her chin from quivering.

"The long face will get you no sympathy, Jarina." Jared said dryly. He pulled the knot tight. "All things considered, you are a very lucky girl. Instead of ending up with a man who is prepared to be more than generous with you if you will only attempt to humor him, you could have fallen into the hands of a captain who would have merely used you for his own gratification, then handed you over to his crew when he wearied of you. You could have been raped on the docks before you ever reached my ship. Or you could have stayed home like a good little girl and meekly accepted the fate your elders chose for you, in which case, you would be spending the rest of your life with the louse-ridden sausage your guardian favored. Or, you could be like that unfortunate Hamilton girl whose father sold her to the Duke of Roswell."

Jarina's head jerked up.

"Yes, Jarina, her father sold her. He sold her to an aging, dissolute, morally corrupt, sexual deviate. In polite circles, it's better known as marriage negotiations. Rumor has it the settlement was a hundred pounds, although I'm inclined to believe the amount was far greater than that." He chuckled. "You need not look so aghast, my dear. It happens all the time, particularly when some obscenely indebted nobleman realizes the only way he can burrow out from under his obligations is to auction his offspring to the highest bidder."

The bald horror of what he was saying crept over Jarina like a glacier, freezing the blood in her veins as it engulfed her with its awful revelation. There was an odd buzzing in her ears that drowned out Jared's voice and black spots danced before her eyes.

Jared's intention had been to make Jarina realize that there were far worse indignities in life than being in his company, and from the stricken look on her face, he appeared to have succeeded. Satisfied that she would not be causing him any more trouble for a while, he lifted her feet off his lap and dropped them over the side of the bunk. "I wouldn't pity Lord Hamilton's daughter very much if I were you," he said, rising. "The witless twit has probably been salivating over the prospect of being a duchess."

Numb with shock, Jarina sat without moving for a long time after Jared left the cabin. She did not want to believe what he had told her, but instinctively she knew it was the truth. She had been aware for years that her father was deeply in debt. But never in her wildest imaginings had she ever guessed he would attempt to exonerate those debts by bargaining away her future to a man she abhorred. *He had sold her!*

A groan of anguish rose in her throat as what remained of her childish innocence came crashing down around her.

Jared placed his napkin beside his plate and nodded to Angus who was waiting to clear the table. "As soon as we receive the bank draft from the sale of the *Pegasus,* I am going to make Samuels an offer on the warehouse at the end of Church Street. With that small addition, we can easily double our asking price for the company."

Stephen looked doubtful. "What if he won't sell?"

"He will. As soon as he hears the terms of the leaseback agreement." Jared looked down at Jarina, frowning as he observed her toying with the napkin on her lap. Except for an occasional mumbled monosyllable when spoken to, she had kept conspicuously silent throughout dinner, and she had scarcely touched the food on her plate. Glancing up, Jared intercepted the troubled look Stephen was bestowing upon her, and his displeasure deepened. "I want the leases on the other warehouses renegotiated by the end of the year," he said brusquely. "Aim for long-term commitments where possible. As long as trade is booming, we might as well take advantage of the general feeling of good-will."

Stephen dragged his gaze away from Jarina. "Do you think Jefferson is going to grant you that government contract to breed horses for the army?"

"That depends upon whether he is able to convince the members of Congress to put aside their sectional politics long enough to recognize the need for a strong cavalry." Jared paused as Angus reached around him to remove his plate. "If Tom can't bring Congress to a vote," he continued, "I'll have to invest my own funds in the venture, and hope it pays off. Jarina?"

She jerked her head up, and the blank look gradually left her eyes as they focused on his.

"Angus just asked you if you were finished eating."

Her gaze dropped to her still-full plate and she stared at it as though seeing it for the first time. Finally, she nodded.

The muscle in Jared's cheek tightened.

Angus met Stephen's gaze over the top of Jarina's head and lifted a questioning brow, but the younger man merely gave him a bewildered look and shrugged.

Angus finished clearing the table. Stephen, sensing that Jared was quickly approaching the limits of his patience, attempted a weak joke about still suffering the effects of the previous night's revelry and excused himself.

After Stephen and Angus had gone, Jared leaned back in his chair, his brows drawn together as he eyeballed Jarina with a mixture of irritation and concern. "You didn't eat," he said, struggling to keep his tone neutral in the face of his mounting frustration.

"I wasn't hungry."

"From the way your stomach was complaining earlier, I would have thought you were famished."

She did not reply. She did not even look at him.

That he was unable to elicit a reaction from her disturbed him. Gone was the feisty, quick-tongued wench ready to spar with him at the slightest provocation, and in her place sat a pale, uncommunicative dullard. Perhaps she just needed some time alone, he thought. It had been a trying day for all of them, and for Jarina in particular. He was accustomed to having to keep one step ahead of the British authorities. Jarina, he suspected, had never even needed to before now. Jared shook his head. He was weary of trying to figure her out. Rising, he came around the table toward her and bent to brush his lips against the top of her head. "The fabrics Angus brought up from the hold are for you, love. You may do what you wish with them. Whatever notions or supplies you require, tell Angus, and he will get them for you. I'm going up on deck. Don't wait up for me."

The door closed softly after him.

Only then did Jarina drop her face into her hands and surrender to the aching misery she had been battling all evening.

It was well past midnight when Jared returned to the cabin. Jarina was already asleep. Taking care not to wake her, he went to his desk and sat down to document Lieutenant Stendhal's boarding of the *Pegasus* in the ship's log; but his attention wandered, and time and again he found his gaze drawn to the bunk where Jarina lay. In the flickering lamplight, he saw the tracks of dried tears on her face, and guilt nagged him. He knew he was responsible for much, if not all, her unhappiness. Only when she was free of him would some semblance of normalcy return to her life.

Jarina's brow furrowed and a whimper escaped her lips. Clenching her teeth, she ground the back of her head into the pillows and kicked at the quilt that was tangled about her legs, trapping them.

With a sigh, Jared put down his quill and rose. He blew out the lamp and undressed in the darkness. Going to the bunk, he disentangled the quilt and lay down beside her, drawing the covers over them both. Jarina cried out in her sleep as he pulled her toward him. "Shhh," he whispered. His hands glided over the warm, firm flesh of her back as he held her close. "It's all right now. It was only a dream." He continued to hold her, stroking her back and kneading her taut muscles until she quieted and relaxed in his arms.

Her breath was warm against his skin as she lay within the protective circle of his arm, her cheek resting on his chest. Turning his head, he pressed a kiss to her brow and a reluctant smile touched his lips as he wondered if she knew she slept with her mouth open.

Then his expression sobered as he debated what to do with her. The thought of her crying herself to sleep night after night caused his stomach to clench. He did not want to let her go, but he knew he could not keep a hold on her, no matter how well he treated her. Nor could he do to her what he had done to Evelyn over the past eight years and avail himself of her charms without any promise of love or marriage in return. Jarina needed—and deserved—the security of marriage.

The best thing for all concerned, he reasoned, would be for him to stay as far away from her as possible. There was nothing to be gained by sharing her bunk and courting temptation. He would rearrange his schedule so their paths crossed as seldom as possible, he decided.

Tomorrow.

Tonight he would enjoy holding her one last time.

Shifting so that his chin rested against the top of her head, he drew her closer against him and closed his eyes, but troubled thoughts kept him from relaxing, and sleep was a long time in coming.

Chapter Six

For the next four days, Jared managed to keep his vow to avoid Jarina. He rose before dawn to go up on deck and did not return to his cabin until long after she was abed, fueling speculation among the crew as to the nature of the discord between their captain and the girl. Twenty hours a day he worked like a demon, and he drove his men to do the same. Tension ran high, hostilities flared, and indolence was swiftly and harshly disciplined. Only Jarina was spared the sting of Jared's temper, but if she escaped his tyranny, she bore the burden of his neglect.

Four days she had spent in the confines of their cabin, with only her sewing to break the monotony of the lonely hours. Jared did not dine with her, and were it not for the indentation his head left on the pillow beside hers, she would have doubted he even shared their bunk at night. Stephen Landon had not been to their cabin since that last evening when he and Jared had conducted business. And when Angus brought her meals, he never lingered more than a moment or two. Desperate for human companionship, she had tried drawing the Scot into a conversation, but he just gave her an apologetic smile and muttered something about having work to do. She was beginning to feel like an exiled convict.

"What do you think, Angus?" she asked when he brought her luncheon, twirling before him in the new gown she had spent the last four days sewing. She smoothed her hands down over the luxurious sapphire velvet and laughed. "More suitable for a lady than boy's breeches, is it not?"

Angus eyed her sadly. He'd seen the pained, vacant look in her eyes too often the past four days not to know that her gaiety was forced. "Ye're a sight to turn any man's head, lass," he said, giving her an approving nod. "The cap'n will be right proud at what ye've managed to do with a needle and thread."

Her smile faded. "Oh, Angus, what am I going to do? What's going to happen to me when we reach the colonies?"

"Why, nothin' untoward's goin' to happen to ye, lass. The colonies ain't so raw as they once was. There's fine cities there now, and—"

"It's been four days, Angus."

He hesitated. "I know, lass," he said gently.

"I have no money. No family. What if I can't find employment? What will happen to me then? I would rather die than become one of those women who scours the docks looking for a man to buy her a meal in return for her services."

The old man gaped at her. He vehemently shook his head. "The cap'n would never let anything like that happen to ye!"

"He's already proven he can dismiss me without a second thought. If he can discard me as easily, that is exactly what will happen."

"But, it won't happen! I'm tellin' ye, lass, ye're under the cap'n's protection now. He won' let nothin' happen to ye. He's a good man, the cap'n. There's none what can say he don' take care of his own."

Just then, the cabin door opened, and Jarina and Angus both started guiltily.

Shock registered in Jarina's eyes at her first sight of Jared in four days. It was evident that he had eaten little and slept less. Dark shadows haunted the hollows beneath his eyes and his cheeks were gaunt, making the bony ridge above them more prominent than usual. The faint lines about his eyes and mouth had hardened. He looked like a man destined for an early grave.

Jared speared Angus with a damning glare. "I am not paying you to gossip with the passengers," he said icily. "If you wish to remain in my employ, I suggest you return to your duties."

The Scot's face flamed with embarrassment. He opened his mouth to protest, but words failed him. His shoulders drooping, he sidled past Jared and slipped silently from the cabin.

Jarina's shock dissipated beneath a surge of anger. "You had no right to speak to Angus that way," she blurted out as soon as the door closed. "He was not gossiping. He was talking to me, something you can't be bothered to do."

As though seeing her for the first time, Jared's eyes moved with agonizing slowness down the length of her, then up again, pausing to visually caress the swell of her bosom above the close-fitting bodice of her gown, and it was all Jarina could do to stand there and endure the humiliating inspection without flinching.

He did not say a word. Turning away from her, he pulled his sweater off over his head and began unbuttoning his shirt.

Jarina seethed. For four days Jared had ignored her. Four days, she had been cooped up in this blasted cabin, struggling to come to terms with her father's betrayal and the prospect of an uncertain future. She glowered at Jared's back as he bent over the wash basin. Not one comment, she thought peevishly, about the new gown she had spent the past four days sewing. *For him.*

Leaving her noon meal untouched, she marched to the door and yanked it open, and on her way out of the cabin, she succumbed to an utterly childish impulse. She slammed the door as hard as she could.

Because he had never had difficulty acquiring a willing bedmate, Jared had cultivated the ability to go for long stretches without even thinking of women. Months at sea without feminine companionship did not adversely affect him. He knew the moment his ship docked, any number of desirable females would flock to his side, eager for his attentions. He never needed to seek out a woman; women invariably came to him. And because he could dismiss them at will, he exercised a mastery over them they were powerless to fight.

Until now.

He could not control his thoughts of Jarina; they controlled him. And because he could not thrust her from his mind, she became a fixation, dominating every waking moment and invading his dreams. He wanted her. He wanted to lose himself in her. He wanted to feel her silken limbs wrap around him, drawing him into her, urging him on. The single taste he'd had of her intoxicating warmth their first night together had left him hungry for more.

So he avoided her. He left her side before dawn, resisting the enticements her naked body offered. He drove himself to the brink of exhaustion. Yet even hard physical labor failed to exorcise his longings, and he returned to their cabin in the small hours of the morning still aching for the feel of her in his arms.

Last night had almost been his undoing. She had rolled against him in her sleep, her small hand landing squarely in the middle of his chest, and his resistance snapped. He had turned to her then with the intention of satisfying his lusts, but the sight of her face in the starlight, soft with repose, abruptly brought him back to his senses. Cursing himself for his weakness, he retreated to the edge of the bunk and spent the next hour damning her for her ability to sleep while he lay sweating like a pubescent schoolboy, his body rigid with unrelieved passions.

Jared rubbed one hand fitfully across his brow. He did not know how much longer he could go on like this. He knew he was being unfair to Jarina and unduly hard on his crew. Both his temper and his sanity were on the verge of snapping. Something was going to have to give.

He was sitting at the table, warming his hands around a mug of hot coffee when she returned to their cabin, and Jarina knew from the iron set of his jaw that her impulsive burst of temper would not go unreprimanded. He inclined his head toward the empty chair across from him. "Sit down."

The cold wind had chapped her lips and reddened her cheeks. Although she tried to appear dignified as she did Jared's bidding, she could not stop shivering. Gritting her teeth to keep them from chattering, she folded her hands in her lap and lifted a wary gaze to Jared's face.

He swore silently. Not since she first tumbled at his feet in ragged curls and boy's breeches had she looked so fetching. The brisk North Atlantic wind that had heightened her coloring and tousled her hair had brightened her eyes as well, making them burn with a brilliant blue light as they stared, transfixed, into his own. There was no mistaking the fear he read in them, and he was seized with an almost overwhelming urge to laugh. If Jarina ever discovered how much power she held over him, he would be a ruined man.

"There are three things I will not tolerate from anyone," he said sternly, pausing to let his words sink in before he continued. "The first is deceit."

Jarina's eyes widened in surprise, and she opened her

mouth to protest, but Jared silenced her with a wave of his hand. "I am merely telling you this by way of warning. To my knowledge, you have not lied to me, but I must caution you, if you ever do, you will regret it."

He stared at her so hard that she quailed inwardly, certain he knew the truth about her father. Her mouth went dry. She wondered if she should confess now, and make right the falsehood she had told him about having no living relatives, but cowardice prevailed, and she kept silent.

"The second thing I will not tolerate is insolence. You have a fondness, my dear, for infantile outbursts which I find extremely annoying. If you and I are going to get along at all on this voyage, you had best learn to control your temper."

Jarina fumed. A fine one *he* was to be telling her to control *her* temper! "I beg your forgiveness, Captain," she said snidely, recklessly casting caution aside. "In the future, I will endeavor to remember that tantrums are a privilege reserved for the owner of this vessel!"

No sooner had the words left her lips than she longed to recall them. Jared's hand closed into a fist and the muscle in his cheek twitched. His fearsome glare bore into her. "The third thing," he ground out, shoving the bowl of stew Angus had brought for her dinner across the table toward her, "is waste."

She did not need to ask what he meant. Angus had prepared her meal, and now she was expected to eat it, regardless of the fact that it had long since grown cold and unpalatable. She stared at the potage, thick with congealed fat, and her stomach rebelled. She could not eat it. She *would* not eat it.

As if reading her thoughts, Jared leaned toward her and lifted her chin, making her look at him. "You will eat it," he said softly.

Her courage fled. Tears of impotent anger glittered

in her lashes and choked her throat. He did not even have to threaten her to force her to his will.

Jared released her chin. He had won, but the victory had left an unpleasant taste in his mouth. "Eat your dinner."

Hating him, hating herself, Jarina obeyed. She wanted to defy him. She wanted to pick up the bowl and hurl it at his face. She wanted to scream at him that she was a lady and deserved to be treated with respect. She didn't want to be a coward, but that was exactly what she was. Were she brave, she would not have run away from home, but would have stood up to her father and refused his command to marry the Duke of Roswell. Were she brave, she would not be sitting here now choking down this wretched stew against her will. She was a coward. She knew it. Her father had known it. Jared knew it.

While it was her misery that she dwelled upon as she ate, it was her anger that manifested itself, so much so that, after several minutes of watching her stab at her food with a vehemence that smacked of effrontery, Jared's patience had reached the end of its tether. He reached across the table and snatched the bowl away from her.

Taken by surprise, Jarina eyed him uncertainly as he went to his locker and retrieved his black woolen cloak. "Come here," he ordered. There was a note of warning in his voice that overrode any notion she might have entertained of defying him, and on a pair of legs that shook like a rickety scaffold, she rose and went to him.

Jared draped the cloak about her shoulders. "You may stop looking at me as though you expect me to strike you. I merely want you to walk outside with me. It is not healthy to remain cloistered in this cabin day after day, and I have no inclination to spend my time nursing an invalid."

Before Jarina had time to digest his words, Jared gripped her arm and propelled her toward the cabin

door. "Besides," he added testily, "I wish to lay to rest
the nasty rumor being circulated that I beat you and
lock you in our cabin."

If Jarina had felt conspicuous up on the quarterdeck
earlier, her discomfort paled beside what she felt now.
She was acutely aware, not only of the probing stares
of the crew, but of Jared's arm wrapped possessively
about her waist. He held her so tightly their thighs
touched as they walked, and when he stopped to speak
with the helmsman, he drew her close and brushed his
lips against her forehead before turning his attention
to the seaman. She nervously moistened her lips and
struggled to keep her rapidly mounting panic under
control. Jared's doting suitor role did not suit.

His business with the helmsman concluded, he led
her to the taffrail. His gaze drifted out to sea as though
he had forgotten her, but his hand still rode her waist,
and through the cloak, she could feel his fingers gently
caressing. "I think you would like Wyeburn," he said
after a while. "The main house is situated on a hill with
a fine view of the valley and the woods beyond. It's
beautiful any time of year, but especially so in the
spring when the azaleas and dogwoods are in bloom."

Jarina's fear gave way to bewilderment, and she
tilted her head back to look at Jared. She did not know
why it mattered whether she liked his country estate;
she was not likely to ever see it.

Ignoring her questioning regard, he went on to tell
her about the towering hundred-and-twenty-year-old
oak tree that shaded the red-brick house that was now
swathed in ivy, and the run he had dammed as a youth
to make a swimming hole. He told her about the vivid
scarlets and golds that engulfed the land in the autumn.

It was the first time Jared had spoken openly to her
of Wyeburn, and he did so with an absence of emotion
in his voice that tore at Jarina's heart. The picture of
tranquility he painted for her did not ring true. She felt
as though he were imbuing his family home with an

idyllic past that did not exist. A wave of sadness swept over her. She had left behind a childhood of happy memories that were lost to her forever. Jared, she suspected, had never even been a child.

He looked down at her and a crooked grin twisted his mouth. "From the look on your face," he said, chuckling, "one would think I was taking you into uncharted territory thick with wild Indians. Virginia is quite civilized, madam, I assure you."

Jarina felt her face grow warm. "There is a manor house near Sherborne that is also called Wyeburn," she said, changing the subject. "It's built of stone rather than brick."

The smile disappeared and there was a flash of intense hatred in Jared's eyes before his expression once more became guarded. "The Wyeburn you speak of is my ancestral home. Or, at least, it was, until the fourth Duke of Roswell had my great-grandfather arrested on trumped-up charges of gunrunning. My great-grandfather was sentenced to hang, but he managed to escape. Eventually, the conviction was overturned and the king granted him a pardon. By then, however, he had married and put down roots in America. He had no desire to return to England."

At the mention of Roswell, Jarina's blood went cold. It seemed that the fourth duke had had no more scruples than the present one. It sent a chill down Jarina's spine to think the Roswell name had brought grief to Jared's family as well as her own. The coincidence was unnerving and she shuddered.

Taking her by the shoulders, Jared turned her to face him. He closed the cloak at her throat and fastened it. "I don't want you to take a chill," he said quietly.

In the wake of his earlier callousness, his apparent concern for her welfare was disarming. Jarina lifted an inquiring gaze and found him studying her, a frown worrying his brow, and she wondered frantically what she had done this time to displease him. His gray eyes burned with a molten heat as they touched upon each feature of her face as though marking her with his brand. Like a rabbit caught in a snare, she stared back at him, unable to move. Beneath the cloak, his fingers lingered on the swell of flesh above the bodice of her gown. The sensation was not unpleasant and when his hands moved downward to circle her waist and pull her against him, she unthinkingly leaned into his arms and lifted her lips to his as his head descended.

"Cap'n Cunningham! You needs come quick! There's been an accident!"

Disappointment surged through Jarina as Jared abruptly released her and spun around to face the seaman who was struggling to catch his breath. "Where?"

"In the galley, sir. It's Tom Darby. The copper tipped off the fire and spilled gruel all o'er him. He's hurt bad!"

Jarina started to follow, but was brought up short as Jared barked a sharp command over his shoulder. "Stay here!"

By the time Jared reached the galley, the injured youth was writhing on the deck. "My hands!" he screamed. "Oh, my God! I can't lose my hands!"

Pushing his way through the circle of curious onlookers, Jared knelt by the boy and placed a steadying hand on his shoulder. "It'll be all right, son. Lie still."

"I can't take care of my Julie if I lose my hands, Cap'n, I can't! Who'll feed my babies? My Julie . . . Oh, God . . . it *hurts.*"

Jared was already fast at work removing the boy's gruel-saturated shirt. Angry red burns covered his torso, but it was his hands that had suffered the worst injury. Tom had tried to catch the kettle as it overturned, and the boiling porridge had drenched his hands and forearms, turning them a vivid red except for his fingers, where the scalded flesh hung in wrinkled white folds. His entire body shook violently.

"Nothing will happen to your family, Tom. You shall draw full wages until you can return to work."

Tom did not even hear him. He was sobbing uncontrollably. "My Julie, Cap'n. Who'll take care of my Julie?"

Jared slid his arms beneath the boy and gently lifted him. The other seamen moved aside to let them pass. Fitch led the way to a long table in the seamen's mess, and Jared laid the boy on the well-worn planks.

From the corner of his eye, Tom saw the cook and screamed. "Not my hands, Cap'n! Don't let him cut off my hands!"

It took all Jared's strength to hold Tom Darby down. He looked up at Fitch. "What do you think?"

"I don't know, Cap'n. Them burns' real deep. Gangrene's likely to—"

"No, no! Not my hands! Please, Cap'n! Not my hands!"

"We can save his hands," Jarina said quietly.

Both men turned at the sound of her voice. Surprise was frozen on their faces. Jared glowered at her and opened his mouth to order her back up on deck, but before he could speak, she was beside the table. She cast a cursory glance at Tom's other burns and dismissed them as minor, then gently touched his shoulder. Immediately he stilled, and his gaze was fixed on her face in wide-eyed terror as though he were seeing an apparition. She gave him a timid smile. "Can you bend your fingers, sir?" she asked.

The youth's frightened gaze darted from Jarina to Jared and back again.

"Try," Jarina pleaded quietly. "Try to bend your fingers."

His hands trembling, Tom attempted to do as she asked, but the effort overwhelmed him and he began squalling like a child. "I c-can't, mum . . ." he sobbed. His teeth began to chatter. His head rolled from side to side and tears streamed down his face. "It hu-urts too much."

Jarina glanced up. "It's a good sign, Jared. If the flesh were burned all the way through, he would not be able to feel a thing."

Turning her attention back to Tom, Jarina unfastened Jared's cloak and withdrew it from around her shoulders. There was a sharp intake of breath from somewhere behind him, and Jared glanced around to find every man in the room gawking at her. She bent over Tom to cover him with the cloak, and her bodice gaped, exposing a daring amount of bosom to curious male stares. Jared's brows drew together in a fierce scowl. "He must be kept warm," Jarina said as she adjusted the cloak around Tom. She was oblivious to the disturbance she was creating. "I'll need soap and water, and clean linen for bandages. There are some small scissors in the surgery that I will also require."

No one budged. Jarina turned her head and threw Jared an imploring glance.

Jared's scowl blackened. In a burst of temper, he ordered everyone out of the seamen's mess, and he sent Angus in search of the implements Jarina had requested.

Over the next hour, Jarina meticulously snipped the loose outer skin away from the blisters on Tom's hands, exposing the raw, weeping flesh beneath. While she worked, she kept up a steady conversation with the injured youth. Between bravely gritting his teeth and sobbing miserably, Tom somehow managed to talk, and Jarina was surprised to discover that, although he was no older than she, he was married and had two children, and was supporting his aging mother as well. "You'll not be trimming sails anytime soon," she told him when he asked her about his hands.

"I guess I won't be playing on my fiddle either," he said unhappily.

"Not for a few weeks. After that, it will be good for you. It will help you regain use of your fingers."

She then applied a paste of cerate and ashes to Tom's hands and began wrapping them with the linen Angus had torn into narrow strips. "The plaster will need to be renewed twice a day," she told the Scot. "And when you wrap the bandages, you must take care to wrap each finger individually, or the flesh will grow together as it heals." She smiled at Tom.

Tears glittered on the youth's lashes, but there was a look of undisguised adoration in his eyes. "God bless you, mum," he whispered.

She finished bandaging Tom's hands. With Jared's promise that he would soon follow, Jarina returned to their cabin. The ordeal in the seamen's mess had drained her. She hoped she had done the right thing. The chances that Tom might lose his hands were still great, and she feared she may have only delayed his loss. She sat down on the edge of the bunk and wearily rubbed the heels of her hands into her eyes. Exhaustion settled over her like a heavy, smothering blanket. When Jared arrived shortly thereafter, she was sound asleep.

Jared stood by the bunk for several long minutes, studying her fatigue-ridden face in the fading afternoon light. She was lying on her side with her head on his pillow and one hand tucked beneath her cheek, and her lips were parted like a child's. At times like this, when her defenses were down, she appeared too young to shoulder a woman's cares, yet today she had done just that. In the midst of chaos, she had administered to Tom Darby's burns with the deftness of a practiced physician. Jared did not know where she had acquired such a skill. He was still not certain Tom's hands would heal, but Tom believed it, and that was what mattered.

Wondering wryly what other surprises that artless façade concealed, he bent to brush the back of his knuckles against her soft cheek.

She stirred and her eyes flew open, and for a moment,

Jared just stood there leaning over her, feeling guiltily like someone who had just been caught doing something disgraceful. Suspicion flared in Jarina's eyes as her gaze focused on his face, and Jared suddenly found himself blushing like a callow youth. Swearing under his breath, he jerked himself upright and went to his desk, putting the safety of distance between them.

Her body aching with fatigue, Jarina dropped her feet over the side of the bunk and sat up. She stared at Jared's unyielding back and sensed that he was vexed with her, but did not know what she had done to provoke his ire. "I am sorry about soiling your cloak," she ventured hesitantly, thinking that might be the problem.

He rounded on her. Beneath the bewildered frown that creased her forehead, her beautiful blue eyes were wide and guileless. Jared cursed himself for being affected by the unsullied innocence in them. Jarina could seduce a man with those eyes, he thought irritably. She was damned close to seducing him.

He struggled to get his traitorous passions under control. "The cloak is not important. What is important is that you defied me. You were told to stay on deck, and you followed me below anyway. If one of my men deliberately disobeyed a direct order, he would be flogged."

She stared at him in stunned disbelief. She had just done everything she could to save a man's hands and his livelihood, and all Jared could call to attention was her failure to heed his orders. She clutched a fistful of quilt and her heart began to pound with wild, unreasoning dread. "I-I'm sorry," she stammered nervously. "It was not my intent to disobey you, only to help. I am not unfamiliar with scald burns and—"

"A ship's captain who cannot control his passengers can hardly command respect from his crew," Jared interrupted. "To allow your defiance to go unpunished is to invite mutiny. This time, I will let you by with a warning, but if it happens again, you will not be so lucky. I will not tolerate willful disobedience, Jarina. Remember that."

That said, he stalked from the cabin and slammed the door loudly after him, leaving Jarina to stare at the closed door in open-mouthed shock.

Two changes took place in the captain's cabin. Jarina no longer ate her meals alone, and Jared no longer approached their bunk whenever she occupied it. He assumed the night watch, returning to their cabin in time to breakfast with Jarina. Then, after assuring her that her presence would not disturb him, he slept during the day while she busied herself with her sewing, and he arose in the evening to dine with her before going up on deck. Spared of Jared's more amorous advances, Jarina began to enjoy both his company and their dinnertime conversations. The arrangement suited her perfectly.

After a particularly pleasant meal, Jared poured himself a brandy and offered her one.

She hesitated to accept. "I've never drunk brandy," she explained a little sheepishly. Jared had been especially considerate throughout dinner, making her feel as self-conscious as an inexperienced schoolgirl enjoying her first taste of male attention. "I'm afraid I would not appreciate it as you do."

He poured a small portion into a snifter and handed it to her. "First, allow the heat from your hands to warm the brandy," he instructed. He showed her how to cup the snifter in her palm. All the while observing her through hooded eyes, he lifted his own snifter and passed it beneath his nose. Jarina followed his lead.

The heady scent of the amber wine assaulted her senses and flooded her head with unbidden memories of her first night on the ship. Time had softened the painful edges of that eventful night, and the visions that now filled Jarina's thoughts were of intimate caresses and brandy-scented kisses. Hot color consumed her cheeks and her hands trembled as she placed the snifter on the table. "I've been wanting to thank you for the new clothes," she said softly.

He smiled at her. "There is no need to thank me. I merely presented you with the cloth. It was your talent and hard work that rendered such beautiful results."

The warmth of his smile made her feel giddy and a little peculiar inside. Looking down at the gown she had completed the previous day, she touched a forefinger to the burgundy silk and said wistfully, "I've never had so many beautiful things."

"A matter easily remedied," Jared said. "There is a modiste in Alexandria, a Madame Bouchard, who will jump at the opportunity to outfit you with a complete wardrobe. We will pay her a visit when we reach port."

Jarina lifted a startled gaze to his face, but before she could say anything, Jared silenced any objection she might have voiced with a slight movement of his hand. "You have made it clear that you want nothing from me," he said flatly. "However, few things bring me greater pleasure than seeing a beautiful woman elegantly clad. Indulge me in this one weakness, Jarina. I am not doing it for you. I am doing it for myself."

Angus came to the cabin to remove the dinner dishes. "Tom Darby says to tell ye he's plum itchin' to get a bow in his hands again," he informed Jarina. "The poultices ye prepared for him have eased his pain. He can bend his fingers now, lass, and he says to tell ye when he's able, he's gonna play a tune for ye, whatever ye likes to hear."

Acutely aware of Jared's gaze on her, Jarina thanked the Scot for the message, and gave him one of her own. "Please tell Mr. Darby I shall be honored to have him play for me. I am glad his hands are healing so quickly."

After Angus left the cabin, Jarina cast Jared an uncertain glance. "I went up for a breath of fresh air while you were sleeping," she explained, fearful he would think she had disobeyed him and ventured belowdecks against his orders. "Tom Darby came up on the quarterdeck so that I might see how his burns were healing. I hope you don't object."

Jared leaned back in his chair, a thoughtful expression on his face as he studied her. "You have not told me where you learned the healer's art," he said. "I am curious to know how you come by such a remarkable skill."

Afraid the untruths she had told him would reflect in her eyes, Jarina lowered her gaze and toyed nervously with her snifter of brandy. "My father was a physician," she said. "I learned from watching him. Sometimes he let me assist him in his surgery."

" 'Twas well he did. I would not have thought it possible to save Tom's hands."

She glanced up at him from beneath her lashes. "Nor I," she confessed shyly.

Jared eyed her over the rim of his snifter as he took a long slow draught of the brandy. "Was your father a good physician?"

A small frown creased Jarina's brow as she struggled to separate her father's betrayal from his skill as a healer. After a moment, she nodded. "He was wonderful," she said slowly. "The villagers loved him. He never turned anyone away, no matter how seemingly trivial the complaint."

Prompted by Jared's questions, she went on to tell him how her father had become a physician against his family's wishes; of her mother's death during childbirth; of life in the sprawling Hampshire country house; and bit by bit, a picture of her childhood took form in his mind. "And your father?" he asked. "What became of him?"

She nervously moistened her lips. Jared must never know that she had lied to him and that her father still lived. "My father was never a very good manager of money," she said in a low, tense voice. "He seldom demanded payments from either his patients or his tenants. Soon he had creditors barking like hounds at his door. His inability to meet his debts and his loss of self-esteem finally broke his spirit. He became old before his time."

"I am sorry," Jared said quietly.

An unexpected wave of homesickness swept over her. Bitter tears pricked behind her eyelids and her throat constricted. "Oh, Jared, I am so scared," she blurted out. "Until now, I had never even been as far away from home as London, and here I am going halfway around the world to a place where everyone will be a stranger. When you and Angus and Mr. Landon all go your separate ways, I won't have anyone—" She broke off, and gave him a wobbly smile. "I forget myself sometimes," she said sheepishly. "Please forgive me."

Jared's expression softened. Putting down his snifter, he reached across the table and took her small hand in his large tanned one. His fingers closed reassuringly around hers. "You will never be alone, Jarina," he said quietly. "No matter where you go or what you do, I will be there for you."

Jarina's smile faded as their gazes met and held in a silent exchange of understanding that needed no words.

The following evening Stephen Landon joined them for dinner. Time and again, Jarina caught herself blushing at the most innocent remarks, and Jared, in turn, treated her with an almost courtly courtesy. Seemingly unaware of the change between them, Stephen regaled Jarina with lively descriptions of Virginia, from the bustling Tidewater cities to the vast tobacco plantations that had been carved out of raw wilderness. He told her of the shrimp boats that plied the Chesapeake, and of holiday parties at the great houses that lasted from harvest until spring. He described New World delicacies of which she had never even heard, of oysters the size of a man's fist, of sweet white-kerneled maize, and she-crab soup. Jarina's eyes sparkled with delight as she listened to his stories, and she felt a stirring of excitement for the colony that was to become her new home. Warmed by the wine she had sipped throughout their meal, she turned a glowing gaze on Jared. "Oh, Jared, if it's as wonderful as he says, I fear I shall grow fat from sampling everything!"

Jared laughed. "If you do, my dear, Madame Bouchard will grow wealthy keeping you suitably clothed."

His smile softened his harsh features, and as their gazes held, Jarina could not help thinking what a fine-looking man he was. He was everything a woman could want. He was handsome and intelligent and successful. He could walk into a room and command attention just by his presence. His men treated him with a respect that bordered upon reverence, and even Stephen Landon, who enjoyed an equally lofty social standing, had deferred to him repeatedly throughout the evening. He was the type of man men emulated and women adored.

Without realizing what she was doing, she allowed her gaze to drop to his lips. He had not attempted to kiss her since that day up on deck, and she suddenly found herself wishing he would do so again.

The silent invitation did not go unnoticed by either man. Jared's eyes grew dark with desire as passions that were becoming increasingly difficult to deny surged through his veins. He did not know how much longer he could keep his hands from Jarina if she insisted upon looking at him with that beguiling mixture of innocence and seduction which he found so unnerving.

Stephen chuckled. "You had best keep a close eye on this one," he said. "As soon as Damon lays eyes on her, your baby brother may be tempted to call an end to his wild tomcat days and propose."

Jared's smile vanished.

Jarina's gaze riveted on Jared. "I didn't know you had a brother."

"Damon is my half brother," Jared said curtly, his good humor gone. "I suggest you keep away from him. He comes by his roving instincts honestly."

Jarina had no idea what he meant by that, but Stephen did. "If he does," he put in, laughing, "it's the only thing Damon does honestly."

Jared glowered at him.

"Well, I can see I've overstayed my welcome," the younger man said good-naturedly. He stood up. "I'll just leave before I'm thrown out. Good evening, Jarina. I enjoyed dinner immensely. When we reach Virginia, if Jared here doesn't take you to Hall's Tavern for a taste of those crabcakes I told you about, you just call on me. I'll be more than willing to accompany you.

"And one more thing, Jared," he added, his warm brown eyes alight with amusement as he stopped with his hand on the door. "I was wrong about my cousin. Evelyn isn't going to be green when she sees Jarina. She's going to be *livid.*"

A choking silence settled over the cabin after Stephen had gone. Jarina sat staring at her hands which were clasped in her lap while Jared poured himself a dose of brandy they both knew was far too liberal for a man about to go up on deck to assume the night watch. It troubled her that Jared had not told her about his brother, and she did not understand why Stephen's reference to him should cause what had been an otherwise pleasant evening to sour. Nor did she comprehend the veiled reference to Stephen's cousin, except to wonder if perhaps she were in love with Jared. She ventured a glance at Jared from beneath her lashes. "You told me of the rest of your family," she said softly. "Why did you not tell me you had a brother?"

Jared downed the entire snifter of brandy in a single draw. "Because he doesn't concern you. You'll see

naught of him except in my company. If you do otherwise, I'll know the reason why."

There was such an undercurrent of bitterness in his
voice as he spoke that Jarina was taken aback. A full
minute passed before she realized what he had said.
When she did, her eyes flared wide and a cry of indignation tore from her throat. "My God, but you are a selfish bastard! You won't have me, yet you would deny
me the happiness I might find with another man. You
have the gall of a horse, Jared Cunningham, to accuse
me of impropriety with a man I've never even met! If
either of us were prone to debauchery, 'twould be you.
You were the one to be found dandling a cheap harlot
on your knee the last day in port, whereas I've never
known any man save you, and that against my will!"

"Molly McGuire might be a harlot," Jared said
coldly, raking her with his hard gaze as he hauled himself unsteadily to his feet. "But she is also a woman.
And that, my dear, is more than you'll ever be able to
claim."

"A woman!" Jarina flew up out of her chair, but before she could say anything, the door slammed, and she
was left alone with her roiling anger. In a snit, she flung
her arm across the table, sending the dishes flying. "Arrogant bastard!" she sputtered, too angry to think
clearly. Balling her hands into fists, she paced angrily.
"He treats me as though I were dirt beneath his feet
and praises that *trollop* for a woman! What does he
think I am, a stupid child with no feelings? Does he
think I cannot feel the sting of his sharp words? Does
he think I will take his abuse day after day with no regard for my own well-being? God help me, you conceited American, I wish I'd married Roswell rather
than ever lay eyes on you!"

It was not true, and she knew it wasn't, but when
Molly McGuire's face flashed before her eyes, anger
and jealousy erupted anew. That the strumpet not only
had a name, but that Jared actually remembered it

made her all the more despicable in Jarina's eyes. She hated being compared to another woman, particularly one whose lot left so little to be envied, but what stung most was knowing that Jared actually *preferred* the company of someone like Molly McGuire over her.

A choking lump swelled in her throat, and Jarina realized with some reluctance that she was not so much angered as she was hurt. Hurt that she could not compete with even a common whore for Jared's affection.

Angus knew even before he entered the cabin that something was amiss; the captain had been venting his ire on the crew from the moment he went topside. Jarina was sitting on the window seat with her forehead pressed against the cold glass. She did not even acknowledge his presence when he came to clear away the dishes. It's not like her to be so quiet and drawn inside herself, he thought, unable to curb his curiosity at the broken dishes she had stacked in a neat pile on the table. She had fallen into the habit of greeting him with a ready smile, a smile he now sorely missed.

Suddenly Jared's voice broke through the working creaks and groans of the ship. Jarina lifted her head from the window and turned a dismal gaze on the rafters overhead, and she and Angus listened uncomfortably to Jared's bellowing up on the quarterdeck as he chastised the first mate, Silas Crawford, in a voice loud enough to be heard all the way to the colonies.

Angus shifted nervously. "The cap'n, he ain't always like this," he said, despairing for something consoling to say. "He's a hard man, aye, but a fair one. He don' do nothin' without good cause. Give him time, lass. He'll come out of it. Ye'll see."

Jarina looked doubtful. "I want to believe you, Angus," she said in a choked whisper that did little to hide her misery. She gave him a weak smile. "But sometimes . . . sometimes, it's very, very hard."

Long after Angus left, Jarina sat, thinking of Jared and trying to find a way to lessen the hostilities that seemed to flare between them with increasing frequency. Sometimes, when his countenance softened and his guard was down, he seemed most affable, and she thought he must have suffered some great disappointment in his life; she was certain his cynicism and his anger were nothing more than armor to shield a very lonely man. Then, just when she felt she was beginning to understand him, he would fly into a rage at the slightest provocation and she wondered why she bothered sparing him any compassion at all.

She sighed. She did not know what to do. She only knew she could not continue like this, with her stomach tied in a perpetual knot of anxiety, always worrying if she were going to say or do the wrong thing. Perhaps if she were a little nicer to him, she thought, he would respond in kind.

A black melancholy settled over her. Deep down inside, she did not think her efforts would bring any worthwhile results. Still, she had to try. For her sake as well as for the sake of the crew.

Chapter Seven

By morning, the weather had turned. The sea swelled and a cold wind blew from the northwest. Jared studied the high, fast-moving clouds and estimated that he had another six hours of full sail before gusting winds necessitated reducing the amount of canvas. He was confident the *Pegasus* would ride out the impending storm without incident. He hoped Jarina fared as well; he had no tolerance for a seasick woman, particularly one who tormented him with her charms, then accused him of seeking elsewhere the pleasures she withheld.

Somewhere in his tired mind, his thoughts had become twisted and irrational. He blamed Jarina for denying him what he in reality denied himself. He blamed her for being an innocent when what he needed was a willing whore to satisfy the lusts that churned within him. Jarina, with her tempting curves and seductive eyes that promised much and yielded nothing, was useless. She was worse than useless. She was a curse, a flaw in what was once an untroubled existence.

And then there was Damon.

The thought of Jarina falling under Damon's influence aroused a murderous rage in him unlike anything he had ever known. Ever since Stephen's mention of him last night, his imagination had tormented him with visions of Jarina and his young half brother. Jarina and Damon, exchanging secretive glances. Jarina and Damon, locked in each other's arms. Jarina and Damon, making love. He felt the blood of hatred pound in his ears. Jarina was his, damn it, and she had best remember that! If she ever betrayed him the way his mother had betrayed his father, he would kill her. He would not do as his father had done, and stand aside to play the roll of forgiving husband while his wife reared her bastard child in his house.

Jared muttered a savage oath. What was wrong with him? Jarina was not his wife, yet he was behaving as if she were. He had no legal claim to her. What she did was her own affair, and he had no right to interfere. Nor did he have any right to condemn Jarina for his mother's infidelity.

Angry, jealous thoughts had left his insides clenched tight, and sleep was the farthest thing from his mind as he descended the companionway stairs.

Jarina whirled around as the cabin door opened. She smiled a timid greeting, but there was uncertainty in her eyes as they fixed on him.

Miraculously, his vile temper began to subside at the sight of her. She was wearing the sapphire blue gown, and her glossy chestnut curls had been brushed back from her face and secured with a ribbon of the same color. It was a small touch, and perhaps an innocent one, Jared reluctantly conceded as he raked her with his scrutinizing gaze, but it played havoc with his passions. Deprived of his anger, he suddenly felt exposed and vulnerable. He felt like an unsuspecting soldier who had just walked into an ambush. He felt defenseless.

His gaze swung from Jarina to the portable tub that had been placed before the stove and filled with steaming water to the table that was set as though for a feast. A bottle of his finest burgundy had been uncorked and tantalizing odors wafted from beneath platters crowned with silver covers. His empty stomach tightened in protest, for it was not food he needed to satisfy his hunger.

Jarina nervously moistened her lips. "I thought you might be growing weary of breakfast fare for your supper," she said, shifting uneasily from one foot to the other as she explained. "So I had Angus prepare you a special dinner. I hope you like it, Jared. Angus assured me the dishes were your favorites."

Jared broke out into a cold sweat. Perspiration beaded across his upper lip and it took every ounce of self-control he had ever possessed to keep his rampaging emotions under control. First the ribbon in her hair and now all this. Damn! Didn't the girl know what she was doing to him? Didn't she know how badly he wanted her? Hours of picturing her in Damon's arms had aroused more than his jealousy, and he was dangerously close to just picking her up and carrying her to the bunk, willing or not. The muscle in his cheek twitched. "Thank you," he said hoarsely. He could not look at her for fear he would forget himself and force himself on her. Again.

He made no move toward the steak he knew awaited him, but went instead to the stove and poured himself a mug of strong black coffee. He kept his back to her as he stood there drinking it.

Her pulse racing, Jarina chewed on her bottom lip and pondered what to do next. She was not certain she could go through with this, for she knew there would be a price to pay for her efforts. If she acted too agreeable, Jared was certain to demand more of her than shared meals, and the intimacy of his bunk still terrified her, far more than she wanted to admit. Yet, if having her would put an end to Jared's bouts of irrational fury and make the voyage a more pleasant one for all of them, it was a risk worth taking.

Taking a deep breath, she went to him and placed a gentle hand on his arm. "I also had Angus ready a hot bath for you," she said softly. "Perhaps you would like to bathe before we sit down to eat."

Jared choked on the hot coffee as his resistance snapped. Jerking his arm away as though her touch had scalded him, he forcefully set down the mug and turned on his heel. "I have to go up on deck," he choked. He elbowed his way past her.

"Jared Cunningham, don't you dare walk out on me!"

Jared stopped with one hand on the door and turned to stare at her in amazement. His expression was pinched and his breathing labored, and his eyes burned with an odd light that frightened her.

More than a little stunned by her own temerity, Jarina thrust out her chin in a gesture that was less an act of defiance than of wounded pride. "Angus went to a great deal of trouble for you," she said, hurt echoing in her voice in spite of her efforts to appear unflappable. "Are you not even going to eat?"

"I'm not hungry," Jared snapped defensively. He felt like a cornered animal. He had to escape.

"But, Jared, you didn't even—"

"I have work to do, Jarina. In case you failed to notice, this ship does not sail itself."

"Can't someone else do that?"

"I am the ship's captain. It's my responsibility."

"But, you've been awake all night! You need to rest."

"Damn it, Jarina! When I want your advice, I'll ask for it!"

Jared yanked the door open and collided with Angus. The Scot took a startled step backward and spilled hot water from the two full pails he was carrying.

Cursing loudly, Jared shoved him out of the way and stormed out of the cabin.

A perplexed frown creased the old man's brow as he stared, first at his master's departing back and then at Jarina who stood looking as though she might at any moment burst into tears. He saw her throat contract as she swallowed hard several times. Then she turned a stricken gaze on him as though begging him to do something. It broke his heart to see the lass like this. Though he knew not why, he was aware that she had been especially anxious to please Jared this morning. No matter what the captain's reasons, the girl deserved far better than she was getting. "I'm sorry, lass," he said gently, seeking to undo the damage his employer had wrought. "The cap'n dinna mean to be so short with ye. He has a heavy load on his mind, is all, what with worryin' about sellin' the *Pegasus* and findin' jobs for the seamen who won' be goin' with the new owner."

Anger flashed behind the misery in Jarina's eyes. "Oh, Angus, stop making excuses for him," she bit out. She clenched her trembling hands in the folds of her skirt. "He does it because I let him do it. We all do. We let him walk on us. We let him treat us shabbily because we are too afraid of him to fight back. He is like a spoiled child who always has his way, and he doesn't care who he hurts!"

"Nay, lass, 'tis not true—"

"I won't stand for it anymore," she interrupted. Her voice shook with humiliation and anger. "I am tired of being talked down to and treated like a child without a whit of sense. I am a human being, Angus, and I deserve to be treated as one." Without waiting to hear what he had to say, she stalked past him and out the door.

There was a wild, crazed look in her eyes that Angus had never before seen, and a dark foreboding chilled his blood as he realized her intent. "Nay, lass . . ."

"Don't try to stop me, Angus."

Up on deck, the wind whipped Jarina's skirts about her legs and tore the ribbon from her hair. Gritting her teeth against the bitter cold, she climbed to the quarter-deck and made her way toward the helmsman. "Where is your captain?" she asked. She had to shout to be heard above the wind.

The helmsman motioned overhead and Jarina looked up to find Jared high above them. He was straddling the mizzen topyard and staring out to sea. Though he was too far away for her to clearly see his features, she could feel the coiled anger that stiffened the set of his shoulders. But she, too, was angry, and she was determined not to back down now that she had come this far. "I need to speak with him," she told the helmsman, wrapping her arms about her in a futile attempt to shield herself from the wind. "Can you send someone up for him?"

The helmsman's jaw dropped as he turned a shocked gaze on her, and for several long seconds he simply stared at her as though he thought she had gone mad. Then his mouth snapped shut and he shook his head. "I can't do that, mum. The captain would have my hide! No one troubles the captain when he goes aloft."

"This is important!"

"Sorry, mum. I can't."

Frustrated by the man's refusal to do her bidding, she impaled him with her fiercest glare, inflicting on him the smoldering fury intended for Jared. "What is your name, sir?" she demanded.

The man's eyes widened slightly. "Er . . . Perkins, ma'am. Henry Per—"

"Mr. Perkins, when your captain decides to come down from his lofty perch, kindly inform him that his *mistress* wishes a word with him!"

Jarina's presence on deck did not go unnoticed by Jared. Watching her confront the helmsman, then stomp away in a huff, brought a ready scowl to his brow. He had a reasonably good idea what had brought her topside, and he was almost surprised that she did not attempt to follow him aloft to do battle with him. Jarina, he was discovering, possessed a rather volatile temper.

An hour later, his own temper under a tight rein, Jared returned to their cabin, but stopped short of entering when Jarina's voice reached him through the closed door.

"You are rude and arrogant and domineering," he heard her say. "You belittle those who are not of your standing, and you are hateful to those who only wish to serve you. You shout at Angus for no good reason, and when you are angry with me, you vent your spleen on the men as though they are responsible for your ill temper. Do you think I cannot hear your bellowing? Do you think it does not pain me to know others are suffering because of me?"

There was a pause, but no response, then she began again. "You are rude and arrogant and domineering . . ." With some surprise, Jared realized there was no one else in the cabin. Jarina was talking to herself. She was rehearsing a rather damning speech, but for whose benefit? His curiosity was piqued and he could not help wondering at the identity of the poor soul for whom she bore such rancor.

It was not Jared's nature to eavesdrop, and he despised those who peeked through keyholes and listened at closed doors, but this time his curiosity won out. Bracing an arm against an overhead rafter, he rested his forehead against the back of his hand and waited, listening, as Jarina continued her tirade. Within seconds, the object of her scorn was revealed when she suddenly blurted out, "Blast you, Jared Cunningham, but you are a pompous ass!"

Surprised, Jared jerked his head up.

"I could be your friend, but you won't let me," she continued. "Nothing I do pleases you. First you force yourself upon me and then you ignore me. You treat me as though I were naught but a foolish child and curse me for being less than a woman because I choose not to sit upon your knee and bare my bosom to your caresses like some common slattern. You criticize and threaten until I dare not even breathe without fear of provoking your ire.

"I am tired of being hurt over and over again by you, Jared. I know you don't care about me, but if wanting a little kindness is a sin, then let God punish me. Not you. You have no right!"

Jared closed his eyes and groaned. Good God! Didn't Jarina know he never meant to hurt her? Had she no awareness of the guilt that churned within him every time he thought of that night and the callousness with which he had taken her?

Jared turned and went back up on deck. Her words had shaken him more than he was willing to admit, and there was a peculiar tightness in his chest as though the breath had been knocked from him.

By nightfall, the storm was fully upon them. Gale winds buffeted the *Pegasus* about as though she were a child's toy cast adrift in a raging sea, and with each wave that crashed across the graceful prow of the merchantman, there were those who prayed that they would not be sent to a watery grave before the squall had blown itself out.

In the close confines of the cabin, Jarina huddled, shivering violently, on the bunk with her arms wrapped about her knees. There was a sick churning in the pit of her stomach. She had changed from her gown into her breeches and flannels, fearful her skirts would prove too heavy a burden should she be forced to swim. Rain and seawater lashed the aft window, seeping past the joinery to trickle down the glass and pool on the window seat. The fire in the stove had long since gone out and the only warmth to be found in the cabin came from the wavering light of the lantern. Jarina stared at the lantern, her eyes glassy with hypnotic fear as she watched it sway violently from side to side with the pitching of the ship. Caution told her she should extinguish the flame before it set the cabin ablaze. She

wished Jared would come, but he did not. It was up
to her to do something. Finally, her heart pounding
with mindless terror, she willed herself to venture from
the dubious security of the bunk.

She was halfway across the cabin when the ship was
lifted high in the air, hovered for several long, madden-
ing seconds, then dropped.

Jarina screamed.

As if her legs had been jerked from beneath her, she
fell, striking the deck with a bone-bruising thud. The
flame in the lantern died, plunging the cabin into blackness, and there was a loud groan of straining timbers.
Water surged beneath the cabin door and across the
plank floor, saturating her clothes.

She was struggling to sit up when Jared pushed open
the door. His sight, already adjusted to the shadows,
immediately focused on Jarina sprawled on the wet
floor, and with an exclamation, he rushed to her.

Never in her life had she been so glad to see anyone.
She cried out his name, all her earlier anger at him forgotten, and her arms went up around his neck as he
lifted her. He carried her across the cabin, but when
he lowered her to the bunk, she clung tightly to him.
"Don't leave me," she begged, terrified to let go of him
lest he disappear. She hated herself for being such a
coward, but if she was going to die this night, she did
not want to die alone.

"Jarina, I must go light the stove before we both
freeze," he said gently. He reached up to pry her arms
from around his neck. "I will only be a moment, I
promise."

Reluctantly, she loosened her grip, but her gaze
never wavered from him as he left her to add coals to
the brazier. Once he had a good fire going, he shrugged
out of his wet clothes and draped them over the back
of a chair to dry. "Take yours off, too," he said as he
returned to the bunk. "You'll be warmer without
them."

She obeyed, and after he had hung her clothes near his, he joined her beneath the quilts.

Quaking as much from fear as from the unrelenting cold, Jarina went willingly into the welcoming circle of his arm, and Jared pulled her close against him. He held her tightly so that the combined heat of their bodies might warm them.

Jared stifled a chuckle. It was ironic that after all his recent longing for Jarina's beautiful body he should find himself lying abed with her in his arms and no desire to avail himself of her charms. He felt no unslakable lust for her tonight, only a deep-rooted need to be near her, to drink in her soft warmth, and to find contentment in comforting her. She needed him tonight. She needed his strength and his courage, and it felt oddly right that he should be her protector.

After a while, Jarina's uncontrollable shivering began to subside. She shifted slightly and lifted her head to gaze up into his lean face in the darkness. "I'm sorry," she said. "I don't mean to be such a coward."

Jared's arm tightened around her. "You're not a coward, love," he said, smiling down at her. " 'Tis better to have a healthy respect for danger than to be a fearless fool, believe me."

His big hand gently stroked her side, and both his nearness and the fact that he had not laughed at her brought her comfort. She wrapped a slender arm about his middle and nestled her head into the hollow of his shoulder. "I will be glad when we reach the colonies," she whispered against his chest. "I much prefer to have my feet planted on solid earth."

Jared chuckled. "Most people do, sweet."

After that, they fell silent, and before many more minutes had passed, Jared's hand stilled on her hip and his breathing changed. He was asleep.

But rest eluded Jarina.

She lay awake, listening to the storm that churned without. Wedged between Jared and the cabin wall, she felt safe in spite of the weather. She felt protected. No harm can ever befall me as long as I am with Jared, she thought; no one can ever hurt me.

Then, William Osterbrook's unwelcome visage intruded, bringing a frown to her brow. A wound slow to heal, her father's betrayal still hurt. Deeply. That she might now be lying in the duke's bed, suffering his demands, in payment of a debt, was an abomination she could not easily forgive.

Jared had been good to her tonight, she thought. In spite of the angry words exchanged earlier, he had held and comforted her when she needed it. He had not belittled her as another man might have done, and made light of her fears.

Against her cheek, she felt the steady beat of his heart as it maintained a soothing rhythm, and she thought how good it felt to be here in his arms. If only the hours we spent together were like this more often, she lamented. She would even be willing to forgo marriage and accept being Jared's mistress if the liaison brought with it tenderness instead of the bitterness and discord that had thus far plagued their acquaintance.

She was not aware of having fallen asleep until Jared eased his arm from beneath her shoulders and rose from the bed, startling her awake as a blast of cold air touched her bare skin where previously there had been warmth.

"I need to go up on deck awhile," Jared explained as he donned his clothes. "I shan't be long. Stay in the bunk. It's warmest there." From his locker, he retrieved a leather harness and brought it to her. "If the storm worsens, put this on," he said. He showed her how to fasten the harness to a grommet in the wall. "It will keep you from being thrown out of bed."

"Jared, wait!" Clutching the blankets beneath her chin, Jarina sat up. It had been on the tip of her tongue to bid him to stay, but she choked back the plea, knowing she had no right to demand his presence when he was needed elsewhere. He had a ship to guide through a storm, and a crew for which he was responsible. The last worry he needed at the moment was a helpless woman who was too cowardly to stay by herself for a few hours. She swallowed hard. "Be careful, Jared."

Chuckling, he bent down and took her face between his hands and kissed the tip of her nose. "Keep this bed warm for me, will you?"

Even though she knew he must, she did not like the idea of his returning topside while the weather still raged. She had a bad feeling that could not be contributed entirely to the storm, a feeling that something awful was going to happen. Keeping her fears to herself, she forced a smile she did not feel and nodded dutifully.

Pulling on a slicker, Jared started toward the door, then stopped and turned back to face her. For a moment, he just stood there looking down at her, his expression inscrutable in the darkness. "I never wanted to hurt you, Jarina," he said at last, his tone oddly quiet. "If I could undo all the pain you've suffered at my hands, I would. I hope you believe that."

After he left, Jarina's head whirled with confusing thoughts as she lay shivering beneath the covers. Something had changed between them tonight, she mused, a truce of sorts, a healing. She did not know what had prompted Jared's apology; she only knew what it had cost him to voice it. To a man like Jared, pride was everything. Yet, for one brief moment, he had put aside that pride and spoken the words she needed to hear, and that small gesture touched her more deeply than all the new gowns, all the riches in the world.

He had come closer tonight than any other night since she had come on board to capturing her heart. Had he tried to seduce her, she knew she would have gone willingly, shamelessly, into his arms. "Oh, Jared," she murmured wretchedly, her emotions torn by this latest turn of events. "Please, don't make me fall in love with you. I couldn't bear it knowing that you do not love me in return."

Several times during the night, Jared returned to the cabin, sometimes to warm himself at the stove, sometimes to catch an hour's sleep before going back on deck. Dressed once more in her boy's breeches, Jarina kept busy mopping up the water that seeped into the cabin and maintained a close vigil over the pot of coffee Angus left on the stove, certain with each lurch of the ship that the pot would overturn.

During one visit to the cabin, Jared attempted to teach Jarina how to maintain her balance during rough seas. "Your heels are like anchors; they restrict your movements," he told her. "Keep them up. Walk on the balls of your feet."

The lesson was hopeless. Although she tried to do as he instructed, she inevitably wound up grabbing frantically for support every time the ship rocked. "No, don't!" she cried out as he started up out of his chair to catch her to keep her from falling. "I-I think I can do it." Holding her arms out from her sides to help balance herself, she leaned into the swell like he had shown her, then eased back off. She flashed him a triumphant smile.

Then the ship plunged, and Jarina, losing her equilibrium, gasped and tumbled headlong into Jared's arms.

Laughing, he pulled her onto his lap. "Do you know you look like a drunk goose flapping your arms about like that?" he teased.

Jarina drew back her head and gave him a wounded look. "Are you making sport of me, Captain?"

Holding her firmly lest she try to flee his lap, Jared grinned lewdly at her. "No, I'm not," he said thickly, his eyes growing dark with arousal as they took in every one of her beautiful features. "But, I should very much like to."

There was no mistaking either the meaning of his words or look in his gray eyes, and Jarina felt her cheeks grow warm. She was no longer an innocent. She knew what Jared wanted, and to her immense discomfort, she found that she wanted it too. She wanted him to touch her in that all too wicked way of his that made her insides quiver and her heart to pound. She wanted him to kiss her senseless. She wanted him, she realized, to make love to her. Her breathing quickened as his hand moved up to caress the side of her throat, but she did not shrink away from him. Nor did she protest when the selfsame hand began a lazy descent down the front of her shirt, slowly, deliberately, undoing each button.

Pleased that she was not going to fight him this time, Jared took great pains to go slowly. He did not want to frighten her or hurt her. He did not want a repeat of the night they had met. Indeed, he wanted to drive that fateful night forever from her memory. He wanted to start anew, to teach her love's joys, to hear her moan with pleasure. He wanted to shackle her to his side, not with irons, but with soft words and tender caresses. He wanted her to want him as much as he wanted her.

The offending shirt at last unbuttoned, Jared made no move to push it aside, but lifted his hands to cup Jarina's face. He gently brushed the pads of his thumbs across her delicate cheekbones, and his expression was solemn as he gazed deep into her eyes. "I will not hurt you," he said softly. "If anything I do gives you pain or makes you uncomfortable in any way, tell me, and I will stop. Understood?"

Jarina compressed her lips and fought a near-hysterical urge to laugh. How could she tell him the only pain she felt was a throbbing ache between her thighs that begged to be assuaged by his touch? Drawing in a ragged breath, she whispered, "I understand."

Pulling her head toward him, Jared brushed her lips with his, lightly, gently. He nibbled playfully at the tempting fullness of her bottom lip, and touched the tip of his tongue to the corners of her mouth. Jarina moaned softly and pressed closer to him as that strange inner hunger multiplied tenfold, and Jared, releasing her face and moving his hands down her back to draw her even closer, possessed her lips fully in a fierce, devouring kiss.

She returned his kiss without reservation, sliding her hands up along the back of his neck and into his hair, clasping him to her as she surrendered herself completely to his ardor. Her lips parted beneath his prompting, and her tongue boldly returned his sparring thrusts with a fevered urgency that matched Jared's own.

Sliding her shirt from her shoulders, Jared tore his mouth away from hers and began pressing hot, teasing kisses to her cheek, her temple, down her throat. "You've been practicing behind my back," he murmured hoarsely into the soft hollow at the base of her throat.

"Oh, no," Jarina protested feebly. "You are the only man I've ever kissed." She closed her eyes and dropped her head back in helpless abandon as Jared's lips descended.

Taking her by the shoulders, he held her away from him, his gray eyes burning with barely restrained passion. "I taught you that?" he asked, incredulous at the change that had come over her.

"Aye."

"Then come here, woman, and let me teach you more."

Her chest rising and falling in breathless anticipation, Jarina caught her bottom lip between her teeth and choked back a moan as Jared lowered his head to her breast and touched his lips to her naked flesh.

A loud knock at the door rudely intruded.

With a gasp, Jarina sprang from Jared's knee and flew to the far side of the cabin. Her hands shook as she hurriedly buttoned her shirt. She lifted an uncertain gaze to Jared's face and her cheeks burned with embarrassment at his pained smile. "It would seem we are to be afforded no privacy at all," he said with a doleful laugh.

If it were possible for Jarina to blush an even deeper shade of crimson, she did. "I-I think you should answer the door," she stammered shakily.

Inclining his head in agreement, Jared rose. "I'm going to throttle whoever it is," he said dryly, and Jarina almost wished he would.

When he turned back to her after speaking quietly for several moments with his first mate, Jarina was disappointed, but not surprised, to learn that Jared's presence was once again required topside.

"I shall not be long," Jared said reassuringly as he donned his slicker. "The squall is fast blowing itself out. When the sails are reset and the *Pegasus* once more on course, I'll be back. And *this* time," he added with a meaningful smirk, "I will not neglect to turn the key in the lock."

After he had gone, Jarina all but crumpled in redfaced mortification. Good God! Whatever had overcome her to prompt her to behave with such depraved boldness? Less than twenty-four hours past, she had been cursing Jared for an unfeeling lout, yet she had practically thrown herself into his arms. She had behaved like a shameless harlot. I behaved, she thought despairingly, like Molly McGuire.

So engrossed was she in castigating herself for her poor showing of common sense that she did not at first hear the unnatural, low-pitched moan of straining wood. Then the sound abruptly became louder. The ship heeled so sharply Jarina was flung against the wall. A sharp retort followed, and, finally, a loud splintering crash.

Chapter Eight

"Watch his leg! Don' drop him now!"

"Out of the way!"

"You, there, hold that door!"

"Go get Fitch!"

Jarina stared in wide-eyed horror as four men carried Jared's limp, sodden form into the cabin and deposited him with extreme care on the bunk. His eyes were closed and his face ashen, and on his forehead a sinister blue-purple bruise was quickly swelling. Angus peeled off his master's slicker and tossed it aside and Jarina pressed a fist hard against her mouth as her gaze riveted on Jared's right thigh where a crimson stain was spreading across the front of his breeches.

He lay deathly still and there was no movement behind his closed eyelids to reassure Jarina that he lived. His pallor terrified her. Dropping to her knees beside the bunk, she grasped his hands and shoved the sleeves of his sweater back from his wrists, and she groaned in relief as her fingertips sought and found a faint but steady pulse. "Oh, Angus! What happened to him?"

" 'Twas the fore topgallant mast, lass. It split clear in two. Smashed the railing to pieces and came down atop the cap'n's head afore he could get out of the way."

"But, his leg!"

"Come away, lass," Angus urged gently. "There's naught any of us can do. Fitch'll be here shortly—"

"No! I'll not let that butcher touch him!"

"Lass, please . . ."

"Get her out of here! This is no place for a woman!" a seaman yelled.

Strong hands closed about her arms and hauled her away from the bunk.

"Let go of me!"

Fitch appeared in the doorway. "Where is he?"

With a shriek of rage, Jarina tried to jerk her arms free of the men who restrained her, but to no avail. "I don't want you here!" she shouted at Fitch. "Get out!"

"Now, lass," Angus pleaded. "Try to understand."

"Get out!" Jarina screamed. "Get away from him!"

The cook took one look at his captain's leg and shook his head. "There's no savin' that one. It'll turn black with rot sure 'fore the week is out. I'll be needin' my saw."

"No! You'll not take his leg!"

"Lass, please—"

"Damn you all, let go of me!" With all the strength she possessed, Jarina delivered a savage kick to one seaman's shins that caused him to lose his grip on her as he doubled over with a howl of pain.

"What the hell is going on in here?"

Several faces turned toward the open doorway where Stephen Landon stood, taking in the scene before him with an expression of open-mouthed amazement.

Jarina tugged hard. "Let go of me!"

Drawing himself up to his full height, Stephen barked a curt order to the seaman still holding Jarina. "Release her."

"Now, lookee here, man, you're not the ship's captain and we'll not be takin' orders from—"

"I may not be captain of the *Pegasus*," Stephen interrupted sharply, his usually warm eyes glittered with af-

front, "but I do own half her cargo. If you wish to draw
your wages when we dock, you will do as I say. Remove
your hands from the lady. Now!"

The instant the man released her, Jarina flew to
Jared's side. There was blood everywhere. She wondered frantically if the main artery had been severed.
Grabbing a handful of quilt, she pressed it hard against
the wound in a desperate attempt to staunch the crimson flow. "I'll need clean linen for bandages," she said
shakily. "There are surgical instruments in the sick
bay, but they—"

"Now, just you wait a bloody minute!" Fitch blurted
out. "No one touches them tools without my—"

"Angus, get the instruments," Stephen ordered, and
the Scot, anxious to be away from the cabin before the
burly cook decided to resort to fisticuffs, scrambled to
do his bidding.

Purple veins throbbed at Fitch's temples and his bulbous eyes seemed ready to burst from his head. "This
ain't no little porridge scald," he spat at Jarina. "That
man just had a piece of railing rammed through his leg.
If you don't let me get at it 'fore the poisons spread,
you'll be the cause of killin' him!"

An angry retort sprang to Jarina's lips, but she was
saved from responding in kind by Angus's timely return. "I dinna know which ones ye wanted, lass," he
said, dumping an armload of the dirty steel instruments
onto the bunk near Jared's feet. "So I brought 'em all.
What does ye want me to do with 'em?"

Jarina cast a quick glance over the items Angus had
brought and picked out the ones she knew she would
need. "Boil them," she said. Acutely aware of Fitch
who was lingering just inside the door, she added ac-
idly, "Hard."

It was not until Jared's breeches were cut away and
the wound cleansed with brandy that Jarina was able
to assess the extent of the damage. To her immense relief, although it had barely missed being severed, the

main artery was intact. She had once heard her father
speak of mending such an artery, with stitches so tiny
he required the use of a glass lens in order to see what
he was doing, something she would not dare attempt.
As it was, the task at hand was no small feat, and the
sight of blood and torn flesh was already forcing her
stomach into her throat. Taking a deep breath to steady
herself, she gripped one of Jared's cold hands and said
brusquely, as though by way of warning, "Jared Cunningham, if you die just to spite me, I swear I will never
forgive you."

Over the next hour, Jarina's hands never stopped
moving. With a pair of bone forceps, she picked every
splinter she could find from the open wound. And then,
with Stephen and Angus looking on in rapt amazement, she eased together the layers of torn tissue and
made them fast with small individually tied knots of
sewing silk, a task made doubly hard by the persistent
rolling of the ship. In spite of the cold, perspiration
beaded across her upper lip as she worked, and she was
beginning to feel quite ill.

By the time the last stitch was knotted and cut, the
cold gray light of dawn was just breaking over the horizon. Dragging her sleeve across her forehead, Jarina
rose unsteadily to her feet. Jared had still not regained
consciousness, and she was torn between feeling grateful and terrified. He was so awfully pale. He had lost
so much blood. What if he never regained consciousness? What if his leg became gangrenous and had to
be removed anyway? What if he died?

Stephen placed a steadying hand on her shoulder.
"Are you all right?"

She pulled away from him. "Please, d-don't . . ." she
stammered. Stephen's face blurred and swam before
her eyes. "Please . . . I-I feel . . . excuse me."

Without warning, she turned and fled the cabin.

Grasping one of the ropes that had been stretched
across the deck to give the men a handhold during the

storm, she stumbled to the railing. Salt spray stung her eyes, but when she blinked, all she could see was blood. Blood and torn flesh. There was blood on her hands. Blood on her clothes. The ship rolled and she felt her self-control break as the night's trials overwhelmed her. "Oh, Jared!" she groaned.

Gripping the rail, she leaned over the side of the ship as painful spasms ripped through her stomach, over and over again.

When she had heaved her stomach dry, she slid to the deck and buried her face in her bloodstained hands. Never, for as long as she lived, would she forget the sight of that proud, handsome man lying helpless, dependent on those around him for his very life. Her father would curse her for a fool if he knew what she had done. Yet, she could not simply sit back and let Fitch saw off Jared's leg. Not when there was a chance, however small, that it could be saved.

She prayed fervently that she had done the right thing. If the wound became inflamed and Jared died, she would be to blame. "Dear God, don't let him die," she whispered miserably. "Not now. Not when I've only just begun to love him."

All that day and throughout the next night, Jarina sat by Jared's bedside. To her relief, his injured leg did not fester, and no telltale streaks of red developed to warn of pending infection. His heartbeat was strong, and he did not become feverish, but his forehead was discolored and swollen where the falling mast had struck him, and beneath his tan an unnatural pallor remained. Jarina wished her father were here; he would know how to drain the injury to relieve the pressure on Jared's skull.

As for herself, she had already seen enough blood to give her night terrors for weeks to come.

When Stephen came to the cabin shortly after dawn the following day, Jared still had not regained consciousness, and it took every ounce of will Jarina could muster not to fling herself into the younger man's arms and sob out her worries. She forced a smile. "He rested peacefully all night," she said, a lightness in her voice that she feigned as she spread an extra quilt over Jared. "It will do him good. He needs the sleep."

"He's not the only one," Stephen remarked. "Allow me to take over here awhile. You can go lie down in my cabin."

Jarina shook her head. "I want to stay here." She reached out to stroke Jared's bearded cheek. "In case he awakes," she added softly.

Stephen watched her as she adjusted the quilt around Jared and he wondered at the gentleness of her touch and the worry that marred her smooth brow. For weeks his conscience had troubled him regarding the precarious relationship that existed between Jared and Jarina. While common decency demanded that he marry her, Jared had never been one to yield to pressure when he was loath to do something. Furthermore, Jared possessed a formidable temper. Marriage to him would not be easy for any woman. For one as young and guileless as Jarina, it could be a living hell.

Still, some perverse, illogical part of him that would not be reasoned with wished Jared would marry her. Jared was his best friend. He deserved happiness. Jarina, he sensed, could bring Jared that. She possessed a quiet strength, a steadfastness that had hitherto been missing from Jared's life. And it was obvious from the way she attended him that she cared deeply for him. She might not love him, but perhaps, given time . . .

Stephen felt his face grow warm with embarrassment as Jarina glanced up to find him studying her. "Jared is lucky you are here," he commented offhandedly. "You did a remarkable job with his leg."

"I only did what any woman would do."

"Not any woman. Jared's mother would never have gone to such lengths for his father."

Jarina's eyes widened in disbelief at the mere possibility that a woman, least of all Jared's own mother, could be so cold and uncaring as to not want to do whatever was needed to save her husband, regardless of her personal feelings for the man. Surely Jared had never done anything to endear her to him during the weeks they had been at sea. Yet, that did not mean she was willing to let him die. Squaring her shoulders, she said tersely, "Then I pity Jared's mother. She must have been a very lonely woman."

A dry smile touched Stephen's mouth. "She was."

Leaving Jared's bedside, Jarina seated herself at the dining table. "Tell me about Jared," she invited, fixing Stephen with a look that almost dared him to refuse her. "I would like to know him better."

Taking the chair Jarina indicated, Stephen shrugged nonchalantly. "What can I say? He is one of the wealthiest, most powerful men in Virginia, perhaps on the entire eastern seaboard. The woman who marries him will want for neither material possessions nor social prominence. The matrons of Fairfax county will outdo themselves petitioning for her favors. She will be the most sought-after guest during the social season, and the most envied hostess. An invitation to Wyeburn will be a treasured coup."

Jarina fixed Stephen with a blank stare. There had been not the slightest trace of sarcasm in his voice to indicate that he was jesting. Indeed, he seemed quite serious. Folding her hands in her lap, she looked him straight in the eye and said firmly, "I want to know about Jared. About his family. The kind of childhood he had. I want to know why he harbors such hostility toward his half brother."

If Jarina had had difficulty determining Stephen's intent, he had no such problem; Jarina's displeasure was written plainly on her face. A fortune hunter she was not, Stephen concluded, and that pleased him greatly. He settled back in his chair. "The last is easy enough.

Damon was the unfortunate result of an indiscretion between Jared's mother and an itinerant peddler."

In that instant, so much that had eluded her suddenly became clear: Jared's reluctance to marry; his distrust of women; his unfounded suspicions regarding her virtue; his pointed threats of what he would do to her should she ever betray him. Turning her head, she sat for several moments, studying the hard lines of Jared's face and struggling with the resentment that accompanied understanding. His mother's betrayal was like a blemish on her own character, for she was the one burdened with earning a trust she had done nothing to destroy. And what of Jared's half brother? Was he not an innocent victim as well? She turned her attention back to Stephen. "Are you trying to tell me that Jared hates his half brother because of the circumstances surrounding his birth?"

"Jared," Stephen said flatly, "would never be so petty. Damon was given every advantage normally granted to a younger son, plus a few that are not. He was raised at Wyeburn alongside Jared. He received the finest education. On his twenty-first birthday, he fell heir to a generous trust. Jared gave him control of fifty thousand acres of prime cropland with the promise of a deed in his name if he made the land productive. Jared made Damon a partner in the company and advanced him a loan, free of interest, toward a shipment with a guaranteed return. Jared even offered to build him a new house should Damon decide to marry."

Jarina was having trouble grasping the extent of Jared's wealth, much less its significance in relation to his dealings with his half brother. Her forehead puckered in bewilderment. "Jared gave Damon everything he could possibly want," she whispered, a note of awe in her voice.

"Everything," Stephen agreed, "except legitimacy. Damon never misses an opportunity to remind Jared of the discrepancy in their birthrights. *He* blames *Jared* for being firstborn, for being the rightful heir. No matter what Jared does for him, it's never good enough. Damon covets everything that belongs to Jared. His social standing. His inheritance. His women."

Jarina sat up a little straighter in her chair and one brow arched in surprise. "His women?" she asked.

Feeling a little like a matchmaking mama plotting her next move, Stephen inclined his head and said solemnly, "His women."

Jarina's brow dropped back into place and her chin inched upward. There was no mistaking the annoyance that flashed in her eyes. "Would you care to explain yourself?"

"Jared has a way with women," Stephen said, struggling to keep a straight face. By God, if the girl wasn't *jealous!* "They fall into his arms," he continued. "They throw themselves at his feet. They hang on his shirtsleeve and drink up every word he utters as though it were gospel. Some, of course, are merely in love with his money. Others, like my cousin Evelyn, would give their eye teeth to be the next Duchess of Wyeburn, a title which—although it no longer exists—has nonetheless lost naught of its attractiveness. You see, we Americans are a bit hypocritical when it comes to titles. We eschew them. We dismiss them as fancy trappings, worthless relics of a feudal society which has outlived its usefulness. Yet, in our hearts, we each long to be lord and master of our own private aristocracy. And Jared, had his grandfather remained in England, would now be a duke." Stephen chuckled. "Jared hates it when people call him 'your grace,' but they continue to do it anyway. It matters not to them that the duchy of Wyeburn is long dead."

Treading lightly lest Stephen fathom the real reason for her interest, she said, "Jared told me a little of his family home in Dorsetshire. He said the fourth Duke of Roswell pressed false charges against his great-grandfather, forcing him to flee England."

"Unfortunately, it didn't end there. Roswell had thought to take possession of the Dorset estate, a ploy that failed when the charges against Lord Wyeburn were overturned. Roswell felt cheated, as did his son, and now, his grandson. The sixth duke has been trying for years to secure a lien against the company. Nothing would please Osterbrook more than to seize control of Jared's ships and his warehouses. Roswell is very much like Damon in that regard. He feels that whatever belongs to Jared should, by rights, belong to him."

Jared's connection to Roswell had intrigued Jarina ever since that day on deck when he had spoken of his great-grandfather's plight; and the truth, when it was finally revealed, was so ironic, so absurd that Jarina might have collapsed in helpless laughter had she not realized the precariousness of her position. If Jared ever learned of her betrothal to William Osterbrook, he would not believe she had been no more than a defenseless pawn in a high-stakes gamble between men. He would suspect her of trickery. He would think she had schemed to entrap him, either to make sport of him or to retaliate against Roswell. Likewise, her whereabouts and, especially, her association with Jared Cunningham, Lord Wyeburn, must *never* become known in Southampton. If Jared did not kill her, Roswell would.

Feeling a bit ill over what she had just discovered, she rose shakily. "I think . . . I need a breath of fresh air. . . ."

Puzzled, and more than a little concerned, Stephen leaped to his feet. "I'll go with you."

Jarina shook her head. "Someone should stay here."

"Jared will be fine alone for a few minutes," Stephen said decisively. He took Jarina's arm, steering her toward the door. "Come. We both need the feel of a good crisp wind on our faces."

When Jared opened his eyes, his first thought was that he had been waylaid in some alley and left for dead. There was a fierce pounding in his head that put to shame the mightiest of hangovers, and his body ached as though it had been trampled by wild horses. But he wasn't in an alley, he realized as his gaze focused painfully on the timbers overhead, and his bearings, along with his memory, slowly returned.

The last thing he remembered was being on deck in the midst of a storm and looking up just in time to see the top mizzen mast come crashing down around him. Though the sea was still rough, he could feel the confident pull of the *Pegasus* through the water, and he knew instinctively that she was once more on course.

Bracing himself against the persistent throbbing in his head, he struggled to sit up, but was able to do no more than raise himself on one elbow before the pain overwhelmed him. He squeezed his eyes shut and fell back on the pillow. He felt so weak. To even draw a breath required an enormous amount of strength.

Gradually he became aware of another, equally aggravating, source of discomfort: his right leg. It did not throb, as did his head. It burned. Near the top of his inner thigh, it felt as though the skin had been stretched taut over a live coal. A very large live coal. Worse, the damned thing itched.

With more effort than he would ever have imagined necessary, he managed to work one hand beneath the quilts only to have his fingers come into contact with a bandage wrapped around his thigh. He frowned. He did not remember injuring his leg, but, obviously, that was what must have happened. With great care, he felt along the bandage, trying to discern the extent and nature of the injury, but all he was able to conclude was that the blasted thing hurt like hell.

Then another thought occurred to him, and he experienced a moment of anxiety before further investigation eased his worry. A few more inches and he would have been doomed to serving out the remainder of his life as a eunuch. Thank God he had been spared *that* unenviable sentence.

He was making a second concentrated effort to sit up when Jarina came into the cabin, Stephen close on her heels.

"Jared! You're awake!"

Pain exploded behind his eyelids.

Jarina rushed to the bunk and grabbed his arm just as he started to topple. "Oh, Jared, please be careful!"

Embarrassed and annoyed by his weakened state, he shrugged off her hand. "Leave me be."

"You'll hurt yourself."

"Damn it, Jarina, unhand me!"

The color siphoned from Jarina's face and she took a startled step backward, feeling as though he had just struck her. She opened her mouth, but whatever words she might have uttered stuck in her throat. All that came out when she tried to speak was a strangled, "Oh!" Whirling about, she pushed past Stephen and fled the cabin.

Clutching the quilts with a white-knuckled grip, Jared glared up at Stephen through the pain that hovered like a red haze before his eyes. "I don't need you fussing over me like some old woman," he growled. "Get out of here."

Ignoring his protests, Stephen gripped his arm and helped him into a sitting position. "You're welcome," he said sarcastically.

Jared eased his aching frame back against the pillows and closed his eyes. "Go away," he said hoarsely.

Stephen folded his arms across his chest and stared down at him, disapproval battling with relief in his expression. "You gave us quite a scare, Jared. It's good to see you are your old cheerful self again."

"I feel like hell."

"You'll feel better once you get a cup of coffee and some food in your belly."

"I'll feel better," Jared corrected him, "once I've had

a good strong drink. Pour me a brandy, will you? I need something to rid my head of this cursed aching." Even his eyelids hurt, and he massaged them with his fingertips.

"I'll have to send Angus down to the hold for a bottle."

Jared dropped his hands. "There is a bottle in my locker."

"It's empty."

"There's another one . . . it hasn't been opened yet."

"Sorry, Jared, but that one is empty too. Jarina used it to cleanse the gash on your leg.

Jared regarded him in disbelief. "Jarina . . . ?"

"Yes, *Jarina.* The same person you just snapped at and sent fleeing your humble presence," Stephen retorted.

Jared slowly drew in his breath. So that was why Stephen was standing there looking at him as though he had just committed some hideous crime. He had not meant to lose his temper with Jarina. He simply disliked being coddled, and he especially did not like having Jarina witness his deplorable condition. He made a mental note to apologize to her later. Right now, he wanted to know what had happened. "How long have I been here?"

"Since yesterday morning. You tried to impale yourself on a section of broken railing. Fitch wanted to saw off your leg, but *Jarina* wouldn't let him. She called him a butcher and wouldn't let him get within spitting distance of you. I do not doubt she would have sliced his throat had he so much as tried."

That he had nearly lost his leg took Jared by surprise, but it was the thought of Jarina taking on Fitch like a gallant little warrior that rendered him speechless.

For once, Stephen had Jared right where he wanted him, unable to retaliate, and he intended to take full advantage of the situation. "Then, *Jarina* proceeded to fish about ten pounds of wood splinters from your hide and sew you back up. She would not let anyone but herself tend to you. Until a few moments ago, when she went up on deck for a breath of fresh air, she has been sitting at your bedside, making herself sick with worry over whether you were going to live or die."

A vision of virginal blue eyes, a slender oval face framed with a cap of unruly auburn curls, and a delicate brow creased with worry flashed through Jared's mind and touched a spot deep inside him that was so vulnerable he seldom left it unguarded. "Jarina . . ." he began, then his voice trailed off.

"*Jarina,*" Stephen supplied for him, "saved your life."

An hour later, his strength vastly improved by a hearty breakfast, Jared was sitting with his shaving mirror propped on the dining table, putting the final touches on a much-needed shave when Jarina slipped quietly into the cabin. Jared wiped his face dry and forced an apologetic smile. "Good morning."

Jarina hesitated a second, then stubbornly lifted her chin. "I came to get some of my things. Mr. Landon has kindly offered me use of his cabin. I shall be staying there for the duration of the voyage."

Before Jared could recover from the shock of her announcement, Jarina had gone to his locker and was removing her belongings. *Staying in Stephen's cabin? Was she insane?*

"And where will Landon be staying?" Jared asked, too stunned to think clearly.

Her arms laden, Jarina turned to face him. "In the surgery. He strung a hammock between the—"

She broke off abruptly at the sudden anger that flashed in Jared's eyes and took a hasty step away from him.

"There is plenty of room for you in this cabin," Jared said sharply. "You will remain here."

She shook her head. "I've already made up my mind." She started toward the door.

"I did not give you permission to leave this cabin."

"I did not ask for your permission," she flung irreverently over her shoulder.

"Jarina!"

She stopped.

"Come here!" Jared commanded sternly.

She wondered briefly just how far she should go in defying him. Deciding against doing so, she turned and took several uncertain steps toward the table.

When she moved into the light, Jared saw that her eyes were red and swollen, and he realized with a pang of remorse that she had been crying. Wincing at the pain the effort cost him, he hauled himself slowly to his feet. "It has been brought to my attention," he said, gripping the edge of the table for support, "that I behaved rather badly. You saved my life. I shall never be able to repay you for that." He took a deep breath. "I did not mean to be short-tempered with you earlier. I trust you will find it in your heart to forgive me."

Not, *I hope you will forgive me*, but *I trust.* Always so sure of himself, Jarina thought dismally, struggling to maintain her composure. It shamed her to know she had fallen in love with a man who had the power to hurt her so deeply. I am no better than those women who make fools of themselves demanding Jared's attention, she thought, biting down on her bottom lip to keep it from trembling. Except that she did not want his attention. She did not want him looking down on her and patronizing her and humiliating her. She wanted him to leave her alone. She wanted to be as far away from him as possible, where she could nurse her bruised heart in private.

Lifting her chin, she swallowed hard and said in a thick, tear-choked voice, "You had best get off that leg and get back into bed. I did not go to the trouble of stitching you up just to have you stumble about and injure yourself again."

She took a deep breath and squared her shoulders. "I shall be in Mr. Landon's cabin if you need me."

Chapter Nine

On the eighth of March, forty-three days after leaving England, the *Pegasus* entered Chesapeake Bay, and Jarina had her first glimpse of the land that was to be her new home, the marshy reaches of Virginia's eastern peninsula. Whatever excitement she might have felt, however, was overshadowed by the discord that remained between her and Jared. He was polite to her, but distant, and he made no mention of her returning to his cabin, even though nearly three weeks had passed since she had walked out on him. She blithely told herself that it did not matter, that she preferred the new sleeping arrangements. She was so successful in feigning content that only Angus—who brought her meals and bits of gossip and reports of the progress Jared made in his recovery—suspected that she was not as happy as she led everyone to believe.

"It won' be much longer now, lass," Angus told her when he came to her cabin that evening to bring her dinner. " 'Twill feel good to plant these old feet again on American soil."

Jarina smiled at the note of lightness in the old man's voice. "You sound happy to be home, Angus. Do you have a family to return to?"

"Nay, lass. The cap'n's the closest I ever got to a real

family. Been with him nigh on fifteen years now. He even offered to set me up on a farmstead of my own when he sells the *Pegasus.* Might just take him up on it too. I been thinkin' it would be kinda nice to have me a wife and a couple of bairns afore I'm too old to watch 'em grow up."

Jarina felt her defenses rise. She knew full well what Angus was trying to do. Subtle he was not. Her expression deliberately guarded, she said, "Jared can be quite generous when he so chooses."

"He's a good man, lass," Angus said gently.

He's also arrogant, stubborn, and condescending, Jarina wanted to reply, but she compressed her lips and said nothing.

Sensing that she was not going to be receptive to anything he had to say regarding Jared, Angus sighed and said wearily, "The cap'n says to tell ye we'll be headin' up the Potomac afore tomorrow night."

It was on a cold gray blustery morning that the *Pegasus* finally dropped anchor in the port of Alexandria on the Potomac River. Jared left the ship shortly after dawn, as did Angus and Stephen, leaving Jarina to learn secondhand of their departure. All day she fretted, wondering where they had gone and why she had been left behind.

They've gone ashore on business, she told herself. Jared owned half the ship's cargo, and Stephen the other half. No doubt they were busy making arrangements for the disposal of the goods they had brought back from England. And did not Jared have plans to sell the *Pegasus?* Perhaps even now he was deep in negotiations with a prospective buyer. And Angus, though he had become her dear friend over the past weeks, was, first and foremost, in Jared's employ. Jared would most likely have need of his services.

Then another thought occurred to her, causing her heart to race and her mouth to feel as dry as sawdust. Suppose, instead of making arrangements to sell his ship and his cargo, Jared was arranging to rid himself of her? She doubted he still felt any responsibility toward her. After all, she remembered ruefully, she was the one who had spurned him. Jared's pride might stop him short of forcing her to return to his cabin, but it would not stop him from seeking to be free of her. When she left the *Pegasus,* she would be entirely on her own—with no money, no means of employment, and no place to live.

By the time Jared returned to the ship late that night, Jarina had worried herself into a fevered state. She catapulted out of bed to answer a knock at the door, and was both relieved and overjoyed to find Jared standing on the threshold. "You came back!" she cried out, barely able to restrain herself from flying into his arms.

Jared's brows drew together and he eyed curiously the rumpled gown and matted curls that made her appear as though she had spent several hours tossing about her narrow bunk. Even in the dim, unsteady light from the cabin's single lantern he could clearly see her distress, and it puzzled him. "Of course, I came back. Did you think I would not?"

"I-I didn't know. You were away so long."

There was more than simple worry in Jarina's eyes as her gaze met his in the semidarkness. There was fear. And uncertainty. But, instead of compassion, Jared felt only annoyance. "If you think I would abandon you here while I seek my pleasures elsewhere, then you do me an injustice," he clipped. "My business ashore delayed me longer than I had anticipated. I was not amusing myself with some waterfront slattern, I assure you."

Jarina's eyes widened slightly. *That* possibility had never even entered her thoughts.

Without giving her a chance to defend herself, Jared shook out a cloak that had been draped over his arm and held it open for her. "There is a livery awaiting us on the wharf," he said brusquely. "My town house has been readied for your arrival. We will be staying there for several days while I conclude my business in the city, and then we will make the journey to Wyeburn."

She had turned to permit him to drape the cloak about her shoulders, and now twisted her head around to look up at him in bewilderment and surprise. "Then I shall be going on to Wyeburn with you?"

"What did you think I was going to do with you? Send you back to England?"

There was so much unbridled sarcasm in his tone that Jarina flinched inwardly and hastily averted her gaze before Jared could see the warm flush that flooded her cheeks. She shook her head and mumbled awkwardly, "No, of course not."

As Jared stared down at both her bowed head and her trembling hands while she fumbled with the fastenings on the cloak, he realized that that was precisely what she had thought. Her unkind assumption rankled. "Whatever else you might think of me, Jarina, I am not one of that breed of men who shuns his responsibilities, so you need not worry that I will neglect my duty to you and cast you off to fend for yourself. I promised to provide for you and I intend to do just that." He held the door open. "Come, our conveyance awaits."

Standing three-and-a-half stories above the street, the rowhouse on King Street was a practical, unpretentious affair of white clapboard with dark shutters framing tall windows. It was simply but comfortably furnished, and in every room there was a fireplace that added a cozy warmth and took the damp edge off the night's chill.

From the moment she took charge of Jarina, Mrs. Hoskins, the housekeeper, never stopped talking long enough to draw a breath. "Surprised I was to hear Captain Cunningham had returned and with a wife, no less!" she tossed gaily over her shoulder as she hefted her broad frame up the stairs. "It'll be all over town come morning that the captain finally got himself hitched! And about time too! If there's anyone who deserves a bit of happiness, it's him. He's a good man, the captain, and a right handsome one too. You couldn't have done no better than to land him for your own."

Jarina opened her mouth to tell the housekeeper that she and Jared were not married, then stopped short. She turned back to look at Jared. He was standing at the foot of the stairs, expression unreadable, and she realized with some surprise that he had told Mrs. Hoskins she was his wife. That he would go to such lengths to spare her the indignity of facing her first days ashore as a fallen women, in spite of the way she had treated him, made her feel ashamed. She started to mouth a silent *thank you,* but he turned away and strode into his study. His coldness stung.

Mrs. Hoskins led Jarina up the stairs to a rear bedchamber on the second floor. "The captain thought you'd welcome a bed of your own after them cramped quarters you were forced to endure aboard ship. The captain's chamber joins to yours right through them double doors, so he won't be far away at all."

Hoping Mrs. Hoskins would not see the flush of embarrassment that stained her cheeks. Jarina turned away and pretended to be busy familiarizing herself with her new surroundings. If the housekeeper only knew the real reason Jared and I do not share the same bed, she thought.

The woven blue and white coverlet on the tester bed had already been turned back. Mrs. Hoskins went to the bed and shoved a meaty fist between the linens, then nodded her approval. "Sally's already run the pan over the sheets to take off the chill and put a nice hot brick down here to warm your feet. There's fresh water in the pitcher by the basin and clean towels in the commode."

On and on, Mrs. Hoskins prattled, pointing out every amenity the chamber offered, from the extra wood for the fireplace to the wardrobe for her clothes to the brand new silver-backed hairbrush on the dresser. Only half listening, Jarina went to the bed and touched a tentative finger to the soft white muslin of the nightgown that had been draped across the foot of the bed. She could not help wondering what errant wife could have left *that* garment behind.

Seeing her troubled expression, Mrs. Hoskins put in hastily, "When the captain gave me the money this morning, he told me to pick out the prettiest nightrail I could find. I didn't know what your tastes were, so I—"

"You purchased the gown this morning?" Jarina interrupted, turning a surprised gaze on the older woman.

The grayed head, half hidden by a white mobcap, nodded vigorously. "And there's a dressing robe to match it in the wardrobe. I hope they're to your liking."

Vastly relieved that she would not be forced to don another garment left behind by one of Jared's former paramours, Jarina smiled for the first time that night. "The gown is lovely, Mrs. Hoskins. Thank you for your trouble."

It was Jarina's smile that convinced Mrs. Hoskins she knew precisely why the captain had lost his head over the little waif with the long-lashed blue eyes and the ragged curls. Give her a good night's sleep and do something with that hair, she decided, and the girl would be a sight to turn any man's head.

"Sally or me, one of us will be up first thing in the morning to stoke the fire and bring you some coffee to warm your bones. The captain breakfasts early, but he said to let you sleep as late as you want. Thoughtful man, the captain, and generous to a fault. If I was but twenty years younger . . ." Mrs. Hoskins sighed and shook her head. "Don't you be running about in your bare feet now. When that old wind blows off the river, it works its way right through these walls. When you get undressed, you hurry up and get yourself in that bed. The last thing we want is to have you catching your death."

When the housekeeper had gone, Jarina dropped her forehead against the door and closed her eyes. She had not thought Mrs. Hoskins would ever leave. Nor stop talking about Jared. If she heard one more time just how wonderful he was, she was going to scream. She was beginning to think the woman was in league with Angus.

Yet, what if they were right and she were the one who was in the wrong? It was true that Jared had been exceptionally generous with her. He had even misled the housekeeper into thinking they were married so she would not be subjected to whispered gossip and side-long glances from the servants. And, although she had failed to honor her part of the agreement to be his mistress in return for passage to America, he continued to assume responsibility for her. If his boorish actions rankled, was she not equally to blame? It was not Jared's fault that she allowed herself to be so thin-skinned and vulnerable. It was not his fault she had allowed herself to fall in love with him.

And love him she did, so much so that her heart sometimes ached with the intensity of the feelings she harbored for him. If only he could love me just a little in return, she thought, then perhaps it would not hurt so much.

She did have one consolation. Jared might not love her, but neither did he love anyone else. Of that she was certain. She was not so certain, however, of the reason. Perhaps he was afraid of being vulnerable. Perhaps he was so disillusioned with women that he had closed his heart to even the possibility of falling in love. Perhaps, she thought sadly, he did not know how to love.

By the time Jarina had washed her face and donned the nightgown and brushed her tangled curls to a high gloss, she had reached the conclusion that this time it was her turn to apologize. She was not looking forward to it. All the time she had been condemning Jared for being too proud, too vain, too stubborn, she had been too blind to see until now that she shared his most aggravating faults in almost equal abundance.

She did not have long to wait before she heard someone moving about the front bedchamber. Taking the dressing robe from the wardrobe, she slipped her arms into the lace-trimmed sleeves and tied the pink satin ribbon at her throat. She had to see Jared now before she changed her mind and beat a coward's retreat.

When she entered the chamber, he was standing by the front window, a glass in hand and an open bottle of whiskey on a nearby table. His cravat was untied and his face flushed, and she knew without asking that he was well on his way to getting drunk. "Perhaps . . . I-I'd better come back later," she stammered. "I-I didn't mean to disturb you."

A look of displeasure passed across Jared's face. "You have already disturbed me. If there is something you wish to say, say it."

There was an undercurrent of cold hostility in Jared's tone that sent a shiver of alarm up Jarina's spine. Plagued by guilt from the untruths she had told him, she wondered frantically if he had somehow learned her real identity. She nervously moistened her lips. "I-I just wanted to thank you . . . for the nightclothes. . . ."

Jared's gaze traveled down the length of her, softening somewhat as it returned to her face. He had not meant to be abrupt with her. She was not to blame for the disquieting news that had reached Alexandria two days past, and of which he had only today been informed. "You're quite welcome," he said, forcing a smile that warred with his still-terse tone. "I trust you found your bedchamber adequate to your needs."

I would rather share your chamber, she wanted to say, but did not. "Yes . . . it's quite comfortable," she said instead. Then an involuntary smile broke across her face and she added, almost shyly, "The floor hasn't stopped moving since I set foot in this house. Are you sure it's built on solid ground?"

A low chuckle sounded deep in Jared's throat and some of the harshness left his expression. "I'm quite sure. By tomorrow you should have regained your land legs and it will feel quite differently, I promise you."

Jarina relaxed a little. Perhaps whatever was upsetting Jared had naught to do with her at all.

"Is there something else?" Jared asked, sensing her hesitation.

Now. She had to do it now. Taking a deep breath, she began haltingly, "I-I wanted . . . to apologize . . ."

He waited.

"You have been very . . . generous . . . to me," Jarina continued. "Back on the ship . . . it was wrong of me to think ill of you, that you intended to be rid of me. I mean . . . you had every right . . . I was not being very fair to you . . ." Her voice faltered. "I-I'm sorry I doubted you," she finished in a pained whisper.

As she stood there with her bare toes peeping out from beneath the hem of her dressing robe, twisting one finger in its generous folds, she looked so young and untouched that Jared almost felt guilty over the lustful thoughts that invaded his consciousness. He wondered if she would protest much if he tried to make love to her now. She had certainly been willing enough that night aboard the *Pegasus* before he had injured himself, but then, perhaps she had not really wanted him after all, but had merely been driven into his arms out of fear of the storm. If he extended his hand to her now, would she come to him? Or would she respond to him with the same loathing and disgust as she had the first time he'd had her?

His tormented mind, weakened by the spirits he had been consuming, shrank from learning the answer. If she recoiled from him now, he was not certain he could endure the rejection. Always, in the past, he had been the one to leave a woman's bed, and he had always been in full control of his emotions when he did so. He had not been prepared to one day have the tables turned on him.

Yet, not only had Jarina been the one to leave *his* bed, she had taken his heart with her. He, Jared Cunningham, known on two continents for his physical prowess and his unsurpassable resistance to the wiles of the opposite sex, had been overset by a blue-eyed moppet who looked hardly old enough to be allowed to wander from the nursery unattended. Were that truth to be known, he would be made the object of ridicule in every establishment he dared venture. Within a span of weeks, he had twice risked being unmanned, first by a broken railing that had barely missed condemning him to a life of monastic abstinence, and now by an eighteen-year-old temptress who had not the slightest inclination of the power she wielded over him. He was shamefully close, he thought, to taking leave of his senses and behaving like a smitten youth.

He took a deep breath, as much to steady himself as to cool the fires that flamed within, and downed his glass of whiskey in a single swallow. "Go to bed, Jarina," he said wearily. "We can talk in the morning."

Jarina turned to leave, but not before Jared saw the disappointment that flashed across her face, and he again cursed himself for being so callous with her. "Jarina."

She blinked several times, and Jared wondered if he had imagined the glimmer of moisture in her eyes. "Rest well, love," he said.

Fragile and fleeting, a hint of a smile touched her lips. "Good night, Jared," she said softly.

After she had gone, Jared eased his weary bones onto the bed and kneaded the muscles in his thigh, wincing at the persistent ache that had been with him ever since the accident. When he looked about the chamber, he

was struck for the first time just how large and empty
the bed looked, and he wondered at his own sanity in
sending Jarina back to her own chamber.

God, how he wanted her . . .

In spite of its less than auspicious beginnings, the
week spent in Alexandria evolved into a pleasant one
for them both. As it neared its end, no one who saw
them together could have guessed that they had ever
been less than the best of friends. Although nighttime
found them in separate chambers, during the day, Jared
seldom left Jarina's side. When his presence was not
required at the warehouses or on the docks, he could
be found escorting her from shop to shop. He produced
his coin purse for so many impulse purchases that
Jarina finally balked before the entrance to Madame
Bouchard's shop. "I refuse to go in," she announced
stubbornly, "until you promise not to buy me another
thing. Every time I look askance at something, you purchase it for me. I have not asked you for a single item,
yet you have already bought me enough clothes and
frippery to last me a lifetime!"

"Frippery!" Jared returned with a pained expression,
feigning insult. "I did not hear you complain, madam,
when I purchased your muff and bonnet."

Infected by his unusually bantering mood, Jarina
smiled inwardly as she snuggled her hands deeper into
the warm ermine. She lifted her chin and met Jared's
dark glower with a look of unrelenting obstinance. Her
cheeks were pink from the cold and her eyes shone with
a merry sparkle that led little credence to the stern look
she gave him. "Promise me," she said firmly.

Jared grinned. "You'll be late for your fitting."

Her eyes narrowed and her lips compressed. "Promise me."

Taking a step toward her, Jared reached over her
head and braced one hand on the doorjamb behind her,
effectively trapping her between himself and the wall,

and said offhandedly, "Of course, I could always pick you up and carry you inside."

She eyed him warily. "You wouldn't dare! Would you?"

One brow arched portentously.

Knowing he would not hesitate to do just that, Jarina sighed and said with an air of exaggerated resignation, "Then I suppose I have no choice but to allow you to spoil me rotten."

"Like an egg?"

A smile tugged at the corners of her mouth, but she wrestled it down. "Like an egg," she agreed solemnly.

"Look at the bright side, sweet. You'll be the best-dressed omelet in Virginia."

"I'll be unbearable to live with," she warned.

"You're an impertinent, stubborn, mouthy little baggage. I'd say you are already unbearable to live with."

She gave him a coquettish smile. "Yet you think I am adorable and you cannot live without me."

A pensive—almost introspective—expression briefly shadowed the twinkle in Jared's eyes and then was gone. "I cannot live without you," he said quietly.

Before she had time to wonder whether he were serious or was jesting with her, Jared gripped her arm and steered her into the shop.

At the jangle of the bell over the door, Madame Bouchard, beaming at the arrival of her best-paying customers, rushed forth in a flurry of silk and rustling petticoats. "Ah, Captain Cunningham! And, Madame! How wonderful you both look this morning." She winked at Jared over the top of Jarina's head. "The article about which you inquired, Monsieur, arrived only yesterday. My girls have been working all night so that it would be ready for Madame's fitting this morning. Would you care to see it?"

"I trust your instincts," Jared said lightly. "You have yet to fail me."

Jarina threw him a look of dismay. "Jared, if you have bought something else, I shall—"

"You shall wear it, and enjoy it," he finished for her. "Madame, do you think you could keep my wife occupied for the next hour while I attend to an errand that refuses to wait any longer?"

There was a teasing note in his voice that immediately aroused Jarina's suspicions. "What errand?" she wanted to know, slipping easily into the ruse they fostered of letting everyone think she was his wife.

Jared only laughed and bent down to kiss her cheek. "You'll see, love," he whispered into her ear.

After he had gone, Madame Bouchard sighed and said wistfully. "Ah, what a man. You are a lucky one, Madame. Most husbands are not so generous. Nor so handsome." Then her expression became serious and businesslike. "Come, Madame," she said, ushering Jarina into the fitting room. "We have much work to do."

When Jared returned to the shop an hour later, he was greeted by the sight of Jarina standing with her arms folded in front of her, her bottom lip curled out in a pout, and the toe of one little kidskin slipper tapping impatiently on the wood floor. "Jared Cunningham, how could you!" she said petulantly. "That watered silk must have cost you a king's ransom!"

He grinned. "But, well worth every pence."

"Jared, it's from France!"

"So?"

"It was *smuggled!*"

"Do you like it?"

Her pout dissolved into a radiant smile. "I love it! I can hardly wait until it's finished."

Satisfaction gleamed in Jared's eyes. He took Jarina by the shoulders and set her away from him. "Turn around. I wish to see if I received my money's worth."

Unbeknownst to Jarina, Madame Bouchard had emerged from the back room, and while Jarina turned a slow circle before them in a rose velvet gown that had just been completed, Madame Bouchard stood in the shadows and watched Jared while he watched Jarina. There was both reverence and lust in the gaze that traveled appreciatively over the girl's slender form, the Frenchwoman noted, and she could not help feeling a stab of sadness for the end of what had amounted to an era. Jared Cunningham had a reputation that extended from Portsmouth to Savannah, and since his return to Virginia, her shop had buzzed with the intelligence that the charming rascal now kept a respectable distance from the establishments of his bachelor days. Upon learning of his surprise marriage, former mistresses fumed, wide-eyed debutantes bewailed their loss, and doting mamas vacillated between relief that their innocent daughters were now safe from at least one of the notorious Cunningham brothers and indignation that he had chosen an English girl over one of their own.

Sighing wistfully, Madame Bouchard stepped from the shadows. "These new styles compliment Madame's figure perfectly," she said, moving to stand beside Jared. "Women who carry too much flesh cannot wear such a high waistline without looking ridiculous, but Madame is slender enough that she looks both youthful and elegant. And deep-rose is a good color for her. It brings out the delicate pink in her cheeks. The gown is beautiful, no?"

Embarrassed by the other woman's frank discussion of what she considered a decidedly intimate subject, Jarina blushed as she peeked shyly from beneath her lashes to find Jared watching her with a warm, approving gaze. Then, the corners of his mouth turned up in an enigmatic half smile and he inclined his head slightly. "I agree," he said in a low, almost caressing, tone. "She is beautiful."

There was a new lightness in Jarina's posture when she left the shop clad not only in her new rose gown,

but also in a new cloak of soft gray wool that contrasted
nicely with her ermine muff and bonnet, and it took
an enormous amount of self-control not to succumb to
the childish impulse to skip a step and twirl around
merrily. In spite of the fact that she knew their deception must someday end and they would travel separate
roads, for now she was happy, happier than she had
ever been in her life. She suspected her lightheartedness
had less to do with the new clothes Jared had purchased for her than the look in his eyes when he had
said, *She is beautiful.*

Taking full advantage of his good humor, she waited
until he had placed her packages inside the carriage and
settled beside her on the seat, then turned to him and
demanded saucily to know the nature of his errand.

One dark eyebrow shot upward. "What errand?" he
asked, pretending ignorance.

"You know good and well what errand! You bought
something else, didn't you?"

"Now, what makes you say that?"

"Because you are like a volcano spewing gold guin-
eas! In the past week, you have bought me no less than
twenty gowns, fourteen petticoats, six pairs of shoes—"

"You needed them."

"No one needs fourteen petticoats."

"I won't buy you another petticoat, I swear."

If any one aspect of the man pleased her above all
else, it was the warm glow of laughter in his gray eyes
when he was in a jovial mood. He was more approach-
able when he laughed. More human. Twisting around
on the seat so that she was almost facing him, she lifted
her gaze to his and fluttered her lashes. "Tell me what
you bought," she begged prettily.

"No."

"Please?"

"No—Jarina, what are you doing?"

"I'm looking for my present."

Not at all put off by her antics, Jared extended one

arm along the back of the seat and stretched out his long legs. Amusement softened his sharply chiseled features as he watched her search out every pocket in his cape. She was like a child in her exuberance, unaffected and unpretentious, and for a second Jared envisioned a passel of dark-haired, blue-eyed toddlers clambering over his knee to seek whatever treat his pockets harbored.

Suddenly, Jarina's eyes flared wide and she let out a squeal of excitement.

In a flash, Jared caught hold of the hand that was busy trying to delve into his waistcoat pocket. No sooner had he gotten one hand under control than the other emerged and pounced. He caught that one too. "Enough, you little minx!" he said, laughing.

Jarina tugged but could not free her hands from his grasp. "I want to see what you bought."

"No."

"Just one little peek?"

"No!"

Jared's grip on her hands relaxed a mere fraction, but it was enough to enable Jarina to wriggle one hand free. It headed straight for its intended target.

"Why, you little—!" Seizing her around the waist, he hauled her onto his lap and yanked her hard against his chest, trapping her arms between them. "You will get your present tonight. Now, settle down or I will put you out on the street and make you walk home," he warned.

A musical little laugh escaped her as the carriage rolled to a stop before the town house. "We're already home," she announced gaily.

They were both still laughing as they entered the house to find Stephen waiting for them in Jared's study.

"I hope you two were enjoying yourselves," Stephen said tersely. He looked from one to the other like a stern schoolmaster who had just caught his two rowdiest pupils conspiring to no good. "*I* have spent the morning working myself like a draft horse."

"That's too bad," Jared said good-naturedly. He helped Jarina remove her cloak. "*We* had a wonderful time."

At Stephen's request, Jarina pivoted before him, and he let out a low whistle as she surprised him with a deep, sweeping curtsy. He looked at Jared and grinned. "Madame Bouchard outdid herself this time. Next time you see her, tell her I want two of those."

Jarina's brow wrinkled in puzzlement, but Jared, one corner of his handsome mouth curving into a cynical smile, merely inclined his head and asked dryly, "Pink or blue?"

Stephen laughed. "My preference runs to blondes."

After a few moments of lighthearted banter, Jarina begged to be excused. Remembering that she had not eaten since early that morning, Jared instructed her to find the housekeeper and tell her to have a luncheon prepared for her, but Jarina shook her head. "I intend to be good and hungry tonight," she said gaily. Noticing Stephen's questioning glance, she explained, "Jared is taking me to Hall's Tavern tonight. I intend to forget my manners and try one of everything!"

After she was gone, Jared turned to find Stephen grinning insolently at him. "Say one word, and I'll have you thrown out on your ear," Jared said testily.

Stephen's face contorted as he struggled not to laugh, but he wisely refrained from voicing the thought that loomed in the forefront of both their minds. If Jared was not thoroughly and hopelessly besotted with his beautiful little stowaway, then he was coming damned close.

Jared crossed the room to the liquor cabinet, and Stephen's mirth abated as he noticed the trace of a limp in his step. It had been a good month since the accident. They had been ashore a week, yet Jared had not seen a physician. "Does your leg trouble you?" he asked.

"Not as much as it would were I to have lost it," Jared said. He poured himself a whiskey.

Jared offered Stephen one, but the younger man shook his head. "Perhaps you should see a leech," he ventured. "It's possible he could drain the wound and—"

"The only thing he would drain is my pockets. There was no sign of infection when Angus removed the stitches, and I see no reason to reopen the wound now that the flesh has healed. Now, I know you did not come here to discuss my health. Tell me what you were able to find out."

With a Gallic shrug of defeat, Stephen relented. "It's worse than we thought," he said. His demeanor became serious. "Not only has the crown placed a lien against the company, but has issued a warrant for your arrest as well. You have been charged with failure to pay import and export duties."

Jared was more annoyed than surprised by the news.

"If the taxes are not paid by the thirtieth of June," Stephen continued, "the crown will claim title to the company and dispose of it at private auction."

"Where Roswell," Jared concluded for him, deliberately keeping his voice low and a firm grip on his rising temper, "will be free to purchase what he has failed these past fifteen years to seize. It would not surprise me in the least if Roswell is the motivating force behind all this. If anything, I expect it from him. For some, there is a great deal of satisfaction to be derived from seeing history repeat itself."

There was no need for Stephen to ask what he meant by that. They both knew it would suit Roswell perfectly to have Jared arrested on trumped-up charges the same way the fourth duke had his great-grandfather arrested for gunrunning. "If it's true that Roswell is behind this," Stephen said, "he will have a hard time proving the charges. Not only were the tax payments witnessed and recorded, you carry the receipts."

"Witnesses can be bought and records destroyed. As for the receipts, if I so much as set foot on English soil, they will be taken from me and I will be imprisoned and condemned without trial."

Stephen nervously moistened his lips. He had invested heavily in the company and if Jared were imprisoned and his assets seized, they both faced financial ruin. "What are you going to do?" he asked, fearing the question as much as the answer.

Jared drained his glass. "I don't know," he said grimly. "But I will think of something."

That evening, Jared was careful to maintain a cheerful front as he escorted Jarina to the raucous waterfront tavern that was renowned throughout the colonies for its savory fare. Hall's Tavern was as much a gathering place for families as for men in search of cheap drink and an easy wench, and though Jarina was at first apprehensive of their boisterous surroundings, the presence of several obviously respectable women accompanying their husbands immediately put her at ease. At her request, Jared declined the private chamber that he had reserved in favor of a corner table in the taproom. He asked for wine, and Jarina again surprised him by countermanding his orders. "What is that woman drinking?" she asked, indicating a well-dressed matron sitting with an equally dignified gentleman two tables away. When the tavern owner told her, Jarina gave him her most dazzling smile and announced decisively, "Then, that's what I shall have."

Had she been with anyone else, Elija Hall would have served her without question, but if there were one man in all of Virginia the tavern owner dared not cross, it was Captain Cunningham, and he now looked to Jared for approval of his lady's request.

The man's hesitation to honor Jarina's request piqued Jared's irritation. "Make that *two* tankards of ale, and make it fast," he snapped ungraciously.

After the tavern owner hurried away to fetch their ale, Jarina turned a wide-eyed gaze on Jared and asked softly, "You don't object to my having the ale, do you?"

Realizing that he had nearly allowed his temper and the day's trials to best him, Jared forced himself to relax. This is Jarina's evening, he reminded himself. He was determined not to spoil it for her. "Of course not," he said, replacing his frown with an easy smile. "You may order anything you wish."

And she did. She had fried crabcakes and fried clams. She had boiled shrimp redolent with a spicy red seasoning that clung to the shells in which they had been cooked. She had sweet white corn dripping with melted butter. She sampled clam chowder and oyster stew and even learned to wield with some dexterity the wooden mallet required to crack open the thick-shelled claws on the boiled crabs. And she loved it all. The only thing she turned up her nose at was the raw oysters that Jared favored, and as he dunked one into red pepper sauce and raised it to his mouth, she eyed him warily. She was certain the disgusting, slimy thing would let out a loud squeal when he bit into it.

When Jarina had finally consumed so much food that her stomach felt full to the point of bursting, she daintily dabbed at her mouth with her napkin and wiped the butter from her fingers. Then she leaned back against the wall and groaned. "If gluttony is a sin," she asked philosophically, "why do I feel as though I have died and gone to heaven?"

Jared chuckled. "You look as though you are in pain."

"I think it's the ale," she said. She rubbed her tortured stomach. "It doesn't seem to agree with me."

"I think," Jared corrected her, "it agrees with you all too well."

There was no criticism in his words; he was merely stating fact, and Jarina could not help feeling a little embarrassed as she met his bemused gaze across the table. "Thank you for bringing me here," she said. There was a warm flush in her cheeks that was not entirely the result of too much ale. "I had a wonderful evening."

For a moment, Jared regarded her without expression, his thoughts carefully hidden. Then a generous smile spread across his face and warmed the gray in his eyes. "The evening is not ended yet," he said softly. He lifted his tankard to her in a silent toast before draining it. "I believe there is still the matter of a *gift* which someone was quite anxious to have."

Jared could tell from the way Jarina's eyes widened that she had completely forgotten about the gift she had been so anxious to see earlier. So intent had she been on relishing sights and tastes and smells of their evening together that nothing else had mattered, something he found particularly appealing. He knew men who planned and dreamed and longed for the future, or who bemoaned the days that had slipped by unnoticed until they became part of an irretrievable past. Few of his aquaintance possessed either the wisdom or the ability to simply enjoy the present. He smiled. "Finish your ale, sweet. As soon as we are alone, I shall present you with your gift. If I attempt to do so now, we are likely to be beset by thieves."

Jarina did not have long to wait.

As soon as they withdrew to the privacy of the coach, Jared drew shut the velvet curtains that separated them from the world without. A pair of lanterns illuminated the interior of the carriage with a gentle light that lent a golden glow to Jarina's face and reflected like twin beacons in her eyes as she turned an expectant gaze on Jared. Although he had been the object of too many adoring gazes in his lifetime to be affected by the unsubtle advances that women invariably threw his way, the closeness of the carriage, combined with the shining anticipation on Jarina's face brought an unexpected rush of warmth to Jared's loins and a rueful chuckle to his lips. "If you keep looking at me like that," he warned as he reached inside his cloak, "I'll not be responsible for my actions."

Before she could say anything, Jared took her left hand, and Jarina's smile faded as she stared in numb shock at the huge, marquis-cut diamond he slid onto her third finger. She had never seen such a beautiful ring, and had certainly never expected to wear one. She was awestruck that he would trust her with such a lavish gift. What if something happened to it? The diamond was so large; what if she should bump it and knock the stone from its setting? What if she lost it?

Yet, even as her mind searched frantically for reasons to refuse Jared's gift, she knew in her heart that they were mere excuses. The ring, far from being a token of his affection, was instead a mark of ownership, a bold, forceful announcement to the world that she belonged to him. As long as she wore it, she would not be free to receive another man's attentions, and she could not forsake her own future, no matter how much she wished Jared could be a part of that future. She slowly shook her head. "It's beautiful, Jared. But, I cannot accept it. It would not be proper for me to wear it."

"It would be if you were my wife."

She jerked her head up to stare at him.

His fingers closed around hers, and he held her hand tightly. "Jarina, I know ours would not be the love match you desire," he said quietly, "but there are other, more practical, reasons for marriage to which I think you should give some thought. I've already promised to provide for you, and I intend to do just that, with or without a marriage license bond. But, as I think you are aware, without the legality of matrimony, you would be subject to gossip and ridicule. You would be a social outcast. I would prefer to spare you that humiliation."

That morning, when he had purchased the ring,

there had been no doubt in Jared's mind that Jarina
would agree to be his wife. Now, he was not so confident. He did not know what he would do should she
refuse him; he did not want to let her go. Feeling as
awkward as an untried youth, he took a steadying
breath. "There is one more thing," he continued. "I'm
not getting any younger, and Wyeburn is in need of an
heir. This would not be a marriage of convenience." He
hesitated. "You already know that I am not an easy
man to live with. . . ."

His voice trailed off, and Jarina realized with a pang
that he feared she would refuse him. *Oh, Jared, I love
you so much,* she thought, but she cautiously choked
back the remark, not wanting to drive him away with
sentimental words he might not want to hear. Her
throat ached with the emotion that swelled in it. Leaning toward him, she lightly touched her lips to his
cheek. "I will marry you," she whispered.

Though her reply was restrained and her kiss more
dutiful than passionate, Jared felt a sudden, insane
compulsion to blurt out every dream, every fear, every
doubt, every longing that had ever sought refuge in his
heart. He wanted to hold Jarina and confess to her
things he had never revealed to anyone else. Yet he said
nothing. For the first time in his thirty-six years, he was
genuinely afraid of making a complete fool of himself.

He met no resistance as he drew her to him. She
raised her arms to encircle his neck as his head bent
over hers, and, with a low groan that was part pleasure,
part loss of self-control, he possessed her lips fully and
forcefully, devouring the sensual promises they offered
with an urgency that bespoke of passions held too long
in check. Her senses starved for his touch, Jarina
molded herself to him. Her lips parted, at first yielding
to his pursuit, then strained against his, seeking eagerly
to satisfy a burning, relentless hunger of their own.

He kissed her again and again, causing her head to
reel and and strange sensations to explode inside her

in a wonderful drunken heat that turned her limbs to liquid. One hand slid beneath her skirt and upward along a shapely calf to stroke her thigh above the top of her stocking. Her own slender fingers acted with a will of their own, threading through the crisp, thick hair at his nape and pulling him closer. His breath was warm and caressing against her ear. "I want you, Jarina," he whispered hoarsely, and his hand moved higher still. Without warning, his tongue darted into her ear. Jarina gasped as a tremor of delirious pleasure rippled through her, and her back arched, driving her warm softness hard against the hand that caressed her.

It was the slowing of the carriage as they neared the town house that alerted Jared to his responsibilities. Not wanting to embarrass Jarina by allowing them to be caught in such an intimate embrace, he smoothed down her skirts and pulled her trembling form against him to hold her close as they rolled to a stop. He would wait, he decided, until they had reached the privacy of their chambers before continuing where propriety demanded they leave off.

Reluctant to leave the warm security of Jared's arms, Jarina settled against him as he lifted her from the carriage. Though her topsy-turvy world had not quite righted itself, she was lucid enough to realize that Jared's carrying her from the carriage to the house was less an act of politeness than of possession. Before the night had ended, she would belong to him completely.

Chapter Ten

Jarina slowly lifted her head from Jared's shoulder and raised her eyes to the night sky. "It's starting to snow," she said softly.

Jared paused on the stoop to follow her gaze, and a pensive smile momentarily touched his mouth as he observed the first swirling flakes. Finally he dropped his gaze to meet hers and one dark brow angled questioningly. "Have you ever ridden a toboggan?" he asked.

Her spirits buoyed by the youthful laughter she saw in his eyes, she shook her head. "I don't even know what that is."

He grinned. "Next winter I shall take you for a ride on one."

"But, what is it?"

"You'll see."

"Jared, tell me!"

With Jarina in his arms, Jared strode into the house. "You'll see," he whispered teasingly into her ear.

"Be you Captain Cunningham, sir?"

Jarina jerked her head around and Jared lifted his to stare in mute surprise at the slicker-clad stranger who greeted them in the foyer hall. Jared released

Jarina's legs and lowered her to the floor, but continued to hold her close. "I am," he replied.

The seaman's sharp gaze came to rest on Jarina, and he stared at her long and hard before turning his attention back to Jared. "I've a message for you from Captain Corrigan of the *Lucky Lady,*" he said in a broad Devon burr. "The captain says to tell you the American ambassador has finally agreed to a meeting before he departs for London. You must meet with him tonight. The *Lucky Lady* sails with the tide."

Jarina felt Jared stiffen, and her startled gaze riveted on his face. "Jared, what's wrong?"

He gave her shoulders a gentle squeeze. " 'Tis naught of your concern, sweet. Will you take me to the *Lucky Lady?*" he asked the seaman.

The man inclined his head. "Aye, sir."

Confusion battling with dismay at having their evening together spoiled, Jarina reached out to place a restraining hand on Jared's arm just as he made to leave her side. "Must you go?" she blurted out without thinking.

"I am sorry, Jarina. This cannot wait."

"But—"

"We will discuss it later."

Bewilderment creased her forehead and her mouth opened, but the unvoiced protest died in her throat as Jared's brow arched meaningfully. She dutifully choked back the myriad of unasked questions that reeled in her head. A small smile softened Jared's features and he could not help chuckling inwardly at the resentment that flashed in her eyes before she averted her gaze. If Jarina ever learned to channel her anger instead of chafing in silence at commands she deemed unfair, he mused, she would be a formidable opponent indeed.

Jared excused himself and strode into his study, leaving Jarina behind with the stranger.

An uncomfortable silence filled the hall and Jarina glanced up to find the seaman staring at her.

He shifted uneasily and looked away, and she did the same. But when she glanced up again, he was again staring at her, this time with a perplexed frown. "You're from England," he said suddenly.

She nodded.

"Hampshire?"

"Yes."

"Is your da a bleeder?"

"I beg your pardon?"

"A bleeder," the man repeated. "A leech. A doctor. Is your da a doctor?"

Her breath caught in her throat and there was a peculiar tightening in her chest that made it difficult to breathe. "Why do you ask, sir?"

"I went to a bleeder once when my ship was docked in Southampton. A real gentleman, he was. A baron. I'd cut my hand and he sewed me up." He held up his hand for her to see the puckered white scar that ran from his thumb clear across his palm.

Jarina fidgeted as a vague, almost forgotten memory tugged at the far reaches of her consciousness.

"There was a little girl at the infirmary that day," the man continued. "No more than a wee mite, she was, with the biggest blue eyes I ever saw. The doc said she was his daughter." He paused. "She'd be about your age now."

Jarina's heart began to pound. Forcing into her voice a nonchalance she was far from feeling, she said off-handedly, "I am afraid you have me confused with someone else."

"I don't think so," the man said slowly. He was still frowning. "I'd never forget them eyes."

Jared returned, carrying beneath his arm the leather case containing the ship's papers he had brought from the *Pegasus*. Mumbling a hasty apology, Jarina skirted past him and started up the stairs, careful to keep her gaze from the seaman. She did not want to look at him. She did not want him to see the color of her eyes again, nor anything else for that matter.

"Jarina!"

Swallowing hard, Jarina stopped on the stairs and turned to face Jared. "It's cold down here," she said, wrapping her arms about herself and shivering. "I thought I would wait for you upstairs."

There was an inappropriate grin on her face that failed to disguise the distress in her eyes, and Jared's brows drew together in concern. "There is no need to wait up for me. I will be late."

A smile flickered across Jarina's face and was gone. "Good night," she said softly.

Puzzled by her unexplainable behavior, Jared watched her through narrowed eyes as she turned and bolted up the stairs.

Jared was not the only one who observed her flight with interest. The seaman too thought the lady had behaved a bit oddly, denying that she was Lord Hamilton's daughter and all when he knew for a fact she was, but he said nothing. There was no accounting for gentry, he knew, and if the Honorable Margaret Hamilton was a bit off her rocker, it was no business of his.

Jarina waited until she heard the front door close before shutting the door to her bedchamber and collapsing against it. The man knew who she was! What if he told Jared? Barring that, how long would it be before someone else recognized her? Tonight she had crossed a barrier with Jared. He might not love her, but she knew he was drawn to her, and had the seaman not been waiting for them when they returned from Hall's Tavern, Jared would be here with her now, making love to her. She closed her eyes and groaned. If Jared ever discovered her deception, if he even suspected that she was connected in any way with the Duke of Roswell, there was no telling what he might do to her. All she knew is that he would hate her. If he ever learned her true identity, her life would not be worth living.

The streets were dark and slick with ice as Jared wound his way through the city toward the town house. Somewhere, he heard the creak of a door opening and the splash of a chamber pot being emptied into the alley beyond. In the distance, a cock crowed. His meeting with the American ambassador had taken far longer than he had anticipated, but he had come away from the *Lucky Lady* feeling as though a weight had been lifted from his shoulders. With a little luck and fair sailing, he should be acquitted of the charges against him well before summer.

It was not yet daylight when he mounted the steps and let himself into the house. Before long, the servants would be up and about, but by then, he hoped to be well on his way. Before he left, however, he needed to speak with Jarina.

He found her, not in her own bedchamber, but in his. She was curled up in the wingbacked chair by the fireplace, sound asleep. The remaining embers on the hearth emitted enough light to illuminate her face. Jared noticed the way her long lashes fanned out across her cheeks and the inviting moistness of her slightly parted lips. Smiling to himself as he bent down, he placed two fingers beneath her chin and gently pushed upward, closing her mouth.

Her eyes flew open and she sat up with a start. "Jared!" she cried out in a hoarse, sleep-choked whisper.

Jared slid an arm beneath her legs and lifted her up from the chair. "I told you not to wait up for me," he chided softly as he carried her through the double doors that separated their chambers.

Looping her arms behind his head, she pressed her face against the side of his neck and let her eyelids droop. "What time is it?" she mumbled sleepily.

As if in reply to her question, the clock in the downstairs hall struck the hour of five.

Jared deposited her on her own bed and tucked the covers around her. "I must speak with you before I leave," he said. He sat down on the edge of the bed.

Jarina blinked up at him. "You're leaving again?"

"I need to meet with Jefferson regarding the army contract he offered me. If I depart now, I can be back before nightfall. But, that is not what I wished to discuss with you. How soon can you be packed?"

Jarina forced herself awake. "It shan't take long. The rest of my gowns will be delivered in the morning. Are we going somewhere?"

"I've arranged for a magistrate judge to marry us as soon as I return from Washington City. Then we will go on to Wyeburn."

Wyeburn!

Jarina's pulse quickened. The longer she remained in Alexandria, the greater the risk of someone recognizing her. Last night her identity had nearly been revealed. Wyeburn offered the perfect refuge.

"If you would prefer to wait and be married in a church—"

"Not at all!" she burst out. Her eyes shone in the darkness. "Having the sacrament read by a magistrate instead of a priest will make us no less wed." Her voice dropped. "Nor will it make me any less a wife," she added softly.

Again Jared found himself confronted with the temptation to open up to Jarina, but he fought back the urge, reminding himself that he was no callow youth to indiscriminately confess his innermost thoughts simply because a woman smiled at him and professed to be interested in his concerns. Trust did not come easily to him, and he preferred to err on the side of caution. "Get some rest, sweet," he said, rising. "You have a busy day ahead of you."

"Jared, wait!" Hugging the covers to her chin, she

sat up, and although Jared could not see her expression clearly in the darkness, he could sense her worry. "Why did you have to go see the American ambassador?" Jarina asked. "Are you in some kind of trouble?"

He hesitated. To deny her a reply would only arouse her curiosity, and the last thing he wanted was to have her prying into matters that did not concern her. More than that, he felt an overwhelming, yet unexplainable, need to protect her from Roswell. He did not want her to know of his dealings with the duke, lest her innocence suffer from that knowledge. Jared knew he was not being logical. It was simply the way he *felt*.

The best solution, he decided, was to tell her the truth.

"I have been charged with nonpayment of British duties," he said dispassionately. He hoped to dissuade her from further questions by downplaying the seriousness of his predicament. "Until I can prove that I paid the proper levies during my last voyage to England—"

"How can anyone even suggest such a thing!" Jarina interrupted. "I *know* you paid the taxes."

Standing beside the bed, Jared stared down at her in surprise. "How do you know that?"

"When I first hid aboard the *Pegasus,* I overheard Angus say you would be lucky to turn a profit because of the taxes and fines you were forced to pay. Jared, do you have any idea what will happen to you if you fail to prove your innocence? The crown can seize your ships!"

"Jarina, I—"

"And you dare not return to England to plead your case, or you will surely be arrested!"

"I am well aware—"

"Jared, I know certain people in high places who have the power to help you. If I write to them, I am sure they will—"

"It is not necessary—"

"Jared, please, you must let me help you!"

"Madam, if you will kindly be silent long enough for me to speak, you might learn that I do not require your help!"

He could not have hurt her more had he slapped her. Stung, she shrank away from him and dropped her gaze. "I am sorry," she mumbled. "It was shortsighted of me not to realize that you would already have the situation well in hand."

He immediately regretted having used so harsh a tone with her. Bending down, he placed his palms flat on the mattress on either side of her. "Jarina, look at me."

Still smarting from his rebuke, she reluctantly obeyed.

"I would hardly call your generosity shortsighted," Jared continued gently. "If anything, it pleases me to know you believe in me. Unfortunately, a woman's word carries little weight in a court of law. Your efforts would be for naught, even if your friends were willing to extend their support."

And all I would accomplish would be to alert my father—and Roswell—to my whereabouts, Jarina thought dismally. "What are you going to do?" she asked.

"I turned my tax receipts over to the American Ambassador to England, who will in turn speak on my behalf when he arrives in London."

If the ambassador's ship doesn't sink before it reaches England, Jarina thought cynically, although she did not say so. Instead, she said, "Lieutenant Stendhal did not take too kindly to being ordered off the *Pegasus* like a petty criminal. Do you think he could be responsible for the charges against you?"

Realizing that she had handed him the perfect pretext, Jared smiled and kissed her cheek before straightening. "I do not doubt it, sweet. The man is certainly capable of such underhandedness."

As he drew away from her, for a mere second, Jared

saw her, not as she was now, but as she had been the first time he laid eyes on her, with her boy's breeches and ragged curls. Had anyone told him then he would soon be thoroughly captivated by the little blue-eyed, auburn-haired ragamuffin who had tumbled so inelegantly at his feet, he would have laughed and denounced the prophet for a charlatan. Yet, that was precisely what had happened. Ten short weeks ago, he could not have imagined returning to Wyeburn with a wife. Now he could not imagine returning without one.

The sky was cloudy and gray as the private coach left the brick-paved streets of the city for the open countryside. Towering oaks and maples lined the road and marked the boundaries of the passing farms. Stripped of their foliage, the trees stood bleak and barren against the dawn, their nakedness relieved only by an occasional pine or holly thicket. The snow that had fallen only two nights before had melted; and although there was the unmistakable scent of spring in the air, the ground was still brown and cheerless in its late-winter guise.

Inside the coach, Jared chuckled low. "If you are watching for wild Indians, sweet, I can assure you, there have been none in this area for more than a hundred years."

Feeling a little sheepish, Jarina pulled away from the window and let the curtain drop. There was a red mark high on her cheek where her face had been pressed to the glass. "I was wishing the snow had not melted," she told him.

He grinned at her. "Unless we get an unseasonably late blizzard, you will have to wait until next winter for your toboggan ride."

Jarina laughed. "After hearing you describe how fast those things go, I'm not certain I even *want* to ride one." Inside her fur muff, the fingers of her right hand closed around the ring she wore on her left. "I fear, my lord, you have married a coward."

Jared silently regarded the woman across from him for some moments before saying flatly, "You are no coward."

"Then explain why I am so fearful of meeting your family," she challenged.

"I wasn't aware that you were."

Jarina nervously looked away. It wasn't Jared's brother she was loath to meet. It was *her.* Evelyn Landon. For the past two days, ever since Jared first told her they would be leaving Alexandria, she had thought of little else except the woman her husband had left behind when he last sailed for England. The woman who longed to be Duchess of Wyeburn.

Was she tall? Short? Fair or dark? Was she beautiful? With an instinctive feminine distrust of women who were beautiful, Jarina promptly decided that Evelyn Landon was probably going to be the most beautiful woman she would ever meet. And, as her imagination conjured up a buxom beauty with long blond tresses and classically molded cheekbones, her spirits sank. No matter that less than an hour ago Jared had stood with her before the magistrate judge and pledged his troth; one look at Evelyn and Jared would be lost to her forever.

"I will allow that Damon is not the most agreeable person to have for a brother-in-law," Jared said suddenly, intruding upon her preoccupation, "but the least you could do is spare him that venomous glower until *after* you have met him. You might even decide you like him. In which case, I may be tempted to reassess my own opinion of the man."

An embarrassed smile played at the corners of Jarina's mouth. "I told you I was a coward," she joked. "See, already I am fretting without reason."

Disregarding her artificial joviality, Jared extended a hand and said gently, "Come here."

"You do not need to baby me, Jared."

"My motives are purely selfish, love. I wish to stretch out my legs."

Liar, Jarina thought dryly as she changed seats to sit beside her husband.

His arm settled about her shoulders and he pulled her close. "Apart from Damon," he said, "the only *family* we need contend with are the servants. First there's Evanston. He has been a part of the family for three generations and is so blind that, as long as we don't tell him about that hideous wart on the end of your nose, he will think you are beautiful."

Jarina's mouth dropped open and she cast her husband an astonished glance.

"Then there's Finley, the gardener," he continued lightly. "He has never forgiven me for riding my pony through his perennial border when I was seven, but if you can convince him you weren't born yet, much less subject to my corrupting influence, he might not hold it against you. If he does decide to chase after you with the hose, rest assured that he is afflicted with rheumatism and cannot run very fast."

A choked giggle rose in Jarina's throat. "Jared, you're terrible!"

"Cook is easy. All you need do is have seconds of her sweetbread pudding and she will be forever in your debt. And Maggie—well, now—Maggie is another story. She has been the housekeeper at Wyeburn for nearly forty years, and was more of a mother to me than my own. For the past fifteen years, she has been after me to abandon my bachelor ways and seek a wife, so you can well believe that she will take a keen interest in you. The only problem you may encounter with Maggie is that she is quite determined to see the nursery wing reopened."

Jared's meaning was not lost on her. A crimson flush spread across her face and she self-consciously lowered her gaze.

Jared gave her shoulders a reassuring squeeze. "Just be yourself, sweet," he said softly. "Everyone will love you."

At midday, they stopped at a roadside inn. This time Jared did not indulge Jarina in her somewhat questionable preference for the noisy common rooms. He promptly led her through the tavern and down a narrow hallway into a private dining parlor. "A bedchamber adjoins this room," he informed her, indicating the connecting door. "I thought you might want to rest."

Recalling his earlier remark about reopening the nursery at Wyeburn, panic surged through Jarina as her imagination jumped to a completely licentious conclusion. "I'm not tired," she blurted out.

"But, I am," Jared said, wondering at her tone. "We still have a good six hours of travel remaining, and I need to walk the stiffness out of my leg."

Jarina's breath left her in a *whoosh* of relief. "I-I'm sorry . . . I never gave a thought to your leg. You must find the coach terribly confining," she added hastily, eager to change the subject.

"It's a minor annoyance, nothing more." Cupping her face in his hand, he brushed his thumb across her cheekbone. "Thanks to you, madam," he said quietly, "I still have a leg."

Jared's eyes darkened as their gazes met and held. Jarina's pulse quickened. For an instant, she wished Jared had not paused to order dinner on their way into the inn. It would be a wondrous thing, she thought crazily, to reopen the nursery at Wyeburn. . . .

A sharp knock at the door brought them quickly back to reality. The innkeeper's wife ushered in an entire procession of servants bearing all manner of covered platters and dishes. "We had a good harvest last year," she proudly announced. She placed another log on the fire. "If anything is not to your liking, just send it back and I'll prepare something else."

Jared discreetly slipped a gold coin into the woman's

palm. "I'm sure everything will be just fine," he assured her.

As they relaxed over a leisurely meal, Jared spoke at length of the contract he hoped to secure to raise horses for the army. "General Washington was an infantryman," he explained. "Had we Americans not been assisted by the French in our fight for freedom, we would have lost to the British simply for lack of a suitable cavalry."

Jarina's brows knitted together. Although she was too young to remember the war between England and the United States, she had heard many stories of the hardships her countrymen had endured while on American soil, and she knew tensions still ran high between the two countries, in spite of the active merchant trade that had flourished in the past decade. "Jared, do you think your friends will resent the fact that I am English?"

Stretching out his long legs before the fire, Jared cradled his coffee cup in his palms and studied her thoughtfully for several moments before answering. "It's an inborn contempt for petty tyranny that distinguishes the American from his European cousins. Your birthright may be English, Jarina, but you have a decidedly independent streak in you that makes you as American as any veteran of the war. Had you not, you would have stayed home and married the nobleman your guardian chose for you rather than run away to seek your own future."

"An act which, at the time, you deemed childish and irresponsible," Jarina reminded him.

Jared grinned. "Ah, but at the time, I did not know what a prize you were. Little did I know that, in addition to a pretty face, I had won a seamstress, a surgeon, a potential toboggan partner, and a perfectly delightful dinner companion." He toasted her with his coffee cup.

Never certain whether he was complimenting or teasing her, Jarina sidestepped the issue and returned to the original subject. "Raising horses will be a great change for you," she said. "Will you not miss your ships and the sea?"

"For a while, perhaps, but I want to accomplish more with my life than wander the globe. While I have been away, my house has fallen into disrepair and my fields have lain fallow. I want to return Wyeburn to its former glory. I want to leave to my children a legacy of which they can be rightfully proud."

Jarina's startled gaze riveted on her husband's face and she found him regarding her with an intensity that made her breath catch.

"I want children," Jared said quietly.

Jarina's heart pounded fearfully. She wanted children too, almost as much as she wanted to be a proper wife to Jared. She had simply not expected it to happen *now*. Wondering if he intended to bed her here in a public inn where privacy was an unattainable luxury, she unwillingly allowed her gaze to be drawn toward the door that led to the adjoining bedchamber.

Jared chuckled. "I merely acquired that room so that you might have an hour's rest before we resumed our journey," he said, rising. "I have no intention of pouncing on you. But I want you to give some thought to what I said. I do want children. And I want you to be their mother. When we reach Wyeburn, there will be no more closed doors between us, Jarina. Tonight you will share my bed. Our bed." He bent and kissed the top of her head. "Get some rest, sweet."

It wasn't until after Jared left the room that Jarina realized she was clutching the arms of her chair. *Rest!* How did he expect her to rest when he had left her with what amounted to an ultimatum? *I want children. I want you to be their mother. When we reach Wyeburn, there will be no more closed doors between us.*

Her eyes closed and she groaned. She couldn't go through with it. She couldn't share his bed and let him do that awful, vile thing he had done to her the night she'd met him. She could not let him hurt her again.

Yet, did it have to hurt? Was it not the breeching of her maidenhead that had caused her so much pain that terrible night, and not the act of coupling itself? She enjoyed Jared's kisses. She enjoyed the way his caresses made her feel all warm and liquid inside. She enjoyed simply being held by him. Perhaps, given time, she might even come to enjoy the union that would make her truly his wife.

Besides, a critical voice in her warned, if she refused Jared, there would be plenty of other women waiting, like vultures, to take her place. Namely, one Evelyn Landon.

An hour later, she was once again seated beside Jared in the coach. Jared extended his arm along the back of the seat and stretched out his leg, propping his booted foot on the seat opposite them, while Jarina settled comfortably against him, her head nestling in the hollow of his shoulder. She had not rested well at the inn and the rhythmic sway of the coach soon lulled her into a peaceful lethargy.

They had been traveling for nearly an hour when Jared broke the silence between them. "You haven't spoken since we left the inn," he said, twirling one dark-chestnut curl about his finger, then letting it spring free. "Is something amiss?"

She tilted her head back to look up at him. "I was trying to remember when was the last time I felt so contented."

Jared chuckled. "I believe it was two nights ago, when you drank enough ale to put a seaman under the table."

She smiled. "I was also wondering what our children would be like."

Jared considered that one a moment. "They'll probably have your blue eyes," he finally said.

"And your black hair."

"They'll be stubborn, like their mother."

She giggled. "And spendthrifts, like their father."

"They'll have warts on the ends of their noses."

"Jared Cunningham, I do not have a wart on my nose!"

Seeing through Jarina's light tone, Jared immediately sobered. "Does the thought of having children distress you?"

She looked away and said, a bit too quickly, "No, of course not."

It was not having children that frightened her, Jared realized as an awkward silence yawned between them; it was him. On their first night together, he had behaved like a rutting boar, with no thought to anyone's desires save his own. He had ruined for her what should have been one of the most pleasurable experiences of her life. With a sigh of remorse, he drew her against him and rested his chin atop her head. He vowed he would make it up to her.

It was well past dark when they left the main road for one that was so seldom traveled it had become rutted, and Jared made a mental note to have it repaired at the first opportunity.

The lurching of the coach jarred Jarina from her slumber. Placing her palms against Jared's chest, she pushed herself upright. "Are we almost there?" she asked sleepily.

"Just a few more miles, love."

"Oh." Panic beat a rapid advance in Jarina's heart and her stomach clenched tight. Soon it would be time. Soon they would arrive at Wyeburn and Jared's family would find out that he was now married. To her. She pulled the lap furs up about her shoulders and settled back into the warm security of her husband's arms.

Though he took quick notice of her apparent lack of enthusiasm, Jared could not fault her. Nearly two years had passed since he had last been home, and as the end of their journey grew imminent, he found himself becoming increasingly ill at ease. He did not know what he would find at Wyeburn. For all he knew, the house could have been ravaged by fire during his absence.

Something told him *that* would be the least of his worries.

Beneath the lap furs, Jarina's hand sought his.

"And what is *that?*" Jonathan Shelby asked.

"This," Evelyn replied, slowly peeling, strip by strip, the exotic, yellow-skinned delicacy, "is a banana. They're very expensive. I had them imported from Martinique."

He laughed. "Bought with Cunningham's money, no doubt."

"Of course. Surely, you don't think I would pay for them myself?" Watching him through half-closed eyes, Evelyn inserted the tip of the banana's creamy white fruit between her red lips and suggestively drew it in and out several times before taking a bite. She held the banana out to him and smiled. "Would you care to sample one?"

He leered at her. Shoving her hand aside, he caught her around the waist and rolled with her on the carpet. "Don't mind if I do," he said huskily.

Evelyn closed her eyes and lay passively, offering neither assistance nor protest as he unbuttoned his pantaloons and groped beneath her skirts.

Thirty minutes later, she slipped from the study and started down the long hall toward the drawing room to rejoin the rest of her guests. Before she had taken more than a few steps, a figure emerged from the shadows and an iron hand closed about her arm. "Amusing yourself with that ale-bellied Republican from Culpeper?" Damon hissed.

Sighing with exaggerated weariness, she slowly

turned to face him and one finely tapered brow arched in speculation. "Jealous?"

"Do you even know his name?" Damon returned sarcastically.

Evelyn's roughed lips budded into a pout. "What you really want to know," she taunted, "is whether he performs as well as you do."

Evelyn's face was flushed and a fine sheen of perspiration covered her skin above the low neckline of her saffron velvet gown. The smell of sex clung to her like a second perfume, mingling with the heady Oriental fragrance she always wore and arousing Damon's desire along with his fury. Grasping her shoulders, he jerked her against him. "You might remember, my dear, to show a little decorum while you are a guest in my house."

She laughed and gave her disheveled black tresses a haughty toss. "Don't you mean, Jared's hou—"

Damon's mouth closed over hers, checking her retort with a punishing kiss. She gave herself up eagerly to him, boldly molding herself to the length of him as his hands eased her gown off her shoulders. Her lashes fluttered against her cheeks and her head dropped back as Damon's lips moved down her moist neck to the naked breasts that strained hungrily against his chest. Calmly observing her through hooded eyes, he moved his hands down to imprison her slender waist and lift her higher against him.

A low groan sounded in Evelyn's throat. Raising up on tiptoe, she arched her back, presenting her coral nipples to him like a sacrificial offering. But it was not a nipple Damon sought, but the soft white swell just above. Surprise, then alarm, surged through Evelyn as his mouth clamped brutally on her flesh.

Uttering a cry of outrage, Evelyn forced her hands up between them and shoved as hard as she could.

Damon's hold on her broke and she stumbled backward. "You bastard!" she spat, her chest heaving in righteous anger. She pulled her gown back up over her bosom, but the revealing bodice failed to cover the red blood-bruise that Damon's sucking had raised on her flesh. Vengeance flashing in her dark eyes, she brought up her hand and her palm cracked across his cheek. "For your information," she ground out angrily, "Jon Shelby is a far better lover than you could ever pretend to be!"

Whirling about, she stomped away.

Chuckling, Damon took a cigar from his waistcoat pocket and bit off the end. He had waited a long time to see Evelyn get her comeuppance, he thought as he watched her throw open the drawing-room doors. He could wait awhile longer.

In the drawing room, Evelyn loudly clapped her hands and demanded her guests' attention. "You are going to be here another month, and I will not have you sitting around growing fat from lack of exertion," she announced. "Charles, get up off that sofa. I want you men to carry the furniture out of the center of the room and roll up the carpets. We are going to dance! Madeline, I elect you to play the pianoforte, and none of that dreadful chamber music, for God's sake. Play something risque. Play a waltz!"

Within minutes, everyone had complied with her wishes. The furniture had been moved and the polished wood floor bared. After several rather clumsy and self-conscious starts, Madeline Carter delved eagerly into one of the new waltzes she was forbidden to play at home.

"May I?"

Evelyn turned and smiled coyly up at the fair-haired man beside her. "Need you ask?"

The man's gaze dropped meaningfully to the angry blemish on her bosom, then returned to meet hers. He shrugged. "You wear another man's brand," he offered in explanation.

"And you reek of Lucy Blanchard's perfume. Are you sleeping with her tonight?"

"Perhaps. Unless, of course, another strikes my fancy."

Evelyn allowed him to lead her onto the dance floor. "Do I strike your fancy, sir?" she asked seductively.

He grinned. "Let us just say, you have awakened my interest."

While the dancers whirled to the lively strains, several of the numerous servants Evelyn had hired paraded in and out of the drawing room, bringing tray after tray of elegantly prepared foodstuffs and glasses of champagne to her guests. Some of the guests were friends, some were friends of friends. Most, Evelyn knew, had come merely to spend the winter enjoying the comforts Wyeburn offered and to ease the burden on their own ill-stocked pantries, but she did not care. It was a common practice among Virginia's landed gentry to simply move in with one another during lean times, and she was not above taking advantage of anyone's temporary descent into poverty.

Meanwhile, in the kitchen, a revolt was rapidly brewing among the servants. "If that Lyman Carter grabs me bum one more time," complained a freckle-faced, red-haired girl of fifteen, "I'm gonna take my tray of whore-derves, and dump it all over him."

No one bothered to correct her pronunciation. "I've had enough of Miss Evelyn bossin' me around like she's the missus here," Cook declared. Rolling her eyes, she mimicked in a high-pitched voice, " '*You ignorant old woman! If I've told you once, I've told you a thousand times, I don't like cream in my tea. I have cream in my chocolate and lemon in my tea.*' Ha! If she wants lemon, all she's gotta do is screw up that sour face of hers and spit!"

Maggie shook her head. "I just hope that boy of mine is not of a mind to marry her like she wants," Maggie said, speaking of Jared as though he were her own son.

She frowned as she tucked a gray strand back beneath her mobcap. "Even with her highfalutin ways, the old Mrs. Cunningham weren't near so bad as this one."

"She kept me practicing for an hour yesterday how to announce her when she enters a room," Evanston said, then demonstrated in his most dignified voice, *"Her grace, the Duchess of Wyeburn."*

Cook wagged a finger at him. "If Mr. Jared marries that . . . that . . . *harlot,* I swear I'll quit! I don't care if they do send me back to the poorhouse."

To everyone's astonishment, the old woman's face crumpled and her eyes filled with tears. "Mr. Jared's the kindest man I know," she wailed. "He took me off the streets, he did, and give me a job when no one else would even turn me a second look. All I had to do was fry him a steak without killin' it, and the job was mine, he said." She dabbed at her eyes with her apron, and added thickly, "I don't want to go back to the poorhouse, but, upon my word, I just can't stay here with that woman criticizin' me all the time and makin' me cook them fancified things I never even heard of. It'll be a sorry day if Mr. Jared was to wed her."

Maggie patted her arm and said consolingly, "None of us is giving that boy credit for having a lick of common sense if we worry about him marrying the likes of Miss Evelyn. He's been turning a blind eye to her all these years, and there's no cause for us to think the manner of things will be any different when he gets back from England. Now, lovey, you take some of that nice barley soup you made up to Finley. That'll cheer him up for sure. Poor old man, sittin' up there in his room with his leg broke and no way to get about."

"Who has a broken leg?"

Cook, who had been unceremoniously blowing her nose into her apron, froze; Maggie spun around; and Evanston fumbled in his waistcoat for his spectacles. His hand shook as he placed them on the tip of his nose. He blinked twice, then his eyes grew round as saucers.

"There seems to be a dearth of tongues in this room," Jared remarked offhandedly. "I asked a question. Who broke a leg?"

Maggie was the first to find her voice. "Good heavens! If you aren't a sight for these old eyes! When did you get home?"

"Mr. Jared, sir!" Evanston blurted out, forgetting himself. "We didn't expect to see the likes of you until after Easter."

"You neglectful boy!" Maggie chided. "Thinking you can just light out for more'n two years without a word to anyone! Get yourself over here and give this old woman a hug!" In spite of her scolding tone, there were tears in her eyes and a catch in her voice.

Jared's arms engulfed her and he hugged her so hard her feet left the floor. "I missed you, Maggie," he whispered into her ear before he set her down.

Jarina had deliberately hung back while Jared became reacquainted with his old friends. Her throat constricted uncontrollably as she observed the reunion. Her father had always said one could learn more about a man from the way he related to his servants than to his business colleagues, and it was obvious that these people loved Jared deeply.

Maggie noticed Jarina for the first time, and a weighted silence fell over the kitchen as each woman took the other's measure.

Jarina's heart thumped so loudly she was certain everyone in the room could hear it. She knew instinctively that Maggie Kilmore could make or break her stay at Wyeburn, for while the woman was not a relative in any legal sense, she had reared Jared, and she would be as protective and defending of him as any devoted mother.

Jared took Jarina's arm and gently drew her near. "Maggie, Evanston . . . all of you . . . this is my wife, Jarina."

Uncertain whether she should curtsy or shake hands,

Jarina decided upon the former, and as she demurely lifted her skirts and bent her knee, Maggie, who had never been curtsied before in her life, turned a deep red. Suddenly remembering herself, she clapped her hands to her flaming cheeks and exclaimed, "Your wife! Mrs. Cunningham! Oh, heavens, if you aren't the prettiest little thing I've ever laid eyes on!"

Turning to the others, she said loudly, "I want you to meet your new mistress. Mr. Jared up and got himself married, and *this* is his *wife.*"

She had put so much emphasis on the word *wife* that Jarina lifted a puzzled gaze to her husband's face. Jared, in turn, raised a brow in displeasure. "We are legally wed," he said dryly. "Perhaps you would like to examine the marriage license bond?"

The servants all exchanged glances, and Cook, who had suddenly caught Maggie's drift, blurted out, "Now that Mr. Jared's already married, I won't have to go back to the poorhouse!"

Jared stared at her. "The poorhouse?" he asked.

Maggie silenced Cook with a look, then turned back to Jarina. "You poor thing, standing there, shivering. You just bring yourself over here to this chair by the stove and sit yourself down and—good heavens, child! What happened to your hair?"

Before Jarina could reply, Maggie brushed her own query aside. "Never you mind," she said crisply. "The first thing we want to do is get some hot soup into you to take the chill off your bones. Imagine! Mr. Jared just up and getting married! And a fine choice for a wife he made, if you ask me. You do justice to the Cunningham name for sure! Heavens, would you look at them blue eyes! Fiona, dish up some of Cook's soup for Mrs. Cunningham here, and—oh!" Suddenly remembering something, she spun on Jared and blurted out, "Finley!"

"Finley?" Jared asked, taken aback.

"It was Finley who broke his leg," Maggie said, finally answering Jared's earlier question. "Stepped in a gopher hole and landed flat on his face. You never heard anyone yell so much in your whole life!"

Warmed by both the barley soup the red-haired girl had brought her and the friendly chaos that pervaded the kitchen, Jarina listened with interest as the servants told Jared of all that had happened since he had last been home, from the fire in the smokehouse to the visitors who had come to spend the winter. Jarina could have sworn she had heard music when they approached the house, and now she understood why Jared had insisted they enter through the kitchens. After spending twelve hours in the confines of the coach, they were both too rumpled and travel-weary to face a houseful of guests.

Yet there was a conspicuous absence of any mention of Evelyn Landon that made Jared uneasy. He was not looking forward to the inevitable meeting with Evelyn. Even though he bore no affection for her, he knew she would be crushed when she learned he had married. And while he wanted to be free of Evelyn Landon, he did not want to hurt her.

"I am almost afraid to ask," Jared said wearily. "Just how many *guests* has my brother invited."

"Oh, it weren't Mr. Damon who invited everyone," Cook interjected. "It was Miss Evelyn. She said that when she saw you in Alexandria before you went to England, you told her she could stay here while Fair Oaks was being fixed up. Although, if you ask me, Mr. Jared, them carpenters have been at work there a mighty long time."

"How long?"

Cook hesitated. "Since Christmas before last."

Annoyance flashed in Jared's eyes and the muscle in his jaw knotted. "I think it's time I had a word with Evelyn."

Jarina rose from her chair. "Jared, wait! I want to come with—"

"No. Evanston, please show my wife to our apartments and have one of the maids prepare a bath for her."

The butler looked alarmed. "But, Mr. Jared, the master's suite isn't—"

"Take Jarina to my bedchamber," Jared repeated firmly.

Angry footsteps sounded in the hall. "What is it with you people?" demanded an indignant feminine voice. Evelyn appeared in the doorway, her color high. "I asked for a tray of hors d'oeuvres over an hour ago, and no one has bothered to bring it. Instead, I find you socializing—" She broke off suddenly and gasped. "Jared, you're home!"

Evelyn rushed forward and flung herself against him. She threw her arms about his neck and kissed him long and hard.

Engulfed in the cloying cloud of her perfume, Jared made no attempt to return Evelyn's greeting, but stood rigidly and without responding while she rubbed her body provocatively against him and devoured his lips with her kisses.

Jarina's eyes smoldered with jealous fury. Silently fuming, she watched the black-haired woman kiss her husband. Even though the woman in her imagination had been a buxom blonde, she needed no introduction to tell her this was Evelyn Landon. Stephen's cousin. Her competition.

Evelyn finally stopped kissing Jared, but refused to relinquish her hold on his arm. "Oh, darling, I've missed you terribly! Why didn't you send someone ahead to let us know you were coming?" Her gaze alighted on Jarina, and her dark eyes widened slightly. Suddenly, she let out a squeal of delight. "Oh, Jared, you've brought me my very own French maid, just like I always wanted. And such a precious little thing, she is. Just look at those adorable blue eyes! Does she speak English?" Without giving him a chance to reply, she turned to Jarina and said with agonizing exaggeration, "Pahr-lay-voo ahn-glezz?"

It was on the tip of Jarina's tongue to reply, *probably better than you,* but she bit back the retort. Stepping forward, she swept into a gracious curtsy. "You must be Evelyn Landon," she said with a honeyed sweetness that soured her stomach. "Stephen and my husband have spoken of you at great length. I feel I know you well already."

Taken aback, Evelyn stared at her blankly. "Your husband?"

Knowing it was too late now to attempt softening the blow, Jared disengaged himself from Evelyn's clinging hold. He drew Jarina's hand through his arm and held it tightly. "Evelyn, this is my wife, Jarina."

Chapter Eleven

The color siphoned from Evelyn's face as she turned a disbelieving gaze, first on Jarina, then on Jared. "Your wife?" she whispered.

"My wife," Jared said quietly.

For a moment, Evelyn simply gaped at them as all her well-laid plans collapsed at her feet. She could not believe Jared was married. Not once, in all the years she had known him, had he shown the slightest interest in a woman beyond what she could do for him in bed, and she did not believe he had undergone any miraculous change, particularly over this skinny little chit of a girl who didn't look old enough to know what a man's cock was for, much less how to ride one. Her nostrils flared as she regarded the unwelcome newcomer with contempt. "*Jar*ed and *Jar*ina," she said snidely, enunciating with pained distaste the shared beginning consonant of their names. "My, my, how provincial. Tell me, Jared, has the great stag grown so old and feeble that he is only able to impress suckling babes with his sorry performance?"

Although she did not completely comprehend what Evelyn was talking about, Jarina felt her husband stiffen. Anxious to forestall a confrontation, she lifted glowing eyes to his anger-congested face and said warmly, "Jared is a wonderful man. I am honored that he chose me to be his wife."

Jared's scowl softened slightly as a look of surprise flickered across his features, but if he was taken aback by Jarina's unexpected announcement, Maggie was delighted. Not only was her boy finally wed, it would seem Miss Evelyn had just met her match. Maggie bit down on her bottom lip and turned away so no one could see the smile that threatened to overtake her.

Evelyn's eyes burned with jealousy. "Honored! You stupid infant! Jared doesn't love you. Jared doesn't know how to love anyone except himself."

For the first time in eight years, Jared felt neither hatred nor revulsion for Evelyn. So many times he had longed to punish her, to make her pay for hurting him. So he had courted her, and bedded her, and let her think he intended to offer for her. Yet now, when it would be so simple to give vengeance a brutal twist by throwing his marriage up in her face, all he felt for her was pity. "Jarina has done nothing to you, Evelyn," he said. "Leave her be."

Evelyn paid no heed to the quiet warning in Jared's voice. Leaning close to Jarina, she said in a sneering tone that was at once conspiratorial and full of spite, "Do you know how many women in this house he has bedded, little girl? Shall I take you to the drawing room and introduce them to you?"

Jared took a step toward Evelyn, his expression murderous, but before he could give vent to the fury building inside him, a man chuckled from the doorway.

Damon snuffed out his cigar. "I think it's a splendid idea," he said lightly. "And while we're at it, we can introduce all the men *you* have bedded, Evelyn. Except, of course, for Jonathan Shelby, who, at this moment, is sound asleep in Jared's study." He approached Jarina. "I'm Damon Cunningham, Jared's half-brother." He took Jarina's hand and bowed low over it. "Welcome to Wyeburn."

Jarina had to stifle the impulse to jerk her hand away. She did not understand why Damon's touch should repel her so. She felt the floor sway beneath her feet, and a cold sweat broke out across her forehead as she stared numbly at her brother-in-law. Had she not known otherwise, she would have sworn that Jared and Damon and Evelyn were brothers and sister. All three possessed the same thick, black hair. The same strong jaw. The same imperious arch to their brows. The only real difference lay in their eyes. Evelyn's were dark and brooding; Damon's were spoked with gold, like cat's eyes; and Jared's were a clear, icy gray. Something here was wrong, terribly wrong, yet she could not define exactly what. She began to feel sick to her stomach. Evelyn's strong perfume seemed to bear down on her, suffocating her.

Jarina felt Jared's hand tighten on her shoulder and she dimly heard him order Maggie to take her upstairs.

Jarina fought to get her reeling emotions under control. "Jared, we should go meet our guests," she said with more calmness than she was feeling. "I'm sure everyone will want to know you returned safely from your voyage to England."

Damon's smile lacked warmth. "Not to mention the fact that you are now married, brother dearest," he said.

Jared did not give a damn whether Evelyn's and Damon's friends knew of either his return or his marriage, but before he could say anything, Damon had taken hold of Jarina's arm. "Allow me to introduce you to some of the most prominent families in Fairfax County," he said smoothly as he led her from the room.

Jarina did not see the venomous look Evelyn fixed on her departing back.

Jared did.

As soon as Jarina and Damon were out of earshot, Jared rounded on Evelyn. "I want everyone out of this house no later than tomorrow morning, and it would please me greatly if those who do not have far to travel were to leave tonight."

Evelyn gaped at him. "Jared, you're mad!" she protested. "I can't tell these people to leave! I invited them to stay until spring planting!"

"And while you're about it," Jared continued, oblivious to the servants who listened to the exchange in fascinated disbelief, "you may pack your own belongings. You have a home, Evelyn. Return to it."

Evelyn's eyes widened, then filled with tears. Pressing a fist against her mouth, she turned and ran from the room.

Jared glowered at the servants who suddenly looked away and pretended to be busy. Shaking his head in annoyance, he turned on one heel and stalked out the door.

The last thing Jared wanted to do tonight was mingle with a pack of lazy, self-centered, spoiled socialites who were spending the winter living off the fruits of his labors, and it galled him to think that Jarina did. He had caught the note of vexation in Jarina's voice when she suggested it, and he had the distinct feeling she was deliberately trying to provoke him, although he did not know why. Perhaps she was upset at finding Evelyn at Wyeburn; he certainly was.

Then he remembered his own prophecy, and he wondered if his wife was finally learning to channel her anger. If so, was he her intended target, and not Evelyn? Perhaps, he thought irritably, Jarina had no intention of sharing his bed tonight and was merely delaying the moment when they would be alone together.

Whatever her purpose, he intended to find out.

Jarina was angry. She did not blame Jared for Evelyn's presence at Wyeburn, but the fact that the woman would even presume to establish residency during his absence rankled sorely, for it served to confirm her fears that Evelyn shared a closeness with Jared that she, as his wife, could never hope to attain.

"Keep a close eye on Lyman Carter's hands," Damon warned as he led Jarina through the hall. "The man is a lecher."

In the crowded drawing room, Damon clapped his hands and called for everyone's attention. He lifted two glasses from a tray and passed one to Jarina. "I have an announcement to make," he said. "One that calls for a toast."

Jarina stared numbly at the glass of champagne in her hand, acutely aware of the man who stood beside her, with one hand placed possessively on her elbow. With his dark good looks and his persuasive smile, Damon was so much like Jared, the resemblance was uncanny. Yet he was also very different. There was something about Damon that made her uneasy. As in the kitchen, she was again gripped with an unexplainable urge to recoil from him.

Damon raised his glass. "Ashton, you asked me earlier when Jared was due to return from England, and I could not tell you. Now, I can. Jared returned today." Damon paused for effect, then added, "A married man!"

In the brief span of silence before anyone could respond, Evelyn flew past the doorway, sobbing bitterly, and ran up the stairs.

Everyone began talking at once.

"What ails Evelyn? She was fine when I last spoke to her."

"Jared is married? When?"

"I'd be willing to bet Evelyn and Jared came to blows. She was dead set on being his wife, you know."

"Did you hear that? Jared got married!"

"Is that his wife?"

Annoyed by the disruption, Damon slammed his glass down on a table. He was still gripping Jarina's elbow, and the abrupt movement caused her to spill wine down the front of her gown.

Swearing under his breath, Damon grabbed a napkin.

"Here, I'll do it," Jarina said hastily as Damon began to blot up the champagne, but he merely shoved her hand out of the way, leaving her no choice but to stand there and endure his ministrations. He dabbed at her bodice and hot color consumed her cheeks as his fingers brushed against her breast.

At that moment, Jared appeared in the doorway. His steely gaze riveted on Jarina and his brother. His face was dark with fury as he closed the space between them in angry strides.

Jarina froze in terror as Jared bore down on them.

Jared seized Damon's arm and spun him around. Before the younger man had a chance to get his bearings, Jared drew back his arm and smashed his fist into Damon's jaw.

A woman screamed as Damon fell.

Jared started toward him, but Jarina clutched his sleeve. "Jared, don't!"

Jared's breath came in painful gulps as he fought to get his raging temper under control. Angry sparks flashed in his gray eyes like cinders dancing off a blacksmith's anvil.

Damon struggled to sit up, and wiped the back of his hand across his bleeding mouth.

Jared leveled a warning finger at him. "Jarina is my *wife*," he ground out. "If you ever touch her again, I will tear you from limb to limb!"

A shocked cry escaped Jarina's lips. "Jared, he didn't do anything! He was only trying to clean up the champagne I spilled."

Ignoring her, Jared turned and faced the guests who were regarding him with a mixture of curiosity and appalled disbelief. Nor was their opinion of their host improved when Jared glared at them and declared icily,

"Your carriages will be made ready tomorrow morning for your departure. You have outstayed your welcome. I don't want to see any of you here again except at my invitation."

In the shocked silence that followed, Jared rounded on Damon and added in a low, menacing tone. "And that includes Evelyn. I don't know what purpose you intended to serve by bringing her here, but I want her out of this house."

Jared took Jarina's arm in a painful grip and spun her toward the door. Too terrified to protest, she half walked, half ran to keep up with him as he hauled her from the room.

In the great hall, they encountered Evanston, whose reddening face betrayed his knowledge of what had just happened. Jared shoved Jarina into the old man's arms. "Take her to my chambers," he ordered brusquely.

"Jared, wait!" Jarina started after him as he turned to go, but the look of blazing fury he gave her stopped her short. Gone was the kind, gentle man she had come to know in Alexandria. In his place was the old Jared who haunted her dreams. The Jared who had taken her innocence. The Jared who had once threatened to make her life hell. The Jared who had sworn he would kill a wife who played him false.

Feeling confused and betrayed by the unanticipated change that had come over her husband, Jarina succumbed to Evanston's whispered prodding, and followed the servant up the stairs.

In the drawing-room doorway, Damon leaned against the doorframe and dabbed a handkerchief to his bloodied lip while he observed the scene before him with thinly-veiled amusement. " 'Tis comforting to know some things are impervious to change," he said dryly as Jared came toward him. "You are still the same heartless bastard you always were. Within an hour of your homecoming, you have managed to fell me, insult your peers, and humiliate your wife. Tell me,

Jared, is there any hope at all that you might acquire the fine art of subtlety at some point in your life?"

Jared stopped before him, his gray gaze smoldering. "If you were not my brother, Damon, I would pick you up and physically throw you from this house," he said in a low, meaningful voice. "As it is, you would be wise to stay out of my way. And if you ever lay a hand on my wife again, I will forget the common blood that flows in our veins, and kill you where you stand. Do you understand me?"

"Perfectly well," Damon replied. "And while you're about it, there are some things it's time *you* understood, Jared. About Evelyn."

Jared met Damon's unruffled gaze with a scorching glower. "I have no desire to discuss Evelyn with you, or with anyone," he said as he turned away. "Good night, Damon."

Some of Damon's earlier impatience snapped in his eyes, but he quickly brought his temper under control. "You'll not be so quick to expel Evelyn from this house and dismiss her from your thoughts when you've heard what I have to say," he said.

Jared turned and his gray eyes narrowed as he regarded Damon in icy silence. Then he motioned toward his study. "I'll give you five minutes," he said flatly.

Damon pushed himself away from the doorframe. "It will take that long just to have Jonathan Shelby carried out," he tossed over his shoulder as he sauntered casually down the hall.

Thirty minutes later, when Jared emerged from his study, his face was ashen, and there was murder in his eyes.

With a weary sigh, Jarina went to the window and stared out the leaded panes at the blackness beyond as her tired mind groped for an explanation to Jared's bizarre behavior. She remembered what Stephen Landon had told her about Jared's mother, but immediately dismissed that possibility as irrelevant. She had never given Jared reason to distrust her, or to suspect her of infidelity.

Then other, less clear memories flitted through her thoughts. *Damon comes by his roving instincts honestly.* Had Stephen said that? Or had Jared?

Damon covets everything that belongs to Jared. His social standing. His inheritance. His women. Stephen had told her that.

Damon doesn't concern you. You'll see naught of him except in my company. If you do otherwise, I'll know the reason why.

Jarina closed her eyes and groaned inwardly as the truth struck her. Jared was not angry because of anything that had happened. He was angry at what he feared could happen. Damon was handsome and charming and persuasive. He was younger than Jared. And Jared had no way of knowing that just being near Damon made her skin crawl.

What hurt her the most, however, was the thought that Jared did not trust her.

"Oh, Jared," she whispered, "I could never be unfaithful to you. I love you."

Earlier, Evelyn had accused Jared of not knowing how to love. But Evelyn was wrong, Jarina thought. Jared knew how to give love. He simply did not know how to accept it in return.

As she waited for Jared to return, Jarina wandered aimlessly about the bedchamber. In spite of the roaring fire on the hearth, the room felt cold. She shuddered. The great bed at the far end of the masculine, dark-paneled room did not beckon. It threatened. I do not belong here, she thought. She felt unwelcome.

She stopped before a broad low chest, cluttered with discarded jewelry and toiletries, and reached out to touch a forefinger to the large ruby of a ring. A woman's ring, she realized uneasily.

Then her gaze fell on a small perfume vial. Drawn

by curiosity, she lifted the stopper and brought it to her nose. She gasped. It was the same scent that had permeated the air when Evelyn Landon had entered the kitchen. It was Evelyn's perfume! Jarina dropped the stopper and jerked her hand away as though she had been burned. Her heart pounded and she began to tremble violently as an anger more savage, more violent than any she had ever known shot through her, frightening her with its intensity. For the first time in her life she knew how it felt to want to kill someone. With a strangled cry, she picked up the vial and hurled it as hard as she could against the wall.

The door opened, and Jarina whirled about.

Jared lowered her travel trunk to the floor and straightened, his displeasure evident as he impaled her with a reproving look. Even though he had not seen her throw the vial, he had heard the shattering of glass, and he knew what she had done. Perfume filled the air with its choking scent. Reaching behind him, he pushed the door shut. "That, madam, was uncalled for," he said tersely.

Jarina's eyes blazed like blue fire as she faced her husband. "How could you?" she demanded. "How could you bring me here to the very same bedchamber you shared with your mistress? How could you even *think* I would consent to sleeping in the bed where you made love to *her?*" She could not make herself say Evelyn's name.

Jared stared at her long and hard, and there was a look of absolute loathing on his face that Jarina knew she would not forget for as long as she lived. "Jarina, even you are not so naive as to believe there have been no other women before you," he said quietly, dangerously. "And yes, Evelyn was one of those women. But, I never bedded her in this house, much less in this room, and certainly not on that bed."

The remark about her naiveté stung. "I may not possess your vast experience, my lord, but I am not stupid." Her voice shook with anger and humiliation. "If your mistress never shared your bedchamber, then do me the courtesy of explaining why her perfumes and her jewels are here." Acting on a hunch that soon proved painfully correct, she marched to the wardrobe and yanked open the door. "And her clothes!"

The sight of Evelyn's gowns hanging in his wardrobe unnerved Jared almost as much as it did Jarina. "I will have Evelyn's belongings removed immediately," he said icily.

Jarina clenched and unclenched her hands, and her throat knotted so tightly, she could not swallow. Her voice dropped to a choked whisper. "Please, my lord, do not trouble yourself. I shall endeavor to find another bedchamber." Her head held high, she stalked to the door and yanked it open. She only took a few steps before coming to an abrupt halt, realizing too late that she was not in the hall, but had entered another room entirely. Trying to gather her bearings, she stared about her in bewilderment. Along one wall stood a huge bathing tub carved from a single piece of marble. Opposite the tub, near the corner fireplace that spilled its warmth into the room, was a round breakfast table and two comfortable-looking chairs. On another wall a washstand stood beside a huge linen press.

Behind her, Jared spoke. "This is a bathing chamber," he said coolly, emotionlessly. "Another room adjoins this one. It was the bedchamber my mother preferred. She found the oak paneling in the master suite too oppressive for her tastes." He went to another door and opened it. "It's through here," he said.

A terrible pain seized Jarina's chest. Even though self-esteem had driven her to seek another bedchamber, another part of her wished fervently that Jared would deny her that request. If he ordered her to stay, she would not give in to him without a fight, but at least her wounded pride would be assuaged by the knowledge that he *wanted* her. Now she did not even have that small assurance. Feeling as though she were being exiled, she followed him to the door.

The second bedchamber was light and airy in contrast to the paneled darkness of Jared's room, but Jarina showed little awareness of her surroundings. She stood in the middle of the room and stared down at her hands while Jared gave instructions to the maid who had been changing the bed linens when they entered.

"Jarina, look at me."

Even though he had spoken softly, Jared's voice blasted through Jarina's misery like a musket shot, nearly crushing her resolve. Blinking hastily several times to banish the bitter tears that grated behind her eyelids, she slowly turned to face him. Her chin stubbornly inched upward. As much as she felt like it, she refused to cry in his presence.

All day, Jared had looked forward to this night when he could take Jarina in his arms and make love to her. He wanted to show her tenderness and passion, not the selfish lust he had inflicted on her before. He wanted to go to her now, and hold her, and kiss away the aching uncertainty that haunted her eyes, but he could not. There was still too much pent-up anger inside him. Seeing Damon touching her had unleashed a jealous rage he had not thought himself capable of feeling. Violence did not frighten him. Loss of self-control did. He took a deep breath. "If you need anything, you know where to find me. Or you may ask one of the servants."

Jarina's throat ached so much she could barely speak. "Thank you," she whispered numbly. She turned away, but not before he had seen the bright glimmer on her lashes.

Jared sighed wearily. How could he expect her to deal gracefully with what he could not yet accept?

Going to her, he gently placed a hand on her shoulder and she flinched.

The muscle in Jared's jaw tightened at her reaction to his touch. *Damn it, Jarina, we have come so far!*

Don't let Evelyn destroy us now! Cursing himself for his weakness, he let his hand drop. Without another word, he turned and left the room.

Back in his bedchamber, he nearly gagged on the heavy cloud of perfume that engulfed him. If he got his hands on Evelyn, he would throttle her. He went to the door and yanked it open. "Evanston, get in here!"

When the servant arrived, he found Jared pacing.

Jared whirled on him. "I want everything removed from this room and destroyed," he ordered. "The furniture, the carpets. Everything!"

Evanston looked aghast. "But, Mr. Jared, the bed was one your grandfather brought over from—"

"Burn it," Jared snapped. "I want nothing that Evelyn Landon has touched left in here." He started toward the door.

Evanston balked. "Sir, you were born on that bed!"

"I said, *burn it!*"

In the hallway, Evelyn hovered in the shadows, tears glittering on her lashes as she observed Jared's angry exit from his bedchamber. She had overheard enough of the exchange between Jared and his new wife to ascertain with a fair amount of accuracy just how matters stood. Jared might be married to the spineless little twit, she thought, but he certainly wasn't sleeping with her.

And he won't. Not if I have anything to say about it, she vowed. Her bottom lip trembled, and she bit down on it to keep from bursting into sobs. Jared had loved her once. She had to find some way to win him back.

She waited until Jared had gone and the hallway was clear before emerging from the shadows and tiptoeing down the stairs.

Jarina knotted her fingers in the folds of her skirt and squeezed her eyes shut against the threatening tears, refusing to acknowledge their existence. Evelyn Landon had accused her of being an infant, and if she cried, she would only prove the woman right.

Even through two closed doors, she could hear Jared's bellowing. The angry words fell on her ears like blows, as though punishing her for the discord between them, and when Jared shouted, *"Burn it!"* her entire body jerked with an involuntary shudder.

Jarina opened her eyes and took several deep breaths as she struggled to regain her composure. Near the foot of the bed stood the maid to whom Jared had spoken before he left the room.

"A bath is being prepared for you, m'lady," the girl said. "Shall I unfasten your gown?"

Jarina wrapped her arms about her aching stomach. "That won't be necessary," she finally managed to get out. "You may go now."

The girl did not move.

"I can undress myself," Jarina said, thinking the girl may have misunderstood her.

"Mr. Jared told me to stay and—"

"I want to be alone." Jarina's voice wavered and the tears she had succeeded in resisting suddenly welled in her eyes. "Please," she pleaded softly. "Just go."

The maid hesitated, then bobbed a curtsy and left the room.

A painful silence engulfed the room.

Jarina's misery began to give way to anger, and she took a frustrated swipe at a tear that streaked down her face. Why did Evelyn Landon have to spoil everything? Why did she even have to be here? How differently the evening would have progressed had Evelyn and her friends not been at Wyeburn when they arrived. Jared would not have fought with Damon. And she and Jared would not have quarreled.

And we would be spending the night together as man and wife, she thought.

"Damn you, Evelyn!" she swore aloud. "I'm not going to let you come between us!"

There was a soft knock at the door, and the maid Jarina had sent away entered the room. "Your trunk, m'lady," she said apologetically. She stepped to one side to allow the two men carrying her trunk to pass. The men lowered her trunk to the floor and left the room, and the maid started to follow.

"Wait," Jarina called out.

The girl stopped.

Jared is yours, you fool. Evelyn can only have him back if you let her.

Jarina reached a decision. "Will you do something for me?"

"Whatever you wish, m'lady."

It's time you stopped being such a coward and took control of your fate.

Jarina had to take several deep breaths to steady herself, but when she finally spoke, there was a note of renewed determination in her voice. "Please, find out where my husband went, then come straight back here. Don't tell anyone I was asking about him."

The girl looked surprised, but if she found Jarina's request unusual, she kept her observations to herself. She hastened to do her lady's bidding.

It was all Jarina could do not to fly after the girl and put a stop to the errand on which she had just sent her, and the effort required to remain where she was caused her to begin trembling uncontrollably. The insanity of what she was about to do astounded her, and she still wasn't sure she had the courage to carry out her own plan.

Yet, if she did not, she sternly reminded herself, the price she would pay would be unbearable.

She would lose Jared forever.

And Evelyn would have won.

After her nerves had been calmed by a warm bath and a cup of tea, Jarina slipped unseen from the house and started down the hill. She did not carry a lantern; the maid who had helped her locate Jared had pointed the way to the bank barn where he was last seen, and the light streaming from the house windows illuminated her path. Her breath fogged in the damp night air. She suppressed a shiver and drew her cloak tighter about her. "Please, still be there," she prayed.

The maze of outbuildings that formed the working portion of the farm were connected by long corridors that sheltered the servants from the weather during the winter. The two-story bank barn was the oldest of the buildings. It was nestled snugly into the hillside so that the lower level was below ground on one side, protecting it from the northwest winds.

Jarina carefully made her way down the steep bank and eased open the door.

The inside of the barn was softly lighted by lanterns that hung from the rafters, well out of the way of the bales of hay that had been stored for the winter.

She did not see Jared anywhere.

Her pulse had begun to race fearfully. What if Jared would not listen to her? Worse than that, suppose he laughed? Even being the object of his anger was better than being ridiculed, especially when her entire future hung in the balance.

Determined not to give up, now that she had come this far, she stepped inside the barn and closed the heavy door, wincing as the rusting hinges squealed a loud protest.

"What are you doing here?"

Jarina whirled around.

Jared emerged from the shadows and drove the pitchfork he was carrying into the hay. He was not wearing either a cloak or a sweater. His white shirt was open at the neck and clung to his sweat-dampened chest. "I asked you a question," he clipped. He took a step toward her. "What are you doing here?"

Jarina's heart stuck in her throat. "I-I need to talk to you," she said, annoyed with herself for stammering when she had already rehearsed her lines a hundred times. She was glad her cloak hid her trembling hands.

"I'm working."

"Jared, please . . ."

The muscle in his jaw twitched, but he said nothing. He glared at her through narrowed eyes.

She nervously moistened her lips. "Are we . . . alone?"

"Damn it, Jarina! Say what you have to say, then get the hell out of here. I have work to do."

Any other time, she would have turned and fled. Perhaps it was a measure of her desperation that she did not. Perhaps she was merely growing accustomed to Jared's temper. Only one thing was certain: she was out of her mind. She swallowed hard. "I wanted to apologize . . . for reacting the way I did . . . when I found Evelyn's belongings in your bedchamber. I was jealous . . . and hurt. I couldn't bear the thought of you holding her and . . . and . . ." *Loving her.* She broke off, unable to make herself say the words. "I'm sorry," she finished lamely.

Jared's expression did not change. "Are you finished?" he asked curtly.

Stung by his uncompromising tone, she bristled. "No, I'm not."

Silence, tense and punishing, stretched between them like the calm before the storm. Were the sky to open and strike them both with a bolt of lightning, Jarina would not have been surprised. She could *feel* the coiled anger that emanated from her husband in heated waves.

And she could feel her own resolve rapidly crumbling.

"My lord," she began slowly. "I know . . . I once said I would never come to you willingly . . ."

She saw Jared's chest expand as the simple act of breathing suddenly seemed to require an enormous amount of effort. "I'm waiting," he said, his voice oddly hoarse.

"I want . . ." She faltered. Wrestling down her rising panic, she took a deep breath and began again. "I want you to make love to me."

Chapter Twelve

The expression in Jared's eyes became hard and unreadable as stone. He did not move, but stood staring at Jarina with an intensity that seemed to slice through her soul.

Why did he not say something?

"I don't want to revert to the way things were aboard the *Pegasus*," Jarina said, her tormented mind groping frantically for an explanation to what must have seemed a bizarre request. "I hate living like this, with walls and closed doors and angry words between us. I'm not asking you to love me, only to let me be a wife to you. I *want* to be your wife. I want to bear your children."

He still said nothing.

Jarina's heart felt as though it would shatter, but she had to try one more time. "I love you," she whispered achingly.

A low oath exploded in Jared's throat.

Jarina froze as he came toward her, his forceful strides reverberating through the plank flooring. A silent scream rose from somewhere deep inside her, and she instinctively braced herself. Her stomach somersaulted. Jared reached for her and her knees buckled.

Jared caught her and yanked her against him. His mouth came down hard over hers.

There was a hungry violence in Jared's kiss that terrified Jarina at the same time that it awakened something in her that was both primitive and unrestrained. She rose up on tiptoe and leaned into him, wrapping her arms tightly about his neck as his hands rushed over her back and hips with frenzied urgency, pulling her to him. She could not control what she was feeling. Her heart raced with fear. Her body burned with longing.

After several long moments, Jared tore his mouth from hers. He gathered her close and held her tightly as he fought to get his own rampaging emotions under control. He warned himself to slow down. He did not want to frighten her. He knew he should take her back to the house and continue this in the privacy of her bedchamber, yet he wanted her so badly, his body refused to be denied. He felt as though he had been waiting his entire life for Jarina; he could not wait a moment longer. He drew her into the shadows and lowered her to the sweet-scented hay.

Jarina's hands moved up over his chest to twine about his neck and she pulled him down with her as he bore her into the hay. Her lips eagerly sought his.

Jared kissed her tenderly. Fiercely. His tongue flicked over her lips, tasting them, teasing them, then gently parting them to explore the honeyed sweetness within. He kissed her with long, lingering, erotic kisses that caused her head to swim and which made her forget everything except the wonder of lying wrapped in his strong arms.

He unfastened her cloak and spread it open. His hands made fast work of her nightgown, and within moments it lay on the hay beside them.

Framing her face with his hands, he brushed his lips over her eyelids, the delicate curve of her brow, and down her cheek. "My God, you are sweet," he breathed, then he tenderly, lovingly kissed her again.

His hand trailed down along her throat, across her breast, and came to rest on her ribcage. His thumb gently stroked the soft underside of her breast, and the touch of his work-roughened fingers sent a delicious heat spiraling through her. Everywhere he touched, her skin tingled with aching need.

Jared cupped her breasts in his hands and lifted them and gently caressed them. He feathered his fingertips across her nipples, coaxing the delicate pink crests into tight little buds. Her skin was warm and still slightly damp from her bath, and as he lowered his head to her breast, Jared drank deeply of the soft clean scent of her. He heard her sharp intake of breath when he touched his lips to her heated flesh. Then his lips parted and he drew her nipple into his mouth. Jarina moaned and threaded her fingers through his hair, holding him there as though she never wanted him to leave.

There was sweet agony in the sharp, almost painful, sensations that shot rhythmically through her body, piercing stabs of desire so intense that she felt as though she were on fire. His hand moved downward over her abdomen and she arched against him, her body straining for the pleasure his fingers promised as they slid possessively into the soft triangle between her legs.

Wave after wave of delirious warmth crested over her, carrying her higher and higher, until she felt as though she were teetering on the brink of something that was both wonderful and terrifying. She felt like a bowstring that had been pulled to the limit of its resilience, then beyond.

Then Jared's mouth followed the same path his hand had forged, and the bowstring snapped. A low scream tore from Jarina's throat and her hips surged upward.

Jared caught her hips and held them fast, denying her escape from his intimate exploring. His hands cupped her bottom and he lifted her even higher, and Jarina thought she would die of pure pleasure. She made soft mewling sounds deep in her throat and flung

her head from side to side as Jared brought her from
one shuddering peak to another, each one more intense
than the one before. Then her body went rigid and she
cried out Jared's name as a liquid fire engulfed her,
driving her over the edge into sweet oblivion.

Slowly, gently, he lowered her to the ground. He
pulled away from her and quickly shed his own clothes,
then rejoined her on the cloak and gathered her into
his arms.

A low sob broke in Jarina's throat and she clung to
him in wonder and confusion as another tremor shook
her body like the aftershock of an earthquake. She felt
as though she were drifting down through a warm mist.
She wanted to ask Jared what had happened, but her
tongue suddenly seemed incapable of speech. Before
she could gather her wits, he was again caressing her
with gentle, skillful hands, urging her back up to the
drugging, dizzying heights from which she had just descended. He stroked her breasts and her back and the
soft flesh of her inner thighs until she was twisting and
moaning incoherently beneath him. He covered her
mouth with his and she tasted herself in his kiss as he
devoured her with a tender violence that left her trembling and aching for more.

Then she felt him part her legs and lower his body
to hers, and the painful memories she had tried to banish from her thoughts suddenly intruded, bringing her
crashing back down to earth. The delirium that had
been so sweet only seconds ago was now a nightmare
from which she was desperately clawing. In sheer
panic, she stiffened and clamped her thighs together.
She placed her palms flat against Jared's chest and tried
to shove him off her, but he captured her hands and
held them against his pounding heart. "Jarina, don't,"
he commanded, his voice harsh with the effort of con-
trolling his own raging passions.

Shame washed over her at the realization of what she
had done. In the soft light from the lantern she saw the

look of tender concern in Jared's gaze, and hot tears filled her eyes. Her bottom lip quivered uncontrollably. "I'm sorry," she murmured wretchedly. "I don't mean to be such a coward."

Regret flashed in Jared's eyes, and he wondered how he could ever have hurt her. Worse, if he continued on his present course, he would only hurt her again, no matter how gentle he tried to be. Fighting down his own body's punishing demands, he gently drew her hands up to his mouth and brushed his lips across the backs of her knuckles. "Jarina, you are no coward," he said with a quiet firmness that defied objection. "The fact that you willingly came to me tonight when I have given you every reason to fear and hate me attests to your courage. On the night we met, I did something to you I had never done to a woman: I forced you. No, that's not accurate. Force is too kind a word for what I did. I *raped* you."

Jared's words so startled Jarina that she opened her mouth to protest, but he silenced her with a slight shake of his head.

"It was rape, pure and simple," he continued in a low, pained voice. "I took my pleasure with no thought for you—or for the price I would pay for my selfishness. The guilt over what I did to you haunts me still. Night after night, I lay awake, filled with self-loathing for having hurt you, yet wanting you so much I ache. I cannot nullify what I did to you. I can only show you that physical love between a man and a woman is something to be enjoyed, not feared. I want to make love to you, Jarina. I want to make you forget what I did to you before. I promise not to hurt you. But, I will not force you. If you are not ready for this, we can wait."

It had never occurred to Jarina that Jared's memories of that night were no less painful than hers. His admission, as well as his willingness to wait until she was ready, made her throat ache. He too was haunted by ghosts, she realized. Only Jared's ghosts were far worse than hers because they were of his own making. She, at least, could place the blame elsewhere; Jared could not.

What she could do, however, was help free him of those ghosts.

Jarina forced herself to relax, and willed her legs to part. "I'm ready now," she said softly, giving him a tremulous smile that asked as well as gave forgiveness.

Her slight movements beneath him nearly broke Jared's control. Sweat dampened his forehead, and his face was hard and dark with the effort of holding back. "Are you certain?" he asked thickly.

So there would be no doubt, no more misunderstandings, Jarina brought her hand down between them, and Jared sucked in his breath as her warm fingers closed intimately around him; then she gently, but firmly, guided him to her. "Yes, I'm certain," she whispered.

Jared's resistance shattered.

Jarina unconsciously braced herself for pain as he eased into her, then gasped in bewilderment when there was none, only an unfamiliar fullness.

Jared pulled partway out, then plunged deeper, and deeper still, until she relaxed and instinctively opened to him; and he drove his full length into her sweet warmth. Ignoring the throbbing ache in his loins, he began to move gently within her, watching her face, feeling her body's responses as though they were his own. He memorized the unguarded emotions that paraded across her lovely face as she met his gaze with one of trusting innocence. He delighted in the way the dazed wonder in her eyes gave way to surprise as his slow, agonizing movements suddenly increased in force and tempo. He wanted to know what pleased her and what did not. He wanted to give her what she had been denied the first time he'd had her. He wanted to make it perfect for her.

If Jared's earlier caresses had brought almost immediate reward with their quick, piercing stabs of pleasure, the feel of him inside her ignited a fire in her belly that slowly uncurled and spread its intoxicating warmth through her limbs, and Jarina found herself arching into him, her body straining for the fulfillment he promised with his deep, driving thrusts. Her breathing quickened. Her fingers closed around a fistful of hay that she clutched with a white-knuckled grip as he coaxed her higher than she had ever been before. She squeezed her eyes shut and threw back her head, and her chest rose and fell with her rapid, frantic gasps. "Oh . . . Jared—" she sobbed.

"Don't fight it, sweet," Jared whispered hoarsely. "Just let it happen. This is the way it should be." *This is the way it should have been the first time,* he added silently. His thrusts became faster and deeper.

The liquid fire that had been slowly building inside her exploded with a force that made her cry out. Her back arched and she drove her hips hard against him. Staving off his own ease a few seconds more, Jared wrapped his arms around her and crushed her to him, his body absorbing the impact of her tumultuous climax as wave after wave of delicious heat washed over her, rocking her with shuddering spasms that seemed as though they would never end. Then he slowly withdrew and drove into her one final time, joining her in sweet release.

Not wanting to crush her with his weight, he eased himself off her and rolled to his side. He slid one arm beneath Jarina's shoulders, intending to take her with him, but his body was sapped of all strength and he collapsed onto his back instead, with one arm trapped beneath his wife and the other flung out at his side. He drew in a deep, restoring breath and stared fixedly up at the rafters. The chill night air played havoc with his heated flesh.

Beside him, he heard a noise that sounded suspiciously like a muffled giggle, and he turned his head to find Jarina watching him with shining eyes. Her face was flushed and bits of straw clung to her hair and he thought she had never looked so beautiful. She bit down on her bottom lip in a futile attempt to smother a laugh. "Oh, Jared," she blurted out, grinning broadly at him, "I feel utterly *scandalous!*"

A less secure man might have been wounded by her laughter; instead, Jared found the corners of his own mouth twitching involuntarily. Before he could respond, a picture flashed through his mind of the two of them sprawled on the hay like a couple of hounds who had exhausted themselves chasing each other through the pasture, and his shoulders began to shake with silent mirth.

Jarina clamped her hands over her mouth as she was seized with a fit of giggles, but the effort to stifle her hilarity resulted in an inelegant snort that brought a hoot of laughter from Jared. He pulled Jarina against him and held her tight, burying his face in her hair and reveling in the warmth of her body against his. Still laughing, she wrapped an arm around his waist and snuggled deeper into the warm security of his embrace. She was happier than she had been in a long time. She felt safe. She felt loved. She breathed a long sigh of contentment and tilted her head up to look at him. Her eyes glowed. "I wish we could stay here all night," she said softly.

Threading his fingers through her hair, Jared lifted her face to his and kissed her tenderly. "Your wish, madam, is my command," he murmured against her mouth. He eased his arm from beneath her and rolled easily to his feet. "Wait here."

Jarina's breath caught in her throat as she watched Jared walk away, and her heart swelled with a fierce pride at the knowledge that such a magnificent man was her husband. Never, even in her wildest dreams, had she imagined she would someday be married to a man who was so splendidly tall, so strong, so commanding. Or—she smiled dreamily—so devastatingly handsome.

Jared returned with the lap furs from the carriage. He spread them on the hay and extinguished the lanterns, and within moments, he lay with Jarina cradled once more against his chest. "*Now* we can stay here all night," he teased in the darkness.

Jared's skin was like cold, smooth marble next to hers, and Jarina shivered as she snuggled against him beneath the furs. Jared kissed the top of her head and gently stroked her hip. His heart beat soothingly against her cheek. Gradually their bodies warmed.

Jarina was the first to break the languid silence that had settled over them. "Is this where you are going to keep your horses?" she asked.

"For a time," Jared said. "The stables need to be expanded, and more stalls added. I thought this would be a good place for the horses while the construction is ongoing." He paused, then added pensively, "This barn will require a great deal of work too. It hasn't been used in years."

Jared's voice trailed off and Jarina could not help thinking he was referring less to the barn than to how long he had been away. "Are you sorry you came home?" she asked.

He smiled at her ability to probe his thoughts. "A little," he admitted reluctantly. "Returning made me remember why I left in the first place."

Jarina absently trailed her fingers across Jared's chest. "Surely not all your memories of Wyeburn are unhappy ones?" she prompted gently.

"Not all." He chuckled. "At least, not of the barn."

For hours, they lay in each other's arms, touching each other with gentle, unhurried caresses and whispering shared secrets in the dark like old friends who had years of catching up to do. Jared talked of his plans for Wyeburn. He told Jarina of the changes he wanted to make to the barn and the other outbuildings. He talked of his ships and his plans for selling the company. And the more he told Jarina, the more he realized he wanted to share with her. Never had Jared felt so at peace with himself, or with the world.

Jarina traced a forefinger along the puckered scar on Jared's thigh. "Does it still hurt?" she asked.

"I seldom notice it anymore. You did a fine job with the needle, madam. I shudder to think what would have happened had you not been there to keep Fitch at bay."

A long moment of silence passed, and when Jarina finally spoke, her voice was so low Jared had to strain to hear her. "I thought you were going to die," she whispered.

Jared's hand stilled on her hip. Suppose he *had* died? Suppose something were to happen to him now? He had not yet changed his will. Not only would Damon inherit his holdings, but now, to a lesser extent, Evelyn would as well. And Jarina would be left penniless and homeless.

First thing tomorrow morning, he was returning to Alexandria to pay a visit to his solicitor. He wanted to be certain that Jarina's future was secure. He did not want to leave her at Damon's mercy.

He also had a score to settle with one Stephen Landon.

"Tell me something," Jared said, changing the subject. "Why you did you have Angus boil the instruments? I have known plenty of leeches, and to my knowledge, not one ever boils a blade before using it."

"It was my father's belief that if tainted meat could be made fit to eat by thorough cooking, then tainted flesh could be freed of infection by the same."

The thought of having his leg lowered into a stew kettle made Jared swear under his breath. "Damn!"

Jarina smiled at his reaction. "Furthermore," she continued, "since the flesh does not become fevered until after it is opened, either by injury or incision, it stands to reason that infection is introduced from outside the body, possibly even by the very same instruments that are used in surgery. So my father boiled his instruments to rid them of whatever malevolent properties they possessed."

Jared brushed a wayward curl off her cheek. "Was it also his practice to use two entire bottles of expensive brandy to cleanse a wound?"

He had spoken with such seriousness that Jarina thought he was angry. She looked at him and caught the bright flash of his smile in the darkness. "I'm afraid not," she answered primly, matching his grave tone. "My father would not have panicked as I did. He would have had the foresight to use cheap rum on the wound and saved the brandy for himself."

When Jared finished laughing, he gave her shoulders an affectionate squeeze. "Your father was a wise man, sweet. It's a pity he did not live long enough to share his discoveries with the rest of the medical world."

Hearing her father referred to in past terms when he was still very much alive brought a lump to Jarina's throat. She no longer harbored any resentment toward him for the part he had played in her betrothal to the Duke of Roswell. She did, however, worry about him. The duke was not a forgiving man. What price would he extract from her father for her disappearance?

Jared sensed the sudden change in Jarina, and her silence disturbed him. "What are you thinking?" he prodded gently.

Jarina sighed. "I was merely wondering at the strange twists and turns my life's path has taken these past months," she said pensively.

A troubled frown creased Jared's brow. "Do you regret not staying in England and marrying the man your guardian chose for you?"

Jarina turned her face against his chest, and he heard her utter a smothered laugh. "What is it?" he prompted.

She shook her head. "Nothing."

"What?" he persisted.

Jarina bit down on her bottom lip, and she felt her face grow unbearably warm. She was glad it was dark so Jared could not see her embarrassment. "I was thinking," she said self-consciously, almost shyly, "that His Grace would not have pleased me nearly so much as you."

Two completely unrelated thoughts sprang to Jared's mind at her remark. The first was that the man to whom she had been betrothed was a duke. The second was that she had enjoyed his lovemaking, and that confirmation brought a satisfied chuckle from him. Raising up on one elbow, he rolled Jarina onto her back and pinned her beneath him. His hand moved up her thigh to stroke her most sensitive spot. "Shall I attempt to please you again?" he asked huskily.

Smiling happily, Jarina reached her arms about her husband's neck and pulled him down toward her. "I think, my lord, I would like that very much . . ."

Later, sated and content, Jarina relaxed in Jared's arms. Within moments her breathing changed and her weight against his side suddenly grew heavier.

Sleep did not come so easily to Jared, and he lay awake, listening to the wind as it gained strength and velocity. His mind raced. He had not wondered in weeks about the man to whom Jarina was once betrothed; now he could not put him from his thoughts. When Jarina had referred to him as *His Grace,* she had unwittingly revealed his position. Now Jared was suddenly obsessed with learning more about the man from whom Jarina had fled.

A particularly strong gust shook the barn's timbers.

Jarina stirred. "Is that the wind?" she whispered.

"It's going to storm," Jared said. "I think, love, we had best forego our night in the barn until we know for certain that the roof doesn't leak."

Jared dressed quickly and helped Jarina put on her nightgown. He gathered up her slippers and her cloak and bundled her into one of the lap furs.

"I can walk," Jarina protested sleepily as he lifted her in his arms.

"I would prefer to carry you."

Jarina wrapped her arm around his neck and nestled her head against his shoulder. Her eyelids drooped. "You're a very romantic man," she murmured.

"No," Jared corrected dryly. "Only a practical one. You are tired, and you can stumble in the dark and hurt yourself.

In spite of his denial, Jarina could tell from Jared's tone that her remark had pleased him. Her arrogant, cynical husband had more soft spots in his world-weary heart than he was willing to acknowledge, and she enjoyed being the one to find them.

The house was dark and still as Jared carried her through the hall and up the stairs.

Jarina lifted her head off Jared's shoulder and wrinkled her nose. "I can still smell the perfume," she said.

Jared chuckled. "You have a powerful right arm, sweet. I'm thankful I wasn't in the way when you lost your temper."

Jarina's expression sobered. "I'm sorry I threw the perfume," she said contritely.

Neither of them saw the gentle glow of a flame in the darkness or smelled the tobacco smoke or felt the intense gaze that followed them up the stairs.

In the shadows, Damon took a long draw on his cigar. Above him, he heard Jarina laugh softly at Jared's whispered remark, and then he heard the door of her bedchamber close. Pushing himself away from the wall, he went to the stairs and bent down to get a closer look at the piece of hay he had seen fall from Jarina's hair. He picked up the seedstalk, and an unpleasant smile curled his hard mouth as he crushed it in his hand.

*   *   *

Jarina awoke to the sound of rain lashing against the window. She rolled onto her side and burrowed deeper beneath the covers, but sleep eluded her. After a while, she turned onto her back and lay listening to the storm. Beside her, the sheets were cold, and she wondered how long Jared had been up.

She yawned and stretched with lazy contentment. When they had returned to the house last night, Jared had made love to her yet again before finally blowing out the candles, and she had fallen asleep in his arms, exhausted but happy. Now she missed him, and she wished he would come back to bed.

The bedroom door opened a fraction and Maggie stuck her head into the room. "So you are awake," Maggie said, beaming at her as she came in carrying an armful of clean towels. "Mr. Jared was up and about hours ago, but he said to let you sleep."

Wrestling with a pang of disappointment, Jarina sat up. "It sounds as if it's raining hard," she said, making a halfhearted attempt at polite conversation.

Maggie put the towels on a low stool beside the bathing tub. "It rained most of the night," she said when she returned to the bedchamber. "The run overflowed its banks. That's why Mr. Jared left the house as early as he did. He wanted to get across the run before the bridge washed out."

Jarina felt as though she had received a blow between the eyes. "Jared's gone?" she asked incredulously.

"He said to tell you he'll be back as soon as he can. There was some business with his solicitor that needed tending to, he said."

A puzzled frown wrinkled Jarina's brow. Jared had not said anything to her about seeing a solicitor.

"He won't have any trouble getting through in this weather though, seeing as how he's on horseback," Maggie continued. "Unfortunately, *they* won't be leaving anytime soon."

Jarina did not need to ask who *they* were. Sighing deeply, she pushed back the covers and dropped her feet over the side of the bed. "Just how many of *them* are there?" she asked.

Maggie's shoulders shook with suppressed mirth at Jarina's dry tone. "Twenty-two, to be exact," she said. "Twenty-three counting Miss Evelyn."

Twenty-three! Jarina's eyes grew wide and round as she stared at the housekeeper in disbelief. How was she going to keep twenty-three people whom she did not know entertained until Jared returned?

As if reading her thoughts, Maggie chuckled softly. "Long as you don't have any objection to using the back stairs, you can slip down to the kitchen with me and take some breakfast without anyone else knowing you're up and about. Before anything else though, let's see if we can't do something about that hair."

An hour later, Jarina sat in Wyeburn's spacious kitchen enjoying a sumptuous breakfast of coddled eggs, Welsh rarebit, smoked sausages, beaten biscuits with thin slivers of Virginia ham, and a compote of peaches, pears, and dark, sweet cherries. Pushing her plate away, she leaned back in her chair and sighed contentedly. "If I eat another bite, I'm going to burst," she told Cook.

"These young girls today, always worrying about their figures," Cook grumbled. "They're scared to death to have a little meat on their bones." In spite of her complaining, she noted with satisfaction that Jarina had put away a healthy portion and was not a finicky eater.

To the astonishment of all the servants, Jarina got up from the table and began scraping the dishes she had eaten from. Fiona threw Cook a horrified glance, and Cook, in turn, looked to Maggie. But Maggie merely compressed her lips in warning and shook her head.

Jarina glanced up just in time to see the silent exchange, and she froze. "Is something wrong?" she asked.

Cook lowered her head over the stew vegetables she was preparing and began chopping furiously.

Evanston coughed and excused himself from the room.

One by one, the servants all turned away and resumed their tasks.

Tears pricked behind Jarina's eyelids and choked her throat. It did not matter to her whether or not she won the approval of Jared's friends, but she had hoped that these people who worked for Jared and who held him in such high regard—who loved him as much as she did—would accept her as one of their own. She could see now that she had been wrong. She put down the plate she had been scraping and wiped her hands on a towel. "Please excuse me," she said shakily. "I did not mean to intrude." With as much dignity as she could summon, she started toward the door.

"If that don't beat all!" Maggie scolded. "Child, you just get yourself back in here and stop all this nonsense about intruding. This is your house and you're welcome to go anywhere in it you want. We just don't know what to make of you yet, is all. The old Mrs. Cunningham would not have been seen dead in the kitchen, and here you are with your sleeves rolled up."

Jarina was genuinely bewildered. She could not imagine a woman *not* wanting to have a hand in the workings of her own home, and she said as much.

"You can help me air the beds," volunteered a timid voice by the fireplace.

Maggie rounded on the little maid whom Jarina had sent to find Jared last night. "Airing the beds is *your* duty, Mary, and don't you go tryin' to get out of it." Maggie turned to Jarina. "If you want something to do, why don't you make up a tray and carry it up to Finley? He's been chomping at the bit to meet you ever since he heard Mr. Jared had got himself married."

If the other servants did not know what to make of Jarina, Arthur Finley had no such difficulty. "If it offends you, clean it up," he said bluntly when he saw her observing his discarded clothes lying strewn about the chamber.

That he was testing her was so obvious Jarina could not help smiling. "It does offend me," she said pleasantly as she placed the tray on the foot of the bed where he sat with his splinted and wrapped leg propped up up against a pillow. "But I'm not your keeper. You'll have to clean up your own mess."

The old man burst out laughing. "Well, if you ain't a cheeky one! Just like that husband of yours. Pull up a chair, girl. You and me got some getting acquainted to do."

Over the next hour, Jarina discovered she liked the gardener thoroughly. He was honest and straightforward. He was not in the least intimidated by her status as his employer's wife, yet he called her Mrs. Cunningham with an ease and dignity that made Jarina feel as though she had been born to the position.

He was also willing to answer Jarina's pointed questions regarding the relationship between Jared and Damon.

"Now, you're a smart enough lady to be able to figure out that your husband did plenty of sowing his wild oats before he wed you; and he wasn't always discrete, either. Well, the old duke weren't no different. Only his galavantin' about the countryside didn't come to an end when he got married."

Now that Jarina had tasted the full draught of Jared's love, it sickened her to think that he might turn elsewhere to satisfy his needs.

"Well, the old duke was a jealous sort," Finley continued. "And because his own actions weren't above reproach, he was quick to point a finger elsewhere. Call it guilt, if you will, but when Mrs. Cunningham be-

friended that poor peddler, the duke swore to high
heaven that she was beddin' him."

Jarina was afraid to draw a breath. "Was she?" she
asked.

"Well, you gotta remember," Finley advised her,
"that the old Mrs. Cunningham weren't like you. She
weren't the kind to sit and chat with servants, or with
anyone else below her station. So when she brung that
man in out of the rain and give him a hot meal, it raised
more than a few eyebrows around here."

Jarina nervously moistened her lips. "You don't believe she was unfaithful, do you?"

Finley shook his head. "Pardon me for sayin' so, but
the old Mrs. Cunningham was a prissy snot. She was
all-fired concerned with what everyone was going to
say about her behind her back, she was tightfisted with
a penny, and she was meaner than hell to anyone who
rubbed her the wrong way." He paused. "But, she
weren't the kind to break her vows. It woulda gone
against her grain."

Jarina toyed with the folds of her skirt. "Then, Jared
and Damon could very well be full brothers," she said.

The old man nodded.

"Does Jared know all this?"

"Sometimes it's not a matter of what you know, but
what you're willing to believe," Finley said quietly.

After giving his words some thought, Jarina shook
her head. "It seems such a waste," she said sadly, "All
these years of discord because of what may have been
nothing more than a simple case of misbegotten jealousy."

The gardener agreed. "However," he was quick to
caution, "I wouldn't go about feeling too sorry for Mr.
Damon, if I were you. There's no accounting for bad
seed, and Damon's a bad one, through and through,
regardless of who his sire was."

In the days that followed, Jarina had little time to
think about either Jared or Damon or the misconcep-

tion that had shaped their lives since birth. There was too much to see and do at Wyeburn.

The rain brought with it a spell of warm weather, and spring erupted into full bloom almost without warning. The grass greened and the trees budded out and everywhere Jarina looked, azaleas announced their presence with brilliant bursts of color. Finley grew restless in the confines of the house, and Jarina had him carried out to the garden where he could oversee the planting. When she was not busy in the kitchen or helping with the other household chores, Jarina could often be found in the garden, digging a flower border or sowing seeds or transplanting a shrub at Finley's direction.

Lyman Carter and his sister left for Richmond, and Jarina was not sorry to see them go. Unfortunately, the rest of Evelyn's houseguests seemed disinclined to return to their own homes, and Jarina found their continued presence at Wyeburn both an annoyance and an inconvenience. She was not certain how much license she had in asking them to leave, and deemed it best to simply let the matter ride until Jared returned. She saw very little of Damon, and that only in passing. And she didn't see Evelyn at all.

"Miss Evelyn took to her bed with a sick headache," Mary told her one night as she eased her sore muscles down into the hot bathwater.

Jarina leaned back in the tub and closed her eyes. "Did anyone make a tisane for her?" she asked wearily.

"Maggie did, but Miss Evelyn refused to drink it. She said Maggie was trying to poison her."

If Maggie doesn't, I just might, Jarina thought. She made a mental note to prepare something for her in the morning. If Evelyn was going to be staying at Wyeburn awhile longer, the least she could do was be civil to the woman.

"I don't know why you'd even *want* to be nice to her," Maggie said the next morning when Jarina asked her for Rosemary and Catmint to make an herbal infusion. "She wouldn't even open her door for me yesterday when I took her that tea."

Although it was the truth, Jarina could not very well say it was because she wanted Evelyn to hurry and recover so she would go home. Instead, she said, "My father had plenty of patients that he did not like, yet he never turned anyone away. I suppose it's a trait I inherited from him."

Maggie snorted. "When you harbor a viper in your midst, you're going to get bit, I always say." She paused, then added meaningfully, "I haven't been wrong yet."

An hour later, when Jarina carried the tea tray up the stairs to the guest wing, she could not help praying that, just this once, Maggie would be wrong.

She received no response to her knock, but the movements she had heard behind the door suddenly ceased. She took a steadying breath. "Evelyn, it's Jarina," she said. "I've brought you an herbal tea for your headache."

A long moment of silence passed, then Jarina heard what sounded like weeping. She heard shuffled footsteps approach the door, and a key turned in the lock.

The door eased open a fraction, then wider, and Jarina nearly dropped the tray. She gasped and her eyes widened in horror. "Evelyn!" she choked. "What happened to you?"

Chapter Thirteen

Evelyn dabbed at her eyes with her handkerchief. "Oh, Jarina," she blurted out. "I didn't know what to do. I couldn't let anyone see me like this, and I don't have anyone else to go to."

Jarina went into the room and set the tea tray down on a small, round breakfast table. "Let me see your eye," she said.

Evelyn sniffled and obediently tilted her head to one side so Jarina could see the purple-black swelling that ringed her left eye and extended down over her cheekbone. Because it had not taken on the yellowish tinge of a bruise well on its way toward healing, Jarina knew it had to have been inflicted within the past day; and it disturbed her to think that whoever had struck Evelyn could be someone they were harboring under their very roof. "Who did this to you?" she asked.

Evelyn's chin quivered and a tear streamed down her cheek. "I-I can't tell you," she stammered.

Jarina's heart went out to the older woman, but she could not allow her personal feelings to stand in the way of bringing Evelyn's attacker to justice. Taking Evelyn by the arm, she led her to the breakfast table and pulled out a chair. "Sit down and drink some of the tea I brought you. Then we can talk."

Evelyn docilely obeyed.

Jarina could not help feeling sorry for Evelyn. Her hair and clothes were unkempt and her face drawn and pinched. She looked far older than she had the night they first met. As she watched Evelyn slowly sip the herb tea, Jarina began to wonder if she had misjudged her. She could not hate the woman anymore than she could blame her for wanting to keep Jared. Jared was her heart and her life. She would fight anyone who tried to take him from her.

Evelyn put down her teacup, and Jarina tried again. "Evelyn, I need to know who did this to you. Is it someone staying in this house?"

Evelyn buried her face in her hands and her shoulders began to shake with sobs. "I can't tell you."

Struggling to keep from losing her patience, Jarina took a deep breath. "Was it one of the guests?" she asked.

Evelyn shook her head.

Then, who? Jarina wondered, her brows drawing together in concentration. Damon? One of the servants? Perhaps later Evelyn would be more inclined to reveal the identity of the person who had struck her. She stood up. "I'm going down to the kitchen to see if Maggie has any Linseed and Comfrey that I can use to make a hot poultice for you to put over your eye. It will help the swelling go down." She paused, then added in a quiet, but uncompromising tone, "Until I know who did this to you, none of the women in this house is safe. If you don't tell me who he is, and he hurts someone else, I will hold you responsible."

Jarina turned and started toward the door.

Behind her came Evelyn's voice, low but distinctly audible. "It was Jared," she said.

Jarina froze. Icy prickles rose up on her skin and made her hair feel as though it were standing on end. There was a sick churning in her stomach as she turned back to face Evelyn.

Evelyn pushed herself to her feet. "I didn't want to tell you," she choked out, wringing her hands. "It happened the night you arrived at Wyeburn. When Jared left your bedchamber, he came to mine. He was so furious. He said the two of you had quarreled. He said he wanted me. When I refused him, he became violent. That's why I've been staying in here all this time. I didn't want you to know . . ." Her voice trailed off.

Angry color flushed Jarina's face. How could she have been so gullible? Dear God! Why had she not heeded Maggie's warning?

Jarina lifted her chin and her eyes glittered dangerously. "If Jared did strike you," she said slowly, her voice unusually calm, "it would be no more than you deserve. You have insinuated yourself into this household; you have abused Jared's hospitality; and you have insulted me. I may be an infant in your eyes, but I am not stupid. Even a child could tell that your bruise is no more than a few hours old, not a week as you would have me believe. Jared did not strike you, but someone did. If you haven't the decency to tell me who, then at least do me the courtesy of staying out of my sight. You are no longer welcome in this house, Miss Landon. The sooner you leave, the better."

Her head held high, Jarina turned and walked serenely out the door.

She heard a shriek, followed by a splintering crash as Evelyn hurled something against the closed door. Jarina fled down the hall to the sanctuary of her own bedchamber and slammed the door behind her. Trembling violently, she wrapped her arms around her knotted stomach and sank to her knees. Rage gripped her insides with a crippling intensity. She wanted to lash out at something. Or someone. She wanted to run back to Evelyn's bedchamber and say all the hateful things she was not able to think of earlier. She wanted to hurt Evelyn as deeply as she had been hurt. She wanted to witness the anguish in Evelyn's eyes when she told her she and Jared had spent a wonderful, exquisite night together.

But to do so would only defile the love you feel for Jared, she sternly reminded herself.

She shuddered. What was happening to her? Why was she allowing Evelyn to affect her so? It was clear the woman was trying to destroy her marriage; she could not allow Evelyn to destroy her instead.

A chilling suggestion invaded her thoughts.

Suppose the bruise on Evelyn's face had not been a new one? An hour had passed from the time Jared stormed from her bedchamber until she found him in the barn. Given a different set of circumstances, would she still be so quick to defend him?

He *had* been furious that night, and with good reason. Yet she had seen him equally furious many times. She had seen grown men quake in fear at his bellowed commands. Time after time, she had been reduced to tears by his cutting rebukes.

Was Jared capable of striking a woman? Yes.

Would he? She thought not. Not once, no matter how angry he had been with her, had he ever raised a hand against her.

She remembered the way she felt when Jared held her in his arms, and her fears calmed. Jared was a strong man, strong enough to kill with his bare hands. Strong enough to make her feel safe. Strong enough to be gentle.

She sighed and leaned her head back against the doorframe. She hoped she was strong enough to persevere until Jared returned.

"Look at you, old man! Tracking mud through my clean kitchen!"

Angus grinned. "Ah, Maggie, ye'll never change, will ye? Harpin' about clean floors when it's a big kiss ye're wanting."

Maggie wagged a finger at him. "You had best keep

your distance, you no-account Scot! And take off those filthy boots!"

Heedless of the curious stares they were drawing from the other servants, Angus crossed the kitchen with quick strides. Maggie let out a squeal of surprise when he seized her around the waist, all but lifting her off the floor as he hugged her to him. He planted a hearty kiss on her lips, then gently set her down, but he did not release her. "I gots it, Maggie," he said, loud enough for her ears alone. "I gots the land, and I've been puttin' up the timbers for a house. *Now* will ye marry me?"

The housekeeper's eyes widened. "The land Jared promised you?" she whispered.

Angus patted his breast pocket. "The deed's right here. A hundred acres of prime bottom land. I wanted the cap'n to put up a paper and let me pay for it a bit at a time, but he wouldn't hear of it. He said it was a weddin' present, Maggie. For us."

Maggie eyed him sadly. "I'm too old to give you children, Angus. You always said you wanted children."

"I want you more. And besides, there's naught to keep us from takin' in a couple of waifs and bringin' them up like our own." He paused, then added. "What do ye say, Maggie? Will ye be my wife?"

"Angus!" Jarina cried out from the doorway.

Angus and Maggie sprang apart, and there was a sheepish look on the Scot's face as he turned around.

Jarina ran across the room and threw her arms around the old man's neck. "Oh, Angus! It's been so long! I thought I'd never see you again!"

Angus hugged her tight. "A sight for sore eyes, ye are, lass. I can see my Maggie here's been takin' good care of ye."

Tears brightened Jarina's eyes, and when she spoke, there was a catch in her voice. "Maggie's wonderful to me, Angus. Just like you were. Oh, Maggie, I can't even begin to tell you how kind Angus was to me during the voyage. When Jared took the night watch, I had no one to talk to except Angus. Sometimes I felt as though he were my only friend in the whole world. He and Stephen Landon." She whirled back to Angus. "How is Stephen? Have you seen him? Is he still in Alexandria?"

Angus laughed. "Whoa, lass! One question at a time! But, first, there's a question *I* want answered."

Jarina opened her mouth to ask him what question was that, but stopped short when she saw that he was not looking at her, but past her. At Maggie. Angus raised one shaggy brow and Maggie blushed profusely. Then the look in the old woman's eyes softened. "Yes," Maggie said quietly.

Angus let out a Highland battle yell. He caught Maggie to him and kissed her thoroughly.

Jarina glanced around at the other servants, but they seemed as perplexed as she was. Fiona held her palms out and lifted her shoulders in a bewildered shrug.

Angus seized Jarina's hand and gripped it tightly. His eyes shone. "There's to be a wedding, lass. Maggie and me, we're gettin' married!"

Before Jarina could respond, Angus caught her about the waist and whirled her around the room until she was dizzy and out of breath. Laughing and gasping for air, Jarina clutched her side. "Angus, you sly fox!" she said breathlessly. "When did all this come about? And Maggie, you never breathed a word. Please, I want to know everything!"

Over the next several hours, they sat at the kitchen table, laughing and gossiping and talking about the wedding. Angus told of the house he was building. Cook surprised them with strawberry tarts and clotted cream, and while they ate, they talked some more.

The hour grew late, and an easy silence settled over them. Angus leaned back in his chair and folded his hands over his contented stomach. He looked at Jarina, and his expression softened. "I've been here nigh on five hours, lass, and not one word ye've asked of your husband," he chided gently.

Jarina's head snapped up. "You've seen Jared?"

Angus inclined his head. "Aye. He said to tell ye he'll be home before the week is out. He'll be bringin' with him the horses he purchased."

"Oh, Angus, that's wonderful!" Jarina exclaimed, but there was little joy in her voice, and her bright smile failed to mask the worry in her eyes.

Angus and Maggie exchanged glances.

"Does Jared know you're getting married?" Jarina asked, neatly sidestepping any discussion of Jared and turning the conversation back to the wedding.

"In a manner of speaking," Angus said. He winked at Maggie. "The cap'n promised to give the bride away if I could sweet-talk her into havin' me."

Jarina looked surprised. "Was there ever any doubt?"

"None at all," Angus replied.

A short time later, Angus excused himself, leaving Maggie and Jarina alone in the kitchen.

Jarina rose from her chair and began stacking the soiled dishes.

"What's ailing you, child?"

"Nothing is ailing me, Maggie. I'm just tired. There was so much excitement today, with Angus arriving, and then finding out the two of you are to be married."

Maggie folded her arms across her chest and eyed Jarina closely. "Mary went up to Miss Evelyn's bedchamber to fetch the tea service you left there," she said meaningfully.

Jarina's hand faltered in midair. She reached for another plate.

"The teapot was smashed into a thousand pieces."

Jarina still said nothing.

"You never did tell me what happened when you saw her this morning."

Jarina's fist came down on the table hard enough to

make the dishes jump. "Blast it all, Maggie!" she burst out. "That woman made me so angry I *still* want to tear her hair out!"

"Good heavens, child! I've felt that way about her for years. What did Miss Evelyn finally do to get you up in arms?"

Anger glittered in Jarina's eyes. "*Miss Evelyn* is sporting a black eye the likes of which any schoolboy would be proud. She claims Jared gave it to her."

Maggie's smile faded. "You can't be serious," she said in a stricken voice.

Jarina flashed the housekeeper a perturbed glance. "Jared did *not* hit her, Maggie. That bruise is new; it hasn't even started to yellow yet. Even an idiot could look at her and know she hasn't had it more than a few hours. A day at the most."

Maggie's shoulders visibly sagged in relief.

"How could she do this?" Jarina demanded. "How could she stay here all these months, spending Jared's money, entertaining her friends at Jared's expense; then accuse him of abusing her?"

"I tried to warn you," Maggie said.

"I know, and I was too stubborn to listen." Jarina sighed, then added ruefully, "Now I must face Jared when he returns and tell him what I did."

Jarina glanced at Maggie and caught the query in the lifted brows. "I told Evelyn to leave," she confessed in a small voice.

The housekeeper's entire body began to shake with suppressed laughter. "Child, if that's all you did, you can stop your worrying. Mr. Jared told her to leave the night you both arrived at Wyeburn. He said he wanted that entire bunch of riffraff out of this house. If anything's going to make that boy angry, it's the fact that they haven't gone yet."

"I wish they would all leave, and take Evelyn with them," Jarina said wearily. "I know it's a terrible thing to say, but I don't want her here. I tried to put myself in her place and imagine how I would feel were someone to take Jared away from me, but it changes naught. I hate her, Maggie."

The housekeeper's brows drew together in concern. "You're not afraid Mr. Jared might look to Miss Evelyn with a roving eye, are you?" she asked.

A wan smile touched Jarina's lips. "I can't help it, Maggie. I fear I am a terribly jealous wife."

Maggie snorted. "Seeing as who you're married to, child, you're better off a jealous wife than an unfaithful one."

"Well, lass, exceptin' Miss Evelyn, that's the last of 'em. Can't say that I'm sorry to see that one go."

Jarina watched Jonathan Shelby's carriage drive away, then she turned away from the window. "Oh, Angus, I hope Jared never finds out what we did. You know how much he hates deceit."

Mischief twinkled in the Scot's eyes. "I'm willin' to wager the cap'n will forgive one wee little fib."

"Angus, it was no wee fib. It was an outrageous lie!"

"Aye, but it worked."

An involuntary smile tugged at the corners of Jarina's mouth. "I wish you could have seen the look on William Reinhold's face when I broke the tragic news to him."

Angus grinned. "I dinna need to, lass. The man nearly broke his neck tumblin' down the stairs in his rush to get away from the house!"

Jarina pressed a hand over her mouth to stifle a giggle. "I'm so glad Damon decided to go to Providence for a few days. We would not have gotten away with this had he been here."

Maggie came into the drawing room. "Child, Finley's been asking for you—" She broke off when she saw Angus, and her eyes narrowed in suspicion. "All right, you two. This makes the second time today I've caught you with your heads together. Would either one of you mind telling me what devilment you're brewing now?"

"Angus wants me to convince you to hold the wedding as soon as Jared returns," Jarina said lightly. It was not entirely a lie; she and Angus had been discussing the wedding earlier that morning. "And, quite frankly, I am in agreement with him. I think you should be married as soon as possible."

"I already told you, the wedding will be *after* the house is built, or not at all."

Angus shook his head. "Ah, Maggie, the house won' be complete for another month or two. And the cap'n did say we could live here until then."

Maggie's expression became militant. "No house, no wedding," she said firmly.

"But, Maggie, love, I'm not gettin' any younger," Angus protested. "If ye waits much longer, I'm gonna be too old and feeble to say my vows!"

Jarina slipped past Maggie toward the door. "I think I shall go see what Finley wants," she said, laughing.

In the hall, Jarina came face to face with Evelyn. Her gaiety faded, and she instinctively braced herself for confrontation. "Hello, Miss Landon," she said coolly. "I trust the headache no longer troubles you?"

Evelyn tilted her head back until she was peering haughtily down her nose. She ignored Jarina's greeting and went straight to the point. "I want to know what you told them to make them depart so suddenly," she demanded.

Jarina noticed that Evelyn had attempted unsuccessfully to disguise her black eye with cosmetics. The bruise was just beginning to change in color. Jarina clasped her hands before her, the gesture exuding an air of serenity she was far from feeling. "I merely pointed out to your guests that they had overstayed their welcome," she said calmly.

Evelyn's face flushed red, and her dark eyes flashed. "You had no right! They were *my* guests!"

"Then *you* should have asked them to leave," Jarina returned. "Since you did not, I took the liberty of asking them myself. Now, if you will excuse me, I have work to do." She started to go around Evelyn, but the other woman stepped in front of her, blocking her path.

"You'll never get away with this," Evelyn spat. "He was mine long before he ever knew you. We were to have been married when he returned from England. He *loves* me."

It took Jarina a moment to realize that Evelyn was no longer speaking of her guests, but of Jared. Inwardly, she began to seethe. "Miss Landon, I am finding this conversation both boring and distasteful," she said. "Whatever once existed between you and Jared was wonderful, I am sure. But it wasn't love. That much I know. Now, if you will kindly step out of my way—"

"He loves me!" Evelyn shouted. "You'll never be able to keep him. Once he tires of your skinny child's body, he will come back to me. I know what pleases him. I know where and how he likes to be touched." Her voice dropped to a murmur and she said smugly, "I know ways to love him you never dreamed of."

Jarina felt a warm flush of color creep into her face. She longed to slap the self-satisfied smirk off Evelyn's face, and it took every ounce of resolve she possessed to keep her hands still. She frowned slightly, drawing her finely arched brows together as though giving the woman's words some serious thought. "That's very interesting," she said, fixing Evelyn with a completely blank look. "Tell me, Miss Landon, do you have any other accomplishments?"

Evelyn's chin shot upward. Her eyes narrowed until they were like slits of dark light, and her nostrils flared, but she said nothing. With a haughty toss of her black tresses, she turned and flounced away.

From the doorway of the drawing room, Angus

chuckled. "I dinna think she did," he said, laughing softly.

The side door to the warehouse opened. Accompanied by a windy gust, Stephen Landon hurried inside, a thick packet tied with string beneath one arm. "You're early," he commented when he saw Jared.

"You're late," Jared amended tersely. He followed Stephen into a private office and closed the door. "Well?"

The younger man grinned. "It's all here," he said. He handed the packet of papers to Jared. "The *Pegasus* and the *Connemara* are now officially listed as having been lost at sea. The *Pegasus* has been reborn as the *Southwind* and the *Connemara* as *Zanzibar*. Most of the men agreed to sign on with the new owners."

"Good," Jared said. "What of the remaining ships?"

"The favor you called in worked. Your name has been removed from the registry, and there's naught to evidence that the ships were ever owned by anyone other than myself. As far as anyone is concerned, you still own the company, but the fleet was always mine." Stephen chuckled. "If Roswell does succeed in getting his hands on the title, he will be acquiring little more than a few near-empty warehouses, and a couple of old saltbuckets that won't stay afloat through the next winter."

A determined glint hardened Jared's eyes. "Roswell won't get the company unless I physically sell it to him, something I have no intention of doing. These other precautions are merely for my own peace of mind."

"And mine," Stephen agreed. An uncomfortable silence fell over them. Stephen shifted nervously. "Jared, I didn't know about Evelyn," he suddenly blurted out. "I swear it."

Jared regarded him in stony silence several moments. Then some of the rancor left his expression and there was resigned acceptance in his sigh. "I know," he said quietly. "And I apologize for believing Damon when he told me you were aware of her parentage. How could I expect you to know when I was so easily deceived all these years?"

Stephen was thoughtful. "Then you think Damon is telling the truth?"

"I think it's possible. We both know what a libertine my father was. What troubles me is why Damon waited so long to tell me what he knew. Apparently, our mother revealed the truth to him just before she died." He paused, then added in a low, taut voice, "That was nearly twelve years ago."

"What are you going to do?"

"What can I do? If Evelyn is indeed my half-sister as Damon claims, then she is entitled to my protection and my support. I cannot simply turn her out to fend for herself."

As if by silent agreement, no more was said of Evelyn. They discussed business awhile longer, then Jared excused himself.

"Are you certain you don't want to go to the Boar's Head to celebrate our latest venture?" Stephen asked, but Jared declined.

"You may still be the carefree bachelor, Stephen," Jared reminded him, "but I now have a wife to consider."

Stephen's brown eyes twinkled. "Would you by chance be in a hurry to get home?"

The jesting note in the younger man's voice did not escape Jared's hearing. "That could be an accurate assessment," he retorted.

Stephen laughed low. "So our little stowaway finally succeeded in domesticating you," he joked.

By the time Jared left the warehouse, it had begun to rain. A cold wind blew out of the northwest, but Jared did not even notice it. The remembered feel of Jarina in his arms warmed him and brought a contemplative smile to his mouth. He was not certain *domesti-*

cate was the correct term for what Jarina had done to him; he only knew that the two weeks he had spent away from her had been unbearably long. He was anxious to see her lovely face, and to hold and kiss her again. His blood ran hot as he thought of seeking his pleasure in the passion he knew he could arouse in her.

Minutes later, observers were to note a lone rider, his collar turned up and tricorne pulled low, goading his great black stallion to a furious gait across the Virginia countryside.

Jared could not wait to get home.

"In this damp?" Maggie asked, incredulous.

Jarina fastened her cloak. "I hate being closed up in the house after the lovely weather we had last week," she said. She did not add that the persistent smell of Evelyn's perfume was making her nauseated. Lately, even her food seemed to have taken on the cloying scent, and she could scarcely take a bite without feeling sick to her stomach. She wondered where Evelyn was obtaining her seemingly unending supply of the essence. "Besides," she said, "I'm only going as far as the garden. If it starts to rain again, I will take shelter in the conservatory."

"Don't you do any planting, you hear?" Finley warned. He was sitting by the hearth with his bound leg propped on a stool. "The ground's too wet. You'll only succeed in packing down the earth, and when the ground dries, it will be hard as mortar."

Jarina laughed. "True, but just think how easily the weeds will pull up."

The brisk April wind felt cool and reviving. Jarina now understood how Jared must have felt aboard the *Pegasus* when he went aloft or when he stood on the quarterdeck with the wind on his face. She took a deep breath. It felt good to be out in the open air.

Gathering her skirts, she made her way across the muddy ground toward the conservatory to fetch a small spade and the protective hand mitts Finley had given her.

The glass-enclosed structure was warm and damp inside, and the seeds she had helped Finley plant were beginning to come up. She touched a forefinger to the delicate green cotyledon of a newly sprouted tomato plant and smiled. She had never tasted a tomato, but Finley had promised her a real treat come summer. Love apples, he had called them, then proceeded to inform her that they were a proven aphrodisiac. "Tomatoes and leeks and oysters," the gardener said, and she had blushed profusely, remembering the quantity of raw oysters Jared had consumed the night he had taken her to Hall's Tavern.

"Good afternoon," came a seductively smooth male voice from behind her.

Jarina gasped and whirled around. Her hand flew to her throat in a gesture that was more defensive than surprised. "Damon!"

Damon sauntered toward her. Even white teeth flashed in his tanned face, but Jarina found little comfort in his smile, or in the gold-spoked gaze that roamed freely over the length of her. "If you will permit me to say so, little sister, you are a welcome ray of sunshine on this dreary day."

She forced a polite smile. "You are very kind, sir," she said. It was the first time she had been alone with Jared's brother since the night she had arrived at Wyeburn. A small part of her still suspected that Damon had been the one to strike Evelyn, and the seclusion of the conservatory from the rest of the house made her uneasy. Skirting around Damon and the profusion of plants that filled the conservatory, she went to the cupboard where the hand tools were kept and opened the door. "I thought you were still in Providence," she tossed over her shoulder. "When did you return?"

Damon moved to stand behind her, and when he spoke, his breath was warm against the back of her head. "Last night," he said silkily. "I couldn't bear being away."

The underlying suggestiveness in Damon's voice raised prickles on Jarina's skin and caused her heart to race. Both Damon's closeness and the humid warmth of the conservatory were making her feel physically ill. She wished he would not stand so near. Damon reached past her, and Jarina's heart slammed against her ribs as their bodies touched. A sick bile rose in her throat. "Excuse me," she muttered, and scooted frantically away from him.

Damon lifted the hand mitts from the top shelf and turned to give them to her. His hard gaze bore into her. "Is this what you were looking for?" he asked.

A hot flush consumed Jarina's face as she realized what she had done. Embarrassed, she reached for the gloves. "Thank you," she murmured.

Damon's eyes narrowed as he contemplated her, and there was little warmth in the subtle smile that touched his mouth. "You're welcome," he said dryly.

Jarina nervously moistened her lips. "Did you have a pleasant journey?" she asked, searching frantically for some safe topic to discuss.

Damon plucked a sprig of mint and rolled it between his thumb and forefinger. "Not especially. Evelyn asked me to find a house for her to rent. Unfortunately, her tastes exceed her means, and I was unable to locate anything that might suit her."

"Why doesn't she simply go home?" Jarina asked, then wished she hadn't. Damon threw her a cutting glance that made her want to bite her tongue.

Damon flung the bruised mint aside. "Evelyn no longer has a home," he said curtly. "Fair Oaks was auctioned for unpaid taxes more than a year ago."

The unexpected news caught Jarina with her guard down. Both the realization that Evelyn might be staying longer and the steamy warmth of the conservatory were making her feel physically ill. "I'm sorry," she murmured. "I didn't know."

"Of course you didn't. Not even Jared knew until a short time ago. Of course, being the trusting soul that he is, the first thing Jared did was ride off to Fair Oaks to find out for himself if I was telling the truth. Odd thing about my brother . . . he despises liars."

The constriction in Jarina's chest was so great she could hardly breathe. She now had no less than two enormous falsehoods to her credit.

Damon's eyes narrowed as he contemplated her. "I would not concern myself with Evelyn if I were you. She will get exactly what she deserves. Nothing more, nothing less."

Before Jarina could ask him what he meant by that, Damon turned and stalked from the conservatory, leaving her to stare after him in a mixture of bewilderment and relief.

Jarina spent the afternoon working in the garden. Kneeling upon a broad plank to keep from sinking into the mud, she weeded the rows of vegetable seedlings she and Finley had transplated the week before. She loved the smell of the damp earth and the way the wind felt on her face; and as she worked, a quiet contentment settled over her. Being in the garden almost made her feel as though she were back at Hamilton Hall.

With a squeal of delight, she dropped the spade and removed the clumsy hand mitts, then dug her fingers into the soft soil to loosen a clump of wood sorrel. "You may be a noxious weed to some," she said as she carefully lifted the shamrocks, "but to me you are the harbinger of good fortune." She set the shamrocks aside to transplant into a pot and leaned back on her heels with a sigh of happiness as she basked in her own good fortune. She had all she had ever wanted, and more. Those first terrifying days aboard the *Pegasus* were but a hazy blur in her memory. She now had a wonderful home in a grand new land, and a husband who was dearer to her than life itself.

From the corner of her eye, Jarina saw Mary coming from the house. She got to her feet and was brushing the dirt off the front of her cloak when the maid reached her. "Maggie says to tell you tea is ready," Mary said. "She wants you to come inside before you take a chill."

Jarina picked up the shamrocks. "I'll come inside if you will find a pot for these," she said, handing them to the girl.

Mary cast the clump of weeds a sideways glance. "You know what Maggie is going to say when she sees them, don't you?"

Jarina laughed. "I can guess."

Jarina was halfway back to the house when a movement in the distance caught her attention, and she stopped and stared as a man slowed his black horse from a gallop to a leisurely walk. Although the distance was too great for her to see the rider's face, her pulse quickened. She would know those broad shoulders, that proud posture, anywhere.

Then the rider lifted his hand and waved.

Jared!

Jarina broke into a run.

When she reached the bottom of the hill, Jared leaned down and caught her around the waist and hoisted her, laughing and breathless, up onto the saddle in front of him. He crushed her to him and his mouth came down fiercely over hers.

Jarina returned his kiss hungrily, wrapping her arms about his neck and molding herself to his hard contours.

Bereft of a guiding hand, Morocco, the black stallion, stopped. He turned his sleek head back toward his master, but when it became evident that no direction was immediately forthcoming, he turned away with bored indifference and began nibbling on the sweet young grass growing at the side of the road.

Jared tore his mouth away and clasped Jarina to him, burying his face in her hair. "God, I missed you!" he murmured into her fragrant curls, then he recaptured her lips and kissed her again.

When at last they reluctantly drew apart, Jared chuckled tenderly. "Were I always guaranteed such a warm welcome," he said, "I would be tempted to venture out regularly, simply so I could enjoy returning again and again."

Jarina's eyes shone. "Jared Cunningham, I was quite vexed with you when I discovered you had gone without telling me!" she laughingly warned. "Don't you even *think* of leaving me again!"

Jared visibly relaxed. While a part of him had secretly hoped that Jarina would be glad to see him, he had dismissed the longing as a sentimental notion, and the unexpected attainment of that wish touched him deeply. He could not explain why, but Jarina's unconditional acceptance meant a great deal to him. He rumpled her wind-tousled curls playfully and grinned. "You'll have a hard time getting rid of me, sweet."

Suddenly Jarina's brows knitted together and she looked past him over his shoulder. She withdrew her arms from around his neck. "Where are the horses you purchased?" she asked.

"I hired a man to bring them from Fredericksburg. One of the mares is in foal, and I wanted her to make the journey slowly. They should arrive tomorrow." He paused, then added with a rueful laugh. "I couldn't wait that long."

Happiness swelled in Jarina's chest until she felt she would burst. It was the closest Jared had ever come to telling her he loved her. Her hand sought his and their fingers intertwined. "I'm glad," she whispered.

Jared brought her hand up to his lips, but stopped just short of kissing it. Arching a brow, he held the grimy, dirt-crusted little fist away from him and eye-balled it quizzically.

Jarina pulled her hand free and hid it in the folds of her cloak. "I was pulling weeds," she said primly, as if that explained everything.

"Jarina, I am paying Finley and two other gardeners a good wage to do that."

"I know. But I wanted to work in the garden. I also want to help you with the horses when they arrive, and I want to help you build the new stables."

Jared could not help smiling at the stubbornness in his wife's voice. "Is there anything else you would like to do, sweet?" he asked indulgently.

With a mischievous grin, Jarina blushed and slid her hands provocatively over Jared's chest beneath his cloak. "Do you think not, sir?" she asked coyly.

Jared threw back his head and laughed fully, deeply. He wrapped his arms around Jarina and held her tight. It had never felt so good to be home.

Still holding Jarina with one arm, he picked up Morocco's reins with his free hand and turned the stallion back toward the house. "In that case, madam," he said huskily, "we had best not tarry any longer. I would not want to be caught granting my lady's wish here in the middle of the road."

Jarina settled contentedly against her husband's chest. " 'Tis a pity you are saddled with such a demanding wife, my lord," she teased.

With Jarina seated before him, Jared slowly led the lathered black stallion up the winding drive. High on the hill before them, Wyeburn's ivy-cloaked walls rose proudly from the ground, and Jared was filled with a fierce pride in his home. As his gaze rested on the giant oak tree that hovered over the house like a watchful guardian, he began to consider having a child's play swing hung from one of the lower branches.

Realizing where his thoughts had strayed, Jared gave his head a sharp shake as though to clear it. Perhaps

Stephen was right. Perhaps he was becoming domesticated.

At his abrupt movement, Jarina tilted her head back to look at him. "Is something wrong?" she asked.

The troubled expression gradually left Jared's eyes. "No," he said slowly, still a little in awe of the changes in his life one drunken night had wrought. He smiled and kissed Jarina's upturned face. "For once, everything is amazingly right."

When they reached the house, Jared dismounted, then reached up for Jarina who slid willingly into his arms. He handed the reins to one of the grooms and issued instructions to rub down the stallion. With Jarina at his side, he mounted the steps, but no sooner had he entered the house than Evelyn came running down the hall toward him, and his good humor vanished. He had hoped he would not have to deal with Evelyn immediately upon his return.

"Jared, you're home!" Evelyn cried out. She would have flung herself into Jared's arms had Jarina not fixed her with a frosty glare that stopped her in her tracks. She did not know what Jarina may have told Jared of their confrontation. "Damon and I were just sitting down to tea," she said with a sweetness that belied the desperation in her dark eyes. "Won't you join us, Jared? I know you must be exhausted after your journey."

Like an actor responding to his cue, Damon appeared in the drawing-room doorway, a half-full teacup in one hand. He leaned casually against the doorframe.

Jared's jaw tightened, and his eyes narrowed as they scanned Evelyn's face, searching frantically for some evidence to disprove that they shared a common sire.

What he saw sickened him.

Not only did Evelyn strongly resemble the man who had fathered them both, so did Damon.

A cold sweat erupted across his brow. *Good God! Had he been so thoroughly misled that he was not only guilty of bedding his own half sister, but of denying his brother his full birthright as well?*

Jared's gaze left Evelyn to rest upon his brother, and he found the answer to his question in Damon's self-satisfied expression. Damon raised his teacup in salute. "Touché," the gesture seemed to say.

Jared felt as though the ground were splitting open and dragging him downward into his own private hell of hate and deception. In that moment, he would have given his entire fortune, his lands, and his identity to simply disappear to some remote corner of the world where he might live out the remainder of his life in peace.

At his side, Jarina shifted nervously.

Drawing a deep, ragged breath, Jared placed an arm about her shoulders and gave her a reassuring squeeze. "Thank you, Evelyn, but I must decline," he said with stiff politeness. He had to make an effort not to stare at her bruised eye. "If you see Maggie, please ask her to send my tea upstairs."

With his arm still securely around Jarina's shoulders, Jared turned toward the staircase.

"I saw Jonathan Shelby when I was in Providence," Damon said.

Jarina's heart missed a beat. Willing herself to be calm, she slowly turned back to her brother-in-law. "I hope Mr. Shelby is faring well," she murmured tensely.

A puzzled frown creased Jared's forehead as he glanced from his brother to his wife.

Damon took an excruciatingly long drink from his teacup. "Jon is doing fine," he said. His hard gaze bore into Jarina. "He sends you his regards."

Jarina forced a tight smile, but said nothing. She turned and started up the stairs. Jared followed close behind.

"Welcome home, Jared," Damon called out behind them. He chuckled, then added dryly, "I must say, brother dear, you look remarkably well for a man who is dying of blackwater fever."

Chapter Fourteen

Jarina froze.

Jared turned to stare at his brother. "Would you care to repeat that?" he said.

Damon drained his cup. "Somewhere, Jared, Jonathan Shelby acquired the misguided notion that you were suffering a recurrence of the malaria you had contracted during a previous voyage to the tropics. He said he would like to have stayed to catch up on old times with you, but he feared catching the fever."

Even Evelyn was staring at Damon in wide-eyed shock. "My God!" she whispered hoarsely. "Who could have possibly told Jon such an outrageous—" She broke off suddenly and whirled around to spear Jarina with an accusing glare.

Jared turned to look at his wife. Her face was pale and she was gripping the banister rail. "Jarina, do you know anything about this?" he asked.

Jarina turned an innocent blue gaze on her husband. "I don't know where Mr. Shelby could have gotten the idea that he was in any danger," she said. "Blackwater fever is not contagious."

Contempt blazed in Evelyn's eyes. "You bitch! That's how you made them leave, isn't it? You told them Jared was ill!"

Jarina said nothing. Her tongue felt like a block of wood in her mouth. She could not have spoken had she tried.

Averting her gaze, she gathered her skirts and turned to flee up the stairs, but Jared caught her arm, stopping her. Taking her chin in a gentle grip, he made her look at him. His probing gaze never wavered. "Jarina, did you tell Jonathan Shelby that I had contracted blackwater fever?" he asked quietly.

Jarina's heart was beating so furiously it felt as though it were pounding against the base of her throat. She had hoped at least a day or two might elapse before Jared discovered what she had done and she was forced to confess her lie; now even that small reprieve was denied her. She swallowed audibly. "Yes," she choked.

Jared stared at her long and hard, but to Jarina's confusion, suppressed laughter danced in his gray eyes and one corner of his mouth began to twitch involuntarily.

Behind him, Evelyn did not see the open admiration in the gaze Jared fixed on his wife; she had only heard the deadly quiet in his voice. Thinking she now had the upper hand, she pressed forward recklessly. "You little trollop! I could kill you for this! How dare you lie to my guests and send them running for fear of their lives! No one will ever accept an invitation to Wyeburn again, and it's all your fault!"

Neither Jared nor Jarina heard her. Jarina smiled shyly at her bemused husband. "I fear my intentions were not very honorable, my lord," she said softly, for his ears alone. "I wanted you all to myself when you returned, and it was the only way I could think of to make them leave willingly."

Jared's gaze smoldered with restrained passion as it swept over his wife. "I think we should discuss this further, madam," he said, then added huskily, "in private."

Jarina blushed beneath Jared's lusty regard. "I agree," she whispered.

Jarina preceded her husband up the stairs.

Incensed, Evelyn rounded on Damon. "Didn't anyone hear a word I said?" she demanded indignantly.

Damon threw her a scorching glance. "Oh, shut up," he spat. He turned and walked away.

Upstairs, Jared was not inclined to let Jarina off without an accounting of her actions. "Blackwater fever?" he asked sternly the instant he had closed the bedchamber door behind them.

Choking back a giggle, Jarina wrapped her arms about her husband's neck and rose up on tiptoe to plant a kiss upon the disapproving line of his mouth. "An extremely debilitating case," she admitted solemnly.

Jared's fingers moved up Jarina's back to unfasten one tiny button after another. He nibbled playfully on her bottom lip. "Then I suppose I shall be confined to my bed until I undergo some miraculous recovery?"

"Only if your physician deems it necessary, my lord."

Jared eased Jarina's gown down over her shoulders and his eyes darkened. "I have a sorceress for a physician," he said thickly. His head descended.

Hours later, after they had both soaked in a hot bath and eaten a light supper, Jarina lay in her husband's arms, recounting all that had happened during his absence.

Jared frowned when he heard that Evelyn had tried to credit him with the blame for her blackened eye. He had been stroking Jarina's bare hip beneath the covers, and now his hand stilled.

Jarina tilted her head back to look at him. The lines of his face were hard and his displeasure evident in the amber glow of the bedchamber hearth. "Do you know who would have had reason to strike her?" she asked.

"It could have been anyone, sweet. Evelyn has more enemies than friends, and her friends are not a particularly loyal lot."

Though his answer was noncommittal, Jarina suspected that Jared knew more than he was willing to reveal. "At first, I thought it might have been Damon," she said. "At times, he seems almost to hate her. Yet, this afternoon when he told me he was trying to find a place for her to live, I had the impression he felt sorry for her." She paused, then ventured hesitantly, "Sometimes I almost pity her myself."

Jarina's admission brought a derisive snort from Jared. "Evelyn is not worthy of your pity, Jarina," he said coldly. "If I catch her in another deception like she tried to work on you, she will find herself without a roof over her head. I will not tolerate having a liar in this house."

Jarina retreated to her own side of the bed, and several long moments passed before either of them spoke again. Jared raised up on one elbow and studied Jarina's face in the flickering firelight. "What's wrong?" he asked, troubled by her silent withdrawal.

"I was wondering if you were angry with me for telling that lie about you having blackwater fever?"

Jared reached out to cup her breast and gently knead it. "If I were, I think you would have known it."

Jarina turned her head to look at him. "I would never lie to you, Jared," she said, her voice oddly subdued. "It would be too easy for you to look into my soul and know I wasn't speaking the truth. I have no secrets from you."

Jared lowered his head to her breast and touched his lips to her hardening nipple. "None, love?" he asked.

Jarina thought of her flight from Hamilton Hall, of her betrothal to William Osterbrook, and of the father Jared must never learn still lived. "None that matter," she said sadly.

The following weeks were busy and productive ones at Wyeburn. From dawn until dusk, the sounds of sawing and hammering filled the air, accompanied by the master carpenter's shouted instructions. The barn was turned into a temporary stable, and the paddocks strengthened and enlarged. The horses Jared had purchased in Fredericksburg arrived.

Jarina immediately fell in love with the pregnant chestnut mare. "Oh, Jared, she's beautiful," she whispered as Lady Beth nuzzled her palm and began eating the oats she held in her hand.

Jarina's approval brought a ready smile to Jared's lips. "If you'd like, you may choose a name for her foal," he offered.

Jarina's head snapped up and her eyes grew wide and round as she stared at her husband. "May I?" she asked, incredulous.

Jared never ceased to wonder at the joy Jarina derived from such seemingly simple pleasures. His expression softened and he reached out to stroke the delicate curve of her cheek. "Yes, love, you may," he said.

If their days were occupied with hard work, their nights were filled with hours of the most pleasurable lovemaking either of them could ever have imagined possible. Sometimes Jared wooed and courted Jarina as though she were an impressionable schoolgirl, plying her with seductive promises that brought a blush to her cheeks; at other times, he took her roughly, driving into her with a hungry violence that made Jarina think he was not making love to her so much as he was *possessing* her, trying to make her such an inseparable part of him that her loyalty could not be questioned. She sensed that while he refrained from telling her what was troubling him, he needed to assure himself that she would not desert him. He was never satisfied until she surrendered to him completely.

Only one thing happened to mar the blissful passing of their days.

They rose early one morning with plans to go riding. No sooner had they finished dressing than Jarina turned and bolted for the bathing chamber. By the time

Jared caught up with her, she was hunched over the wash basin, heaving up her breakfast.

Jared fetched a cool, damp cloth, and Jarina stood helplessly while he bathed her face.

"I think it was the ham," she said shakily. "The smell of it didn't agree with me this morning. I should not have eaten it."

Jared was not convinced. "There will be no riding for you today," he said firmly.

Disappointment flashed across Jarina's face. "But Maggie has already packed us a picnic lunch and—"

"No arguments, sweet. I don't want to take a chance on you becoming ill again." Ignoring Jarina's protests, Jared picked her up and carried her back into the bedroom. "I can show you Wyeburn another time," he said as he gently lowered her to the bed. "You are going to stay in this bed today, and that's my final word on the matter."

Jared helped her remove her gown.

"But, I'm not ill," she insisted as he tucked the covers around her. "It was the ham."

Relieved to see that some of the color had returned to Jarina's face, Jared placed his hands on either side of her, and his gray eyes sparkled as though he were enjoying some private joke. "Madam, has anyone ever told you that you make a most disagreeable patient?" he teased gently.

He closed the drapes and went to remove the soiled wash basin. When he returned to the bedchamber a few minutes later, Jarina was sound asleep.

She is still such an innocent, he thought, worry clouding his eyes as he gazed down at her slumbering form. He had not yet told her about his relationship with Evelyn, and the longer he delayed, the less inclined he was to speak of it. He did not think he could bear the revulsion he knew he would see in Jarina's eyes when she learned he had committed a sin against nature.

Bending down, he pressed a kiss to her brow.

If he had his way about it, she would *never* learn the truth.

It was midday when Jarina finally ventured downstairs. She found Jared in his study going over the household accounts. He looked up and smiled when he saw her. "Feeling better, love?" he asked.

"I'm still a little tired."

Her face was pale and there were dark shadows beneath her eyes. Her listlessness troubled him. "Shall I have Maggie bring you some tea?" he asked, but she declined.

"The thought of food doesn't sit too well right now," she said. "Perhaps later."

Sensing that she needed to be held, Jared put down his quill and pushed his chair away from the desk. "Come here," he said.

Jarina went to him. He put his arm around her and she did not resist when he drew her onto his lap. Looping her arms about his neck, she settled against him and rested her cheek against the top of his head. "I'm sorry I spoiled our ride."

"We can go riding anytime," Jared said. "It's you I worry about. You work too hard. Sometimes you don't realize your own limits."

Jarina lifted her head and stared at him in disbelief. "I lead a life of lazy indulgence here, and well you know it."

"You have been doing the work of three strong men," Jared corrected her. "If we were still aboard the *Pegasus,* I have no doubts you would be attempting to sail the merchantman singlehanded. From now on, you are to take things a little slower. And that's an order."

Jarina still could not believe he cared so much about her. She placed one hand against his lean jaw in a gentle caress and a pensive smile touched her lips. "Sometimes I think I am the luckiest woman in the world to have such a considerate husband," she said softly. "You are a wonderful man, Jared Cunningham."

Guilt sliced through Jared like a blade.

God, don't ever let her learn the truth! he prayed.

He turned his head and pressed a kiss into her palm. "Those are mighty potent words, madam, coming from a woman who once called me a pompous ass."

Jarina's eyes widened slightly.

Jared grinned at the startled expression on his wife's face. "If I remember correctly, you also said I was rude, arrogant, and domineering." He paused, then added as an afterthought, "And hateful."

Jarina's heart pounded in her chest. There was only one time she remembered ever speaking such thoughts aloud, aboard the *Pegasus,* and then she had thought herself safe from prying ears. She did not know Jared had overheard her that day. Regret flashed across her face. "Oh, Jared, please forgive me. I never meant those awful—"

He placed a forefinger against her lips, silencing her. "You did mean them, and you were quite justified in voicing them. I was terribly cruel to you, Jarina. If either of us should seek the other's forgiveness, it is I."

Jarina shook her head. "There is nothing to forgive. I know it could not have been easy for you, to suddenly find that the mistress you had engaged was an inexperienced maiden who had not the slightest idea how to please you."

"No, love, it was not an easy time for me, particularly when the maiden in question had the body of a goddess and the morals of a saint. However," he added with a sincerity that came from deep within his heart, "do not fear that I am not pleased. You please me more than I ever thought possible. I'm finding I rather enjoy being married to you."

And I love you, Jarina thought.

An easy silence settled over them as their thoughts

drifted along different paths, and they each found comfort in the other's presence.

For a long time, Jarina stared idly at the piles of bills and correspondence lying on Jared's desk, and she wondered in awe at the vast amounts of money he controlled. How differently her life would have turned out had her father had such funds at his disposal. He would not have needed to bargain away her future to Roswell; and she would not now be exiled from her childhood home. She might have met Jared under entirely different circumstances. On the other hand, she might never have met him at all.

Suddenly, she sat up a little straighter and her gaze focused on a particular invoice. "Is that what you paid for my gowns?" she asked, incredulous that anyone would spend so much money on a trousseau.

Seeing where her attention had strayed, Jared chuckled. "No, love," he replied. "That's what I paid for *one* of your gowns."

Jarina let the discussion drop at that, but Jared could tell she was not happy.

The last day of April dawned warm and sunny. Maggie went with Angus to view the progress he had made on the new house, and most of the other servants were given the day off. Damon and Evelyn remained at Wyeburn, and to escape their annoying presence, Jared went down to the stables.

Shortly afterward, Jarina followed.

Jared was leading his great black stallion to one of the paddocks and Morocco was tossing his head and tugging on the bit like an untamed colt. Jarina climbed up on the fence to watch.

Opening the gate, Jared led the stallion inside, then unbuckled the bridle and slipped it off over his head. Free of restraint, Morocco charged, kicking up clods of dirt behind him. With his neck arched high and his nostrils flared, he pranced across the paddock toward one of the mares Jared had purchased in Fredericksburg, a dainty bay with a white blaze in the middle of her forehead.

Jared closed the gate and strode around the paddock.

Jarina smiled happily in greeting, then placed her hands on Jared's shoulders while he lifted her off the fence and set her on her feet. "You should not be climbing on fences," he scolded gently. "I told you to be careful. You don't listen very well, madam."

She threw him a reproachful glance. "I wish you would stop coddling me, Jared. I've not been sick once since the other morning, and that was because of the ham."

Although Jared said nothing, he had a few theories of his own about that day, and he had been watching both Jarina and the calendar closely ever since. If his hunch played true, the baby would be due around the first of January.

A loud whinnying drew their attention back to the horses. "Oh, Jared, look!" Jarina cried out in dismay as Morocco backed the mare into a corner and bit her ear. "He's hurting her!"

"He's not hurting her, love; he's courting her," Jared said thickly, his voice low and softly seductive. His arms went around Jarina from behind and he gently pulled her against him. "He's been wooing her for several days. See the way he dances around her and tries to win her favor? When the time is right, he will mount her."

A rush of pink stained Jarina's cheeks. In spite of herself, she could not tear her gaze away. A hot ache grew between her thighs and spread like wildfire through her limbs as she watched in red-faced fascination while Morocco and the mare played out an elaborate courtship ritual before her eyes. The stallion nuzzled and nipped at the mare, and she in turn bolted beyond his reach and led him on a wild chase around the paddock, then stopped and stood docilely to receive his ardent attentions.

Jarina's heart hammered furiously. She clamped her thighs together, but the fire that burned in her loins would not be quelled.

Jared's hand slid downward over her belly and Jarina gasped. "Oh, Jared, someone will see you," she protested.

Jared bent and pressed his lips against the soft white flesh at the side of her throat. "No one will see us."

Everywhere his kisses touched, her skin burned. She felt him working her skirts up between them, and when his hands touched her bare flesh, she choked back a groan. Her knees trembled so badly, they threatened to buckle beneath her. She closed her eyes and dropped her head back on Jared's shoulder as he stroked and caressed her until she was almost sobbing with pleasure. She sagged weakly against him, unable and unwilling to fight the uncontrollable desire he was arousing in her.

In the paddock, Morocco let out a shrill, screaming neigh. Jarina's eyes fluttered open in time to see the stallion rise up on his hind legs behind the mare.

Then Jared eased his fingers into her wet warmth and a violent tremor rocked Jarina's entire body.

Jarina was just coming back down to earth when a harried voice intruded on their privacy. "Mr. Jared, come quick! It's Lady Beth!"

A panicked cry broke in Jarina's throat. Coloring hotly, she shoved her skirts down. Jared signaled to the groom who turned and ran back toward the barn.

Jarina's hands flew to her warm cheeks. "Do you think he saw us?"

"I doubt it."

Vowing silently to exercise more caution in the future, Jarina frantically tried to smooth the creases from her skirt. "Oh, Jared, look at me! I'm a mess!"

Jared straightened her collar. "Quite the contrary, madam," he said huskily. "You look adorable."

"Jared, don't tease! Look at my gown! I'm all wrinkled. Everyone will *know.*"

He chuckled. "Stop blushing, and no one will suspect a thing."

When they reached the barn, Lady Beth was lying on her side. Her ribs were heaving and a fine sheen of sweat covered her chestnut coat.

Jared knelt beside the mare.

"She's been pacing the past hour," the groom said. "I thought it might be something she'd ate, seein' as how it weren't her time. But then her waters broke."

Jared spoke gently to the mare as he moved his long, tanned fingers over her distended belly. Lady Beth lifted her head and regarded him with large woeful eyes. A strong spasm gripped her abdominal muscles and she whinnied in discomfort.

"Is she going to be all right?" Jarina whispered.

Jared's expression was somber. "It's too soon," he said quietly. "Lady Beth will be fine, but the foal won't survive."

"Oh, Jared, no!"

Jared got to his feet. Taking Jarina's arm, he steered her away from the laboring mare. "Love, I want you to go back to the house and wait for me. Sloane and I will manage here."

"But, I want to help!"

"No."

"Jared, please—"

"Jarina, I'll not argue with you. This is no place for a woman. Go back to the house. I'll send word as soon as it's over."

Jarina's chin jerked up and mutiny flashed in her eyes. "If a birthing were not a woman's place, we would have all sprung full-grown from our fathers' loins," she said petulantly.

Realizing the futility of trying to reason with her,

Jared relented. "All right, you may stay," he said. "But if anything should go wrong and I tell you to go back to the house, you are to obey me."

She nodded hastily in agreement. "I promise."

"Mr. Jared, it's coming," Sloane called out.

Releasing Jarina's arm, Jared went to Lady Beth.

After several long, agonizing moments, the forelegs appeared, encased in whitish membranes, and then the head. Lady Beth's distended sides suddenly contracted and there was a wheezing sound deep in her diaphragm.

Standing well back so that Jared would not change his mind about letting her stay, Jarina clamped her teeth down on her bottom lip to keep from crying out in sympathy as Lady Beth's abdomen contracted in hard labor. *Come on, Lady Beth! You can do it!* she urged silently. Her eyes were wide with fear and wonder as she watched the foal's shoulders and chest slide free of the mare's body.

The foal began to struggle and gasp for air.

A moment later Sloane let out a loud whoop. "A colt!" he announced. "Lady Beth's got herself a son!"

Something burst inside Jarina's chest.

An emotion she could not define swept over her. Tears welled in her eyes, and her shoulders began to shake with soundless sobs. In all her years of assisting her father in his practice, not once had she ever witnessed a birth.

The colt was perfect. His wet, wavy coat was a dark, rich chestnut, almost red, his legs were long, and his eyes clear and bright.

He was also lying very, very still.

Lady Beth began to lick the colt, but he would not move. His breathing was shallow and uneven.

Confused, Jarina looked at her husband. His brows were drawn together and his expression was grim. "Jared?"

She saw his shoulders stiffen. "Go back to the house," he said quietly.

"Jared, what's wrong with him?"

"I will explain later."

"Is he going to die?"

"Damn it, Jarina! Do as I say!"

Suddenly, and with unprecedented clarity, Jarina *knew* what her husband intended to do. Without thinking, she blurted out, "You can't! I won't let you!"

Jared rounded on her, but Jarina failed to heed his murderous expression. "I won't let you do it!" she cried, her voice quavering with near-hysteria. "I know he's weak, but that's no reason to kill him. You must give him a chance!"

That Jarina would even *think* he intended to take the colt's life infuriated Jared. He had hoped she held a higher opinion of him than that. "I told you to go back to the house," he ground out.

"I'll feed him," Jarina insisted. "I'll sit with him at night and keep him warm. He'll get stronger. You'll see."

"He is not going to get stronger just because you *want* him to," Jared spat. "A horse is not like a human; no amount of care is going to save him. He came too early. His lungs are not completely formed. *He is going to die.*"

"I don't believe you!"

Sloane's head whipped around and he gaped at her in stunned disbelief. His alarmed gaze met Jared's, and there was no mistaking the dismissal he read in his employer's frosty stare.

Without a word, Sloane left the barn.

As if to prove Jared wrong, the colt lifted his head and whinnied softly.

Jarina pushed past her husband and knelt beside the colt. "See, I told you. He's getting stronger already. All he needs is a little—"

She broke off abruptly as Jared's hand closed around

her upper arm. He jerked her to her feet and spun her around to face him, and Jarina recoiled from the savage fury in his gray eyes. "If you ever question my word again," he warned, shaking her so viciously her head snapped back, "I will turn you out with nary a stitch on your back nor a pence to your name! Do you understand me?"

Surprise, then anger, then horror flashed across Jarina's face in rapid succession as she realized what she had done. Not only had she openly defied Jared in front of one of his servants, she had practically called him a liar. Her face burning with mortification, she opened her mouth to apologize, but Jared had already released her and turned his back on her.

Tears welled in her eyes and a lump too big to swallow lodged in her throat. She felt as though she were drowning in a sea of shame. Today had been spoiled, and she was to blame.

Her stubborn, unyielding pride, however, would not allow her to relinquish having the last word. Her chin inched upward and she squared her shoulders. "Fitch said you would die if I didn't let him take your leg," she said achingly.

Jared crashed his fist into the wall. "Damn it, Jarina! Do you think I *want* him to die?"

The rent of emotion in Jared's voice caused Jarina's throat to tighten and her eyes to brim over. She shook her head. "No," she croaked.

Disgusted with himself for making her cry, Jared pressed his fingertips against the throbbing ache behind his closed eyelids as he fought for control of his own rampaging emotions. He did not know what was happening to him. A few months ago, he could have handled the doomed birth of a premature colt with level-headed indifference; now, he was in danger of crumbling like a sentimental old woman.

He dropped his hand and drew a deep, steadying breath. "My intention was never to kill the colt," he said hoarsely. "Only to spare you the torment of watching him die."

"He's not going to die," she said wretchedly.

There was a painful, unaccustomed constriction in Jared's chest. "Jarina—"

"I won't let him die, Jared. I'll take good care of him. I'm begging you, please, just let me try."

Her plea tore at him. "Darling, don't do this . . ."

"Jared, *please.* You promised I could name him."

Jared's heart slammed against his ribs. Swearing savagely, he turned away from her, his great frame shaking as he dragged his hand across his face in a gesture of impotent frustration. Never before in his life had he felt so fractured. If he sent Jarina back to the house, she would never believe that he'd not had a hand in hastening the colt's death. Yet, if he let her stay, he needed to be strong for both of them. And right now, he did not feel very strong at all.

"All right," he heard himself say, almost as if the decision had been made for him, "we will wait together."

It was Jared's begrudgingly given assent that finally broke Jarina's control. Her shoulders wrenched forward and a sob shattered in her throat. "Thank you," she murmured.

"Don't thank me yet," Jared said harshly. "It's going to be a long wait."

Neither of them knew how true that prophecy was going to prove. An hour passed, and then two, and the colt made no effort to stand. Nor would he nurse. Jarina ran back to the house to fetch a sugar-teat, but after several licks of the knotted handkerchief, the foal seemed to lose interest in the sweet treat. "Oh, Jared, what are we going to do?" Jarina whispered brokenly.

"There is nothing we can do, sweet, except wait," Jared said, with more calmness than he was feeling.

The hour grew late.

Jared lighted the lanterns. One of the servants came

to inquire about dinner, but neither Jared nor Jarina were hungry. Jared considered taking the situation in hand and ordering Jarina to return to the house, then decided against it. As much as he wanted to protect his wife from the harsh realities of life, he knew she was going to have to learn the hard way that not all hurts could be bandaged and kissed away. "Have you settled upon a name for him?" he asked.

Jarina shook her head. "I had thought of Rob Roy because of his red coat," she said woodenly. "But there doesn't seem to be much of the Highlander in him, does there? He's not a fighter like the first Rob Roy."

Because he could find no argument against that, Jared said nothing.

The rustling of straw drew their attention to Lady Beth's stall. The foal was making his first attempt to stand. First, he stretched out his forelegs and pushed himself up. Not daring to breathe, Jarina pressed her fist against her mouth. Her heart beat rapidly and her eyes were wide as she watched the colt raise himself up on his hindlegs. He tottered for several long, unbearable seconds, then collapsed back to the ground.

Jarina's breath tore from her chest in an agonized sob. "Oh, Jared!" she cried out.

Jared's arm went around her shoulders and he pulled her close. "Give him time, love," he said, a little unsteadily. "It usually takes several tries before a foal can stand without falling."

The sun was just streaking over the horizon when Jared knelt beside Jarina and aroused her from a nap. "Look," he said.

Clutching the blanket she had wrapped herself in, Jarina placed a palm against the ground and pushed herself upright. She had to blink several times before her sleepy gaze began to focus on the scene before her.

In Lady Beth's stall, both colt and dam were standing; and the gangly, long-legged infant was feeding heartily at his mother's udder.

"He certainly has the appetite of a Scot," Jared said with a throaty chuckle. "Do you still want to name him Rob Roy?"

Joy and relief washed over Jarina like a tidal wave. She staggered to her feet. "I think we'll have to," she confessed. "Every time I said a prayer for him, I called him Robbie."

Jared enfolded Jarina in his embrace and buried his face against her tangled curls. "I apologize for losing my temper with you earlier," he said quietly.

Jarina tilted her head back to look at her husband with tear-brightened eyes. "I never meant to challenge your word, Jared. Please believe that. I was just so scared you would be right."

"I'm glad I wasn't."

Jared lowered his head to hers and took her lips in a sweet, gentle kiss, but the intimacy of the moment was interrupted by a low, torturous rumble.

Jared jerked his head back, and Jarina's eyes widened in embarrassed surprise. "Was that your stomach, or mine?" she asked sheepishly.

Jared chuckled. "I think it was yours, madam. Are you hungry?"

"Famished."

"So am I. Mrs. Cunningham, would you care to join me for breakfast?"

Jarina laughed. "As long as it doesn't include ham."

They were slowly making their way up the hill toward the house when they spotted Stephen Landon coming up the drive.

"It's like Stephen to arrive just in time to eat," Jared said dryly. "Let's hope he has some good news for us."

Jarina threw her husband a startled glance. "About the charges against you?"

"What else?"

Stephen reined in his horse and dismounted. His brown eyes gleamed warmly. "You two spend the night

in the barn?" he asked, noting the bits of straw that
clung to their rumpled clothing.

Jarina beamed. "Lady Beth gave birth to a colt!" she
said excitedly. "We named him Rob Roy."

Stephen looked surprised. "A little early, isn't it?"

Jared inclined his head. "More than a month. We
didn't think the foal would make it, but he seems to
have pulled through the critical stages."

Stephen let out a long, low whistle. "Thank God for
that. That mare cost you a princely sum."

One of the grooms came to take Stephen's horse.
Jarina slipped her arm through her husband's, and the
three of them continued on up the hill toward the
house.

"The place looks good," Stephen commented, noticing the recently raised timbers for the new stable. "You
have done a lot of work."

"There's a great deal more to be done," Jared said.
"I heard from Tom Jefferson last week. General
Kearns expressed an interest in the Morgan as an issue
cavalry mount."

"I thought you preferred the American Saddle
Horse."

"I do. But the Morgan is worth investigating for his
stamina alone."

A comforting feeling settled over Jarina as she listened to Jared talk. It filled her with wonder to think
that her husband was on familiar terms with his country's president; during all the years she lived in England, she had never even been to court.

When they reached the house, Jarina excused herself
to go change her gown and find Cook. "I don't think
you want to contend with my cooking," she said
lightly.

Stephen's brows lifted in mock horror. "Is it that
bad?"

Jared laughed. "As usual, my wife's modesty is mis-
placed," he said. "Jarina is an excellent cook."

As they watched her go, Stephen said in a low voice, "If I didn't know any better, old friend, I would think you had broken your cardinal rule."

Jared led the way to his study. "What rule is that?"

Stephen declined the drink Jared offered. "Never to fall in love," he said.

A muscle in Jared's jaw tightened. "What Jarina and I share is a friendship based upon mutual respect. I like her, and I enjoy her company. I am not in love with her."

Stephen lowered himself onto a chair and stretched out his legs. "You could have fooled me," he said, grinning.

After that, the conversation turned to business, but Jared's attention span was unusually short, and time and again he found his thoughts wandering. Stephen's jesting about being in love had touched a nerve, and Jared was not at all pleased to discover that merely discussing a subject from which he had previously thought himself immune made him feel exposed and vulnerable.

After several moments of discussing matters of little import, Stephen took a deep breath. "We received a letter from Roswell's solicitor," he said. "Roswell has doubled his offer on the company."

Jared's eyes narrowed. "No."

"Aw, c'mon, Jared. You'll never get more than what Roswell's willing to pay."

"I'll sell to anyone else; not to Roswell."

Never before had Stephen known Jared to allow personal feelings to interfere with common sense when it came to logical business judgments. Usually Jared was amazingly astute. He decided to try one more time. "If you wait much longer," he said, "you'll not be able to sell at all. There's talk that England and France may go to war. If that happens—"

"If that happens, investors in either country would welcome a foothold on our shores. I'll sell the company for a good price, but it will be a cold day in hell before I sell it to Roswell."

A short time later, Jarina appeared in the doorway to announce that their meal was ready. She had changed her gown and brushed out her thick, glossy curls. He went to her and pressed a tender kiss to her brow. "You are beautiful," he whispered.

The next hour passed so pleasantly that Jarina did not even mind when Damon and Evelyn joined them.

Damon showed a vague interest in the news about Lady Beth's foal, but Evelyn's face only registered disgust. "The two of them spend hours at the stables," she said derisively. "I've never known anyone to show so much concern over a dirty animal."

"I'm surprised the foal lived," Damon said, helping himself to a cold meat turnover. "The premature ones usually don't."

"No doubt Jarina was the one who saved him," Evelyn said peevishly. "After all, what else would one expect of someone who has such an *extensive* knowledge of medicine?"

Evelyn's waspishness irritated Jared. "Jarina's knowledge of medicine has proved invaluable on more than one occasion," he said meaningfully.

"Before I forget," Stephen said, recognizing the need to change the subject, "in my saddlebag is a copy of the *London Times,* fresh off a merchantman that docked just last week. I thought those of you here in the wilderness might be interested in knowing how the civilized world is faring."

"Oh, Stephen, Fairfax County is hardly wilderness," Jarina gently chided.

"But it *is* far enough away for us to lose touch with the rest of the world," Damon said. "Tell me, is England still trying to seize our ships and press our seamen into service?"

Embarrassed that Damon would even mention such a thing in Jarina's presence, Stephen dodged the question. "I haven't had an opportunity to read the entire paper," he said. "There was one interesting piece though concerning Roswell. It would seem he and Lord Hamilton have had a falling out of sorts."

Jarina's head snapped up.

Evelyn frowned. "Lord Hamilton? I've heard that name, but I can't recall where."

"It was in the papers a few months ago," Damon reminded her. "His daughter married the Duke of Roswell."

"*Was* to marry Roswell," Stephen corrected him. "She vanished the night before the wedding, and no one has seen her since."

"Was she abducted?" Evelyn asked.

"Not likely," Stephen said. "Roswell seems to think she went into hiding. He had Hamilton thrown into a debtors' prison and intends to keep him there until either the girl reappears or his lordship repays the one hundred and seventy-five thousand-pound marriage settlement Roswell bestowed upon him."

Had Jared not been watching Jarina, he would have missed the sudden evacuation of color from her face. His brows drawing together in tender concern, he reached across the table and took her hand in his, but she seemed not to notice. Her fingers were like ice.

"A hundred and seventy-five thousand pounds!" Evelyn blurted out, incredulous. "The girl must be an idiot not to want to marry him."

"From what I've heard," Damon said, "Roswell is a most unpleasant sort."

"He's a duke, for God's sake!" Evelyn shot back. "And it's apparent that he's extraordinarily wealthy! What does it matter what the man looks like?"

Stephen chuckled. "Not all women are as mercenary as you, cousin dear. Some of them even manage to look beyond a man's purse and his family crest when seeking a husband."

"Not Evelyn," Damon retorted. "Evelyn would marry a jackass if he were titled."

Evelyn's eyes narrowed menacingly. "Better a jackass than a bastard!"

With a strangled cry, Jarina surged to her feet, knocking over her coffee cup in the process. She stared in mute horror at the brown stain that spread across the white linen tablecloth. The room seemed to bear down on her, making it impossible to breathe. There was an odd buzzing in her ears.

Jared pushed back his chair and stood up. He placed a steadying hand beneath her elbow. "It's all right, love," he said quietly. "The stain will wash."

Jarina lifted her gaze to his face, and the raw pain he saw in her eyes sliced into his soul. "Please, my lord," she whispered achingly. "Forgive me . . ." Pushing past him, she fled the room.

Stephen rose from the table. "Jared, what's wrong?"

Without answering, Jared turned and followed after his wife.

Evelyn snorted inelegantly. "Stupid child," she spat. "Crying over a little spill."

Jared stopped at the foot of the stairs, his dark brows knitting together as he watched his wife run up the remaining steps and disappear down the hall. He heard the door to their bedchamber slam after her. Pivoting, he strode across the foyer and into his study. He unlocked his desk and removed the marriage license bond from the top drawer. His hands shook as he unfolded the document.

Margaret Jarina Hamilton. The rounded feminine script leapt off the page at him, striking him like a blow between the eyes. A savage curse exploded in Jared's chest and he flung the license away from him.

He gripped the edge of the desk. She had betrayed him. She had betrayed him as surely as his father had betrayed his mother. Not with her body, perhaps, but with a lie. From the moment she had tumbled at his feet, she had let him think she was someone else. All the time she had been arousing his passions with her body and piercing his armor with her quick wit, she had in truth belonged to Roswell. *She had lied to him.*

Yet, what choice had he given her?

He had inflicted his will on her. He had threatened and browbeaten and humiliated her, and he had tried to break her spirit.

In return, she had saved his life. She had touched him with her innocence and awakened in his breast a tenderness that he had thought himself incapable of feeling. He thought of the way she took him inside her body and surrounded him with her sweet, unselfish love. He recalled the aching uncertainty in her voice that night in the barn when she had told him she loved him. He thought of her unflagging determination to save one premature, spindly legged, red-coated foal, and the last of his defenses shattered.

"Damn, but I am a mindless fool!" he realized aloud.

He strode from the study and bounded up the stairs.

He found her in the great empty room that had once been his bedchamber. She was standing at the window, with her back to him and her forehead pressed against a diamond-shaped pane.

I love you, he thought, and the revelation was as painful as it was sweet.

Without a word, he went to her and drew her into his arms.

Jarina turned her face against his broad chest, seeking comfort in the strong arms that enveloped her. Her body quaked with the effort of holding back the tears that threatened. "Oh, Jared . . . I'm so sorry. . . ."

Jared tightened his hold on her and buried his face in her soft hair. "It's all right, sweet," he murmured. "for as long as you need me, I'll be here."

For a long time he stood there with Jarina in his arms, stroking her back. Gradually her trembling subsided. After a while, when she tilted her head back to look at him, her eyes were unexpectedly dry. Yet there was a quiet sorrow in them that went beyond mere tears. "Jared, there is something I should tell you," she said softly.

The hesitation in her voice ripped through his heart. *Dear God! What kind of monster am I that has made the most precious being in the world afraid to confide in me?* Determined to mend the damage his callousness had wrought, he cupped her face between his hands and bent to press a kiss to her forehead. "You can tell me anything," he gently assured her.

She blushed self-consciously and lowered her gaze. "I did not want to tell you until I was certain," she said shyly. "But if I am going to keep embarrassing myself by getting sick and running from the room, it is only fitting that you know." She took a deep steadying breath and lifted her artless blue gaze to his face. "I think we're going to have a baby."

Jared's expression became closed and unreadable as he struggled with Jarina's announcement. He had hoped she would trust him with the unhappy secret she had kept so close to her heart these past months.

Bewilderment creased Jarina's brow. "Are you not pleased about the baby, my lord?" she asked, sensing Jared's disappointment.

Realizing how closely he had come to hurting her again, Jared quickly checked his troubled thoughts. Her trust he had yet to earn. For now, he just wanted to keep her safe. He must, at all costs, protect her from Roswell.

He pulled her back into his embrace. His smile belied the solemnity of his gray gaze as he looked deep into her eyes, and when he spoke, his voice was thick with emotion. "There is nothing in this world that could please me more."

Evelyn found Damon in Jared's study. "What do you think you are doing?" she demanded. "You were supposed to go after them, you stupid fool! While you're just sitting here, twiddling your thumbs, Jared is up-stairs with *her.* How in the hell am I supposed to win him back if you won't cooperate!"

Evelyn began to pace angrily. "It's not fair!" she wailed. "Jared is the only man I ever really loved, and I'm going to lose him to that little tramp who seduced him. I could kill her for taking Jared away from me. I hate her!"

Damon sat with his feet propped up on Jared's desk, his gold-spoked eyes narrowing in amusement as he witnessed Evelyn's tantrum. A contemplative smile curved his mouth, and when Evelyn saw it, she shrieked.

"Damn you, Damon Cunningham! Don't you dare laugh at me! If you hadn't hit me and given me that awful black eye, none of this would ever have hap-pened!"

"The mistake," Damon retorted, "was yours. Don't blame me because you were stupid enough to try to ac-cuse Jared of slapping you."

Evelyn's eyes glittered with hatred, but she said nothing. Satisfied that he had finally silenced her, Damon leaned forward and shoved Jared's marriage li-cense bond across the desk toward her. "If you can stop thinking of yourself long enough to remember that you are not the only one who stands to lose all because of Jared's marriage, take a look at this. I think, Evelyn dearest, I have found a way to put our little duchess in her proper place."

Chapter Fifteen

Behind the locked doors of Jared's study, Stephen listened to Jared in rapt incredulity, unmindful that he was holding his breath until it tore from his chest in a shuddering gasp. "Good God!" he swore. "I would never have suspected that Jarina is Lord Hamilton's daughter! And to think she might have married Roswell!"

That same thought caused Jared's hand to shake as he refilled his brandy. "Jarina isn't aware that I know," he said tautly. "For the time, I would prefer to keep it that way."

Stephen ran his fingers through his hair. "You're right, of course." He groaned and shook his head in disbelief. "Do you realize what Roswell's reaction is going to be when he learns his intended betrothed is now wed to his worst enemy?"

"Do you realize what his reaction is going to be when he realizes he helped finance Hamilton's release from prison?"

"And I thought you'd gone daft when you said you'd changed your mind about selling the company to him! Jared, if Roswell ever finds out that your share of the proceeds has gone toward repaying Lord Hamilton's debt to him—"

"Which is precisely why I cannot trust anyone but you to negotiate the sale. I want Roswell to think he is dealing with the company's primary proprietor. As far as he is concerned, my hands are tied because of the charges imposed against me by the crown."

Stephen looked doubtful. "I just hope he falls for it."

Later that evening, during dinner, Stephen's announcement that he planned to sail to England was met with a mixture of surprise and apprehension.

"Are you sure it's safe to make such a voyage with the escalating hostilities between England and France?" Jarina asked.

"About as safe as it's always been," Stephen said with casual indifference. He did not want to give Jarina additional cause to worry. She had enough of a burden on her shoulders as it was, knowing her father was languishing in a debtors' prison because of her refusal to marry Roswell.

"But, why?" Evelyn demanded to know. "You just returned from England. I was under the impression you were going to sell the company and give up the sea for good."

"I intend to. The problem is, until we can get Jared here absolved of the charges against him, we are powerless to even *lease* the company, much less sell it."

A small frown puckered Jarina's brow. She glanced at her husband, but Jared seemed withdrawn and disinclined to contribute to the discussion.

Damon, too, had been unusually quiet all evening, although more than once Jarina had caught him studying Jared with a feral gleam in his strange, gold-spoked eyes, and his smug silence set her teeth on edge. The more she saw of Damon, the less she liked him, although she could not explain why. She recalled what Finley had said about Damon being a bad seed, and she wondered uneasily if perhaps the gardener had been right.

It was Evelyn, however, who succeeded in upstaging

even Stephen's unexpected announcement with one of her own.

"I've decided to return to Alexandria with Stephen," she said. "That is, if Jared will consent to letting me stay at the house on King Street," she added demurely, giving Jared a sidelong glance from beneath her lashes.

Jared's eyes narrowed ominously as he regarded Evelyn over the rim of his wineglass, and it was all Jarina could do not to shudder at the cold animosity she saw in their gray depths. There was an undercurrent of hatred in this house that made her physically ill.

Jared put down his glass. "You may stay at the town house," he said.

"The country becomes so boring in the summer," Evelyn said. "There is nothing to do here, and I do miss my shopping expeditions. Even the stores in Providence are lacking. And, of course, since I don't have this obsession with horses that—"

"I said you may stay at the town house," Jared interrupted tersely. "Let the matter drop."

Evelyn bristled. "I was merely trying to explain—"

Jared pushed his chair back and stood up. "If you will excuse me, I have work to do."

Jared left the dining room, and a few moments later, they heard the front door slam loudly after him. Hurt flashed across Evelyn's face, and for a moment, she seemed genuinely confused. "Touchy tonight, isn't he?" she retorted. Her voice wavered.

It was late when Jared finally returned to the house. He undressed in the dark and slipped into bed beside Jarina. She turned and snuggled against him. "I thought you'd be asleep," he said, pulling her close and planting a kiss on her forehead.

Jarina wrapped one arm around his waist and settled her head in the curve of his shoulder. "I was waiting for you," she murmured sleepily.

"I was out at the barn with Rob Roy and Lady Beth."

"How are they?"

"Doing well. I think the foal is going to survive."

Jared made no mention of his burst of temper at dinner, and although Jarina was hesitant to bring up a subject he was obviously loath to discuss, her curiosity won out. "What do you think is Evelyn's real purpose for going to Alexandria?" she asked.

She felt Jared stiffen beside her.

"If you want the truth, Jarina," he said slowly, "I really don't give a damn. I'd gladly pay Evelyn's passage out of the country if I thought we'd finally be rid of her."

Then why have you allowed her to stay here so long? That and a host of other questions regarding Evelyn sprang to Jarina's lips, but she cautiously bit them back. Instead, she broached another worry that had been troubling her. "Jared, why is Stephen going to England?"

A low, throaty chuckle rumbled in Jared's chest as he rolled onto his side, pinning Jarina beneath him. "Woman, has anyone ever told you you talk too much?" he teased. Gripping the hem of her nightgown, he began working it up over her hips.

He lowered his mouth to hers, but she turned her face aside, dodging his kiss. "Jared!"

His lips moved provocatively down her throat. "Hmmm?"

Jared's caresses were causing a tantalizing heat to unfurl in the pit of Jarina's stomach. "Jared, I asked you a . . . a question . . ." she stammered, unable to think clearly.

Jared pulled her nightgown over her head and flung it aside.

"I want to know why Stephen—" A giggle burst in Jarina's throat and she nearly doubled over at the tickling sensation Jared's fingers made on her sensitive skin as they trailed down over her abdomen. "Jared, stop that!" she blurted out, grabbing his hand and holding it tightly to keep him from tickling her. Her chest rose and fell rapidly as she struggled to catch her breath. "I wish you would answer my question," she said petulantly.

Raising up on one elbow, Jared studied her face in the darkness. "And what question is that?"

Even as Jarina released her breath in an exaggerated sigh of exasperation, she sensed that Jared was not teasing her so much as he was stalling for time. "I don't believe Stephen is going to England to prove your innocence and to get the charges against you dropped, because you have already made arrangements with the American ambassador to do that," she said. "So I want to know the *real* reason Stephen is making this voyage."

"I don't expect to hear from the American ambassador for at least another two months," Jared explained patiently. "In the meantime, I have received an offer to buy the company at a good price, and I want to sell. Since the prospective buyer resides in England, Stephen's journey will serve two purposes. First, Stephen will secure my pardon from the king, if the American ambassador has not already done so; then he will negotiate the sale of the company. By sending Stephen now, rather than wait for a reply from the American ambassador, I will be able to finalize the sale as soon as possible, hopefully *before* there is any serious trouble between England and America."

Although Jarina did not believe Jared was lying to her precisely, she suspected he was deliberately omitting a rather large portion of the truth. And after what happened the last time she questioned Jared's word, she was reluctant to do so again. "Do you believe there will be trouble between our two countries?" she asked instead.

"If the Royal Navy doesn't cease with their unlawful searches of our ships, there very well might be."

Jarina chewed on her bottom lip. "I hope there isn't," she said in a small voice.

"So do I, love," Jared replied. And, because he knew there was no point in telling Jarina not to worry about it—she would do so anyway—he lowered his head to hers and brushed his lips against the throbbing pulse at her temple. *"Now* may I make love to my wife?" he whispered huskily.

Spring turned into summer. Angus and Maggie were married, and Jarina was left with the task of training Mary to take Maggie's place as housekeeper. Jared finally received the long-awaited contract from the army and turned his attentions to his horses. Evelyn moved her belongings into the town house on King Street, and, except for the outrageous bills that arrived monthly for purchases she had charged to Jared's name, they were hardly aware of her existence.

And Jarina's pregnancy began to show.

"You're getting a rather nice little belly on you, my dear," Jared teased her as they were dressing one morning. Embracing her from behind, he allowed his hand to travel downward to caress her newly rounded abdomen through her chemise.

Jarina closed her eyes and let her head drop contentedly back on her husband's shoulder. "You won't think it's so nice when it begins to interfere with your lustful ways," she returned.

Jared jerked his head up to eye her reflection in the looking glass. "Lustful?" he asked, and Jarina could not help laughing at his wounded tone.

"Amorous?" she amended.

He grinned at her. "That's better," he said.

God, how I love you! Jared thought.

Jarina had not told him she loved him since that night in the barn when he had first made love to her, and inwardly Jared knew it was because he had never said it to her in return. He did not know why he held back, except that some small part of him rebelled at his insatiable need for her. Nor was his hunger entirely physical. If anything ever happened to Jarina, he was not certain he could go on living. If he lost her, the pain would be as great as if someone had cut out his heart.

Jared cupped her breast and nipped playfully at her earlobe. "I could stay here all day with you," he murmured.

Love shining in her blue eyes, Jarina laughed and scooted out of his embrace. "Jared Cunningham, you are incorrigible!"

They were enjoying a leisurely breakfast when Evanston informed them that a messenger from Washington City had arrived and wanted to speak with Jared.

Alarm coursed through Jarina's veins, and she had to struggle to keep her expression neutral. "Perhaps he is bringing you more orders for horses," she said with a nonchalance she was far from feeling. She did not know why she should suddenly feel so frightened.

Jared rose from the table. "There is only one way to find out," he said. In spite of his light tone, Jarina saw his jaw tighten ominously.

Several moments later, when Jared returned after speaking with the messenger, his expression was grim. "I must go into Washington for a few days," he said. "Jefferson wants me to testify before Congress regarding Lieutenant Stendhal's boarding of the *Pegasus* last winter."

Jarina's eyes widened in surprise. "But, why? I thought you reported that incident to the British Naval Attaché while we were still in Alexandria."

"I did. Unfortunately, the British have become more brazen in recent weeks. They broadsided the U.S.S. *Chesapeake,* killing three seamen and wounding eighteen. In addition, they seized four American sailors as deserters and removed them to His Majesty's fleet. One of the men was hanged."

As if in sympathetic reaction, Jarina's hand flew to

her throat. And then she remembered Stephen, and a cold knot of dread formed in her stomach.

"I'll be leaving right away," Jared said brusquely. Then, as if reading her thoughts, his tone gentled and he said, "Landon should be in England by now; his ship would not have been involved in the altercation."

Perhaps not this time, but what of the next? Jarina thought uneasily. "Will you be away long?"

"Only a few days." Jared did not add that he also intended to pay Evelyn a visit. He had never told Evelyn why he did not marry her eight years ago, and he doubted she knew the reason they could never marry. While he no longer loved her, he felt she deserved an explanation. He owed her that. "Is there anything you want me to bring back for you?" he asked instead.

"Good morning," Damon greeted from the doorway. "Mind if I join you two for breakfast?"

The look of hatred that streaked across Jarina's face was gone so quickly Jared wondered if he had imagined it. Jarina indicated a chair. "Not at all," she said politely, her expression unreadable.

Damon sauntered into the room.

"Unfortunately, I cannot stay," Jared said, regarding his wife with a troubled frown. "Jarina can explain everything to you." He bent down to place a kiss on her cheek. "Are you going to be all right here?" he asked in a low voice.

Ashamed that she had given Jared cause to worry by allowing her dislike of Damon to show, Jarina gave Jared her warmest smile. "I'll be fine," she assured him. Then she laughed and patted her stomach. "*We* will be fine."

During the journey to Washington, Jared wondered if he should have brought Jarina with him rather than leave her at Wyeburn during his absence. In spite of the fact that Damon had given him no specific reason not to trust him, Jared was not comfortable leaving Jarina alone with him. A lifetime of suspicion had taken a hefty toll, Jared realized, and he reluctantly dismissed his misgivings as absurd. He did not want to risk either his wife's or his baby's health by letting Jarina travel during her pregnancy. Still, that brief flash of hatred he had seen in her eyes disturbed him greatly.

Jared spent the first four days of July testifying before the Senate and hearing the testimonies of other ships' captains. The attack on the U.S.S. *Chesapeake* was merely the latest of a long series of British assaults on American vessels. While the *Pegasus* had merely been boarded, other captains had suffered losses of both men and property. But whether his good fortune was due to luck or careful planning, Jared neither knew nor cared. By the end of the fourth day, he was anxious to return to Wyeburn.

He was packing to leave when a hotel page brought him an invitation to a Fourth of July banquet being held at the White House that night.

Any other time, he would have regarded the invitation as his due. Tonight, however, it felt like a summons, and he was loath to accept. During the past four days, he had come to the realization that the fast-paced, often vulgar, world of politics bored him. Because it was the seat of government, Washingtonians tended to regard their city as the sacred core around which the rest of the world revolved, a narcissistic attitude which he was beginning to find extremely irritating. Once, in the midst of a discussion on horsebreeding, he had caught Senator Cranston—a handsome, successful bachelor whose company he had once enjoyed—eyeing him with something akin to pity.

"It must be a dreadful bore, living so far away from everything," Cranston said, and Jared found himself gritting his teeth in annoyance. He wondered wryly if he should tell the senator that his favorite pastime was watching the way Jarina's lashes curved against her cheeks while she slept.

It was still daylight when Jared's coach turned down Pennsylvania Avenue. Militia paraded before the White House, and from the Navy Yard, Jared could hear the booming of cannon. A fight broke out on the White House steps as Federalists and Republicans struggled to be first in line at the reception in the East Room. And at the banquet later that night, there was a frenzied cheering when someone proposed a toast declaring that the United States stand up and fight for its principles.

"It would appear that the requirement for a cavalry may come sooner than any of us anticipated," a weary, grim-lipped Thomas Jefferson told Jared.

While the merchant in Jared was mentally calculating the profits he was likely to make from the sale of his horses to the army, the husband and father in him rebelled against the mere idea of war. He did not want to place his family in jeopardy for the sake of quarreling nations. "I assume you are aware the people are calling for a special session of Congress to deal with the issue," Jared told his old friend.

Jefferson inclined his head in acknowledgement. "Unfortunately, between those factions who accuse me of being in the pay of Napoleon and those who would like to see the English permanently driven from our shores, there is precious little room for negotiation. If I submit to a special session of Congress now, with the country's present mood, there is certain to be a vote to declare war on both France and Great Britain."

Although it was late by the time he left the banquet, Jared decided to go on to Alexandria rather than return to his hotel room. As soon as he had spoken with Evelyn, he wanted to go home.

The sun was just breaking over the horizon when Jared crossed the Potomac into Virginia.

"Miss Evelyn left yesterday afternoon with all her finery," Mrs. Hoskins told Jared when he arrived at the town house. She made no effort to disguise her contempt. "And good riddance too," she said. "There was never a woman more trouble than that one, I'm telling you. Kept the maids hopping day and night to do her bidding."

"Did she say where she was going?" Jared asked.

The housekeeper shook her head. "She paced all morning, waiting for a delivery from Madame Bouchard's. And when the new gowns arrived, she tore out of here with nary a mind your leave. Stuck you with the bill, she did. It's on the desk in your study."

Jared ran his hand through his hair in a gesture of frustration. He had not the slightest idea where Evelyn might have gone, but gut instinct told him she was up to no good. It had never been otherwise with Evelyn, he thought wearily. Why should she change now?

"There is one thing you might find to your interest," Mrs. Hoskins said, not caring what damage she might wreak with her gossip. As far as she was concerned, Evelyn Landon was long overdue for a scathing set-down. "For the past two weeks, Miss Evelyn's been going around here making us announce her presence as, 'Her Grace, the Duchess of Roswell.' "

Jarina sat back on her heels and turned her face up to the blazing July sun. She had spent most of the morning working outside, and was finally beginning to realize some visible results with the overgrown rambler that grew in a thorny tangle along the garden fence. Perspiration trickled down her neck, and she dashed it away with her hand. She was hot and tired, but happy. Earlier that morning, she had thought she felt the baby move, but when the sensation was not repeated, she decided she had been mistaken. She knew it was still too early, that the fetal quickening would not come for at least another month, but she sometimes became impatient in her eagerness to experience each new stage of pregnancy. The mere thought of Jared's baby growing in her womb filled her with a joy unlike anything she had ever known.

A sweat bee swarmed around her face. She took a swipe at it, but it persisted in its annoying assault, and she finally gave up the battle and got to her feet. "All right, you win," she said, laughing.

The rose thorns had scraped the bare flesh of her hands and arms in several places, causing it to sting annoyingly, and Jarina absently scratched at a troublesome itch on her forearm while she let her gaze wander down the hill toward the road. She wished Jared would come home. Although Damon had kept to himself during Jared's absence, she did not like being alone in the house with him. Even the constant presence of the servants failed to ease her fears. She told herself that she was allowing her imagination to run wild, and that she was basing her dislike of Damon on nothing more substantial than malicious gossip. But gossip, a tiny voice in her head reminded her, was often rooted in truth.

With a weary sigh, she turned her attention back to the rose hedge. By the time Jared returned, she hoped to have it pruned into shape and the weeds cleared from around it.

At midday, an excited Mary came running out to the garden. "Mr. Jared's come home," she said breathlessly. "He's in his study with Mr. Damon now."

Jarina's hands flew to her hair, then to her gown, and a look of horror flashed across her face as she realized how she must look. She snatched up the gardening tools she had taken from the conservatory and shoved them into Mary's arms. "Please, Mary, hurry! As soon as you put those away, you must help me change my gown. I don't want Jared to see me like this!"

Dragging her sleeve across her heat-flushed face as she ran, Jarina hurried back to the house.

Jared was home!

After the smothering midday heat, the interior of the thick-walled brick house was cool and inviting. Slipping off her shoes so they would make no sound on the wood floors, and thus betray her presence, Jarina picked them up and padded noiselessly across the foyer.

From the study, Jared's voice blasted like a cannon, rocking the walls of the house with its violent anger. "Damn you, Damon Cunningham! May God curse the ground you walk on!"

Jarina froze.

"If you think," Jared continued, "that Wyeburn will *ever* be yours, by whatever means, you are sadly mistaken. You'll get a settlement of one hundred thousand pounds, and not a pence more. When that runs out, you'll have to learn to *work* for a living. I want you out of this house and off this property now!"

"I'll go," Damon said. "But you'll not be able to keep me away. Wyeburn is as much mine as it is yours, and someday, it will be *all* mine. You have cheated me out of my inheritance long enough!"

The study doors crashed open, and Jarina ducked into the shadows to keep from being seen as Damon stormed from the house. Her heart pounding, she crossed the hall to her husband's study. Jared was pouring himself a liberal drink, and she saw his hand tremble as he put down the decanter.

"Jared?"

He rounded on her, his face dark with barely constrained anger. He seemed almost surprised to see her. He forced a brittle smile, and she saw him struggle to get his temper under control. There were shadows beneath his eyes, and he had not shaven. "Jared, what's wrong?"

His smile faded, "Let it lie, Jarina. It doesn't concern you."

"But, I saw Damon—"

"Jarina, I have no wish to discuss the matter with you, now or ever."

Sweat formed a muddy rivulet down her temple and

she reached up to wipe it away. This was not the home-coming she had planned, and she had to fight to keep the tremor of disappointment from her voice. "Jared, I'm sorry. I didn't mean—"

"Get your hand away from your face!"

The biting fury behind his words slammed into her like a physical blow, nearly sending her to her knees. She jerked her hand back down to her side, but even that hasty movement did not seem quick enough to suit Jared; and he bore down on her, closing the distance between them in three angry strides. A pained gasp tore from her throat as he gripped her elbow with enough force to crack the bones and spun her around to face the sunlight streaming in through the window. He held her arm up to the light. "Look at you!" he barked. "What in the hell have you been doing?"

She blinked up at him in confusion. "I-I was working in the garden."

"And where was Finley?"

"I don't know—"

He turned her roughly toward the door. "Get out of those clothes and burn them. You are not to wear them again!"

Thoroughly shamed at being dragged through her own house like a naughty child, Jarina wrenched her arm free of her husband's grip. "I don't know what has gotten into you," she hissed, glaring at him through a haze of angry tears, "but if you ever touch me like that again, I'll . . . I'll kill you!"

"Jarina, wait!" Jared shouted, but she bolted past him.

Running after her, Jared collided with a wide-eyed Mary, who stood trembling in the middle of the foyer, nearly knocking the frightened housekeeper down. He caught Mary by the shoulders and set her back on her feet. "Do you know of a cure for poison ivy?" he demanded impatiently.

Mary vehemently shook her head. "No, sir, I—"

"Then, find out!"

Jared took the stairs two at at time.

He caught up with Jarina just as she fled into their bedchamber. She hurled the door shut, but he blocked it with his shoulder, sending it crashing back into the wall. He caught Jarina's arm and she screamed.

"Let go of me, damn you!" she shrieked, giving a hefty jerk that nearly yanked her arm from its socket. The tears that she had been trying to contain spilled over. Angry with herself for crying, she reached up to dash them away.

Alarm streaked through Jared. "Jarina, for God's sake, keep your hands away from your face!"

Jarina's hand stopped in midair, and for the first time she saw the angry red blisters that covered her fair skin from her fingers to her elbows.

Jared could not help chuckling at her appalled expression. "Jarina, darling, somehow you managed to get into a patch of poison ivy," he said gently.

She lifted brimming eyes to his face. "Poison ivy?"

"Poison ivy. Virginia is infested with it. It thrives in our climate. Unfortunately, some people are highly sensitive to it. It will spread wherever you touch, and if you get it in your eyes, it can even blind you."

Jarina bit her bottom lip and tears streamed down her face. Her shoulders hunched forward and began to shake.

His eyes darkening in concern, Jared started toward her. "Don't cry, sweet."

The corners of her mouth tugged involuntarily and Jarina smiled sheepishly at him through her tears. She wasn't crying; she was *laughing!*

She held her arms gingerly out at her sides, not daring to touch anything. "Oh, Jared . . . Until today, I'd never even *heard* of poison ivy!"

Jared motioned to her to turn around, and he began to unbutton her gown. "It's an invasive weed that greatly resembles the Virginia creeper you English are so fond of letting climb all over your houses, except that its leaves grow in clusters of three instead of five. I would venture to guess there was a healthy patch of it growing quite contentedly along the garden fence with the roses until you came along and tried to root it out."

Jarina tilted her head back to look at him. "Am I going to be scarred for life?"

"No. Just miserable for a few days." Jared chuckled, then added in a low, suggestive tone that both teased and threatened, "And completely at my mercy."

He eased the gown off her shoulders, letting it fall in a rumpled heap on the floor. Still wearing her shift, Jarina stepped free of the gown and turned to face him, and her expression became somber. "Jared, I'm sorry I said those terrible things to you. I thought you were angry with me and I didn't understand why—"

Catching her face between his hands, he pressed a silencing kiss on her lips. "No apology is required, sweet," he murmured against her mouth. "I wasn't angry with you before, and I'm not angry now."

Rather than comforting her, the reprieve weighed heavily on Jarina's conscience. It tore her apart to keep on lying to him about her past, yet it frightened her more to think of what Jared might do should he ever learn the truth. Her throat worked convulsively as she swallowed. "You are so good to me," she whispered. Without thinking, she reached up to wrap her arms around his neck, but Jared stepped back, deftly dodging her poison ivy-tainted embrace. He wagged a warning finger at her. "Don't you dare!"

"You're awfully quiet," Jared told Jarina late that night after he had blown out the candles.

Jarina frowned at the buttermilk and tansy-soaked rags that had been wrapped around her hands and forearms. "How long will I have to wear these?"

"A few days. Longer if you don't leave them alone."

With a sigh, Jarina obediently placed her hands at her sides so she would not be tempted to scratch.

The bed creaked as Jared joined her. He lay on top the sheet to allow his body to cool off in the elusive breeze that ruffled the sheer cotton curtain at the open window. "Now," he said firmly, "tell me what is *really* troubling you."

Outside, the crickets had taken up their nightly vigil, and Jarina cocked an ear to listen to one in particular whose drone seemed to be coming from behind the wardrobe. "I think we have a cricket in here," she said."

"Jarina, you're hedging."

She sighed. "If I tell you what is on my mind, you will only say 'tis none of my concern," she said wearily.

Jared did not miss the note of pique in her voice. He knew it annoyed her when he kept matters from her, and while his intentions had been honorable, he had begun to wonder of late if he was doing the right thing in trying to protect her from the harsh realities of life. Perhaps it was time, he thought, that they stopped keeping secrets from each other. "Why don't you allow *me* to decide what I will say?" he said.

Jarina turned her head to look at him in the darkness. The challenge he had thrown her was too great to resist. She took a deep breath. "I want to know what you and Damon were quarreling about this afternoon."

"Are you certain you want to know?"

"What do you mean?" Jarina asked, surprised by his reply.

Jared rolled onto his side and raised himself up on one elbow. Jarina's hair had grown in the months since their marriage, and now it framed her face in soft waves. He reached out to caress her cheek, then allowed his fingers to slide into her soft hair. "The truth is not always pleasant, love," he said quietly.

Jarina said nothing. She knew Jared was trying to

prepare her, but for what? Even though she had heard Jared banish Damon from Wyeburn, she had thought he would retract his edict as soon as he'd overcome his anger. Surely the quarrel he'd had with Damon could not be *that* serious?

"Evelyn is no longer in Alexandria," Jared said, coming straight to the point. "Unless I miss my guess, she is at this moment aboard a ship bound for England. With Damon's prompting, and Evelyn's weakness for position and prestige, Evelyn has decided that she would make a very good Duchess of Roswell."

Jarina's heart skidded to a standstill.

"After all," Jared continued in a low, meaningful voice, "Lady Margaret Jarina Hamilton is no longer free to marry his grace."

Jarina squeezed her eyes shut and groaned inwardly. There was a terrible pounding in her ears and she felt as though she would be sick. It hurt to breathe.

Jared turned her face toward him. "Why did you not tell me?" he asked gently.

Jarina's entire body began to shake as though she were cold. "I-I was . . . afraid. . . ."

"Of me?"

She swallowed hard several times. "Yes."

Jared slid one arm beneath her shoulders and rolled her against him. She even *felt* cold. Wrapping his arms about her, he held her trembling form close to him. He gently stroked her hair. "I apologize for making you afraid of me," he said quietly.

Jarina took a deep, quivering breath. "How long have you known?"

"A few months."

"You never said anything!"

"I was hoping you would learn to trust me enough to come to me with the truth."

"Oh, Jared, do you realize what will happen if Evelyn tells Roswell where I am? He will kill my father!"

"Actually, your father is more valuable to both Roswell and Damon if he remains alive. Not only does Roswell want the company so badly he would kill for it, Damon has been trying for years to coerce me into giving up Wyeburn. When he discovered who you really are, he concocted a scheme whereby Evelyn would convince Roswell to marry her in return for telling him where to find you."

Jarina was horrified. "Jared, no! Roswell won't marry Evelyn! Not when he can employ other means to get the information out of her!"

"You and I both know that, love. But Evelyn was easily duped. All Damon had to do was tempt her with a title and a life of aristocratic ease. As for your father, to save his life, I would have to relinquish all claim to both Wyeburn and the company."

Jarina shuddered.

Jared tightened his hold on her. "Fortunately for us, Evelyn's greed provided the one flaw in Damon's plan. Instead of going straight to England as Damon told her to do, she decided to delay in Alexandria and replenish her wardrobe."

"Which explains all the bills you have been receiving."

Jared snickered. "Judging from what she spent, I would say Evelyn now has a trousseau befitting a duchess," he said dryly.

"Jared, if she has already departed for England, how are we going to stop her?"

"We can't, sweet. What we can count on, however, is Landon's two-month lead. As soon as Stephen confirms that I have been cleared of the charges against me, he is under directions to sell the company."

"But, how will that—"

"To Roswell."

Jarina stiffened. "I thought you didn't want to sell to him?"

"I don't. But he made me an attractive offer, and I'm not above using his money to repay your father's debt to him. By the time Evelyn reaches England, Lord Hamilton will be a free man."

Jarina's throat tightened as she realized what he was saying. "You would do that for me?" she asked.

Jared smoothed her hair away from her face. "When I lay unconscious with a piece of deck railing through my thigh, you not only saved my leg, you gave me back my life," he said quietly. "The least I can do is give your father his."

Several long moments of silence passed while Jarina grappled with all Jared had revealed to her. Although Jared may never have told her he loved her, proof of his love went well beyond words. And never in her life had she felt as unworthy of that love as she did now. "I thought you would be . . . angry . . . when you found out about me," she struggled to get out. She felt overwhelmed with guilt. "I'm sorry I lied to you."

Jared expelled his breath in a long, weary sigh. "You are not the only one who has been living with deceit," he said. "There is something about me you have a right to know."

Wondering what dark secret he could possibly be keeping from her, Jarina tilted her head back to look at him. His eyes were closed, yet even in the darkness, she could see the grim set of his jaw.

"Jarina, in spite of the fact that we are brothers, Damon and I have never been close. He envied everything I had, and I, in turn, resented his existence. To me, he was simply another reminder of my mother's faithlessness."

Even though his voice was steady as he spoke, Jarina knew what it cost Jared to speak of his mother. "It's all right," she said softly. "You don't have to tell me about your mother. I already know."

Any other time, Jared would have demanded to know who had told her. Now it no longer seemed important. "What you know, and what I always thought

I knew, is a lie," he said. "It wasn't my mother who played my father false, but the other way around."

Somehow, that revelation did not surprise Jarina. "So, Damon is in truth your brother," she said.

"Yes," Jared said, his voice oddly hoarse. "And Evelyn is my half sister."

Jarina felt as though the air had been knocked from her lungs. Wriggling out of Jared's embrace, she pushed herself away from him and sat up. "Your sister?" she asked in a small, choked voice.

Although he had braced himself for her censure, having her retreat from him in disgust was almost more than Jared could bear, and he had to fight himself to keep from giving in to the urge to plead with her to try to understand. Good God! He swore inwardly. He had never before abased himself to anyone! Now it was all he could do to cling to what remained of his pride. "Evelyn and I share the same father," he said woodenly.

Suddenly, all that had been so vague before now seemed painfully clear to Jarina—the uncanny resemblance among Jared and Damon and Evelyn; Jared's reluctance to make Evelyn leave Wyeburn; Jared's tolerance of the debts Evelyn generated in his name.

Jared's sudden aversion for a woman who had once been his mistress.

Feeling his dilemma as acutely as though it were her own, Jarina reached out and placed one cotton-swathed hand against his chest. "Why didn't you tell me before?" she asked softly.

Jared took her hand in his and held it close to his rapidly drumming heart. "Jarina, Evelyn and I were *lovers*. I *bedded* her."

"I know."

"You're not repulsed?"

"I have always disliked Evelyn," Jarina said slowly, carefully choosing her words. "Her kinship to you doesn't change that."

"Jarina, what I am trying to say—"

"And it doesn't change how I feel about you," she interrupted, her tone almost militant. "While your roving bachelor's ways cannot be placed above reproach, I have never held them against you. Nor do I fault you for not knowing that Evelyn is your half sister. You have paid handsomely for both your father's passions and for your own, first with bitterness, and then with guilt. I'll not add to that toll by condemning you. What is done is done; we cannot go back in time and undo what we don't like."

A tired smile touched Jared's mouth as he reached out to trace the delicate line of Jarina's cheekbone with a forefinger. "You are a remarkable woman, Mrs. Cunningham," he whispered.

Sensing instinctively Jared's need to know that his touch did not now repel her, Jarina lay down beside him and nestled into the comforting circle of his arms. "I know I am not as sophisticated or as worldly as the other women you have known," she purred softly against his chest, "but I am, you must admit, an avid student. And if I did not have these cursed bandages on my hands, I would use every hedonistic, lascivious trick you have taught me, and *show* you how much I love you."

Although he did not believe it possible that Jarina could still love him after what he had just told her, the sheer relief that surged through him at hearing her say it was almost Jared's undoing. If her words were a lie, it was a lie he needed to hear. His arms tightened around her, and he said thickly, "Thank you."

Long after Jared had fallen asleep, Jarina lay awake, listening to the persistent chirping of the crickets. In the distance she heard the eerie hoot of an owl. Fear touched an icy finger to her spine and she shivered. She swallowed hard, but the ache in her throat would not go away. In spite of Jared's reassurances that her father would be safe, she could not help feeling that something terrible was going to happen.

Chapter Sixteen

In November, Jared received word from the Department of State that all charges of criminal activity imposed against him by the government of Great Britain had been dropped. Stephen Landon had been gone seven months, and while Jared was careful not to let Jarina see his concern, he was becoming worried. He sent a servant into Alexandria for news of any ships that might have been lost at sea, and was both relieved and puzzled when the reply was negative. What had become of Stephen? And, for that matter, of Lord Hamilton?

Damon, for all anyone knew, may as well have fallen off the face of the earth.

The light of the full moon struck Jared in the face when he rolled over and opened his eyes. Jarina was standing at the window with the drapes pulled back, the moonlight illuminating her pensive profile and her well-rounded form. "Jarina, is something wrong? Is it the baby?"

She shook her head. "I was just trying to imagine Wyeburn covered in white," she said, not looking at him. "In England, it would have snowed by now."

The hollow note in her voice wrenched at Jared's heart. He knew she was worried about her father, and it pained him that there was naught he could do to ease her fears. He patted the mattress beside him. "Come back to bed, love, before you take a chill." he said gently.

Her movements were slow and ungainly as she did his bidding, and Jared gripped her arm to support her as she lowered her weight to the bed. He tucked the covers in around her and drew her head into the hollow of his shoulder. Her feet were cold, and he clasped them between his own to warm them. "Do you have any idea how beautiful you look in the moonlight?" he whispered into her sweetly scented hair.

His compliment was not well received. "I feel like a beached whale," Jarina mumbled ungraciously. Jared had stopped making love to her in recent weeks, and although Jarina's logic told her he restrained himself out of concern for her and the baby, vanity told her it was because she was fat and ugly. The changes in her body no longer thrilled her, and more often than not, she was ill-tempered and out of sorts.

Jared chuckled softly. "Then you're a very beautiful beached whale, sweet," he reassured her.

"And you, Jared Cunningham, are a hopelessly inept liar."

As if in protest at her unkind remark, the baby kicked strongly. Jarina gasped and her hand flew to her abused side. Jared laughed and hugged her tighter. "That'll teach you to call your lord and master vile names," he chided gently.

When Jarina did not respond, Jared drew back his head to look at her, and he was surprised to see the glimmer of tears on her lashes. His brows knitted together. "Jarina?"

"I'm scared," she said in a small, choked voice. "I wanted this baby so much, yet now that the time grows near, I find myself thinking more and more of how my mother died—"

"Jarina, don't," Jared said sternly.

"I can't help it, Jared. My mother was in labor for three days before the doctors finally decided to take the baby. They thought they could save her life. . . ."

Jared wrapped his arms around her and held her tightly. "Please don't be afraid, darling. I won't make you go through this alone. I'll stay by your side every step of the way. God knows I've helped deliver enough foals. I'm not one of those weak-kneed souls who faints at the sight of an afterbirth."

Jared was holding her so tightly Jarina had to struggle to free her head so she could catch her breath. She tilted her head back to look at him, and even in the darkness a determined light seemed to burn in her eyes. "Jared, if anything happens, and you have to choose between me and our child, promise me you will save the baby."

"Nothing is going to happen," Jared said fiercely.

"But, if something does happen—"

"Jarina, please, for God's sake, *don't.* "

"Promise me!"

Jared's breathing was hard and fast. He had threaded his fingers through Jarina's hair, and without realizing it, was now gripping a fistful of hair so tightly it brought tears to her eyes. "Do you realize what you are asking of me?" he whispered.

Jarina's voice cracked. "Yes . . ."

A silent battle of wills raged between them. Had the choice been left to him, Jared would have sacrificed even his own life for Jarina. She had become such a part of him, he could not imagine living without her. The law gave him, not Jarina, the right to decide whether it was wife or child who lived. In his heart, Jared knew the law was wrong. He sighed and pressed his lips against her forehead. "I promise," he said wearily.

At that, the tension seemed to leave Jarina. Her eyelids drifted shut and she relaxed in his arm.

Between them, the baby kicked lustily.

*   *   *

Two days before Christmas, winter descended upon Wyeburn with howling fury. Outside the house, a storm raged. Snow banked against the southwest side of the house and blocked the view from those windows.

The kitchen door flew open and Jared stomped into the warm, cozy room, dragging with him a freshly cut, ten-foot Balsam fir that was covered with snow. Thinking he had lost his mind, Jarina hastened to shut the door behind him. "Jared Cunningham, why on earth are you bringing a *tree* into the house?" she demanded.

Jared stood the tree upright and gave it a hearty shake that sent snow flying in all directions. Fiona and Mary squealed and ran to dodge the icy spray, but Jarina merely grimaced as snow peppered her face and the front of her gown.

Looking uncannily like a small child seeking his mother's approval, Jared gave her a sheepish grin and asked, "Well, love, what do you think of our Christmas tree?"

"Our what?"

Jared's brows dipped and he eyeballed her suspiciously. "Don't tell me you've never had a Christmas tree?"

Jarina had fallen into the habit of folding her hands atop the broad shelf of her abdomen, and she did so now. "I haven't the slightest notion what you are even talking about," she said primly.

Jared turned to Mary and Fiona. "Do you believe it?" he asked. "This woman has never seen a Christmas tree!"

Mary covered her mouth with her hand to smother a giggle, but the red-haired Fiona looked afronted. "I've never seen one neither, sir," she said.

Jared chuckled. "Actually, the decorating of a Christmas tree is a wonderful pagan custom my grandfather acquired from a Swiss Lutheran family he once boarded with in New York. They had one put up in the hall of their house, and my grandfather liked the practice so well he adopted it for his own. We have a Christmas tree at Wyeburn every year."

Jarina's forehead puckered in bewilderment. "Jared," she began slowly, not quite certain how she should break the news to him, "Lutherans are not pagans."

Amusement dancing in his gray eyes, Jared leaned close to her. "It used to be called a Passion tree," he said in a low, seductive voice, causing Jarina to redden with embarrassment at his double meaning. "I favor a return to the old name."

Wrestling to contain the smile that threatened to burst across her face at any moment, Jarina patted her rotund stomach and said with mock disapproval, "I think, my lord, proof of your *passion* is already far too evident."

With Evanston's help, Jared managed to get the tree set up in the drawing room.

"Are you certain it will stay upright?" Jarina asked, studying the painted wood stand with wary reserve.

"It has every year," Jared replied lightly. He could not recall a Christmas that promised to be as joyful as this one. Even the cloud of Stephen's and Lord Hamilton's whereabouts hanging over them could not diminish the pleasure Jared felt at the turn his life had taken. He enjoyed his work. He felt contented and fulfilled. After a lifetime of licentious wayfaring, marriage and impending fatherhood agreed with him immensely.

Mary fetched the delicate crystal and brass ornaments from the attic and Fiona carried in a large platter of crisp brown gingermen she had spent the morning baking. A thimble had been pressed into the top of each one to form a hole through which a ribbon had been threaded. The cookies and ornaments were to be hung from the tree limbs, Jared explained to Jarina, and candles affixed to the tips. Because of the danger of fire, the candles were lighted only once, on Christmas Eve, when the presents were exchanged.

To Jarina, exchanging gifts on Christmas was unheard of. "Don't you hang a stocking from the mantel on Twelfth Night?" she asked.

Jared grinned boyishly. "A very large one, love," he replied.

They spent the afternoon decorating the tree. By the time the last gingerman was hung and the last popcorn garland strung, the servants had tactfully disappeared, leaving Jared alone in the drawing room with his wife.

Jarina gasped as Jared unwrapped a silver filigree star. "Oh, Jared, it's beautiful!"

He passed it to her. "Would you like to put it on top the tree?" he asked.

She smiled a little ruefully. "I'd likely fall and harm the baby."

"You won't fall. I'll hold you."

With Jared holding her legs as she stood atop a sturdy chair, Jarina placed the silver star on the tree's uppermost tip. When the star was positioned to her satisfaction, she braced her hands on Jared's shoulders and he carefully lifted her off the chair.

Wrapping his arms around her from behind, Jared rested his chin atop her head. "It's a lovely tree," he said.

Tears pricked behind Jarina's eyelids and her throat tightened. "I wish my father were here to see it. I think he would like these pagan customs."

Jared kissed the top of her head. "We've heard no bad news, sweet," he reminded her. "All we can do is wait."

Jarina caught her bottom lip between her teeth and blinked hard as the shiny brass decorations blurred and swam before her eyes. "I know," she whispered.

Fiona was just bringing in afternoon tea when a loud commotion from the kitchen drew their attention. Excusing himself, Jared started to go see what had happened, but was nearly plowed down in the doorway by Maggie, Angus close on her heels.

The old woman's clothes were covered with snow, and her face was ruddy from the cold, but her eyes were bright as they swept over the Christmas tree. She nodded her approval. "I was wondering if you'd remembered to put up the tree."

Jarina twisted around on her chair. "Maggie!"

"Good God!" Jared swore. "How did you two get through in this storm?"

"If ye'd bothered to look out the window," Angus said, "ye'd have noticed the snow stopped hours ago. My Maggie got this dusting comin' in the kitchen door."

Jarina lumbered up off her chair. "You must be frozen," she admonished. "Please, come in by the fire—don't worry about your wet shoes, Angus. The snow won't harm the carpet."

As Maggie joined Jarina in the drawing room, Angus motioned to Jared. "Can I speak privately with ye a moment, Cap'n?"

Jared followed Angus into the hall.

"Maggie 'n' me, we went into town so's Maggie could buy some trimmings for the clothes she's been makin' for Miss Jarina's babe," Angus said. "We tried to get back here last night, but we got laid up in the storm and ended up spendin' the night at a farmhouse halfway between here and Alexandria."

"Are you all right?"

"Aye, Cap'n, we're fine. 'Tis Mr. Landon what's in a bit of a pickle."

Alarm surged through Jared's veins. "Stephen's back?"

Angus nodded. "He sent word ashore with one of the longboats. The *Zephyr*'s anchored in the middle of the Potomac without permission to dock. President Jefferson signed an embargo yesterday." Angus went on to tell him of the chaos that had erupted on the docks. "American vessels canna leave port, and the foreign ones canna come in," he finished.

"But the *Zephyr* is an American ship," Jared protested.

"Not any more, Cap'n. She's flyin' His Majesty's colors. I asked around the docks, and one of the men told me she belongs to the Duke of Roswell now."

Every muscle in Jared's body felt tensed and ready to spring. "Was there any word of Lord Hamilton?" he asked.

"Nay, Cap'n."

If anyone knew Jared almost better than he knew himself, it was Angus, and although the Scot did not know who Lord Hamilton was, he recognized that something was amiss. Jared turned to go back into the drawing room, but Angus placed a gnarled hand on his arm, stopping him. "Lad, I've been with ye a long time," Angus said in a low voice. "Whatever we've been through, we've been through together. I'll not abandon ye now."

For several long moments, Jared stared at the old man without speaking, overcome by a realization that humbled him and at the same time made him proud. Of all the people he had known in his life, the ones he had treated the worst were the ones who had stayed by him and returned his shabby treatment of them with a deep, unfaltering loyalty. They were also the ones dearest to him. Jared took a deep breath. "Will you return to Alexandria with me?"

Angus nodded. "Aye."

"Jarina was telling me how much that red colt of yours has grown," Maggie said when they returned to the drawing room. "I hear he's been living up to his namesake." Her gaze sought her husband's and a silent message passed between them.

"Oh, Jared," Jarina said excitedly, "Maggie is going to stay here until I have the baby. I told her it wasn't necessary, but she insisted. Isn't she wonderful?"

Jared flashed Maggie a grateful smile. "Yes, she is."

Not wanting to delay his departure any longer than

necessary, Jared broke the news to her as quickly and as gently as possible about his sudden decision to go to Alexandria.

Bewilderment clouded Jarina's eyes. "Jared—"

"Jarina, the embargo has halted everything. No ships can enter or leave port. Nothing can be loaded or unloaded. The cargo I had planned to ship out is sitting on the docks right now, probably being picked over by thieves. If my men walk away from their jobs, my warehouses will be looted." Jared said nothing about Stephen's return. He did not want to raise Jarina's hopes that her father might be on the *Zephyr*.

Although she could not completely hide her disappointment that Jared was leaving, Jarina somehow managed to force a tight smile. "I understand," she said.

Jared hunkered down before her so that their eyes were on a level, and took one her hands in his. "Keep the bucket under the tree filled with water and it will stay fresh," he instructed. "I'll try to be home for Christmas. If I cannot, we will celebrate when I do return."

Jarina's troubled gaze searched Jared's face, and suddenly it seemed imperative to her that she memorize his every feature. If something happened to him, she would be devastated. She could not imagine living without him. She tenderly placed her free hand alongside his weather-bronzed cheek. "Please be careful," she said.

Jared's fingers tightened about the small slender hand he held, and the expression in his gray eyes softened. Gone was the child who had stowed away on his ship, he realized. In her place was a warm, loving woman who had given him more than he had ever dreamed of having. Lifting Jarina's hand, he brushed his lips across the backs of her knuckles. "I'll not stay away a moment longer than necessary," he promised her.

* * *

Jarina spent a troublesome night. She had trouble getting comfortable. When she lay on her right side, she could not breathe. When she turned onto her left, the baby kicked mercilessly. It was nearly dawn when she finally drifted into a restless slumber fraught with unpleasant dream images. By the time she finally arose, there was a dull ache in her lower back that made even the slightest movement a chore.

Maggie eyed her closely when she entered the kitchen. "You look peaked, child," she said with maternal concern as Jarina lowered herself onto a chair, one hand pressed to the small of her back. "Perhaps you should go back to bed. Mary can bring you up a breakfast tray and rub some liniment into your back."

Mary was sitting beside the fireplace, peeling parsnips. She glanced up questioningly at her mistress, but Jarina shook her head. "I'd rather stay down here," she said, drawing her shawl tighter about her shoulders. "It's warmer. Besides, I don't like being in that bed alone." Realizing too late what she had said, she tried to correct herself. "It's not the same with Jared gone," she said, coloring hotly. "What I mean is—"

Maggie chuckled. "I knew what you meant, child."

Jarina frowned. "Maggie, you're not supposed to be working. You're our guest."

"Ha!" the old woman snorted, drying her hands on her apron. "I've been cooking my own breakfast in this house since long before you was even a twinkle in anyone's eye. I'm not about to let anyone coddle to me now. Are you hungry?"

The smell of bacon sizzling in the iron spider on the hearth made Jarina's stomach queasy. She shook her head. "Maybe later, Maggie."

Fiona came into the kitchen, her russet brows drawn sharply together in a perplexed frown. "There's a man at the front door," she told Jarina. "He stinks to high heaven like that waterfront riffraff what used to come to the tavern on Saturday nights. He won't leave, and he says he won't talk to no one but Mr. Jared."

Mary had been so quiet, Jarina had almost forgotten she was in the kitchen. She put down her bowl of parsnips and started to get up. "I'll find out what he wants," she said.

"No," Maggie intervened. "*I'll* get rid of him. You fix Miss Jarina a cup of tea."

Jarina did not miss the look of resentment that passed across Mary's face the instant Maggie left the room. Since her arrival yesterday, Maggie had taken charge of the kitchen, usurping Mary's position as housekeeper, and Mary had once more found herself following orders rather than issuing them. Jarina gave the girl a sympathetic smile and pushed herself up off the chair. "I had best go see what he wants," she said.

When Jarina reached the hall, Maggie was trying to herd the man out the door. Fiona was right; he did smell as though he had not washed in months. Still, he had come on legitimate business, and Jarina was not about to treat him like a social outcast, regardless of how he looked and smelled. To Maggie's mortification, she invited the man into the drawing room where a fire warmed the hearth.

"I'll only talk to the master 'imself," the man warned her. His eyes were wide with curiosity as he followed Jarina into the drawing room.

"I'm afraid my husband is not available," Jarina said. She motioned toward a chair, and tried not to cringe as the man accepted her offer. Holding onto the arm of another chair for support, she carefully lowered herself to the seat. "Is there something I might be able to help you with?"

The man eyed her warily. "You be Mistress Cunningham?" he asked.

Jarina nodded.

"I was told to talk to Cap'n Cunningham, and no one else."

"You will either have to deal with me, or come back when my husband is free to speak with you."

"But, I came all the way from Alexandria!" the man protested.

Jarina lifted her hands in helpless resignation. "I'm sorry."

In spite of the fact that he was being paid good money to deliver his message according to precise instructions, he was not looking forward to making the journey a second time. He squirmed on the chair and flexed his fingers to thaw them. "Well, I don't know," he said. "If I knew the message would find its way to the cap'n . . ."

Jarina gave him her most charming smile. "You can rest assured I will speak with my husband the moment he returns." She paused, then added with artless cunning, "Sir, you must be chilled to the bone after your long journey. Would you care for a cup of hot coffee?"

The man looked taken aback, and Jarina surmised it was because he was not accustomed to either being invited into people's homes or being called *sir*. He rubbed his jaw. "Well, now, that would be real nice."

From the corner of her eye, Jarina could see Maggie standing in the doorway, vehemently shaking her head. Pretending she had not noticed, Jarina turned to the older woman and said, "Maggie, please see that a tray is prepared. This gentleman would like coffee, and perhaps some dried apple tarts?" She arched a querying brow at the man, and saw his face light up at her mention of the tarts.

Looking suspiciously like she was going to have an attack of the vapors, Maggie returned to the kitchen, shaking her head in disbelief and mumbling under her breath.

Jarina turned her full attention on the man sitting opposite her. "Now, sir, what were you about to say?"

"Well, ma'am," he said, wondering if he was sealing his own death warrant by not following his directions

to the letter, "if you could pass on to the cap'n that Mr.
Landon and Lord 'Amilton 'ave got into town. 'Is lordship'll be stayin' at the cap'n's house on King Street
'til someone can come into town to fetch 'im."

The color drained completely from Jarina's face,
then returned with a rush that made her feel light-
headed. "Sir, are you absolutely certain it's *Lord Hamilton* we are speaking of?"

The man nodded. "That's what 'e said."

Jarina leaned back in her chair, with one hand
pressed to her side and her breath coming in short
bursts as though she had been climbing stairs. "Oh, sir,
you don't know how wonderful your news is! You can
be certain—*absolutely certain*—that I will inform my
husband of your visit."

For the next thirty minutes, it was all Jarina could
do to sit still and endure the man's company while he
wolfed down two cups of coffee and no less than six
apple tarts. Finally, after stuffing two more tarts inside
his coat to carry with him, he took his leave.

Moving more quickly than she had in months, Jarina
fairly flew to the kitchen. "Maggie, please tell one of
the men to have the coach made ready," she said
breathlessly. "I'm going to Alexandria."

Maggie's mouth dropped open. "You're not going
anywhere in your condition!" she blurted out, but
Jarina was already halfway out the door.

"You may come with me if you like, but you had better hurry," Jarina called out over her shoulder. "As
soon as I can pack a few belongings, I'm leaving!"

In spite of Maggie's protests, it soon became evident
to her that Jarina very much intended to go to Alexandria, with or without her blessing, and alone if necessary. "Good Lord! Has the child gone daft?" she
muttered as she flew to pack a few belongings of her
own.

By the time the coach left the boundaries of Wyeburn and turned east onto the main road, the sun was

high. "We'll never make it to Alexandria before night-fall," Maggie said, no more disposed toward making the journey now than she had been before Jarina explained its purpose to her. "We'll most likely have to spend the night at one of those dirty taverns."

Jarina shifted her weight on the seat in an attempt to get comfortable. "There's an inn halfway between here and the city that's nice and clean," she said, remembering the place where she and Jared had stopped for their midday meal when he first brought her to Wyeburn. "We can stay there."

Her disgruntled mind groping for further proof that this journey was a terrible idea, Maggie said, "What puzzles me is why your father and Mr. Landon didn't come here themselves. Seems like a waste of time and money, if you ask me, hiring someone to carry a message when you could as well deliver yourself."

Although that too perplexed her, it was a puzzle Jarina preferred not to dwell upon. There was only one reason she could think of why her father would not have attempted the journey, and that was because he was ill. Perhaps the voyage had been too hard on him. Perhaps—and this was what she feared most—his months in prison had sapped both his strength and his health. Already she was bracing herself for what she might find upon seeing him for the first time in nearly a year. "I'm sure there's a good explanation for it," she said, her enthusiasm tempered with caution.

Fortunately, there were few travelers on the road, and rooms were available at the inn. Jarina surprised the driver of the coach by reserving a room in the inn for him too.

"But, ma'am, I always sleep in the livery," Simms said, not quite certain he'd heard right when she'd told him the room had a *fireplace*.

"It's too cold in the livery," Jarina said. "You will sleep in the inn. Furthermore, since you were kind enough to volunteer to drive so that Blakely could be home with his family for Christmas, I will see that Mr. Cunningham includes something extra in your wages this month."

Simms silently vowed to take Miss Jarina anywhere she wanted to go after that.

Even though she had slept little the night before and was exhausted from the hours spent in the coach, Jarina was too tense to sleep. The excitement of seeing her father again battled with her apprehension over what she would say to him when they finally came face to face. While she had long since forgiven him for trying to barter away her future to the Duke of Roswell, she was not certain her father would be so understanding of her running away from Hamilton Hall and disrupting the pattern of *his* life.

By daybreak, the ache in her back was so pronounced she could not get into the coach without assistance.

Maggie's eyes narrowed suspiciously. "What's wrong, child? Is it the babe? It wouldn't surprise me if the poor thing came ahead of its time, what with all the jouncing about we're doing in this carriage."

Giving her a tired smile, Jarina leaned her head back on the seat and closed her eyes. "No, Maggie, it's not the baby. It was the bed. The ropes needed tightening. I could have slept on my stomach and even my great belly would not have filled the sag in the mattress."

In spite of her reassurances that she was fine, Jarina was overwhelmingly glad when the rooftops and the church steeples of Alexandria at last came into view.

The house on King Street seemed unusually quiet when they arrived. The drapes were drawn and no one responded to Jarina's persistent application of the brass knocker. Jarina tried the door, and was relieved to find it unlocked since she did not have a key.

"Do you think anyone's here?" Maggie said in a hushed voice as they stepped into the darkened hallway.

Embarrassed to be whispering in her husband's house, Jarina replied in as normal a tone as possible. "I don't know," she said shakily, her voice sounding unnaturally loud in the stillness. "Perhaps Mrs. Hoskins went to the market."

Her heart beating unnaturally fast, Jarina called out the housekeeper's name, but there was no response. "Mrs. Hoskins?" She paused. "Father? Stephen? Is anyone here?"

Silence.

As she neared Jared's study, Jarina could have sworn she heard something, but the more she strained to listen, the more she was convinced she had been mistaken. Yet there was something peculiar about the silence that she could not define. Something familiar, yet oddly out of place.

She realized with a start that it was not a sound that had her senses suddenly alerted. It was a smell. Elusive, yet unforgettable, the scent of cigar smoke seemed to pervade the house.

Jarina pushed open the study door, and the smell became abruptly stronger.

Before she could scream, a hand closed over her mouth, and she was dragged into the darkness.

Jarina clawed frantically at the hand that covered her face, smothering her. Iron tendons trapped a slender wrist and yanked her hand down, and a choked scream exploded in her throat as her arm was wrenched cruelly behind her back.

Damon's voice shattered the darkness. "Light a lamp," he ordered tersely.

Jarina twisted her head around, and in the sudden flicker of light from the lamp, she saw Maggie lying on the hallway floor. A man stood over her still form.

The hand moved away from her mouth, and Jarina cried out in horror, "What have you done to her?"

Damon gave her arm a vicious jerk that brought her around sharply. Knotting his fingers in her hair, he yanked her head back, forcing her to look at him. "Behave yourself, and I may let the old woman live," he ground out.

Without warning, he spun Jarina about and shoved her toward a chair.

Her coordination impeded by the child she carried, Jarina stumbled against the chair. Her hands shot out in a futile attempt to break her fall, and a searing pain shot through her knees as they struck the floor.

"For God's sake, don't hurt her!"

The man's voice knifed through her senses. Pushing herself upright, Jarina lifted her head and stared through a haze of pain and confusion at the familiar face that shifted in and out of focus before her eyes. She gasped. "Father!"

Lord Hamilton's feet were tied together and fastened to a leg of the chair on which he sat, and his hands were bound behind him. His hair had grayed considerably since Jarina had last seen him. He was pale and thin, and when he spoke, there was a tremor of fear in his voice. "Jarina, are you hurt?"

Clinging to the chair for support, she struggled to her feet. "I'm fine, but what of you? What have they done . . . to . . ."

Her voice trailed off as her gaze traveled to the big, fleshy figure of a man standing in the shadows behind her father.

As the man moved out of the shadows, the lamplight reflected off his oily, boil-inflamed skin. A sneer curved his cold, cruel mouth. His possessive gaze raked Jarina's form.

Jarina's lips went white.

"Merry Christmas, Lady Margaret," said the Duke of Roswell.

Jarina's knees buckled beneath her and she fainted.

Chapter Seventeen

"I apologize, sir," the officer in command told Jared, "but I cannot allow you to visit the prisoner without permission from the duke."

It had taken Jared two days to obtain clearance to board the *Zephyr,* and he was not about to leave without Stephen. "I want to see Roswell," he said tersely, masking his unease with arrogance. He wondered where Roswell could have taken Jarina's father.

"That is impossible, sir. His grace went ashore with Lord Hamilton."

"Then, perhaps you can enlighten me as to why Mr. Landon is being confined," Jared said, his frustration mounting.

"I'm sorry, sir, but I—"

"Then, I will wait for him to return," Jared interrupted impatiently. Pivoting, he started toward the aft companionway, with Angus close on his heels.

"Sir, you can't go down there!"

Jared stopped and turned. He meaningfully arched a brow at the officer, and the man visibly shrank away from him.

"What I m-meant," the officer stammered, "is that his grace's . . . er . . . feminine companion . . . is staying in the duke's cabin. . . ."

Evelyn?

Jared noted that the man did not say *wife* or *mistress*. He had said *feminine companion*.

Jared studied the man with cool detachment. "Would we be speaking of one Evelyn Landon perhaps?" he asked.

The officer looked taken aback. "Why, yes . . . how did you know?"

"Lucky guess," Jared said sarcastically. He turned back toward the companionway.

"But, sir—"

"Miss Landon will receive me," Jared snapped.

Without waiting for the officer's permission, Jared descended the companionway stairs.

The door to the ship's aft cabin was locked. He pounded on the door. "Open up," he demanded.

He heard a movement inside the cabin. "Jared?"

"Open the door, Evelyn."

"I can't. It's locked from the outside."

Jared swore under his breath. He was in no temper to put up with Evelyn's games. "Then, get away from the door," he said impatiently.

Jared stepped back, and the officer seized his arm. "Sir, you can't do this! His grace will have me flogged if you—"

His face dark with rage, Jared flung off the man's hand. "And I will have you thrown overboard if you don't keep out of my way!" Steeling himself for the impact, Jared hurled his full weight against the door.

The door burst open with a splintering crash.

Evelyn screamed and threw her arms up over her face.

Prepared to shake the truth out of her if necessary, Jared closed the distance between them with angry strides. His hand snapped about her wrist and he jerked her hand away from her face.

The shock of what he saw knocked the fury from his veins.

Evelyn's face was bruised and distorted. It seemed to pull to one side as if she had suffered a stroke. Her nose looked as though it had been broken. Her once dark, flashing eyes were now dull and void of life. "Thank God you're here!" she croaked hoarsely.

Jared had to fight himself to keep his horror from showing on his face. He released her wrist, and she flung herself against him and threw her arms around him. "You must help me! I can't stay here with him."

For a moment, Jared just stood there, dumbstruck. He saw his hands, poised in midair as if awaiting his orders, and he was torn between wanting to take Evelyn in his arms and comfort her, and wanting to shove her away from him in revulsion. Instead, he took Evelyn by the shoulders and pulled her away from him. "I need to know where Roswell is," he said with forced detachment.

"Please take me away from here. *Please!* I can't bear being with him anymore. The man is a beast!"

Jared shook her gently, but firmly. "Where is he?"

"I-I don't know—"

"Damn it, Evelyn. This is no time for another one of your lies!"

Her face crumpled and her shoulders began to shake with bitter sobs. "He w-went ashore . . . to y-your house."

"Is Lord Hamilton with him?"

"Ye-es."

Jared released her and turned to leave.

"Jared, wait!" Evelyn grasped his arm. "You can't go there. It's a trap!"

He turned back to face her.

"William *wants* you to go there. That's why he sent you that message telling you Lord Hamilton had arrived," Evelyn blubbered frantically. "He and Damon plan to hold Jarina's father prisoner until you sign away your rights to Wyeburn."

Jared stared at her long and hard. Any message Ros-

well may have sent to Wyeburn would likely have fallen
into Jarina's hands. And Jarina, he knew, would not
wait for his return. She was probably at this moment
on her way to Alexandria, if she had not arrived already. His heart pounded with cold fear. If anything
happened to Jarina, he vowed, Roswell and Damon
and Evelyn would pay with their lives.

"If William finds out I told you, he will beat me,"
Evelyn said, sobbing. "Jared, I'm sorry! I'm sorry I let
Damon talk me into this. I only did it to make you jealous. I never wanted to hurt Jarina. I just wanted to pay
you back for marrying her. Please take me with you.
You don't have to marry me. We were lovers once. We
can be lovers again."

Jared wrested his arm from Evelyn's grip. "If anything happens to either my wife or my unborn child,"
he said shakily, "I will never forgive you."

Her beleaguered mind searching for something to
make Jared stay, it suddenly occurred to Evelyn that
Jared had told her Jarina was expecting. Jared turned
to go, and Evelyn blurted out in desperation, "It's not
yours!"

Jared froze.

"I saw them together in the conservatory," Evelyn
continued frantically to Jared's back. "It was when you
went to Fredericksburg to buy your precious mare."
Evelyn wrung her hands together. "The baby isn't
yours, Jared! Jarina betrayed you just like your mother
betrayed your father. Your father was forced to raise
his wife's bastard son. If you go back to Jarina now,
so will you!"

Jared slowly, deliberately turned to face her. His pupils had contracted until they were almost invisible in
his cold granite eyes, and his face was white with rage.
At his sides, his hands flexed murderously, and he
wished they were around Evelyn's neck. "You disgust
me," he ground out between clenched teeth.

Panic erupted across Evelyn's face as Jared turned

and walked out the cabin door. "She won't admit the baby is Damon's!" Evelyn screamed at Jared's parting back. "She will lie about the baby the same way she lied about the blackwater fever! Just like she lied to you about her father and who she really is!"

Angus stopped Jared on the companionway stairs. "Ye canna leave her here, lad," he said. "Like her or no, she's kin."

Jared knew if he did not get himself topside, he was going to be violently ill. He didn't trust himself around Evelyn. He wished he'd never told Angus of his relationship to her. "Then *you* stay here with her," he choked.

When Jared reached the maindeck, he came face to face with the frightened officer who had tried to stop him from seeing Evelyn in the first place. He seized the officer's coat front and lifted him until the man's toes cleared the deck. "My man will remain on board until I return for him," he said in a low, dangerous voice, oblivious to the muskets that were trained on him with unerring precision. "If any harm comes to him, or to Mr. Landon, I will hunt you to the corners of the earth and tear you apart with my bare hands."

Jared released the man and barked an order to a seaman who scrambled to drop a rope ladder over the side of the ship to the longboat that awaited him below.

Never had the short distance to shore seemed so great, or a longboat seemed to move with such lumbering slowness. Jared urged the oarsmen on, and when their increased efforts failed to please him, he snatched the oar away from one of the men and began rowing himself.

He had to reach the house on King Street before Jarina did.

A lieutenant and two enlisted men from the shore patrol awaited Jared on the docks. "Are you Jared Cunningham?" Lieutenant Griswold asked.

Jared's blood ran cold. Was he too late? "I am," he heard himself say.

"Sir, if we could trouble you to come with us—"

"What happened?" Jared interrupted.

"A carriage bearing your crest was driven off one of the piers no more than an hour ago. There was a man trapped inside with his hands tied behind his back. We need your help in identifying him."

Jared immediately thought of Lord Hamilton. Had Roswell killed him? "Of course," he said with a calm he was far from feeling. "I will accompany you."

The man turned out to be Simms, one of his drivers, and Jared felt his rage mounting at his servant's needless death. With a voice completely lacking in emotion, he apprised the officer of the situation on the *Zephyr,* and requested the navy's help in getting Stephen, Angus, and Evelyn off the ship.

Lieutenant Griswold readily agreed. "We'll call out the big guns if necessary," he said. "This won't be another pitiful *Chesapeake* affair, I promise you."

Try not to sink the ship in your eagerness, Jared thought sarcastically, but he kept his thoughts to himself. He had no patience for political dogfights or for the fools who instigated them.

"Is there any other way in which I might help you?" Griswold asked.

"Yes," Jared said without hesitating. "You can lend me a gun."

By the time Jared reached the town house, dusk had settled over the city. Between the drapery panels, he could see a lamp burning in his study. The rest of the house was dark. After checking the street to make certain no one followed him, he slipped stealthily into the alley.

The kitchen door was unlocked. Armed with a pair of French duelling pistols the officer had lent him, Jared slowly made his way through the back hall, testing each floorboard carefully before allowing it to accept his weight. One untimely squeak, and his presence would be betrayed.

He could hear voices coming from his study, and then his brother's taunting laugh. "It would appear your beloved husband may not be coming for you tonight after all," Damon said. "And I was so looking forward to giving him his Christmas present. You are aware, are you not, that we exchange gifts on Christmas rather than on Three Kings' Day? 'Tis a custom our grandfather started, although I never could comprehend the importance my family always seemed to attach to it. Perhaps it was because my mother wanted everyone to think we were all one big happy family, with a long history of intimate familial traditions."

Standing well back in the shadows, Jared could see Damon standing by the fireplace, a half-smoked cigar dangling from his fingers. Jarina was sitting on a wing-backed chair, with her hands folded serenely on her lap, staring at the fire, and Jared was proud of her. If she was afraid, she did not show it. Behind her, peeking surreptitiously through the drapes at the street beyond, was William Osterbrook, the Duke of Roswell.

Damon took a long draw on his cigar. "Do you know what I have planned for my dear brother this Christmas?" he inquired of Jarina.

Jarina lifted her tired gaze to Damon's face, but said nothing.

"I had intended to give him your father in exchange for the deed to Wyeburn," Damon answered his own question. "Then you arrived and threw all my well-laid plans into a quandary. Why would Jared accept your father in trade when he could very well have you?"

"Why, indeed?" Jared asked calmly from the doorway.

Jarina gasped.

Roswell spun away from the window, and Damon's head snapped around.

Three pairs of eyes riveted on Jared.

Exhausted relief passed over Jarina's face.

Jared leveled a pistol at Damon, and the other at Roswell. "Get away from that window," he ordered Roswell.

Exchanging uneasy glances with Damon, Roswell did at he was told.

"Out here . . . in the middle of the room," Jared instructed. "That's right. Now, down on the floor. On your belly."

Raw hatred burned in Roswell's eyes. "If you think you have won, Cunningham, you had best think again," he said as he awkwardly lowered himself to the floor. "I have both title to the company *and* the money you thought to use to free Hamilton. You have *nothing.*"

Damon had begun to surreptitiously move away from his position by the fireplace, and now Jared swung both pistols on him. "Not so fast, Damon," he said tersely.

Damon drew himself up to his full height. "I believe the rules outlining proper use of duelling pistols, brother dearest," he said, "dictate that each party involved have possession of one. You are being a little selfish, are you not, in keeping both of them for yourself?"

Jared was not amused. He motioned toward Roswell with one of the pistols. "Get over there with your friend," he barked.

Damon flung his cigar into the fireplace. With an air of unhurried nonchalance, he started across the room.

Jarina's eyes flared wide and she sucked in her breath. "Jared, watch out!"

The back of Jared's skull exploded into white-hot pain. His grip slackened. The pistols slid from his hands and one of them discharged as it struck the floor.

Jarina screamed.

Jared reeled drunkenly and plummeted into peaceful oblivion.

Damon hurried to him and rolled him onto his back. Swearing at the loss of a shot, he kicked aside the pistol that had fired and picked up its match. "Go search the alley," he ordered the man who had hit Jared from behind with a brick. "Make certain he wasn't followed."

Jarina pushed her way past Damon and fell to her knees beside her husband. Her hands shook as she felt his neck for a pulse. She pulled her hand away and there was blood on her fingers. "My God! What have you done to him!" she cried out.

Damon gripped her upper arm and hauled her roughly to her feet. "He's not dead, you little fool," Damon snapped. "Get back to your chair, and don't leave it unless you wish to join your companions in the cellar. Go!"

Her stomach wound into a tight knot of fear, Jarina obeyed.

Roswell stumbled to his feet. "Arrogant bastard," he spat.

"Get a bucket of water," Damon said tersely. "I want him conscious for this."

Roswell bristled. "I take orders only from my monarch," he returned with icy disdain.

Damon cast him a withering glance. "At this moment, *your grace,* you are in no position *not* to follow my orders. Get the water before I forget we are in this together and decide to use the remaining ball on you."

As if his threat needed reinforcement, Damon aimed the pistol at him.

The duke needed no further encouragement.

Jarina closed her eyes and gripped the arms of her chair as a sharp pain gripped her lower back and her abdomen. The pain lasted several long seconds and was the strongest she had felt so far. She heard the clock in the hall strike the quarter hour. The pains were coming regularly now, every five minutes. She opened her eyes and slowly released her breath as the discomfort subsided. She wished Maggie were here with her, but the old woman had been locked in the cellar along with her father and Mrs. Hoskins. She did not know what had become of Simms.

Roswell returned with the water.

Damon motioned toward Jared's unmoving form.

Gritting his teeth at being ordered about by a common colonial, Roswell dashed the water at Jared's face.

Jared groaned.

Jarina instantly started to her feet, but was brought up short as Damon impaled her with a warning glance. Her heart lodging in her throat, she sank back down on the chair.

Gasping for air over the water that had gone down his nose and throat, choking him, Jared struggled to sit up. The back of his head felt as though it had been split open. He coughed and dragged his sleeve across his wet face. "I should have known one of your henchmen would be lurking in the shadows waiting to crack my skull," he said, studying Damon through narrowed eyes. "You've never been one to do yourself what you could as easily pay another to do in your stead." He paused, then added meaningfully, "The way you enticed Evelyn into your scheme to lure Roswell to Virginia."

Damon threw back his head and laughed. "Ah, yes, our dear sister. Actually, Jared, Evelyn required very little convincing. She warmed to her part in the plan quite readily. Unfortunately, a woman who is willing to sleep with damned near anyone in order to get what she wants is someday going to get more than she bargained for."

There was a cryptic meaning in Damon's words that caused Jarina's heart to miss a beat. She glanced in bewilderment from Damon to her husband. "Damon, what are you talking about?" she asked, anxious to draw attention away from Jared, who was slowly working his way to his knees. "Has something happened to Evelyn?"

Damon turned his head to look at her. A cold smile twisted his mouth as he regarded her with those odd, gold-spoked eyes. "Evelyn," he said smugly, "got precisely what she deserved."

Jared lunged.

Damon reeled backward as Jared's head plowed into his belly, sending him crashing into Jared's desk. The gun in his hand fell to the carpet. Papers flew everywhere as the two men, locked in a deathgrip, rolled across the top of the desk.

Sick with fear, Jarina pressed a fist against her mouth to keep from screaming as Jared and Damon rolled to the floor behind the desk. Her gaze fell on the pistol lying on the carpet. Without thinking, she pushed herself up out of her chair and started toward it.

A strangled cry tore from her throat as a hand knotted in her hair, and she was yanked cruelly backward.

Roswell's meaty arm encircled her neck, and he jerked her against him. The garlicky, unwashed odor of him filled Jarina's nose and made her gag. She kicked and tried to pry his arm loose, and was rewarded with the sharp cold jab of metal against her spine. "Your brother-in-law is not the only one with a gun," Roswell hissed in her ear. He gouged the tiny pocket pistol he had been concealing beneath his coat harder into her back.

Jarina groaned and sagged helplessly against him as yet another contraction gripped her belly.

Jared seized the front of Damon's shirt and and hauled him to his feet. Before Damon could get his bearings, Jared drew back and smashed his fist into Damon's jaw.

Through a blur of pain, Jarina saw two of Damon's men run into the room. She shrieked, "Jared!"

The men leapt on Jared from behind.

With a massive effort, Jared shrugged one man off.

The other man wrapped his arms around Jared's neck
and his legs around Jared's waist, and clung piggyback.
His face purple from not being able to breathe, Jared
turned his back to the wall. Then, without warning, he
threw himself backward as hard as he could, and the
awful crunch of breaking bone reverberated throughout the room. Crushed between Jared and the wall, the
man screamed. His grip on Jared's neck slackened, and
he slid to the floor, unconscious.

Damon dove for the pistol lying on the carpet.
Clutching it, he slowly straightened. Blood trickled
from the corners of his mouth as he met Jared face to
face. He raised the pistol and pointed it straight at
Jared's heart.

Jared's remaining assailant scrambled to his feet.
Jared did not resist as the man grasped his arm and
twisted it behind his back. He felt dizzy, and his limbs
were like lead. Before his eyes, everything started to go
black.

Damon motioned toward a chair. "Get over there,"
he barked.

Gradually the room began to come back into focus.
The man released Jared's arm. Biding for time as he
regrouped both his wits and his strength, Jared feigned
a limp as he staggered across the room and collapsed
onto the chair.

Damon wiped his mouth on his sleeve. "Ah, Jared,
it would seem even you are not invincible. Amazing,
is it not, how persuasive one small weapon can be?"
In mock reverence, he brought the pistol up to his
mouth and kissed the polished brass barrel, before lev-
eling it once more at Jared.

Jared leaned his head against the back of the chair
and regarded Damon through half-closed eyes. His
mind raced as he plotted what to do next. "All right,"
he said slowly. "You win. You may have Wyeburn. Let
Jarina go, and I will sign the deed over to you tonight."

One dark eyebrow quirked upward, and Damon

began to laugh, softly at first, then in earnest. He pulled
a sheaf of papers from his waistcoat pocket. "I'm afraid
not, brother dearest. You will sign the deed first, and
then I may consider releasing Jarina."

"No."

Damon stared at Jared in disbelief. "It would appear
that my brother requires a little convincing," he said
portentously. He inclined his head toward his hired assailant. The man went to the fireplace and picked up
an iron poker. Moving to stand behind Jared's chair,
he raised the poker high over Jared's head.

Realizing what was happening, Jarina screamed.
"No! Don't!" She struggled against the hold Roswell
had on her.

The man waited, ready to strike.

An evil grin spread across Damon's features. Keeping the pistol leveled at Jared, he tilted his head to one
side and spoke over his shoulder for Roswell's benefit.
"But then, perhaps there is a more effective way to convince Jared to sign the papers," he suggested. "Perhaps
our dear friend Roswell would like to take Jarina upstairs and enjoy a sampling of what he was denied on
his wedding night?"

The color drained from Jarina's face.

Roswell needed no further encouragement. Gripping
Jarina's arm, he propelled her toward the doorway.
Panic stricken, Jarina tried to twist away.

Jared lurched up out of his chair. "Leave her be!"

The man behind Jared raised the poker higher and
brought it down on Jared's shoulder with a sickening
thud. Jared's eyes rolled back in his head and he
dropped to his knees.

The man raised the poker again, and Jarina
screamed. "Don't!" she cried out, sobbing hysterically.
"Don't hurt him! I'll do anything you want. Please,
don't hurt him! *Please!*"

Roswell needed no further prompting. For eleven
months he had chafed at being left standing at the altar.

For eleven months, his bruised pride had dwelled upon the wedding night he had been denied and the rebellious little chit who had slipped through his fingers. Even that Landon wench who had thrown herself at his feet like a bitch in heat failed to satisfy his lusts. Tonight he was finally going to have his revenge. Revenge against one Margaret Jarina Hamilton. Revenge against Jared FitzHugh Cunningham.

Reveling at the prospect of making Jared listen to his bride's screams as he had his way with her, Roswell shoved Jarina out the door and into the hall.

Jarina felt as though she were clawing her way through a nightmare. Her feet would not move, and she stumbled several times as Roswell pushed her up the stairs ahead of him. Another contraction seared her middle, and she clutched the banister rail for support.

"Hurry up!" Roswell snapped impatiently. He gave her arm a cruel pinch that wrested a cry of pain from her.

Beneath them, a commotion erupted in Jared's study. Jarina and Roswell both turned back in time to see Jared spring. From where they stood on the stairs, they had an unobstructed view into the room. The man behind Jared leapt forward. Damon lost his footing and fell, and his pistol discharged, the ball striking his hired man in the shoulder. The man grabbed his shoulder, and the poker clamored to the floor. Jared pounced on Damon and the two men rolled.

Damon got a foothold first. Locking his hands about Jared's neck, he slammed Jared's head against the floor. Jared pressed his hand against Damon's face, keeping him at bay by digging his fingers into Damon's eye sockets. With a loud grunt, he shoved as hard as he could, breaking Damon's hold on him. Jared rolled to his knees, his back toward the door.

Roswell lifted the pocket pistol and took aim.

There was no time to think. With every ounce of

strength she possessed, Jarina hurled her full weight against Roswell.

In the terrible, endless, suspended seconds that followed, Jared's tortured cry of anguish rocked the very walls of the house. *"Jarinaaaaa!"*

Two sheriff's deputies led Damon away. One of Jared's attackers had fled on foot, and the sheriff assured Jared that a search would ensue. The unconscious man had already been removed from the house.

The sheriff wrapped the two French duelling pistols in his cloak. "You may claim these in the morning," he told Lieutenant Griswold. Then, to Jared he said, "My condolences regarding your sister, Mr. Cunningham. I will send word as soon as her body is recovered."

"Thank you," Jared said coolly. He still had not fully absorbed the news of Evelyn's demise. Even as angry as he had been with her, he had never wished Evelyn dead. Yet, her efforts to make him believe Jarina carried Damon's baby still made him seethe. Of all Evelyn's lies, her last had been her most malicious, and the most incredible.

From the corner of his eye, Jared saw a movement in the hall, and he turned his head to watch while four men lifted Roswell's lifeless body and carried him from the house. In his fall down the stairs, Roswell had broken his neck.

Lieutenant Griswold and his men left with the sheriff.

"I'm sorry, Jared," Stephen said the instant the door closed behind them. "We tried to stop her from jumping. The shore patrol searched the river for over an hour, but they could not find her."

"It's not your fault, Stephen. You and Angus did all you could." Lowering his exhausted form onto the wing chair, Jared dropped his face into his hands.

Stephen and Angus exchanged worried glances.

"She'll be a'right, lad," Angus said soothingly. "There's three doctors up there with her now. Before ye knows it, both she·and the babe'll be givin' all three of 'em fits. Remember how ornery she was when she came down with the poison ivy?"

Jared lifted his head and dropped his hands between his knees. "I don't know how anyone could survive that fall," he said woodenly. "She literally threw herself at Roswell to keep him from shooting me in the back." Jared's voice caught. "This is the *second* time she has saved my life, damn it, and I can do naught but sit here like a useless child, unable to even help her."

"Jared, there is nothing any of us can do, except wait," Stephen said. "Lord Hamilton is a fine physician. Jarina has said so herself numerous times. We should be glad he is the one attending her."

Lord Hamilton came down the stairs. Jared surged up off the chair. "How is she?" he asked.

Torment showed in the lines of Lord Hamilton's face. "I have tried every method I know to revive her, and she responds to none of them," he said. "I must have your permission to either perform a cesarean delivery, or to destroy the child."

Jared stared at him in appalled disbelief.

"Time is running out," Lord Hamilton said tersely when it became apparent that no response was forthcoming. "Jarina is in hard labor now. If I don't do something soon, both she and the baby will die."

"If you perform a cesarean, Jarina will die anyway!" Jared shot back.

"Actually," Lord Hamilton countered, "she has a better than twenty percent chance of surviving. And if it's any consolation to you, most surgical fatalities can be attributed to sepsis and uncleanliness. My own technique involves boiling of the surgical instruments prior to—"

"I am well aware of your damned techniques!" Jared

snapped. "They helped save my life once, even if you were not present to perform the surgery!"

"You need not shout at me," Lord Hamilton ground out, his own composure dangerously close to breaking. "In case you have forgotten, Mr. Cunningham, Jarina is my daughter. I do not wish her death any more than you do."

Jared fought to get his temper under control. "I apologize," he said stiffly. "If you were in my place," he asked, "what would you do?"

Lord Hamilton shook his head. "I was forced to make that decision once, and I chose wrongly. This time, the decision must be yours to make."

If anything happens, and you have to choose between me and our child, promise me you will save the baby.

Jared's entire body had begun to tremble uncontrollably. The promise he had made to Jarina pounded inside his head and filled his mouth with a foul taste. "If you take the baby," he asked shakily, "what are Jarina's chances of surviving?"

Lord Hamilton was a long time in answering. "Very good," he said quietly.

Jared squeezed his eyes shut.

Promise me!

"I think, son," Lord Hamilton ventured hesitantly, "you might do well to ask yourself what your wife would want. If you choose Jarina over the baby, you could very well spend the rest of your life enduring her hatred."

Jared ran one hand through his hair in a gesture of tortured frustration. "If Jarina dies, I have no life!" he argued.

Lord Hamilton waited.

Jared took a deep, shuddering breath. "Do the cesarean," he whispered.

Jared thought he saw traces of Jarina in the curve of his infant daughter's brows, and in her delicate, pink

lips. She sleeps with her mouth open, he thought, and
tears choked his throat.

His hands were shaking as he passed the tiny bundle
back to Maggie.

In the hall, the physicians who had assisted with the
surgery were preparing to leave. One of them handed
Jared his card. "The University of Maryland Medical
School desperately needs teachers," he said. "Your
father-in-law would be a valuable addition to the fac-
ulty. His methods are among the most advanced I have
ever seen, and his theories on infection are worthy of
further study. Please have him contact me if he is interested in establishing a practice here in the United
States."

Jared thanked the doctors and bade them good-bye.
The moment the door closed behind them, Jared pivoted and took the stairs two at a time.

Lord Hamilton was just coming from Jarina's bedchamber when Jared reached the upstairs hall. There
was a pronounced slump to his shoulders and his face
was pale with exhaustion. "We were able to stop the
bleeding," he told Jared. "You may sit with her if you
wish. Dr. Morgan left some laudanum on the lowboy,
with instructions on the proper dosage. Jarina is going
to be in a great deal of pain when she regains consciousness. If you need him, Morgan lives only two blocks
away. Send one of the servants for him." He turned and
started toward the stairs.

Jared glowered at him. He could not believe Jarina's
father was leaving after all he had gone through to get
him here. "Where are you going?" he demanded.

Lord Hamilton never even looked back. "I am going
to get drunk," he said wearily over his shoulder as he
began descending the stairs. "I am going to get very,
very drunk."

A lamp burned beside Jarina's bed, bathing her face
in its soft glow. She was deathly pale; the only color
in her face at all was in the long dark lashes that fanned

out against her cheeks. Her breathing was shallow and uneven.

Jared sat down on the chair beside the bed and picked up one of her hands. It felt cold. He had never really noticed before what delicate, slender hands she had. The huge diamond he had given her suddenly seemed oddly out of place on such a slender hand. His gaze came to rest on the faint mottled scarring that remained of her bout with the poison ivy, and his throat tightened spastically as he realized just how fragile she was. Indeed, without the great belly he had grown accustomed to seeing on her over the past months, she suddenly seemed very fragile, and very small. His fingers closed about her hand, engulfing it, and he held it tightly, as though he might through some miracle be able to impart his strength to her along with his warmth.

He did not know what to say to her. Should he tell her they had a daughter? Should he plead with her not to die? Good God, if *she* died, *he* would die! Didn't she know that? Didn't she know how much she meant to him?

He nervously moistened his lips. "You are not going to get out of taking that toboggan ride this way," he said with mock sternness, and his attempt at humor sounded feeble even to his own ears. Taking a deep, unsteady breath, he tried again. "You saved my life, Jarina. A second time, you saved my life. I am indebted to you, sweet. If you die on me now, I will never be able to repay that debt. You would be sending me to my own grave with a price on my conscience, and you know how that would sorely wound my pride. I *hate* to owe anyone. I hate to lose. I'm not a good sport at all. I even hate to let anyone have the last word.

"But, then, you already know that," Jared continued, swallowing hard. "How many times did I try to keep you from having the last word? How many times did I threaten you and humiliate you and try to bend you to my will? Dear, sweet Jarina, how I hurt you! If I could turn back the clock and undo all the pain I've caused you, I would. Please believe that, love. I cannot bear knowing that I hurt you."

Jared's eyes glittered with unshed tears. "Did you know there were times on board the *Pegasus* when I deliberately provoked you just so I could get a rise out of you? I hated it when you cried, but when you stuck that damned stubborn chin of yours up in the air and defied me, you were magnificent. No one else had ever openly defied me before, and there you were, a mere child, plunging into dangerous waters where grown men dared not tread. God, how I admired you, yet I was too damned proud to admit it."

A low chuckle sounded in Jared's throat. "I'll never forget that day you looked me straight in the eye and asked me what I would do should my wife ever play me false. I had no wife, so I thought of you. Even then, after a single night of holding you in my arms, the thought of you with another man made me insanely jealous. From the very first night, love, you had a hold on my heart that I was powerless to fight."

Jared's tone became very quiet. "I never once believed Evelyn's lies, sweet. If there is one thing I know you are incapable of, it's infidelity, and doubly so where Damon is concerned. Love, do you know how many times I saw you recoil from his nearness, or the look of hatred that flashed in your eyes whenever you saw him? I know you would never go willingly into Damon's arms, particularly when you could not even bear to be in the same room with him.

"If you die on me, Jarina Cunningham, I will never forgive you. I will know you did it just to spite me. If you die—" His voice cracked. There was an aching hole in his chest where his heart should have been, a tangible, burning pain. "If you die," he choked, "I will never get a chance to tell you . . . to tell you . . . how much I love you."

Jarina's face swam before his eyes.

"I love you, Jarina," he said, his voice harsh with desperation. Somehow, he had to make her understand. "Darling, do you hear me? I love you. *I love you!*"

Sliding his fingers into her hair, he gently turned her head toward him. He tenderly, gently kissed her lips, her eyelids, her smooth white forehead. He had to kiss her again before it was too late. He pressed his lips to the erratically beating pulse at her temple. "Please don't leave me now, sweet," he begged. "Please . . ."

His bottom lip quivered and his nostrils flared as he fought for control. "I love you . . . *so much,*" he whispered brokenly. "I love . . . you. . . ."

A sob splintered in Jared's throat, and his entire body began to shake uncontrollably. Burying his face against the side of her neck, he did something he had not done since he was four years old: he cried.

He wept like a baby. An entire lifetime of being strong and unbending crumbled as all the aching misery inside him erupted like a pent-up volcano. Sobs of impotent rage rocked his broad shoulders, and scalding tears ran like molten lava down his face to saturate Jarina's hair and the pillow on which she lay. He wept until the desolate, burning pain in his heart had numbed to a dull ache. He wept until he thought there could not possibly be any tears left inside him, and then he wept some more. He wept until his body hurt from the effort.

A small, gentle, trembling hand covered his.

Jared sucked in his breath, and his head snapped up.

Jarina touched his wet face and there was bewilderment in her pain-glazed eyes. "The baby . . ." she whispered.

Jared turned his face against Jarina's hand and pressed a kiss into her palm. "She is fine, love," he said shakily. "Our daughter is just fine."

Relief that the baby was safe flickered across Jarina's face. A daughter, she thought. Her hand dropped to her side, and she closed her eyes. Her breaths gradually became fuller and more regular.

Jared removed his boots. Careful not to jar the bed and hurt Jarina, he stretched out beside her on top of the covers. He lay on his side, with his gaze fixed on her face. He did not want to let her out of his sight for even a moment.

But relief and exhaustion combined to overwhelm him, and within moments, he had fallen into a deep, dreamless sleep.

The lamp had burned itself out, and in the dim gray light of dawn, Jarina lay watching her husband sleep. Worry and fatigue had deepened the lines of his face, and she could only guess at the tumultuous night he must have spent. She wondered what had become of Damon and Roswell. The last thing she remembered was the jolting impact of her body slamming against Roswell's before they were both hurtled violently down the stairs. She remembered thinking she was dead, and then rationalizing that she must still be alive or her body would not hurt so much.

She also remembered Jared saying he loved her. Over and over, he had said he loved her. And he had cried.

Her expression gentled. "I love you, too, my dear, precious husband," she whispered.

There was a dry scratching in her throat that would not go away when she tried to clear it. Not wanting to awaken Jared, she turned her face away from him and, as quietly as possible, she attempted to cough.

A cry of agony tore from her throat as a crippling pain gripped her entire body.

Jared awakened with a start and bolted up on one elbow.

The tickling in Jarina's throat found no relief in the pitiful little gasps that were all she could manage. She ground the back of her head into the pillow, and her eyes were dark with panic. "Jared—!" she croaked.

Jared seized her hand and gripped it hard, as if by doing so he could absorb her pain. Jarina doubled over in pain as the cough that had been trying to manifest itself wrenched from her chest. She clutched Jared's hand, and he was amazed at the strength of her grip.

Fighting for air, Jarina fell back on the pillows.

"I'll get the laudanum," Jared said, but Jarina only clutched his hand tighter and shook her head vehemently from side to side.

"No," she gasped. Her face was ashen. "I-I'll be . . . fine. . . ."

Jared tried to massage some warmth into her cold little hand. "Your father had to deliver the baby surgically," he explained hoarsely. "You are going to be very uncomfortable for a few days, love."

Gradually, Jarina's breathing evened out and some of her color returned. Remembering the baby, she turned her head to look at Jared. "You said we have a daughter. Where is she?"

Some of the worry left Jared's face. "Maggie took her downstairs last night so you could rest, and Dr. Morgan sent over a wet nurse. I'm afraid you are going to have a hard time reclaiming our daughter, love. Maggie has already taken over the role of the doting grandma. When I last saw her, she was compiling a list of names for your approval."

A small smile touched Jarina's mouth. She could easily visualize Maggie taking charge. "Our daughter . . . is she . . . pretty?"

Jared's chest swelled with fatherly pride. "She's beautiful," he said with deep feeling. "She has your blue eyes."

Jarina blinked at him. "All babies have blue eyes, Jared," she patiently informed him.

"Not *your* blue eyes, madam."

Their gazes met and held. In her husband's gaze, Jarina saw a love and a warmth that made her wish this moment could last forever. Still clutching Jared's hand, she brought it to her face and rubbed it against her cheek, reveling in its rough warmth against her skin. "I am afraid you will have to wait until Three Kings' Day before you get your present," she said softly. "I didn't get you one for Christmas."

A chuckle that began deep in Jared's chest evolved into a low rumble of pleased laughter. "Darling, not only did you save my life, you gave me a beautiful, healthy daughter. A man cannot ask for more than that. I fear, love, it is I who comes to you empty-handed this Christmas. Your present is back at Wyeburn waiting to be placed beneath the tree."

Sudden tears welled up in Jarina's eyes, making them glisten like huge, liquid stars. She squeezed Jared's hand. "You already gave me my present," she whispered achingly. "You told me you loved me."

Epilogue

"My father writes that he is more than pleased with his new position at the University of Maryland Medical School," Jarina said. "The donation you gave the university is going to be used to open an obstetrics and surgical hospital in Baltimore."

When she did not receive a response, Jarina lifted her gaze from the letter she held to find Jared staring down into the cradle at his four-month-old daughter. He offered a finger, and Jarina saw it eagerly seized by a tiny dimpled fist.

Jared looked up at her and smiled. "I told you Jessica was going to have your blue eyes," he said.

Jarina could not help laughing at the note of smugness in his voice. "She has your black hair," she countered.

"And your stubborn chin."

Jarina snorted. "She gets *that* from your side of the family."

Completely enraptured by the beautiful infant who had stolen his heart, Jared allowed little Jessica to draw his finger into her mouth. "It's a pity she has that awful wart on the end of her nose," he said softly.

Jarina set aside the letter from her father and joined

her husband and daughter. "What did you say?" she asked.

"I said, she has a wart on her nose."

"She does not!"

"See for yourself," Jared said. "It's right there, on the end. It's just a tiny one now, but, in time . . ."

The solemnity in Jared's voice sent a chill of apprehension down Jarina's spine. Unable to bear the thought that *their* baby could be anything less than perfect, Jarina leaned over the cradle and ventured a peek.

Silent laughter shook Jared's shoulders.

Jarina jerked upright and impaled him with a damning look. "Jared Cunningham, you are utterly hopeless!"

"You are right," he readily agreed. Extricating his finger from Jessica's determined grasp, he turned to Jarina and drew her into his arms. "I am utterly, hopelessly, in love with my wife. . . ."

If you enjoyed this book, take advantage of this special offer. Subscribe now and . . .

GET A *FREE*

NO OBLIGATION (a $3.95 value)

If you enjoy reading the very best historical romances, you'll want to subscribe to the True Value Historical Romance Home Subscription Service. Now that you have read one of the best historical romances around today, we're sure you'll want more of the same fiery passion, intimate romance and historical settings that set these books apart from all others.

Each month the editors of True Value will select the four very best historical romance novels from America's leading publishers of romantic fiction. Arrangements have been made for you to preview them in your home Free for 10 days. And with the first four books you receive, we'll send you a FREE book as our introductory gift. No obligation.

free home delivery

We will send you the four best and newest historical romances as soon as they are published to preview Free for 10 days. If for any reason you decide not to keep them, just return them and owe nothing. But if you like them as much as we think you will, you'll pay *just* $3.50 each and save at least $.45 each off the cover price. (Your savings are a minimum of $1.80 a month. There is *no* postage and handling – or other hidden charges. There are no minimum number of books to buy and you may cancel at any time.

HISTORICAL
ROMANCE –

—send in the coupon below—

To get your FREE historical romance and start saving, fill out the coupon below and mail it today. As soon as we receive it we'll send you your FREE book along with your first month's selections.

Mail to: 557-73398-B
True Value Home Subscription Services, Inc.
P.O. Box 5235
120 Brighton Road
Clifton, New Jersey 07015-5235

YES! I want to start previewing the very best historical romances being published today. Send me my FREE book along with the first month's selections. I understand that I may look them over FREE for 10 days. If I'm not absolutely delighted I may return them and owe nothing. Otherwise I will pay the low price of just $3.50 each; a total of $14.00 (at least a $15.80 value) and save at least $1.80. Then each month I will receive four brand new novels to preview as soon as they are published for the same low price. I can always return a shipment and I may cancel this subscription at any time with no obligation to buy even a single book. In any event the FREE book is mine to keep regardless.

Name _____

Address _____ Apt. _____

City _____ State _____ Zip _____

Signature _____
              (if under 18 parent or guardian must sign)
Terms and prices subject to change.